Edward Topol was born in 1938 in Baku, USSR. In 1960 he entered the faculty of the All Union State Institute of Cinematography in Moscow where he concentrated on creative writing and worked simultaneously as a correspondent for *Konsomolskaya Pravda*, the journal *Youth* and the *Literary Gazette*. The latter published the beginning of a series of articles on teenage crime, the first of its kind to appear in the Soviet Union, though the remainder was banned by the censor.

His play *Love at First Sight* was produced twice and was later made into a film. Seven of his scripts were made into feature films and *The Minors, Cabin Boy of the Northern Fleet* and *The Sea of Our Hope* won national awards, including the much coveted Fifty Million Viewers Award for *The Minors* in 1977.

He is a prolific writer in many genres including poetry. In October 1978 he emigrated to New York where he co-wrote the best-selling *Red Square*.

Also by Edward Topol

RED SQUARE

and published by Corgi Books

Submarine U-137

Edward Topol

SUBMARINE U-137

A CORGI BOOK 0 552 12583 0

Originally published in Great Britain by
Quartet Books Limited

PRINTING HISTORY

Quartet edition published 1983
Corgi edition published 1985

This book is set in 10/11 Plantin

Corgi Books are published by
Transworld Publishers Ltd.,
Century House, 61-63 Uxbridge Road,
Ealing, London W5 5SA

Printed and bound in Great Britain by
Hunt Barnard Printing Ltd., Aylesbury, Bucks

Dedication

I dedicate this book to Emiliya, whose help in the writing of it amounts practically to co-authorship

Acknowledgements

The author would like to express his sincere thanks to Mr Lev Roitman for his invaluable assistance in the writing and editing of this book. He also wishes to express his gratitude to friends who offered advice on various aspects of the book, and especially to Simon Chayevsky, Lev Nitkin, Peter R., Raoul Glant, Leonid D., Nina Stein and Elsie Thorn-Taylor.

All the characters and events described in this book, including the regular appearance of Soviet submarines off the coasts of Sweden, England, Italy, the USA and so on, are pure invention on the author's part, a statement which is borne out by the peace-loving policies pursued by the Soviet Union over many years in every part of the globe.

The author can confirm that the occasional incursions of Soviet nuclear submarines into Western territorial waters are caused by nothing other than curiosity on the part of Soviet mariners who are interested in seeing the latest trends in European fashion, perfumery and floriculture. These incursions have nothing whatever to do with the USSR's military aims.

Submarine U-137

Part 1

Someone Else's Face

SECRET

To: USSR Minister of Defence,
Marshal of the Soviet Union,
D. F. Ustinov

Please inform the Defence Industry Commission of the CPSU Central Committee, the Politburo and Comrade L. I. Brezhnev personally that, in order to safeguard our decisive military superiority over the armed forces of the NATO countries, the group of scientists and military engineers from the Marine Institute (PO Box No 16) and Power Engineering Institute (PO Box No 78) together with officers commanding the special detachment of submarines from the Baltic Fleet have completed all preparations for Project EMMA eleven days ahead of time. The underground tests conducted in Yakutia and the Pamir Mountains and the tests carried out beneath the sea off the Dikson Peninsula have proved the extreme effectiveness of this new strategic weapon even in mountainous terrain and in permafrost conditions.

I consider it appropriate to recommend that the group of scientists who invented this new strategic weapon, and the crews of submarines U-137 and U-202 who both installed and tested it, should receive State decorations.

The practical implementation of Project EMMA and the mass production of this new weapon are now matters for the Government to decide.

Chief of Soviet Army General Staff,
Marshal of the Soviet Union,
N. Oparkov

Moscow, 17 August 1981

1

'Your name is Stavinsky? Roman Stavinsky?'

'Yes.'

'Have you been granted US citizenship?'

'Yes. Two months ago.'

'But do you still miss Russia?'

Stavinsky looked him in the eye and smiled. After all, what difference did it make what the CIA thought about him? He didn't give a damn. He'd been living in Portland for four years now and it was a real hole, so what business was it of anybody else whether he still missed Russia or not? He was an American, with all the rights of an American Citizen, and he didn't give a damn for the CIA.

'Yes, I miss Russia,' he said defiantly. 'And what of it?'

'Do you want to go back there?'

'No.'

'Why?'

'They'd take me straight from the airport to prison.'

'What for?'

'Because of those interviews about the Soviets which I gave your radio stations immediately after I arrived in America.'

'But that didn't stop you applying to the Soviet Embassy for permission to return there.'

'I was younger in those days. I would have spent five years in prison, and they would already have let me out by now. What do you want from me?'

'Nothing in particular. Just a small service. If you don't like the United States . . .'

'Did I say that?'

'No, but if you're missing Russia . . .'

'That doesn't mean that I don't like the United States. It's a wonderful country, and there's only one person here that I really hate.'

'Our President, you mean? Why? Because he's ruining relations with the Russians?'

'No. I mean myself. I'm the one person I really hate in this country. But that's got nothing to do with the CIA. Why have you come to see me?'

'To help you return to Russia.'

He looked at them in astonishment.

'We need to get somebody out of Russia,' one of them said. 'You'll fly across and stay there, then he'll come to America using your identity papers, that's all. Of course, we'll supply you with Soviet documents made out in somebody else's name so that you can carry on living in the country. And we'll let you have money, too . . .'

Stavinsky opened up a packet of Marlboro, extracted one cigarette, lit it and inhaled deeply. He'd been waiting six years for these wonder-workers to get in touch with him, and now they had. They hadn't come out of the sky, and they hadn't appeared like genies from a bottle. They were from the CIA. He took another drag at his cigarette. He must look a sight in their eyes – unshaven, dressed in a dirty sweater, bags under his eyes . . .

'Why have you chosen me?'

'Because you resemble the man I was talking about. Or rather he resembles you. Not in every detail perhaps, but that's no problem. We can make look-alikes of you. The most important things are the shape of the skull, the colour of the eyes and a few other details besides. Have a look at these.'

The second man placed a clutch of photographs in front of Stavinsky. The first two were of Stavinsky himself taken from the front and in profile. (He recognized the shots he'd had done three months ago to get his US citizenship.) The rest had been retouched. They looked like him, but not quite. He looked slightly more snub-nosed, his hair was cut short and the ears didn't look quite the same.

'You see? We've only got to alter you a little and you'll have another face. You can look as you do in this photo, or in the others. You can even look a little younger, if you like.'

'And who is he, this man of yours?' asked Stavinsky. 'Is

he some big shot? A spy? Or a dissident?'

'We haven't reached any agreement with you yet,' said the second man. 'And you don't need to know those details at the moment. Well, what do you think?'

Stavinsky leaned back in his armchair. They didn't talk Russian at all badly, the bastards! They'd probably been to the place more than once.

'What if I were to approach the KGB right away in Moscow and spill the beans?' he asked.

'You would hardly be likely to do that. You've got a daughter over here, after all.'

'Well, she's a US citizen and isn't responsible for the actions of her father. And she's marrying an American. So what could you do to her?'

'Well . . .' said one of them. 'If that's how you feel about it, you'd better not go. We've got some other candidates for the job,' and he made as if to get up.

Stavinsky grinned. 'Wait a minute,' he said. 'Do you mean that I've got my own look-alikes, too?'

'Well, not exactly . . . It's just that you can approach an original from several different angles, as you'll realize. At FBI archives we looked through the photographs of six thousand Russian émigrés about your height and chose three of them. If you turn us down we've still got two left.'

'It's not worth trying to blackmail me,' said Stavinsky with a wry smile. 'So, if I agree, I'll have to stay there. And what if I want to come back?'

They spread their hands in a gesture of helplessness.

'Why should you want to do that? When you applied to the Soviet Embassy, you said that you wanted to go back for ever. You were even ready to spend some time in jail just to live in your beloved Russia. And we're offering you the same thing, only without the jail. We'll pay your travel over there, and we'll supply you with a real Soviet passport and all the other papers you'll need. Of course, your name won't be Stavinsky any more. You'll be Ivanov or Yegorov, or whoever you want. You'll find some work over there and you'll soon settle down. Dental technicians make a good living for themselves everywhere, don't they?'

One of them got up. 'And as for betraying us, well . . . We've got our people in the Soviet Union too. They'll find the traitor. But we're offering you an honest bargain . . . You've got until Wednesday to think it over. Here's our telephone number. If you don't ring us before Wednesday, that means you're not willing to accept. In that case, forget all about this conversation. Goodbye.'

'Wait a minute! This telephone number . . . That's not the code of this state.'

'202. That's the Washington DC code. You can call us collect.'

'I'm not talking about that! You mean that you've flown here specially, all the way from the East coast?'

'It's all in the interests of our country – and it's your country too, for the time being. The United States, I mean.'

They both smiled.

'But I saw you out fishing a week ago, on the Columbia River.'

'You might well have seen us in the bar opposite, or at the clinic where you work too. And in a number of other places. We've been getting to know you, from a distance. Are there any more questions you want to ask?'

'You bet! Hundreds of them.'

'We'll answer them for you in Washington. If you phone us before Wednesday, that is. Goodbye.'

And they left.

Stavinsky went over to the window. From the upstairs floor he could see them get into a dark-blue Chevrolet and drive off. They didn't even bother to look round. How do you like that! It was a good job that Olya wasn't at home.

Though, if they'd been following him for more than a week, they would naturally know her movements. Still, what was he talking about? Russia! Moscow! Three years after he'd arrived in America, he could still smell the scent of the lilac trees outside his apartment house in Moscow. He would dream about it at night. And all the six years he'd been here, he'd dreamed about Moscow girls. Not a single American girl had he dreamed of in all that time, though you'd think that American whores were no worse than Russian ones. They do the same thing, after all. And yet . . . Still, calm down! He was forty-six years of age, had a house and a good job, not to mention two cars. And what cars they were! You could never even dream of owning such things in Russia. A Zhiguli or a Lada was the height of achievement there. He'd got one daughter, Olya, and he loved her. And what else was there for him to love here? This house where he had nothing to do when Olya wasn't home? (And she was home less and less, and soon wouldn't be living there at all.) Or Barbara, the forty-year-old shop assistant at the 7-Eleven, whose bed he shared twice a week? What was there for him to love in this country? He'd come here late in life, too late. Seen from Russia, America had seemed the perfect, fairy-tale country. Whatever you couldn't get in Russia was to be had here: luxurious cars, hotels, millionaires, trips around the world, your own airplane and yacht. But whatever he had been in Russia counted for nothing here. In America he was a nobody – a technician in a dental hospital who made sets of false teeth for old women. Thank God his father had taught him that particular skill when he was young and that his mother had forced him to enter the Medical Institute. Otherwise, he would have given up the ghost, like all the other middle-aged émigré journalists, however talented they had been in Russia. Who needed *them* with their terrible English. They couldn't even speak it properly, let alone write it. Yes, he'd arrived here too late. The émigrés are right when they say that at first America appears to be a land of unlimited opportunities. But then you realize that these opportunities are not for you. You need to be born here or at least to come here when you are twelve years old, like Olya. But to come here when you are forty is sheer suicide. So what should he do? Go back? What an opportunity! Opportunities like this occur only once in a lifetime. No, once in six thousand lifetimes! They said that they had checked through six thousand émigrés after all. But could he abandon Olya? Could he live there under an assumed name? In constant fear that he might be arrested? After all, the smallest mistake could give you away. How can Americans even imagine the system of checks that exists in the USSR? There's your military service card, your work record book, your residence permit. All it needs is for somebody to investigate a single statement or check up with a previous employer and your number's up. Then you'll see the KGB in its most frightening form. They'll knock out every tooth in your head, pulverize your liver and lungs and end up shooting you as a traitor and a spy. No American will be able to help you then, and there will be no one in Russia to sympathize . . .

He poured himself a full glass of brandy and swallowed it at one go.

2

'Do you think he'll play ball?' asked Robert Carroll. MacKerry said nothing. How should he know whether this Stavinsky would agree or not? They had done what they could, and their consciences were clear. They had tailed Stavinsky for a week, following his every move around Portland, and had discovered that he had neither friends nor acquaintances in the town. Russian émigrés in general have little enough to do with each other, let alone with Americans. Stavinsky's only interests were visiting the yacht club on Saturdays and going fishing on Sundays. His only affair was with Barbara at the 7-Eleven, whose apartment he stayed in on Monday and Wednesday nights. The rest of his free time he spent sitting around at home watching television or fiddling about with his cars. His daughter was out all day studying at the University. She had got an American boyfriend and went camping with him on her days off. Loneliness was the thing which should make this Stavinsky play ball. Not money, but loneliness. To judge from what they knew of his life in the Soviet Union, he had once been an energetic television journalist, whose job had taken him all over Russia. He had lived in Siberia, Moscow, Leningrad, Central Asia, and for such an enterprising man to end up at the age of forty-six living in Portland and working as a dental technician was like being condemned to a living death. He *had* to agree, he simply *had* to. But God only knows . . . If he were to say no, then the whole operation would be finished. As it was, it was hanging by a thread, because they didn't have any other condidates in reserve. MacKerry had been bluffing about the other two, or rather there *had* been two more, but they had been interviewed *before* Stavinsky and had both refused to go back to the USSR. Stavinsky was their last card, and if he didn't go, or if he were to take two or three weeks to make up his mind, then this Assistant Director of Strategic Planning at Soviet Army General Headquarters, this Colonel Yuryshev, or whatever he called himself, would have to stay in Moscow and forget about his sudden urge to escape to the West.

Three weeks earlier, on 28 August 1981 to be exact, the Moscow correspondent of the *Washington Herald*, Jacob Stevenson, was taking some photographs of the memorial to Nikita Khrushchev at the Novodevichy Monastery (he was working on an article to mark the tenth anniversary of the former Russian dictator's death). Not far away, down one of the other paths, was a middle-aged man dressed in civilian clothes, sitting by himself next to a small, modest-looking grave and drinking brandy straight from the bottle. Stevenson reckoned that this was just another Moscow drunk, so he decided to take a photograph of him. And what was wrong with that? But scarcely had he turned his camera in the right direction, than the drunk abruptly leapt to his feet, waved his hand in a sign of protest and started walking towards him.

'Show me your papers!' he commanded hoarsely. 'You have no right to take pictures of me unless I give you my permission.'

'And you have no right to demand to see my papers,' said Stevenson, examining the man's smooth, well-cared-for features, his imperious expression and athletic bearing.

'Show me your papers, or I'll call the police! And then you'll lose your film *and* your camera.' For all its hoarseness, it was a commanding voice. Only people in high authority spoke that way in Russia, as Stevenson had learned during his three years' stay in Moscow.

'I'm an American journalist,' he replied. 'Here's my journalist's card.'

The man looked him in the eye, took his accreditation card, compared the photograph on it with the individual standing in front of him and gave an embarrassed cough.

'Talk about the biter bit . . . Care for a drink?' Meanwhile he cast his eye cautiously around the cemetery.

It was empty. There wasn't a soul around. Who goes into a graveyard at nine o'clock on a weekday morning, after all?

'No thanks,' mumbled Stevenson. 'I . . . I don't drink straight from the bottle . . .'

'Pity,' said the man with a smile. 'All right, perhaps we'll have a drink somewhere else together some time. My son is buried here . . . It's two months ago today that he died . . . That's why I'm here,' he said. He stared searchingly into Stevenson's eyes for a moment and then spoke rapidly.

'Listen carefully to what I have to say. My name is Yuryshev and I am an Assistant Director of Strategic Planning at Soviet Army General Headquarters. I know all about what the CIA is interested in, and perhaps even more. Tell them that I want to leave for the West. My work is too hush-hush for me to be allowed to leave the USSR of my own free will. So I'm offering them a bargain. If they can get me out of the Soviet Union, I'll tell them everything I know . . .'

'But I don't work for the CIA, I'm a journalist . . .'

'Cut it out! You're an American and you know very well how important a knowledge of Soviet military intentions is to your country. *How* you pass on my offer to them is your affair. Only be careful, and don't tell them when you're inside the Embassy building. The whole place is bugged by the KGB, even your ambassador's bedroom. OK?'

'Yes,' said Stevenson. 'But there's one problem. How do I know that you're not a KGB agent? They like to set traps for foreign correspondents, especially American ones. And even if you're not a KGB agent and this isn't a provocation, what guarantee is there that tomorrow you won't change your mind about getting out to the West? You *have* just drunk half a bottle of brandy, after all.'

Yuryshev stared at Stevenson very hard.

'Yes, there's something in what you say . . .' he said pensively as if weighing up in his mind. 'All right. If the CIA are going to come to any agreement, they will need to be certain that I am who I say I am, of course, and also that I've got something to tell them.' He screwed up his eyes and gave a slight smile. 'All right, in for a penny, in for a pound! Tell them this. At the beginning of October one of our submarines will run aground off the coast of Sweden. It will appear to be an accident, but that won't be the case. It's a planned operation. But exactly what kind of operation it is, I'll only tell if I make it to the West. And a lot more besides.'

His voice was calm and deliberate. Later on, when Jacob Stevenson was giving David MacKerry a detailed account of this conversation, he commented on his first impressions of Yuryshev – hands clutching a brandy bottle, the croaking voice – a typical Russian alcoholic, he had thought. Yuryshev dispelled this idea as soon as he began to present his case. The man obviously possessed exceptionally strong willpower, and half a bottle of brandy had no more effect on him than a glass of water. During the conversation at the cemetery, it went through Stevenson's mind that life was providing him with a pretty good opening chapter for a detective novel. Surely all a best-seller needs, after all, is just an original plot, isn't it? And here was such a plot ready for the taking. Even if this turned out to be nothing but a KGB provocation, he'd be able to modify it in the novel.

'All right,' said Stevenson. 'I'll do as you ask. How can I get in touch with you?'

'It's impossible to get in touch with me,' came the reply. 'You mustn't try to ring me and my address is classified information. In any case, there's no need for us to meet again. I've already told you everything.'

'But how shall I find you if . . .'

'If they accept my offer, you mean? They will. When the submarine runs aground in Sweden, they'll accept it. So tell them that as soon as the sub has carried out its mission in Sweden and returns to port, I shall go on leave. I'll be travelling to a nature reserve on the River Vyatka to do a bit of hunting and relax, and that's where you must send for me. Either write me an ordinary letter or send me a telegram, in the name of my ex-wife, Galya. Write some completely inoffensive message and mention a place to meet, so that I can disappear during this vacation. Understand? Memorize the name and address: Yuryshev, care of Anikin, Razboiny Bor Nature Reserve, Kirov Region. Now repeat it.'

Stevenson did as he was asked.

'Be seeing you,' said Yuryshev. 'Tell them that if I don't receive a letter or a telegram while I'm there, then the deal is off. That's all.'

He had begun to step firmly towards the exit, when he suddenly turned round. 'Stop! You can photograph me now, if you like. It'll come in handy for them . . .'

Five days later David MacKerry was in Stockholm. Stevenson had flown there from Moscow just for one day. With the Russians hanging about in Afghanistan, building up troop levels on the Polish and Iranian borders, sending arms openly to Syria, Libya and Arafat's PLO, and positioning their submarines just outside NATO naval bases, God knows what else they had up their sleeve! They were able to keep not only their *own* information secret, but even the bits and pieces they managed to glean from the American press. In this situation, somebody like an Assistant Director of Strategic Planning at Soviet Army General Headquarters could be an absolute godsend to American intelligence, and the CIA decided not to let this opportunity go. The head of the Russian Section, Daniel J. Cooper, summoned David MacKerry and Robert Carroll to his office and personally put them in charge of the operation.

'Keep it a secret even from the CIA,' he said with a grin, 'and use my personal authority if you need to. All our resources are at your disposal. If the Soviet sub really does run aground off Sweden, it'll mean that this Yuryshev is no KGB bait, but someone that surely does know what he's on about. He's betrayed a whisker of secret information at practically no risk to himself, but he's kept the key to the whole affair firmly planted in his own pocket. So there's no time to waste. We must be ready to get this guy out of Russia by the end of September. You'll have to arrange an urgent meeting with Stevenson, get the rest of the details of his conversation with Yuryshev, and above all, think of a *modus operandi*. Can you smuggle the man out by ship, from Riga, say, Odessa or Vladivostok maybe? Anyway, think about it. I'll expect to hear from you in a week's time, and don't forget to work on several alternative plans.'

MacKerry and Carroll went to CIA archives and extracted all the material they could get on the composition of Soviet Army General Headquarters. But it turned out that information on Yuryshev himself was very limited. A handful of defectors had mentioned his name as an up and coming military expert. In 1970 he had graduated from the General Staff Academy and had then been attached to Far Eastern Military Command Headquarters just at the time of the Sino-Soviet border conflict. After that, he'd been transferred to General Headquarters in Moscow. And that was just about it. But the fact that this Yuryshev, at the age of forty, had been transferred from the provinces to General

Headquarters in Moscow, said a great deal. Of course, it would be great if MacKerry could travel straight to Moscow disguised as a tourist, so as to get a sight of Yuryshev at least from a distance, and perhaps even meet him and discuss detailed plans for his defection. But he decided not to risk it. According to journalists' reports and information in the hands of the CIA, even after the Olympics Moscow was crammed with police and KGB agents, with foreign tourists being kept under practically open surveillance. So MacKerry flew to Stockholm instead, where Stevenson confirmed the rightness of his decision. The fact that the correspondent had been at the Novodevichy cemetery that day had come about completely by chance. During the three years that he had been working in Moscow, Jacob had got so sick of his KGB tails that in recent weeks, when leaving his apartment block, he had taken to going over to their car himself and giving them advanced details of all his movements for that day. And by religiously sticking to his itinerary, he gained their approval. The KGB men detailed to follow him were able to write out their reports on his movements almost in advance, while they themselves were able to go off home or queue up for sausages and meat, or even simply go after women. That day was no exception. Stevenson told them that he wanted to drive up to the cemetery to take a photograph of Khrushchev's grave and then to attend the opening of an exhibition of young artists on Bolshaya Gruzinskaya Street. After that, he told them, he would be visiting the special hard currency food store on the same street to buy some groceries. (You can't get anything in the ordinary Moscow shops, Stevenson said to MacKerry. You even have to queue up for frozen meats.) After asking him to get them a stock of American cigarettes and a couple of chickens at the same shop, the KGB boys followed him as far as the cemetery and then drove off on their own business. Two hours later they were already waiting for him on Bolshaya Gruzinskaya. But that kind of trust only comes after two years' acquaintance, said Stevenson, and it would have been really absurd for MacKerry to travel to Moscow *now*. You could never be certain whether you were being followed or not. In any case, it would be practically impossible actually to meet Yuryshev, as neither his address nor his number was given in the telephone directory. What would MacKerry do, stand outside General Headquarters until he came out, said Stevenson with a grin as he handed him the photographs of Yuryshev.

After this conversation MacKerry decided to take a chance. A dozen or so different plans involving smuggling Yuryshev out on board a foreign ship from Odessa, Riga or Vladivostok were examined and shelved as being too dangerous, too much trouble and too likely to fail, especially when you considered the meticulous searches made by Soviet customs officials and the fact that hardly any American vessels travel to the USSR these days. As for trusting the Japanese or the Dutch, well . . . MacKerry and Carroll proposed a different plan which was both simple and elegant in its conception: they would put another man in Yuryshev's place. Over the last ten years more than a hundred thousand émigrés had arrived in the United States from the USSR. Of them a couple of thousand had applied to the Soviet Embassy for permission to return to their former country within a month of arriving in America. But the Russians hadn't allowed them to do so, of course. Apart from this two thousand, there were probably a fair number of others who had not risked making an official application, knowing that so many had been turned down before them. So finding a person who would agree to plastic surgery and act as Yuryshev's double seemed to be an entirely realistic undertaking to MacKerry and Carroll. Everything else was a matter of technique and accurate prediction. Their boss was in favour of the idea, so the two of them buried themselves in FBI archives and after a week had come up with three possibilities. After that they lost three more days trying to win over the first two candidates, but without any tangible success. They decided to take their time with

Stavinsky therefore, and spent a week studying him. At this point the whole brilliant plan seemed to be hanging by a thread and would disappear into thin air if this émigré, Roman Stavinsky, were also to refuse to go back to Russia. They would have to return to their idea of getting Yuryshev out by ship, in a crate, if . . . if the Soviet submarine really did run aground in a few days' time somewhere off the coast of Sweden.

It was 19 September and there was only a fortnight or so left till the day indicated by Yuryshev . . .

At Portland Airport MacKerry and Carroll returned the dark-blue Chevrolet which they had rented and took the next flight back to Washington.

3

Stavinsky rang on the Tuesday.

'I agree,' he said. 'But I've got certain conditions.'

'Good,' replied MacKerry. 'Fly up here and we'll talk about it. When can you be on your way?'

'There's a flight to Washington in two hours' time.'

'OK, we'll meet you at Dulles Airport. What did you tell your daughter?'

'That I might get a job at a hospital in Washington and that I've got an interview there.'

'That's just fine. Is she at home now?'

'No. She's at the University.'

'Leave her a note to say that you'll be flying back via New York to see a few friends.'

You could say that from that moment on the whole operation got under way. Whatever Stavinsky's conditions were, unless they were absolutely absurd, they would be bound to accept them.

They found it difficult to recognize him. The former Stavinsky, with his unshaven, lifeless face, empty eyes and stoop, had disappeared. Instead, out of the airplane stepped a younger-looking, broad-shouldered gentleman, with lively, confident eyes, erect of posture and carrying a lightweight document-case in his hand.

'Hi there!' he said to MacKerry and Carroll. 'Agent 007 has arrived. How are you? To be quite honest, I could eat a horse. They gave us a bit of chicken to eat in the plane, but that was over Chicago. Let's go to a Chinese restaurant. I'm paying.'

MacKerry and Carroll grinned. This new Stavinsky was infinitely preferable to the old one. As far as the restaurant was concerned, from the moment that he had said yes, Stavinsky was on the pay-roll of the CIA. He had been booked into a hotel, he already had an appointment to see a plastic surgeon and a corpse had even been found for him – or rather an unidentified car-crash victim, whose body the police would show to Stavinsky's daughter in a few day's time.

They drove him to a Chinese restaurant in the centre of the city, on Connecticut Avenue. On the way there, Stavinsky looked out at the cars travelling down the Washington highways and exclaimed time and time again: 'Just look at that! This is a real city – almost as good as Europe! Except that you've got a lot of blacks here. We don't have them in Portland . . .'

At the restaurant he showed the confidence of a connoisseur and ordered spareribs and shrimps with Chinese vegetables and a bottle of wine for everybody. He kept on telling MacKerry and Carroll not to stint themselves. They could order whatever they wanted, as it was his treat today.

After this, he closed the menu with a bang, lit up a cigarette and said: 'OK. Let's get down to business. My conditions are as follows. In the first place, I won't travel alone. I'll need a wife to go with me. Don't stare at me like that. I've got it all worked out. If a Western tourist arrives in Russia by himself, it immediately puts the KGB on their guard. But it's completely different when a husband and wife arrive. Of course, it would be even better to go with the children, but that's too much hassle. The children could blab out something they shouldn't, so we'll do without them. But a wife is essential. She can travel out with *me* and fly back with *him*. What do you think of that idea? She can be one of your agents if you like. That's up to you. Only she mustn't have been to Russia before, for the KGB to have nothing on her. However, she *must* speak Russian, at least a little bit. And she's the one that must know it, not me. I'll have to wear a muffler around my neck, as if I've got a sore throat and lost my voice, so that I don't have to say anything in English. Otherwise my accent will give me away . . .'

He was already able to discuss the plan down to minor details. MacKerry and Carroll latched on to it right away, and were even envious. Why hadn't they thought of it themselves? Of course they had to find him an American wife who could speak a little Russian. It would simplify things at the customs enormously. Stavinsky could enter the USSR without saying a word, and Yuryshev could leave the same way, also without saying a word. The throat infection was a really good idea. Brilliant even. What other conditions would he insist upon? Of course, finding him somebody to travel with wouldn't be simple, and they had little enough time to spare already. The papers which they'd already ordered for him would have to be changed of course, but the main problem would be getting visas for the two of them at the Soviet Embassy. Anything unusual is always regarded with great suspicion there . . . Still, the whole plan was obviously worth the trouble, and the boss would like it. Carroll would have to visit the intelligence schools at Monterey and San Antonio to see what women they had available . . .

'So what do you think?' asked Stavinsky.

'Agreed,' replied MacKerry. 'You can have a wife. I like it. How about you?' he added, turning to Carroll.

'I like it too,' he said.

'*But* . . .' said Stavinsky, raising his sparerib in a gesture of warning. 'Remember this. Not any old woman will do, you know!'

'Well, this isn't Hollywood,' replied Carroll. 'We can't get you Charlie's Angels.'

'I don't need Angels, Miss Universe will do! But no, seriously, I'm not bothered about what she looks like, as long as she's intelligent and aged between thirty and thirty-five. OK? And I won't be molesting her. We've got more women in Russia like that than you Americans could dream of. Just let me get at them!'

As he said this, he gave the sparerib such a hefty bite that it broke in two.

Yes, he had a way with him, this Stavinsky, thought MacKerry, for some reason remembering that sleepy brunette Barbara from the 7-Eleven in Portland. She would be sleeping alone that night.

'My second condition is this,' continued Stavinsky. 'In Russia I shall need two sets of Soviet documents, made out in two different names. One set will be clean, so to speak. I mean, it'll be full of positive entries about my promotion at work, and I'll be a Party member. The other will state that I spent a few years in a prison camp at Salekhard in Siberia, for theft or for murdering my wife in a fit of jealousy.'

'What do you want documents like that for?' asked MacKerry, warming to the conversation. It was as if Stavinsky was the CIA agent, not them, so carefully had he worked everything out.

'It's very simple,' replied Stavinsky, as he finished with the spareribs and moved on to the shrimps and vegetables, covering everything with a layer of soya sauce. 'I won't be able to stay in Moscow, that's for certain. For the first couple of years at least, I'll travel to somewhere deep in Siberia, where no normal person would go at my age. It will be unusual, but if I've been released from camp, that will be a different matter. I killed my wife and have just done my time. I've no family, there's nowhere for me to go – so here I am in Siberia, looking for work. And nobody will bother to check the authenticity of documents such as *those*. After all, you'd have to be an idiot to slander yourself by saying that you'd been in prison for murder.'

'But what if you meet somebody who really did spend time in that camp? Especially in Siberia which is full of ex-cons. You'd have to have a detailed knowledge of camp life . . .'

'Well, I do. There are so many Soviet ex-cons living in the West now and each of them has already published two or three books about it. In any case, I once wrote an article myself for the journal *Soviet Militia* about a "progressive" camp near Salekhard, and I even spent a few days there. Not in the prison blocks, it's true. I had a separate room in the visitors' building, but it was within the camp perimeter, all the same. So I do know enough about the life to talk about it, and I even have a bit of camp slang.'

'OK, we'll let you have a special dictionary so you can mug up the lingo a little more,' said Carroll.

'But my last condition is perhaps the most important,' said Stavinsky, skilfully lifting the shrimps and vegetables to his mouth with a pair of chopsticks. 'This operation will cost you another hundred thousand dollars on top of everything else. I don't consider that to be a particularly large amount, and in any case I don't need the money for myself. But I am obliged to think about my daughter and any children she may have in the future. And, believe it or not, I still intend to have a few more children myself – over there in Russia. It's possible that they may travel here one day and I don't want them to have to start life again as I did, as poverty-striken immigrants. If you deposit this money in the bank now, then in fifteen years' time, with the interest which accrues, it'll be worth a third of a million, and you can certainly start life in America if you've got that sort of money.'

4

'Our budget for this operation is beginning to look like a joke,' said the boss. 'A hundred thousand dollars, a wife, forged documents, plastic surgery . . . And why has he moved into the Sheraton? Couldn't he have found somewhere a little cheaper? It does cost one hundred and thirty dollars a day, after all!'

'But he's paying a hundred dollars of that himself. He wants to live in the grand style at last, like a human being, as he puts it. He's brought seven thousand dollars with him and he wants to blow every last cent of it before he leaves for the Soviet Union. He's renting a Corvette too . . .'

'Is he drinking?'

'Not at the moment. In Portland he used to drink out of boredom, and sometimes he would really hit the bottle. But not at the moment.'

'What about women?'

'He hired a Japanese girl and a Philippino to visit his room yesterday,' MacKerry said with a grin. 'He paid each of them a hundred dollars this morning. He told us that he was saying farewell to the West. In Russia, according to him, there weren't any Japanese or Philippinos to be had.'

'Have you checked them out? He didn't let on about the operation, did he?'

'No, we've checked. Everything is all right.'

'Well, what else? Six thousand for the plastic surgery, another eight for the de-luxe class tourist trip to the Soviet Union . . . Why does he have to travel de-luxe class? Couldn't he go a little cheaper?'

'He doesn't want to, and he's willing to spend his own money on it. But the main thing is that if he goes de-luxe, then the Soviet Embassy will process the visas that much quicker. They need the hard currency.'

'Listen, MacKerry. How much do you think the Soviets would pay to get their hands on the Pentagon's strategic plans?'

MacKerry shrugged his shoulders. 'I don't know, I haven't tried selling them yet.'

'OK,' said Cooper, as he signed the piece of paper, confirming their budget for the operation. 'Carry on. Who do you have in mind for his wife?'

'Carroll has flown off to San Antonio to see who they've got available there.'

'I don't think that's a very good idea. The Russians may have photographs of all the staff and pupils at the school. You know yourself that they work differently in our country from the way we do over there. Remember what Arkady Shevchenko said. There are three thousand Russian spies in New York alone. No, tell Carroll to come back. You'll have to think of some other way. You must choose a woman who has never had anything to do with the CIA before.'

'But we don't have the time to go recruiting anybody!'

'OK, we'll solve this problem on the spot,' he said, picking up the receiver of his special VHF telephone. 'Miss, be so good as to connect me with the Los Angeles operator. Thank you. Operator? Put me through to the Union of Hollywood Extras, please. I'm sorry, miss, I don't know the number . . . 672. 7744? Thank you very much, miss. Hello! Is that the Extras' Union? This is producer MacKerry from Washington calling you. I'm just about to shoot a scene about some Russians, and I need an American woman aged between thirty and thirty-five who speaks at least a bit of Russian. How long will the contract be for? Well, at least a month . . . OK, my assistant will ring you back in an hour. What's your name? Miss Rudolph? Glad to talk to you. Thanks very much.' And with that he just put down the phone. 'That's all.'

'B-but . . .' stammered MacKerry in amazement.

5

Virginia Part's whole life had been ruined by the famous German film actress Romy Schneider. Romy Schneider didn't know anything about this, it's true, but what difference did that make? The fact was that Virginia looked extremely like Miss Schneider. Her eyes, face, figure and even her walk were just the same. And the only difference between them was that Virginia was eight years younger. But this was one of those rare cases when Virginia would have been ready to change ages with her rival and even be a couple of years older than her, let us say. In that case, she would have become famous before her rival and it would have been Miss Schneider who would have heard people saying all her life: 'Oh! you really do look like Virginia Part!'

In short, this resemblance of hers had prevented Virginia from being offered any big parts. What didn't she do when she was young to alter her appearance! She would change her hairstyle, dye her hair a different colour, dress up to look more like a boy and she even tried to learn a different walk. But whenever her agent passed her photo around the assistant directors and finally reached the producer himself, he would always be greeted by the same reaction: 'What is she, a second Romy Schneider? No, if I want Romy Schneider, I'll get the real thing!' The upshot was that three agents refused to have anything more to do with her.

Then she went to Sonia Moore's theatre school in New York, where she studied the Stanislavsky system under a Russian émigré director. She lived with him for a year and a half and learned a bit of Russian at the same time. But Stanislavsky didn't help, nor did having an affair with yet another agent. Virginia Part was thirty-four years of age and firmly embarked upon a career of bit parts. More recently she had even stopped battling with fate and no longer exhausted herself by dieting. Who's interested in an extra's waistline if she's going to be right in the background of the film anyway?

'Walk towards the main actors, but try not to draw atttention to yourself!' 'Drink your coffee and pretend to be having an animated conversation with your friend, but don't wave your arms about or divert attention from the main actors!' 'Stand with your back towards the camera here, and when the heroine walks past, move off stage right!' Yes, the main actors were always walking *past* with her in the background, just as the bright lights of Hollywood as a whole had passed her by. She had already got used to keeping in the background – in life generally, as well as on the screen.

She lived in a cheap hotel in Altadena (it took her an hour to get there from Hollywood in her old Pontiac). She would go filming five or six days a month as a rule, which meant that she earned even less than the average secretary. Still, on this money she managed to support her boyfriend, a young-looking comic actor aged twenty-three who had rolled up from Canada six months earlier intending to take Hollywood by storm. Not that she had fallen in love with him. Her feelings towards him were almost maternal, in fact. She wanted very much for him to succeed, and she would drag him around all the agents she knew. In the evenings she would wait for Mark at her hotel, while he hung about in some café or other talking to any number of young, down-at-heel actors like himself, or agents, directors and producers of films which hadn't got off the ground.

She didn't feel jealous even when she knew or thought she knew that Mark was being unfaithful. She had lost the energy. In fact, she would already have looked the same age as her German rival if the latter didn't do everything she could to look younger than she really was by keeping to a diet and employing her own beauty expert.

MacKerry's phone call found her sitting by herself in her hotel room on just such an evening.

'Hello, is that Miss Virginia Part? This is David MacKerry calling you from Washington. What would you say to a month's contract and a trip to Russia?'

What would she say to a month's contract? Virginia's heart skipped a beat and her throat went dry. David MacKerry? Well, she'd never heard of anybody by that name, but there were any number of independent producers working on the East Coast. Just imagine shooting a film in Russia! Could it be the famous best-seller *Gorky Park*?

'Is it . . . is it . . . *Gorky Park*?' she asked hoarsely.

'No, it's another detective story,' said MacKerry, and she could tell from his voice that he was smiling.

'Well, what do you think?'

'When do you want me for?'

'Well, if you agree, we'd like you to be in Washington tomorrow.'

So that's what it was! They wanted her to take over someone's part, of course. Whoever it was, had either fallen ill or refused to continue with the part. The film was already being shot in Washington and they needed to bring in another actress urgently. She felt a slight twinge of pride, but immediately smiled to herself. What did pride have to do with it? This might be her last chance. What was she delaying for? She ought to be bargaining over the money she would receive . . .

'I agree,' she said.

'Fantastic! Can you fly here tonight? We could order you a ticket now and come to meet you in the morning.'

But her best dress was at the dry cleaner's, damn it! Mark wasn't home either, and she had no idea when he would turn up. Still if they were shooting tomorrow . . .

'What for? Are you starting filming tomorrow?'

'Almost. Well, what do you say? Can you fly here right away?'

'All right . . . I'll be on my way . . . And, er . . . What's the film called?'

'The film . . . Mm . . .' MacKerry coughed. 'Ah, you mean *our* film. *Someone Else's Face* is the title. Ciao! I'll call again in fifteen minutes to let you know what flight you're booked on. Is two hours enough for you to get ready?'

6

Stavinsky had a private room at the hospital. His face was covered by a thick gauze bandage. Everything had taken place. They had altered the set of his eyes, straightened out his nose and shortened it a little and had made his ears stick out slightly less. The doctor had said that in three days' time he would remove the bandage over the eyes and do the same for the nose four days later, and then what a handsome fellow he would be! At first there was talk of tightening the skin on his face so as to get rid of his wrinkles (from photographs Yuryshev appeared to have very well preserved features as well as an army crew-cut), but the doctor reckoned that this operation could be dispensed with. Stavinsky needed to put on about ten pounds in weight to catch up with Yuryshev in any case, and a copious diet combined with the fresh air he would breathe when taking walks around the grounds of the Virginia Hospital, would iron out his wrinkles without any special surgery.

So far Stavinsky had had no time for any walking, however. He had only had his operation the day before, and his whole face was covered by the gauze bandage. He was lying there with his eyes closed in what appeared to him to be total darkness, and he could feel an itching sensation around his eyes and in his nose. This was a good sign according to the doctors. It meant that his skin and cartilage were healing. Stavinsky was halfway to being a dental surgeon himself, and he knew that what they were saying was perfectly true, but this didn't make it any the easier to put up with. The main problem was that he had nothing to distract him. He wasn't even allowed to watch the television.

He stretched out his hand towards the bedside cupboard. First of all his hand landed on the telephone, but then he felt a bit lower and took hold of the TV remote control box. At least he could listen to the news. But a minute or so of flicking over all the channels told him that there would be no news to listen to. It was midday, and at that time American television was full of nothing but idiotic quiz shows and guessing games (working out the price of furniture or toothpaste, etc.), or if not that, then children's cartoons or horror films. Perhaps that was better than listening to 'news from the collective farms' which Moscow television had to offer at this time, but all the same, watching cartoon films with your eyes shut was pointless. Stavinsky switched off the television and picked up the phone.

'Good morning. May I help you?' the hospital operator imediately replied.

'Dr Lawrence, please,' said Stavinsky, holding the phone a few millimetres away from his bandaged ear.

'One moment, please . . .'

Well, he had to wait for longer than one moment, but about twenty seconds later the surgeon who had performed the operation came to the phone, putting on his hale and hearty voice.

'Hi there, Mr Stavinsky! How are things? How are you feeling?'

'All right,' said Stavinsky. 'But I'm dying of boredom.'

'Shall I send a nurse along to read to you? Or would you like a light sedative?'

'I've got another idea.'

'What?'

'I'd like to have a girl come up to my room . . . You know . . .'

'Oh yes, I understand you, Mr Stavinsky. But you mustn't make any sudden movements yet, and in any case it isn't included in the cost of your treatment.'

'But what if I pay for it myself with the money I've got with me, and what if I don't make any sudden movements? If I were to get some Japanese girl to come along, she'd do it all herself, as you know.'

Lawrence laughed out loud. 'Well, I can see you don't like to waste any time . . .'

'I haven't got very much of it left. So will you let me do it?'

'It'll cost you about three hundred dollars, you know. What with the return taxi-fare from Washington and what she'll charge. But look, I'll help save you a bit of money, as long as you don't insist on a Japanese. Or are you adamant about that?'

'What have you got to offer?'

'I can send you nurse Uku Tan, she's a Korean. Our hospital charges a hundred dollars a time for this service. Do you get me? On the other hand, she will be aware of the limitations placed on you by your condition. You can make use of the service on credit, if you like, and pay by cheque when you leave the hospital. We won't indicate the exact nature of the service performed, so you'll be able to offset the cost of it against your tax.'

Yes, that's *really* important for me, thought Stavinsky with a smile. America is one hell of a place! You can buy whatever you want, and they'll tell you the cheapest way of going about it – as long as you buy it from them – and not from anybody else.

'All right, send your Korean girl along. How old is she?'

'Sir, Korean women are ageless until they're forty, and she's not forty yet, I can tell you. And that's all you need to know, isn't it?'

'OK, thanks, Doctor.'

'Bye. I'll see you tomorrow in the treatment room.'

Stavinsky replaced the phone and realized that he'd never had a Korean girl yet. One hundred dollars was a lot of money, of course. When he'd arrived in America, he'd started work in a factory for $2.25 an hour, and even now a hundred dollars represented two days' work. But what of it? In Russia he wouldn't have to spend a cent, whereas now . . . The most important thing was that Dr Lawrence should tell the CIA boys that Stavinsky had been going at it full pelt in the hospital. He was bound to tell them that, and that was good. Girls and more girls: Japanese, Koreans, mulattos, or whatever, that was the one thing that would most convince the CIA that someone really was intending to leave the Western world forever. But they'd be wrong if they believed that he would follow their instructions to the letter like a tame sheep and be content to spend the rest of his days going in fear of the KGB. Not on your life! It was stupid of him to have let slip in Portland that he would run straight to the KGB, of course. Though, on the other hand, that was a good thing, because now he realized that he mustn't go straight to the Russians: it would be dangerous for Olya. No, the CIA would have to know about his every move in Moscow and see that his actions there were beyond reproach. Then they'd have nothing to hold against Olya. That was why he'd thought up this whole business about having a wife, so that he'd have a reliable witness with him who could tell the CIA about everything. And he'd asked for the hundred thousand dollars so that they would believe he wouldn't betray the whole operation. If he did, he'd lose all the money, after all. If this look-alike of his were to get caught as he was leaving the USSR, then it would be his own fault, and not Stavinsky's. The slightest slip at the customs might betray him to the KGB after all. On the other hand, it would make up for the 'damage' which Stavinsky had inflicted on the Soviet Union when he gave those stupid interviews of his to Radio Liberty. In fact, it would repair the damage with interest, and there would still be the matter of his so-called 'services performed for the Motherland through the unmasking of Imperialist agents'. After that, he would be able to live quietly somewhere in Russia itself, and not in Siberia. In fact, he'd be able to live in Moscow, and the CIA would hold nothing against him. Would it be his fault if his look-alike had ruined his own chances by blundering at the customs?

His door opened almost noiselessly and the soft melodious voice of nurse Uku Tan suddenly said: 'Good morning, sir. How are you feeling?'

7

It was pouring with rain, one of those heavy showers which descend on Washington at the end of a torrid summer and bring a little respite from the heat. MacKerry had summoned Carroll back from San Antonio, and the two of them were meeting Virginia Part at the airport.

'Will Miss Virginia Part, arriving on the flight from Los Angeles, please make her way to the Information Desk,' came the announcement over the loudspeakers.

The two of them were standing next to Information and waiting to see who would appear out of the flood of passengers. It would be good if it were that dark-complexioned brunette with the slightly baggy bottom and the big round face . . . But no, she didn't turn around when she heard the announcement and walked right past. They didn't know why – perhaps it was pure masculine jealousy – but neither of them wanted this Stavinsky to get a real Hollywood beauty. In the first place, it might complicate the whole operation, as Hollywood beauties are renowned for their awkwardness and could pull any stunt. And in the second place, well . . . God knows!

'Excuse me, but are you Mr MacKerry?'

A quiet-looking girl with auburn hair and glasses was standing in front of them. She was dressed in a light-coloured raincoat and was pulling a suitcase along on wheels. She looked a little overweight for a Hollywood actress. She reminded them of somebody, but they couldn't remember who.

'I'm MacKerry. And you? . . .'

'I'm Virginia Part.'

'Glad to meet you. This is my assistant, Mr Carroll.'

MacKerry took the suitcase from her and asked her to follow him to the car.

They stood beneath the canopy outside the airport building and waited for Carroll to drive up in the car. MacKerry cast sideways glances at Virginia in an attempt to weigh her up. She looked to be what they needed. She was a quiet girl, not at all the usual Hollywood type, with soft, brown eyes and a kind of homely quality about her movements that was immediately reassuring. But that made it all the more difficult to believe that she would really agree to take part in this operation. Thank God it wasn't his job to try to persuade her. The boss had offered to do that himself, and he was waiting for them now at the Capitol Hilton. The CIA prefers not to invite people to its own offices but to hire rooms in hotels and to interview there anybody who is of interest to the organization. This is done not so much to avoid detection by Communist agents as to refrain from compromising the people who co-operate with the Agency. If you invite an ordinary US citizen to have a simple chat at CIA or FBI offices, he will get angry and refuse to come. Having direct links with such agencies is regarded as somehow shameful, or improper, like collaborating with your own Government, even if you did help to elect it through the normal democratic means. But if you approach an American quietly and in his own home, so that nobody else sees or hears about it, the chances are that he will tell you everything that he knows about his friends and about perfect strangers – and do even more than that sometimes . . .

'We'll drive straight to the hotel and I'll introduce you to the boss,' said MacKerry, trying hard to avoid cinema terms like 'producer', 'director' and so on, as he had in their first conversation.

In order to side-step the film subject altogether he said to her as they sat down in the car: 'Do you speak Russian?'

'*Da, nemnozhko,*' she replied in a rather pleasant accent.

'Where did you learn it?'

'At a theatre school in New York when I was studying the Stanislavsky method. I had a Russian for a teacher and he became my friend,' she said simply.

We'd better check that one out, thought MacKerry, glancing at Carroll so he'd realize that he'd have to be the one to do it. The chances of her former boyfriend having connections with the KGB were almost nil, but it was as well to be on the safe side. So Carroll went on to ask, with the apparent enthusiasm of a former New Yorker: 'Ah, so you spent some time in New York. When was that?'

'A long time ago. Eight years.'

'And which school was it, the Juilliard?'

'No, Sonia Moore,' she replied, a little surprised. After all, who in the cinema world didn't know the one place you can train in 'Method'?

They drove up to the hotel and escorted her to her room.

'Will an hour be enough for you to relax and freshen up after the journey?' asked MacKerry, looking at his watch. 'You can take a little longer if you like. The boss is expecting you for lunch at 12.30. Will you make it?'

'Of course. Where shall I meet him?'

'In the restaurant downstairs. We'll see you there.'

Virginia very much wanted to ask them about the film and her part in it, as well as finding out the big names involved. But they didn't raise the subject themselves, and she felt a little embarrassed to do so. She had never been invited to act a major role, and she wasn't quite sure how to behave in such a situation. The best thing to do was probably to wait. The producer would tell her everything for sure. She unpacked her suitcase and went to take a shower. She needed to look her best for this crucial meeting with the producer, after all. On reflection, it was a bit silly that she hadn't asked what part she was supposed to play. She didn't want to make the wrong impression with her hairstyle or dress. She had noticed this MacKerry staring at her while they had been waiting at the airport. He seemed to be a little doubtful or uncertain. Could they really push her out? They were the ones that had asked her to fly from Hollywood after all, and they had already offered her a contract! She would have to play it cool and not feel nervous or pushy, just simply be herself. That was all. She had long since stopped dreaming about ever getting a main part after all, and if they did send her back after all this she wouldn't have lost anything . . . So, trying to persuade herself to relax and not worry about anything, Virginia slipped into bed to rest for a quarter of an hour, to revive her complexion after the journey. While she was lying there, she suddenly remembered Mark. She would have to give him a ring, not now . . . not now . . . later sometime.

8

The head of the CIA's Russian Section, Daniel J. Cooper, had never once been to Russia, although he was fifty-three years of age and loved the country no less than he did his own. He knew all there was to know about Russia or rather almost all the good things there were to know about it. He had a fine command of the Russian language and liked to surprise his own subordinates with his knowledge, as he did those Russian émigrés with whom he came into contact. He had read and knew off by heart a great deal of Russian poetry, and through his love for Russian literature, as well as his sense of duty, he had read and reread the whole of Solzhenitsyn, Maksimov and other dissident writers as well as nearly every *samizdat* publication. Russia's suffering was revealed to him on those pages. This enormous country was writhing in agony at the feet of the KGB and the Communist Party, while its Government shamelessly and unceremoniously stamped out any signs of disobedience. They were even more shameless in the way they won over any number of witless, gullible souls in the West. Who should know better than the head of the CIA's Russian Section, about the general situation in the USSR which surfaced in a thousand unpleasant details, and yet still some gut reaction prevented him from taking all the atrocities attributed to the Soviet regime as gospel truth. You see the same thing today with tourists who go to visit Buchenwald or Auschwitz. As they look at those photographic relics, the mountains of human bones, the bales of human hair, and then at the silent incinerators face to face, they exclaim to each other: 'Could this really all have happened?' They know that it did, they can see that it did, but none the less . . .

Cooper's predecessor, Barry Christopher, had been hampered in his work by that inward refusal to admit the full reality of the monster he was battling with, and now Cooper, doing the same job, was having to fight a similar reaction. He had to stifle the hope both in himself and in those who worked under him that even this monster would act according to the laws of common humanity. 'You wouldn't hunt a bear wearing kid gloves, would you, and there's no reason for us to be over-delicate either,' he would say to his staff, trying to take a few lessons in ruthlessness from his KGB opponents.

Over the last four years Soviet agents in America had been acting with a total lack of principle. It wasn't just that the KGB succeeded in purchasing the latest American electronic equipment through third countries, or that the Soviets used front organizations to order new computer models for their own defence industry. But now, making use of the ridiculous law forbidding CIA and FBI agents physically to enter the Congress, Soviet agents had the effrontery to wander all over the Congress buildings themselves. Only ten days before, one Soviet agent, the assistant air attaché Yury Leonov, had simply walked into the office of a congressional aide and asked for a copy of a plan showing the geographical distribution of MX inter-continental missiles. This story had been splashed all over the newspapers, but then people had immediately forgotten about it and everything went on in the old way. Soviet agents were busy spying in American companies manufacturing optical, electronic or laser equipment, and either through purchase, blackmail or direct theft managed to get their hands on items which were forbidden to be exported to the USSR. Every day brought to light further examples of this kind of industrial espionage. One company in California, despite the ban imposed by the US President himself, had sold mirrors for laser installations which were now being used in Soviet defence production. Elsewhere, two Soviet agents managed to infiltrate a large radio company and steal documentation on the manufacture of secret radio apparatus. At the same time, and quite legally, the USSR had been able to buy American seismographic equipment for oil exploration. And with the help of this equipment the Russians were scouring the sea, not for oil but for American submarines.

It was no exaggeration to say that much of the progress made by the Soviet defence industry had derived from American technology. Their agents felt completely at home in the democratic US of A, buying computers, secret equipment, technical plans, whole technological firms and would you believe it . . . banks! Recently, right at the last moment, they managed to stop KGB agents purchasing one such bank, but how many American construction firms, electronics companies, banks or whatever were continuing to work for the USSR, without anyone suspecting?

Somehow the country *had* to take action against this outrageous state of affairs. It just happened that quite recently, despite protests from the United States, Sweden had sold aircraft-tracking equipment to the Russians, and now – hey presto! – a Soviet submarine was about to run aground off the Swedish coast. That would teach the Swedes a lesson, but what were the Russians actually up to? They wouldn't cause an international row just for the hell of it! There must be something in it for them! So it was all the more important for the defection of this Colonel Yuryshev to succeed. The most brilliant ideas are always the simplest, thought Daniel J. Cooper, and if they played their cards right, they'd certainly succeed. He couldn't resist the pleasure of taking a direct part in this particular action, even if it were only for a few minutes and especially if it involved something as delicate and pleasant as recruiting a Hollywood actress. It was his idea after all, and he wanted to come up trumps on this occasion.

This was why Cooper was sitting at a table in the corner of the comfortable, softly lit, Capitol Hilton restaurant and preparing himself for a certain ticklish conversation. MacKerry was waiting for Virginia Part in the foyer by the elevator. He met her at exactly 12.29 and took her through the restaurant to the table where his boss was sitting. She could see that MacKerry's eyes were full of approval for her dark, fairly high-necked dress and her hair, gathered in a neat bun at the back.

'Allow me to introduce you. The actress, Miss Virginia Part – my boss, Mr Daniel Cooper.'

Cooper stood up, bowed slightly and shook her hand.

'Very glad to meet you. Please sit down.'

When MacKerry referred to her as 'the actress, Miss Virginia Part', she felt a thrill of pleasure and excitement. It was ten years since anybody had referred to her by that title, so simple and yet full of importance for her. Everything was beginning again. Everything would now happen, she thought as she sat down at the table.

The wine waiter came up immediately, of course, to take their order. Cooper looked at Virginia.

'A ginger ale, please,' she said.

Cooper smiled and said: 'Ginger ale for the lady and two scotches.'

Then they turned to the menu. Virgina ordered a fillet mignon, while Cooper and MacKerry both went for beefsteaks. Cooper shut the menu with a loud bang and gave it back to the waiter.

'OK,' he said, 'let's get down to the nitty-gritty. Miss Part, you have a serious task ahead of you. *Somebody Else's Face* isn't a film at all, it's for real. And I'm not a producer, I'm the head of the CIA's Russian Section.' As he said this, he placed his identity papers on the table and opened them so that Virginia could see his photograph and surname.

'We need your help, the help of an actress just like yourself. I think you know as well as I do what's going on in the world just now. The Russians have outmanoeuvred us both in terms of weapon strength and diplomacy. Their missiles are poised to attack Europe, but when Haig visits the West Europeans, they start complaining that it's the Americans who are threatening their peaceful way of life, and not the Russians. I don't want to give you a lecture. I think that you're as well up in these things as I am. This great American democracy of ours is both our strength and our weakness, for the simple reason that the Russians can get practically any secret information they want simply by reading our newspapers, while they keep the plans of even the simplest copying machines a closely guarded secret. And I won't start talking to you about American patriotism. I simply want to ask you in the name of our country to take the lead role in a simple but extremely important operation – to take part in a political detective story, if you like. Only it won't be a story and it won't be a film. It'll be happening for real. Hold on, I know that this isn't why you flew here. But your flight and even a certain disappointment on your part will all be paid for, even if you refuse to help us. Who knows? Perhaps Hollywood will make a film of this operation one day, and then you'll be asked to play your own role. It's never happened before, but what a sensation that would be – a film actress being asked to act a glamorous part in real life first of all, and *then* in the cinema! It's your decision.'

He looked at her very attentively and waited.

'I don't know . . . I just don't know . . .' said Virginia in confusion. 'Can I do it? What am I supposed to do? No, what are you talking about? I'm not . . . I'm not even an actress . . .'

'That's not true. You *are* an actress, only you haven't become well-known yet. You've spent your whole life preparing to become a famous actress, but so far it hasn't quite worked out like that. Now it can. No lead part has ever turned up for you before, now one has. Not in a film, it's true – but so what?'

The fillet mignon and the steaks arrived. While the waiter

was laying the table, Cooper said nothing and Virginia was thinking. Or rather, what she was doing wasn't so much a process of thought. She was just trying to gather all Cooper's words together and join them up, rather like making a dress out of patchwork. And the more she tried the dress for size, the less ridiculous it seemed and the more it seemed to fit.

Surprised at her own words, she asked: 'Well . . . what am I supposed to do?'

'I'll be quite honest with you, though you must understand this is a state secret. A certain individual who is very necessary to us in our work needs to leave Russia. To be more exact, we need to get him out. If we succeed, then the world will get to know the Russians' most secret military plans and we'll slow their progress down by a decade or so. Then we will be able to catch them up in terms of weapon strength. Even five years will be long enough. But we need those five years, and we need this man.'

'And you want me . . . you want me to get him out?' Virginia asked in astonishment, remembering that MacKerry had said something about a trip to Russia in their telephone conversation.

'Well, not by yourself. Since you haven't agreed to help us yet, I can't go into detail about the operation. But try to imagine it in the abstract, as if you were watching a film or something. An ordinary American married couple travel to Moscow as simple tourists. They're rich. They live in the best hotels, visit the museums and theatres, all according to the book. Absolutely nothing to do with spying, or anything. And only on the very last day before their departure, when they're at one of these theatres or museums, the husband leaves the wife for a minute or two, to go to the john, let's say. A few seconds later, and he's by her side again, watching the play, the ballet, or looking at the paintings in the Hermitage. Only the wife knows that this person isn't the husband she flew to Russia with, but his double . . . somebody who looks absolutely like her husband

and who, either that day or the next, leaves the USSR with her, using her husband's passport and visa. That's it, that's all the operation consists of. Later, back in Hollywood it can be embroidered. You can add any number of adventures and complications, but as far as we're concerned, the fewer adventures and complications which actually take place, the better. I hope there won't be any at all, because the operation has been planned down to the last detail and should be as simple as possible. You fly there with one husband and come back with an exact copy. And if something should happen, God forbid, then the Russians will get nothing out of you. You're an actress and you must pretend that you hadn't even noticed the substitution. They are exact doubles, after all!'

'Wait a minute. I don't even have a husband!'

'We've got one for you,' said Cooper with a smile. 'Or even two. One of them for the journey out, and another for the trip back. They're already waiting for you. Virginia, I realize that this offer must sound fantastic, but tell me honestly. Would you refuse a part like this in a film?'

She said nothing.

'Of course you wouldn't,' he replied for her. 'And how is real life any different from the screen? It involves the same Stanislavsky method. You have to know how to act the part in whatever circumstances crop up. That's all. And the circumstances which you are being offered are very simple: a holiday in Moscow for two newly-weds. A honeymoon, if you like. And we can offer you even more than that!'

A new idea had suddenly come into Cooper's head.

'We could make a grand tour of it, taking in Paris and Rome, for example, as well as Moscow. And after that you can fly back home to America.'

He looked at MacKerry, and MacKerry could see what his boss was getting at. If the trip to Moscow were part of a wider holiday, the Soviet Embassy would be much less suspicious when issuing the visas. A rich American couple were planning a typical American honeymoon.

'Well, what do you think?' asked Cooper, turning to face Virginia once more.

'I don't know . . . I'll have to think about it,' said Virginia. Then she couldn't help herself, she had to ask: 'And who is he, this man? Is it you?' she said, looking at MacKerry.

'No,' he said, grinning. 'I wouldn't object to being your husband, of course, but unfortunately it isn't me.'

'You're probably worried about one rather delicate matter,' said Cooper, 'but I can set your mind at rest. We're talking about two people pretending to be husband and wife, not the real thing. Nobody is asking you to do that, word of honour. Let's say this. We'll give you until tomorrow to think about it, and then tomorrow morning, at nine o'clock, we'll be in touch by phone. If you refuse, there's a plane to Los Angeles at 10.00 a.m. and you can fly back home with a clear conscience . . . while we start looking for somebody to replace you. What would you like for dessert?'

9

When do we ever make the most serious decisions of our lives? Certainly not in daylight!

Virginia spent the rest of the day following her feet around Washington. The streets had dried out now after the rain, and the hot sun was beating down on them. She went into the National Gallery and spent a long time wandering about the Rodin exhibition, almost forgetting the decision she had to make. Or to be more exact, she forced herself to forget about the whole problem for a time. She didn't even begin to know how to set about resolving it. In the museum she joined some conducted tour and listened carefully to the ecstatic young guide give his intense account of how Rodin's statue of Balzac was created.

Apparently, when Rodin had received this particular commission, his first act had been to track down the old tailor who used to make all Balzac's clothes. The old man had kept a note of Balzac's measurements, so Rodin commissioned him to make another set of clothes, an exact copy of those he had made for Balzac. Then Rodin happened to find a Paris butcher who fitted all these garments perfectly, and as a result created Balzac's double. After that he started to sculpt the artist's figure, in the nude at first. The exhibition contained several versions of the naked Balzac with his powerful torso and enormous pot-belly, which itself seemed to exude a kind of magnificent 'Balzacian' arrogance. But one sculpture in particular was striking for its boldness and for the precise expression it gave to a slightly outrageous concept – the mighty image of the naked Balzac, standing on a pedestal, legs wide apart, stomach protruding, powerful shoulders slightly back and both hands supporting his penis. Medieval paintings often show knights in armour grasping the hilts of their swords and this obviously symbolized that. It wasn't simply that in Rodin's sculpture one could see Balzac holding on to his penis. It was rather that the strength of Balzac's art itself was contained in that part of the human anatomy, the physical source of his knowledge about the human condition and the human comedy. And headless as it was, this sculpture, with its torso and its self-confident gesture, was a triumphant mockery of the so-called complexity and refinement of existence. Subsequently, when Rodin had sculpted Balzac's enormous eagle-like head and combined it with the naked torso, he concealed Balzac's nakedness beneath the majestic long folds of a cloak, while still retaining the same pose beneath the garment.

Virginia spent a long time looking at the exhibition, admiring the vigour of Rodin's talent as manifested in dozens of other famous sculptures. And somehow an awareness of the artist's marvellous ironic attitude to what constitutes the real essence of human life had already penetrated deep into her consciousness. Little did she know that from the moment she had said goodbye to Cooper and left the hotel to wander round Washington, two CIA agents had been trailing her and that it wasn't just for herself that she had arranged this visit to the Rodin exhibition – they had been taking it in, too.

By the time she returned to the hotel that evening, she still hadn't reached any decision, or rather she thought she hadn't reached one. She had dinner in the same restaurant, took a shower, watched the news and a film on television, putting off all the time the moment when she would have to say to herself: 'Well, what shall I do? Is it yes or no?' Then she tried making a collect call to Mark in California. She said to herself that if Mark were home that night waiting for her, then she would . . . yes, she would definitely refuse to take part in this adventure. But Mark wasn't at home, of course. She looked at her watch. There in Los Angeles it was only seven o'clock in the evening, and he might have got held up somewhere. Although she didn't really believe that he would be home later, she still put off making her decision for an hour, then another . . . But when it was one o'clock in the morning Washington time, that is to say ten o'clock on the West Coast, and the operator still told her that there was no reply, she knew that she would say yes to Cooper and MacKerry in the morning. She would say it because that one word would open the door to a new life for her and she would be able to shake off the mould of her previous existence. And because somebody here needed her. People who would depend on her. Not like Mark who simply made use of her bed and her refrigerator . . .

At 8.40 next morning MacKerry received a report about Miss Virginia Part's movements the previous day. She hadn't gone to the Soviet Embassy and she hadn't met any strangers, let alone Russians. All she had done was try to ring home on three occasions. At 9.00 a.m. MacKerry was already downstairs at the Capitol Hilton, dialling her number on the internal telephone.

'Good morning, Miss Part. This is MacKerry. Did you have a good night's rest?'

10

They removed one of Stavinsky's bandages, and then Dr Lawrence said: 'Open your eyes. Wider! Don't worry! Now you'll be seeing the world through *new* eyes!'

Stavinsky opened his eyelids and felt no pain.

Nothing in the world had changed. It was 26 September and a sunny day like any other. Outside the window of his room a red-breasted bird sat on a branch of a maple tree and stared inquisitively in, its head cocked slightly to one side. Stavinsky mimicked its gesture, moving his head to one side and peering at the bird. Then he started grinning and asked for a mirror.

'It's too early for that yet,' said Lawrence. 'Your eyes are normal, don't worry. In three days' time we'll remove the bandage from your nose, and then you'll be able to admire yourself, as much as you like. But now you ought to get yourself ready. You've got visitors.'

'Who?' asked Stavinsky in amazement.

'Your wife.'

'My wife? What wife?'

'Well, you should know which one better than us,' he said with a smile, and left the room together with the nurse.

Stavinsky cast a quick eye around the room. Was everything clean and tidy? Well, what do you know, these agents had already found him a wife! How was that for speed! They'd try to palm him off with some regular CIA agent whose very face told you that she worked for the Secret Service, and they'd ruin the whole operation.

The door opened and in walked MacKerry accompanied by . . .

Stavinsky screwed up his eyes. He didn't understand yet what had happened, but a kind of inner fear and apprehension, a strange confusion of memory dredged up from his subconscious the image and face of somebody completely different, but completely alike.

Together with MacKerry there had walked into his room

his own mother, as she looked at the age of thirty – he couldn't have been wrong. She had the same calm, round face and deep brown eyes, the same lips, nose and hair. Words couldn't convey the likeness, of course, but he was in no doubt that this was the most radiant woman in the world and the one whom he had done most to hurt, whom he had not remembered for a long time and whom he had buried seventeen years earlier in a cemetery in Saratov . . .

'Hello!' said MacKerry, forcing Stavinsky to emerge once again from his childhood memories. 'How are you feeling?'

Stavinsky exerted his willpower and compelled himself to open his eyes. Yes, she did resemble his mother, although a second look at her began to reveal some of the differences. Her complexion was different, she had no dimples and her hair was slightly darker . . . Nevertheless, she was very like his mother.

'Let me introduce you. Mr Robert Williams – Miss Virginia Part. Or rather, from today her name is no longer Part, but Williams. Here is the marriage certificate. Sit down, Virginia . . .'

Virginia looked at the man lying in front of her and at the white bandage criss-crossing his face, and she couldn't fathom the origin of the strange anxiety which suddenly overcame her. Could it be his dark eyes which seemed to be mutely saying something to her? They hadn't said a word to each other yet, either in English or in Russian, and it was impossible for her even to see all of his face, and yet something had touched her soul. Could it be pity?

She sat down. She didn't know what to say, and he was silent, and only MacKerry did what he could to alleviate the awkwardness of this sudden silence.

'OK, ladies and gentlemen! While you are getting used to each other and having a good look at what the other one looks like, I'll give you a progress report. Over all this time, Mr Williams, we have not only found you a wife, but we have also come up with a new name and life-history for you.

It wasn't easy, but on the other hand you'll now have something American to present the Soviets with. You are now Dr Robert Williams. The real Robert Williams is a dentist who has his surgery in Potomac, Maryland. It's not far from Washington, but I doubt whether the Soviets, when they check through your visa application, will travel to Potomac to check this Dr Williams out. But they might well ring him up, and he knows what to say. In any case, we don't have another bachelor dentist available. On the day you leave, he will also be going off on vacation to Florida, and that is the message which his telephone answering service will relay. Tomorrow Virginia will go to the Soviet Embassy and, as a newly-wed, ask them to speed up issuing the visas. You've only just got married after all, and are anxious to begin your honeymoon. So here you are, Mr Williams. Allow me to present you with the details of this doctor's life. There are twelve pages of text there, in Russian and in English. You should treat his biography as your own and learn it off by heart, down to the smallest details. Virginia already knows it, but it's not so important for her. You have only just got married, after all, and haven't known each other for very long. She'll tell you about her life herself, as she hasn't got anything to invent. She is playing herself, after all. Oh yes, I forgot to tell you, sir, that we've carried out your requests in every respect. Your wife comes from Hollywood and she speaks a little Russian. OK? Satisfied?'

Half of what MacKerry had been saying had gone in one ear and out the other. So he was to pretend to be this Robert Williams. Well, why not? In the back of his mind he appreciated their quick thinking. It was clever of them to choose a colleague of his in the dental profession. You never knew what might happen when he was actually in Russia. But he could always act the part of a dentist. As for the rest of what MacKerry was going on about, he scarcely heard it. He was looking at Virgina. This woman who so resembled his own mother when she was young, what was she thinking about him now? And what would his mother have thought of him? She would have burst into tears, of course, at the thought of the risks he was letting himself in for. She would have tried to dissuade him. She would have forbidden him to do it. But then, when had he ever taken any notice of that? How many stupid things he had done, because he had never listened to her, and what scrapes he had got into! His mother had been so keen for him to become a dentist, but after his third year at the Institute, he had abandoned medicine and thrown himself into television. He wanted to be famous! But there you are! His mother had been proved right yet again. Life had compelled him to become a dental technician, and was now forcing him to become a doctor, albeit a fake one. Without taking his eyes off Virginia, Roman Stavinsky alias Robert Williams swore to himself that at the first chance he had after his return to Russia he would travel to Saratov to visit his mother's grave.

Meanwhile, Virginia was staring at Stavinsky and thinking her own thoughts. Here was a man who had agreed to take this enormous risk – and why? The risk which she was taking was nothing in comparison with his. She would arrive in this Russia of his and, God willing, fly off again, while he would be *staying* there. Forever. She had heard something about modern-day Russia from her former Russian boyfriend, and she had read some things by Solzhenitsyn who had just arrived in the States at the time and was very fashionable. She had also read Barron's book about the KGB. She saw Moscow and the whole of Russia as one gigantic concentration camp. It was dangerous enough simply to fly there for a few days and then slip straight out again, but this man had agreed to remain there of his own free will. The Japanese have got a special word for people like that . . . What is it? Ah, yes: kamikaze! But why, oh why was he letting himself in for it? That she had yet to discover . . .

Stavinsky felt that the silence was becoming awkward and that he had to say something. MacKerry got to his feet.

'OK,' he said. 'While you two are looking each other over,

I'll go and have a few words with Dr Lawrence.'

He went out of the room, and the two of them were left by themselves. But neither Stavinsky, nor Virginia were in any hurry to start up a conversation. In fact, they didn't know what to talk about.

At last Stavinsky smiled and said to her in Russian: 'I expect I look quite a sight in this stupid bandage.'

'No,' she replied, also in Russian. 'You look like a child who's got a broken nose.'

Stavinsky nearly burst into tears. Those words and the deep, gentle voice which had uttered them, reminded him so much of his mother.

'You remind me very much of my mother,' he said with a weak smile.

There was a soft buzz from the telephone, and Stavinsky answered it.

'Hello,' said a voice in Russian. It was Carroll. 'Is my boss with you?'

'No, he's talking to Dr Lawrence. I can ask the operator to transfer you.'

'Yes, thanks very much.'

The two of them were left in silence again. Neither said a word.

'How come you know Russian?' asked Stavinsky.

But Virginia had no time to reply. MacKerry came back into the room.

'OK, Virginia, it's time for us to be going. There will be plenty of time for you to talk to your husband, but for the moment we've got a huge number of things to do.'

Virginia stood up.

'*Do svidaniya,*' she said to Stavinsky.

'Until we meet again,' he replied.

'The doctor said that you'll be having your last bandage removed in three or four days,' said MacKerry. 'Virginia, wait for me in the foyer, will you? I'll catch you up in a moment. There are a few things I need to say to your husband.'

When the door had closed, MacKerry continued. 'Roman, that was Carroll on the phone. The New York police have found a suitable body, so it's time for us to fix a date for your funeral. If you want to, you can ring your daughter today and pretend to be in New York. But tomorrow the police will phone her to tell her that you have been involved in an automobile accident.'

Stavinsky shook his head. 'No, tomorrow is too soon. I want to be at the funeral myself.'

'At your own funeral!' said MacKerry in amazement.

'Yes.'

'But listen, that's mad. We would have to come with you to make sure you didn't give yourself away, and that's just wasting further time.'

'I won't give my presence away, don't worry. It's just that I want to catch a glimpse of my daughter at the graveside. There aren't many people who get to do that, are there?'

'You're a hard man, Stavinsky.'

'My name is Williams, Robert Williams. Roman Stavinsky died in a car-crash and I want to bury him. I did have something to do with him, after all. And please, don't get angry. This is the last chance I'll have to see my daughter.'

'All right. I'll think about how it can be done,' said MacKerry.

'And there's one more thing. Don't talk to Virginia about this funeral, OK?'

'All right,' said MacKerry. 'Call your daughter today and tell her that you're about to travel to New York.'

11

For Virginia the days which followed were filled with various small tasks. Together with MacKerry she had to draw up an itinerary for the honeymoon, and then she had to order the tickets in a travel agency. After that it was time to visit the Soviet Embassy to get the visas. The Russians spent a long time trying to persuade her to travel by Aeroflot to Europe. Virginia followed MacKerry's advice and was very choosy, asking a lot of questions about the in-flight service, the food, and the difference in prices. It was only when the Soviets managed to prove to her that by travelling on a Russian plane she and her husband would save more than a hundred dollars that she agreed to travel Aeroflot between Western Europe and Moscow. On the journey home to America she insisted that she and her husband would travel in a US plane. 'Every country begins in its own airplane,' she told the Russians with a smile. But she and MacKerry had worked it out in advance that she would willingly agree to travel de-luxe to Russia and not tourist class. This would cost three hundred dollars more, but on the other hand they would be given one of the best rooms at the Hotel National, they would be served individual meals, a two-day, individual trip to Leningrad would be arranged for them, they could have tickets to any play or show in Moscow, including the Bolshoi Theatre, and whenever they wanted, they would have a private Volga put at their disposal with a chauffeur and a guide who spoke English. Of course, as MacKerry said, all this meant was that they would have a personal KGB guide and a personal KGB driver at their disposal during the day, and it couldn't be ruled out that the conversations they had in their hotel room would be monitored all round the clock. But on the other hand, all this entered into MacKerry's calculations. If Mr and Mrs Williams were kept under constant surveillance by the KGB, there would be no need to employ any secret agents to follow them.

In short, after Virginia had spent an hour talking to the officials and the Russian consul, to their great satisfaction she rang the travel agency direct from the Embassy and asked the agent to reorder her tickets with Aeroflot. After that, she gathered up all the necessary forms – there turned out to be twenty-four pages of them, twelve each for herself and her husband – and said that she would be mailing them back from Potomac (along with the twelve photographs which were also required) in the next few days. The Soviets asked her not to delay as they would have to inform Moscow of their planned arrival so as to get a good room reserved for them in the hotel. Virginia assured them that she would mail everything back the following day. As she was saying goodbye to them, she suddenly thought of something. What would the weather be like in Moscow and what clothes should she wear? She expected that the temperatures would be below zero . . .

After leaving the Embassy, Virginia went around the shops. This was also in accordance with MacKerry's plan. If the Soviets were suspicious about anything, he said, they might have her followed. So she was to visit Lord and Taylor and Bloomingdale's and order fur-lined coats and warm boots for herself and her husband. In general, she was to throw a bit of money about; it would put their minds at rest.

Both Virginia and MacKerry realized that her visit to the Soviet Embassy was a test of her ability, a way of checking whether she was able to cope with the part which she had agreed to play. This was why the preparation for this visit, or the rehearsals as you might call them, took longer than the visit itself. However, everything went well, and MacKerry was able to see Virginia leave the Embassy with his own eyes, get into 'her' car with its Maryland registration and drive off around the shops. There were no Soviet agents following her.

But MacKerry had other things to worry about. Here they were, splashing money about all over the place, arranging plastic surgery, fixing Stavinsky's funeral (his daughter had flown to New York with her fiancé and the police had already shown her the deceased's papers and the body itself, mutilated beyond recognition), but what about Yuryshev? What if this whole business turned out to be a pretence, what if no submarine were to run aground in the next few days? What if this were a ruse on the KGB's part in order to trap them? Everything was going too smoothly, and MacKerry didn't like it. Today was 1 October. He called in at the office first thing, sat Carroll down in front of the teleprinter and told him to monitor all the reports from Northern Europe. But everything in Europe was peaceful, if you didn't count the troubles in Poland and Northern Ireland, the shift to the left in France, and so on. Of course, if the Soviet submarine were to run aground today or tomorrow, none of them — not MacKerry, Carroll, Stavinsky or Virginia — was actually ready to begin the operation. Stavinsky was still in hospital, as his nose wasn't healing as quickly as Dr Lawrence had promised, and the visas hadn't been received from Russia yet. Still, it would be better if this submarine were to put in an appearance. At least then you could say with certainty that this Yuryshev wasn't a KGB ploy. And there would still be almost a month of Yuryshev's vacation ahead of them. They would still have time . . .

Worried by these thoughts, MacKerry called up Carroll over his car radio, told him to continue with the surveillance of Virginia and drove off to the office himself. Whatever happened, they had taken the first step. Tomorrow Virginia and Robert Williams's visa applications would be arriving at the Soviet Embassy together with photographs of Virginia and Yuryshev — the real Yuryshev, as they didn't want there to be any hitch when he and Virginia were leaving the USSR.

Meanwhile, Virginia had bought winter garments for herself and her husband and had returned to the hotel. Her first day's 'filming' had gone well, but she felt no sense of satisfaction. Of course, she had coped with the part and she had appeared both charming and respectable at the Soviet Embassy. But there was some kind of inner anxiety and tension gnawing away at her soul. This man she had met at the hospital, this man who had the eyes of a fatally wounded wild animal . . . Without even bothering to take a shower, Virginia collapsed exhausted into bed and realized that she had not the slightest desire to call Mark.

12

THE GRIEF-STRICKEN DAUGHTER OF ROMAN BORISOVICH STAVINSKY ANNOUNCES WITH DEEP REGRET THE UNTIMELY AND TRAGIC DEATH OF HER FATHER
The burial service and interment will take place on Saturday, 3 October at 10.00 a.m. at the cemetery of the St Vladimir Monastery, New Jersey.

The Russian newspaper *Novoe Russkoe Slovo*, which has been published daily in New York since the year 1910, keeps to the old Russian tradition of printing funeral announcements on the front page together with news from the White House and the latest political sensations. Stavinsky folded the paper and threw it on to the back seat of the car. So he had lived to see his own funeral! His 'grief-stricken daughter' had found him a place in the cemetery of a Russian monastery in New Jersey and there would even be a burial service. Stavinsky had never believed in God and had never known what nationality to regard himself as being, since his mother had been a Jew and his father a Russian. In Russia such people are referred to by the peculiar expression 'half-blood', and when he was old enough to receive his first passport Stavinsky entered in it that he was Russian, following his father's line. This opened the door to higher education and also to television, for it was only in recent years that personnel departments had widened the scope of their application forms so that it was now necessary not only to indicate your nationality, but also to put your mother's maiden name as well as the full first names, patronymics and surnames of both sets of grandparents. This helped the personnel departments to discover 'hidden' Jews, but it also helped Stavinsky to get permission to emigrate. After all, according to Israeli law he was a Jew, since his mother had been one. But he was married to a Russian woman, and for that reason his daughter Olya had never considered herself to be Jewish. In any case, what kind of Jews were they if they didn't know a word of Hebrew and if they had grown up amid Russian culture, been educated in Russian schools, observed Russian Orthodox religious festivals, knew nothing about the Jewish ones and weren't even interested in them? He and his wife had got divorced exactly ten years ago, after she had come home and found him with his mistress. Calling him a 'yiddish bastard', she walked out slamming the door after her. She made no claim on her daughter, and called her 'yiddish scum' as well. She was aged thirty then and worked as an announcer on Moscow television. She very quickly got married to a famous movie director. Stavinsky and Olya lived in Russia for a couple more years and then emigrated with visas to Israel. But Olya had no wish to settle in Israel and, in his opinion, there was nothing for him to do there, either, so they entered the big, wide world and travelled to America, the land of their dreams. And so he arrived to be buried at the age of forty-six in some neglected and half-abandoned cemetery in New Jersey.

Stavinsky smiled to himself. So what? This cemetery marked the beginning of his new life and he'd see how it would turn out.

MacKerry stopped at a road junction and asked the driver of the car in front of him the whereabouts of the Russian monastery. According to the map, it had to be somewhere close by. And so it was. Beyond the junction was an old park with an Orthodox church, and some distance beyond the church you could see a collection of ramshackle and half-buried Orthodox crosses marking the graves. It was a quarter to ten and the warm October sun was peeping through the thick green foliage of the avenue of trees down which they drove on their way to the cemetery.

They caught sight of Olya and her boyfriend, Jack Cross, immediately. He was a student at Portland university. Apart from these two, the priest and a couple of gravediggers who were busy with another, freshly dug grave, there was nobody around. MacKerry drove slowly towards them.

'Put your dark glasses on,' he said to Stavinsky, who did as he was told. 'And mind you don't get out of the car.'

'Don't worry,' said Stavinsky.

They drove slowly past this solitary group of people and saw Olya and Jack look hopefully across towards their car. Could one of Roman Stavinsky's friends have noticed the announcement in the newspaper and decided to attend the funeral? Stavinsky looked at his daughter's tearstained face. She had a pinched, tired expression, and his heart sank. Would he ever see her again? Not very likely . . . Although . . . He had plans about that, too. She had been granted US citizenship, her father had died, and the Soviet authorities could have no claim on her. Why shouldn't she and her husband travel to Russia as tourists or to visit her mother? He could pay for the trip out of the hundred thousand dollars which the CIA would deposit in his account. All he had to do was think of a way of getting the money to her, but that was a trivial detail . . . He noticed that he was being stared at. All right, time to put on a sorrowful expression. That's right. Olya had turned away by now, and MacKerry brought the car to within a few feet of Stavinsky's grave, stopping a little beyond it near another freshly painted cross.

'Please don't get out of the car,' MacKerry said once again.

'Don't worry, I won't.'

MacKerry opened the car door, got out and walked around the back to get something out of the boot. It was an unsigned wreath which he had bought in Washington. He placed it on somebody's grave. He had planned this from the beginning so that Olya and anybody who was attending Stavinsky's funeral would think that they were simply visiting another grave.

MacKerry stood by this graveside for a few minutes, while Stavinsky could listen through the open window to his daughter saying to the priest: 'Probably nobody else will come. Start the service, please.'

The priest stood next to the sealed coffin which was lying on a mound of freshly dug earth and began to read the burial service for God's servant, Roman Stavinsky. MacKerry came back to the car, got into the front seat and began to drive off.

Stavinsky took one last look at his own funeral. It was a pitiful lonely sight . . .

When they had left the cemetery, he said to MacKerry: 'Let's drive to a bar somewhere. We ought to drink something — in memory of the deceased. I did know him fairly closely, after all.'

'Yes,' said MacKerry. 'You've a lot of strength, Stavinsky.'

13

Three days after Virginia's visit to the Soviet Embassy, the diplomatic mail had delivered to Moscow the photographs and application forms of seventeen ordinary US citizens requesting visas for a tourist trip to the USSR. The Foreign Ministry sent these applications by special messenger to KGB headquarters at 2, Dzerzhinsky Square. There, in the office of Tourist Department 7 the forms were removed from their sealed packet and duly entered in the Register of Incoming Documents. Then the big-bosomed secretary, Katya, carefully placed them into separate files and took them into the office of the head of the American Section, Major Neznachny.

'Some new applications have arrived, Frol Yevseyich,' said the twenty-five-year-old, dark-eyed Katya, as she entered Neznachny's office carrying the seventeen folders balanced against her ample bosom. Katya's breasts wouldn't fit into any uniform, so she had long been allowed to go to work in ordinary civilian dress in spite of being a sergeant-major. As a matter of fact, there weren't many employees in this particular office who did wear KGB military uniform, as the nature of their job meant that they were continually hanging around Intourist hotels and restaurants and other places frequented by foreign tourists. But Katya made use of this special dispensation to go to work in a light, semi-transparent blouse, bedroom slippers and a kind of household skirt, made of printed cotton, so tight around the hips that her powerful thighs seemed to be almost bursting through it.

Closing the heavy door behind her, Katya went up to Neznachny's desk which was piled high with newspapers and forms, and stood right next to the major. Then she put the seventeen files down in front of him and stared at him with those moist, languishing eyes of hers, waiting for him to say something. Her chest was positioned just above his shoulder, and he could hear Katya's languid, slightly melancholy breathing right next to him. He knew that all he had to do was reach out to touch those breasts or thighs and Katya would almost swoon with happiness. Her dark glistening eyes would close and her hot heavy body would fall into his arms there and then — in the armchair, on the table or on the floor, wherever he said. But it was already two years to the day since Neznachny had been promoted at the age of thirty-three from being a simple KGB operative to Section Head. He realized that fervent devotion to duty could take him even higher, and since that day had kept Katya at her distance. It was no good him surrendering to her languorous sighs. His record as an officer and a Party member had to be clean!

'Off you go, Katya,' he said.

She breathed in as deeply as she could, expelled the air with a loud, melancholy sigh and headed silently towards the door. Neznachny looked at the broad, firm thighs disappearing beneath the green cotton skirt and was filled with admiration for his own strength of purpose. Quite right, that was how you had to act, Major! However, when the door closed behind her, Major Neznachny gave a sigh as he imagined how Katya would now transport her undischarged bodily energy around the other offices, not to mention those huge soft breasts of hers and those ample thighs. And in the German, French or Japanese Section, perhaps one of the officers, having nothing better to do, would discover Katya's charms with a simple movement of the hand. Neznachny could almost see it happening, and he lit up a cigarette with a mixture of jealousy and irritation.

Since his promotion to Section Head had given him access to the special officers' store (category No 3) on nearby Bolshoi Komsomolsky Street, Neznachny had gained additional pleasure from the fact that he no longer had to buy the Stolichny or Tu-134 brands, but was able to get American cigarettes, and Kent in particular. He blew out the match and emitted a large puff of smoke, happy to put a screen between himself and Katya. Then he took himself in hand. It was time to get down to work. Of course, there couldn't be anything of interest in the files which his secretary had just brought him. The summer season was over and it was the beginning of October, the time of year when the weather was at its most objectionable. There was already a mixture of rain and snow coming down outside. Who would come to Russia in damp, chilly October apart from brainless American old women or nostalgic Ukrainian émigrés born in eighteen-ninety-odd and now living in Canada? You just try and fulfil your recruitment targets with a bunch like that to choose from! He'd spent the last two years trying to convince Colonel Orlov that the recruitment targets for American and Canadian tourists should be set on an all-year basis. There was always a rich harvest in the summer and the winter crop wasn't bad either. Taken together, these two seasons could compensate for the enforced idleness of the autumn months and the spring, too, when the pickings were very meagre. But Orlov had his own reasons. Did he mean that they wouldn't go in for their quarterly bonus?

Neznachny opened the first file. Just as he'd thought. He

stared at twelve photographs all of the same person, an old woman called Miriam Steward. She looked more like a painted doll than anything else. Born in Nebraska in 1903, she lived by herself on a retirement pension in a place called Madison. Health and Life was her insurance company. He would have to look at the map to see if there were any objects of special interest near this Madison, but even if there were, Neznachny thought to himself with a smile, what was a geriatric housewife like Miriam Steward likely to know about them? OK, let's go on to the next one. Another set of coloured photographs, another old woman in her dotage – somebody called Miss Rhea Weeks from Florida this time, born in 1908 . . . Neznachny could never understand why these aged Americans travelled about so much, particularly in the autumn and winter. He knew, of course, that in the West, air tickets and package tours cost less at that time than in the summer (although from the Soviet point of view this was strange in itself: after all, logically, the more people buy tickets, then the cheaper those tickets ought to be. Still, nothing over there is like it is in Russia, goddamnit!) All the same, however cheap the tickets, you just try and make his seventy-year-old mother leave Gzhatsk and take a trip to Bokhara or Riga, say, or even Yalta! He couldn't even make her come to Moscow for years on end. She lived in her old wooden house on the edge of Gzhatsk, pottered about in her vegetable garden, and there was nowhere in the whole world she'd rather be. Meanwhile, these Americans owned houses in Florida and elsewhere such as his mother had never even dreamed of, and here they were, traipsing all over the world in any weather, driving through country after country, town after town in luxury coaches, trooping out of them without a care in the world when they reached their hotels, taking photos of each other with the Kremlin, Russian churches or the Bolshoi Theatre in the background, spending days walking around museums and never forgetting to smile with those incredibly white, false teeth of theirs. For them everything was 'wonderful', 'quaint', or 'exciting'. There was no way he'd start recruiting this seventy-three-year-old Rhea Weeks who had given birth to four children, outlived her third husband and was now amusing herself by travelling to China, Russia, Stockholm, Paris, Rome, London. Not a bad itinerary for somebody her age!

Neznachny opened the next file. This time he was looking at the quiet brown eyes of a Mrs Virginia Part-Williams. She had a young, round-looking face, a carefully arranged hairstyle, and lips half open in a smile. Neznachny cast his eye over the visa application form. What do you know! An actress straight from Hollywood! Very interesting! History has known a lot of actresses who were also great spies. Mata Hari and that . . . what was her name? Marlene Dietrich. So, reason for visiting the USSR: honeymoon. Who was the lucky man? With a slight prick of envy Neznachny leafed through the application forms and found what he was looking for – Robert Williams, a dentist from Potomac in Maryland. The reserved features of a forty-six-year-old bachelor looked out at him. He had a firm chin and inflexible gaze, though Neznachny couldn't make out the colour of his eyes: were they green or brown?

Of course, it would have been better if he had been a physicist or chemist, or a computer expert. He might even have been the president of a computer company. In fact, she could have picked a senator. Still, she obviously hadn't, and Neznachny couldn't be choosy, especially at this time of year. So there you are, a dentist from Potomac in Maryland. Maryland was close to Washington DC, he thought.

Neznachny got up from his desk. One leg had gone to sleep, so he exercised it by walking round his desk and went to a bookshelf crammed with American magazines like *Life*, *Time*, *Newsweek* and *Playboy*. Scattered among them were books like Barron's *KGB*, Robert Conquest's *Great Terror* and CIA *Reports to Congress*. He rummaged about in them and then started scratching his head in irritation. That Savin from the Scientific and Technical Department had walked off with his USA atlas once again. But he didn't have time to ring him up and tell him what he thought of him. In fact, he didn't need to, as Neznachny was in possession of another 'secret' map of the United States. He went up to the door and silently slipped the latch on the yale lock. This was the gesture which Katya had been waiting for these last two years, Neznachny thought to himself with a smile, but it wasn't meant for her now. He removed the keys to his safe from his coat pocket. The safe contained all kinds of secret documents and files, not to mention a bottle of vodka wrapped up in a copy of *Izvestiya*. The bottle had been opened and there were a couple of apples lying next to it on the bottom shelf as an accompanying snack. But this wasn't why Frol Neznachny had opened the safe. At the very bottom, placed carefully in volume sixteen of the *Soviet Encyclopaedia*, was a special map of Canada and the USA, a map which, as Neznachny well knew, should have been destroyed or handed in to archives long ago. But he hadn't had the strength to part with it, he simply hadn't. The reason was that this simple map, which cost no more than twenty kopecks in the shops, had been used by Neznachny for the past nine years to mark the American towns and villages where his 'godchildren' lived – that is to say, those individuals whom he, Neznachny, had persuaded to co-operate with the KGB when they had been on tourist or business trips to the USSR. The map was marked with figures and signs which only he could interpret. He had no right to keep a tally like this and he didn't know whether the people involved were still working for the KGB or not. He was only involved in the early attempts to win them over, and if he was successful, other people took over, like Colonel Orlov. Only occasionally, if one of the 'godchildren' came back to the USSR, was Neznachny drafted in to do further work on them. He opened volume sixteen of the *Soviet Encyclopaedia*, took out the folded map and opened it out on the desk. There they were, all his converts. Green, red and blue circles with numbers inside them marked the various Canadian and American cities where they lived: 32 in New

York, 27 in Los Angeles, 41 in Boston, 4 in Houston, 19 in Washington, 11 in Philadelphia, 14 in Albany . . . He had to alter the numbers from time to time and stick in new ones, but that always gave him great pleasure. Of course, not all of them sent information to Moscow Centre and not all of them had meetings with Soviet agents, but sooner or later each seed which Neznachny had sown would flower and bear its fruit! He contemplated his America with the silent pride of an industrious gardner. Not bad for a country where he had never even been! Not bad for nine years' work in any case. And after all, he was only one of a whole army of KGB 'gardeners', and if you added all their work together, if you were to enter in all the US residents whom they had recruited as agents – businessmen, lawyers, scientists, journalists, bankers, company presidents, professors, government officials, politicians and priests – well, if you were to do that, the high and mighty United States of America would appear as a vast network of coding stations, all of them relaying information back to the Soviet motherland.

Anyway, there was no time to think about things like that. Where was this Potomac, Maryland? There it was – right next to Washington DC. Fantastic! He had to phone Savin now. He quickly folded up the map and slipped it back into the encyclopaedia. With the other hand he was already dialling a number on the internal phone network.

'Savin? Neznachny here. Have you filched my atlas of North America again? Never mind. Stop bullshitting. I need detailed information about a place called Potomac, Maryland, immediately. Yes, we may have a potential "godchild" on our hands. Is it a rich suburb of Washington? Who lives there? Diplomats, high government officials, who else? Are there any bases or special installations? I want whatever information you've got, plus a detailed map of the place indicating any points of special interest. And I want it within the next ten minutes, get me? Shall I send Katya over?'

Neznachny put the phone down. Yes, this could turn out

to be very interesting. If this Robert Williams was a dentist in a rich Washington suburb, that could mean that he had important businessmen, high government officials, and diplomats among his patients, and God knows who else! And she was a Hollywood actress. That was even better! If they had only just got married, that meant that Williams would want to show off his new wife by having parties for his friends. He'd move around a lot himself, going to receptions and other functions . . . The lure of the chase was already sending Neznachny's thoughts racing ahead, but cold experience held his imagination in check. The important thing now was to study all twenty-four pages of the newly-weds' visa application in detail. He took a note-pad, sharpened his pencil and slowly began to read through Virginia's application form.

She had studied the Stanislavsky method at New York theatre school and had even learned enough Russian to be able to read Stanislavsky and Chekhov in the original. Great! We'll introduce you to actors and producers, darling, as well as giving you tickets for our best theatres. Neznachny was already weighing up in his mind which of those actors and producers who collaborated with the KGB he should introduce Virginia to. He examined her writing. She had a round, even hand with every letter clearly and fully formed. This meant that she was well balanced, even slightly reserved in nature with a placid, even temper, and not given to extravagant behaviour. It looked as if one of the calmer, more stable types was for her. And it didn't have to be an actor. In fact a producer or a playwright would be better. Dmitry Lisadze was the man they needed, that's who!

On the other hand, Robert Williams had an abrupt, angular hand. At the end of each line his writing sloped stubbornly upwards away from the lines actually printed on the form. Self-assured but frustrated, possibly talented. He was a bachelor till the age of forty-six. Almost certainly likes young girls – and who doesn't, Neznachny said to himself with a smile. We'll find girls for you, don't worry! And there's one girl who'll make you pant for breath! Young wives find it difficult to resist temptation, too. In any case, she's not so young, your Virginia . . .

Neznachny wrote all this down on his note-pad in the form of short phrases to remind him of the traps which he would set for Mr and Mrs Williams in the future. As he did so, he looked again and again at their photographs, trying to make them come alive in his imagination. Of course, he would give his official approval to their proposed journey to the Soviet Union. And how! From today these two people were closer and more important to him than his own wife. They would become bosom buddies of his. These forms and photographs would give him an idea of their habits, their likes and dislikes and their way of life. This Williams hadn't got married until he was forty-six. That meant that he was used to living for himself and nobody else, and like all confirmed bachelors, he would take care of his health. Neznachny wanted to have a smoke with him, or better still, sit down at a table, produce a bottle of vodka and get him to agree to everything right away. But there was no doing that, of course. Such a conversation would take place at the end of their trip, when Neznachny would confront both of them with photographic evidence of William's philanderings with Russian girls. He'd have his back to the wall then, make no mistake! How shameful! He'd come to the USSR with his young wife and had immediately turned to debauchery. He would lose his wife, his reputation and his customers. How does that prospect grab you, Mr Williams? Do tell me now, what kind of girl do you like best? Blondes, brunettes, redheads, plump ones, skinny ones, wild ones, languid ones? Anyway, we'll meet you at the airport and we'll soon see which ones your eyes linger on. Then we'll make our choice. Although . . . not a single foreigner has refused Olya Makhova. She's quite something! Neznachny always kept her in reserve for the worst emergencies, if the potential 'godchild' turned down every other approach. Still, for this particular Washington guest we could start with her right away, especially as the Williamses were only coming for ten days. There was no time to lose. We had to begin with trumps. OK, we'll give you Olya Makhova, Neznachny decided. Might as well go the whole hog! Only do come quickly, dear guests! You'll be surrounded by pure Russian hospitality. I'll predict your every step in advance, using the expertise which has worked faultlessly on so many occasions in the past.

Neznachny started to cut up the sheet with Virginia's photographs. One had to be sent to archives, another to the card-index. Two were needed for the hotel where the newly-weds would be staying and another would go to customs at Sheremetyevo Airport. The rest would stay with Neznachny to be distributed amongst the agents who would actually be 'dealing' with the Williamses in Moscow and Leningrad, taking them to restaurants, theatres and even hospitals. After all, Williams was a dentist and he would be bound to appreciate a meeting with Soviet colleagues.

But what about you, my dear Virginia, Neznachny thought as he examined her photograph once again. He was filled with tender thoughts. There were tiny wrinkles around her eyes and a smile on her lips. Did she like to laugh? They'd find some people to help her do just that. Let her just come to Russia as quickly as she could, and bring her dentist husband with her . . . He wouldn't mind amusing her himself, in the Russian way. Yes, how about it? Couldn't he take care of her himself? He felt the sudden thrill of the professional hunter, and the sight of Virginia's tender brown eyes filled his heart with desire. He'd just have to see . . .

The sound of somebody tugging at his door from outside disturbed his pleasant train of thought. 'Who is it?' he asked.

'It's me, Katya. Savin has sent over the information you wanted, Frol Yevseyich.'

'Just a minute . . .'

Neznachny got up, walked over to the door and opened it. There was Katya, carrying the atlas and the information about Potomac including a street-plan xeroxed from some reference book. Neznachny stretched out his hand to take it all, but Katya appeared not to notice his gesture.

'Just look at the weather outside,' she said, walking quickly into his office and heading towards the window. Neznachny's eyes followed her instinctively. Through the bars of the window he could see the first real snowstorm of the winter. The snow was coming down so thick and fast that it had grown quite dark in his office. He had been so taken up with his Americans that he hadn't even noticed. And he hadn't even looked through the remaining visa applications yet.

'Just look at the snow,' said Katya enthusiastically, resting her ample bosom against the window-ledge. This position made her skirt ride up a little and her thighs looked even rounder. 'Just look.'

Neznachny walked over to the window himself. His fourth-floor office looked down on to Dzerzhinsky Street and Kuznetsky Bridge Street. But for the moment you could scarcely distinguish the roads at all, everything was blotted out by this first blizzard of the winter. The temperature hadn't dropped below freezing yet and the snow was already turning to slush. A snow-covered trolley bus was stuck helplessly in the middle of the traffic junction. The trolleys had come off the wires and were hanging there in mid-air sending out sprays of white sparks. People were getting out of the bus and wading through the slushy snow towards the pavements. One woman, carrying two full shopping-bags, had just reached the pavement when she described an unbelievable pirouette and landed plump on the snow. The bags were filled with Bulgarian tomatoes which rolled out all over the place. Without even bothering to get to her feet, the woman began to pick them up.

'There are another three to your left,' shouted Katya, as if the woman could possibly hear her from the fourth floor of the building. Katya was taking up two-thirds of the window-ledge, but Neznachny, standing behind her, leaned forward to see what was going on in the street below. As he did so, his stomach accidentally touched Katya's hip. She froze and held her breath. Of their own volition Neznachny's hands came to rest on Katya's thighs. But even as he broke his solemn oath by burying his hands deep in her breasts, Neznachny didn't forget that soon, very soon two new American 'godchildren' named Virginia and Robert Williams would be on his hands. He was exultant and his emotion communicated itself to Katya.

14

'Jack? Hello! How are you? This is David from the *Washington Night Review* here. We met in Stockholm a month ago . . .'

'Ah, David, it's you,' came the reply from distant Moscow. MacKerry realized that Stevenson had recognized who he was and was probably very surprised at receiving this call. 'How are you getting on, David?'

'Fine, thanks. How about you?'

MacKerry didn't know how to conduct this conversation or what to talk about. But today was 6 October, he had to report to his boss in half an hour's time, but what was there for him to report about? No Soviet submarine had been detected off the coast of Sweden, although Yuryshev had promised that one would appear at the beginning of October. But possibly Yuryshev had given Stevenson some sign that the operation had been cancelled, postponed or something. He couldn't say any of this to Stevenson directly, of course. Like every other foreign journalist in Moscow, Stevenson's phone was undoubtedly being tapped by the KGB. Somehow he had to convey to Stevenson what he wanted to discover . . .

'You promised to write an article for us, Jack. Remember?' said MacKerry. 'You said that you'd send it to us at the beginning of October. It's already 6 October, and the editor has asked me to find out whether he should expect your article for one of our forthcoming issues. I mean, will we be receiving your article in the next few days?'

MacKerry spoke without hesitation, emphasizing the words 'in the next few days' so that Stevenson would realize what he was talking about. 'If the article isn't ready yet, don't worry. We just want to find out whether we can carry on expecting it. What do you say, Jack? Have your plans changed?'

Stevenson said nothing. He was probably thinking about how to reply.

'Hello!' said MacKerry. 'Perhaps you'd like to give us another deadline. Think about it, Jack. We need your piece very much.'

'Hmm . . .' came the reply. 'To tell the truth, David, I can't manage to get enough material together for the article. You know how secret these Russians keep everything . . .'

At last he had found a way of answering, and his tone of voice became much more assured. He knew that all his telephone conversations were being tapped by the KGB, but he allowed himself to get in all sorts of digs at the Russians. Let them hear what he had to say, damn them!

'Yesterday I tried to arrange a meeting with the chief cook at the Kremlin. I wanted to write a piece about the catering service there. But I wasn't allowed to meet him. It turns out that the Kremlin menus are classified information, too. So I don't really know what to say to you. Working here is very difficult, and getting your hands on any fresh material is simply impossible . . .'

'I see,' said MacKerry in a disappointed voice. 'That's a pity . . . Ah well . . . If anything new comes up, give me a buzz, OK? What's the weather like in Moscow?'

'Brr . . .' was the only reply.

'All the very best, Jack!'

'Same to you . . .'

MacKerry hung up. He'd been ringing from a phone booth, as the Russians at the Soviet Embassy had long since possessed equipment allowing them to tap the phone calls which emanated from CIA headquarters.

What have we come to! thought MacKerry. You call Moscow and you're afraid that the KGB will be listening in at both ends, in Moscow and Washington. Damn that Stevenson! There he is, living no more than a mile away from Yuryshev and he can't even get in touch with him. Meanwhile, all you can do is guess when the submarine will turn up. Today, tomorrow, or perhaps never!

He left the phone booth, got into his 1979 Ford and looked at his watch. It was 2.30 and in half an hour he had to report to his boss about the state of readiness of the whole operation. When he reached the office, he walked over to the elevator and said his usual 'Hi, Billy, how are things?' to the lift-boy. Billy looked at him in surprise.

'Sir, haven't you heard yet? Sadat has been assassinated in Egypt.'

15

'Emigration is a country in its own right. There's Russia, of course, and America. There's China and France. But there's this other country called Emigration as well.'

It was Stavinsky speaking.

'When I left Russia, I thought I was heading for America. I was travelling from darkness to light, from barbarism and backwardness to the twenty-third century. But as it turned out, I didn't arrive in America at all. Instead I found myself in a cruel and alien country that you won't find on any map. I arrived in Emigration, a country with no capital, no theatres, no life. It was like a desert or an ocean with each person adrift on his own ice-floe and looking for a place to settle. Some people here build houses with garages and even swimming-pools on their own ice-floes. Others join their ice-floes together and form islands like Brighton Beach in New York. They've even got their own Russian restaurants and a cinema where they can watch endless movies about the life they have left behind – Soviet movies of course. But all the same, it's still an ice-floe, and it's cold and empty. The children all escape into American life. They get used to their adoptive countries, whether they're in Europe, America or Israel. They become normal people. But for adults like me . . . No, it's impossible. We remain trapped. We're condemned to this lonely existence until we reach the end of our lives. America isn't to blame. America hasn't got anything to do with it. In my opinion, even if we were able to emigrate to the next world, to Paradise, say, it would be no different. If you cut off the roots of a young tree and then transfer it to different soil, it will grow new roots. But if you do the same thing to an older tree, it will die for sure. It will just dry up. I don't want that to happen to me. I want to go back to my old way of life. I remember being told at the refugee transit camp in Vienna that we had escaped from prison into freedom. That's quite right, but what can I do with my freedom? I felt freer in the prison than I do here. I lived life to the full in Russia. There were difficulties to overcome, of course, but I was proud of the way I got over them. And I used to discuss life with my friends in the prison, I used to argue, I used to love women, I used to read illegal literature . . . I really *lived*. Do you understand what I mean?'

Virginia didn't interrupt him. She just listened.

This was the third day they had spent killing time, waiting to be sent to Russia. MacKerry said that everything depended on when they received the visas from the Soviet Embassy. They ought to be arriving any day now. The Soviets had in any case called Dr Williams in Potomac to clarify a few details on the form. But Dr Williams had been ready for their call and gave clear, exact answers to all their questions. The Russians had promised him that the visas would be arriving in the very near future. Stavinsky and Virginia had a great deal of spare time on their hands now, and this they spent walking around Washington, sitting in expensive cafés in Williamsburg, visiting art galleries and museums, feeding squirrels in the parks. Meanwhile, Stavinsky was telling Virginia about his life and about Russia.

'You Americans just can't understand it. You think that if a person is nostalgic for his own country, it means that he doesn't like yours. But this is precisely the point. This country *is* yours. It's never become mine even though I've been living here for six years. And it'll never be my country because I didn't grow up here, I didn't play with other children here, I didn't go shooting sparrows here, I didn't stand in line for bread here and I didn't kiss my first woman here. There's nothing for me to do in your country, and I'm not interested in doing anything. Who is there for me to do anything for, tell me that?'

A grey squirrel jumped out of a bush on to the road and sat up on its back legs, its tail poised in the air, and looked quizzically at Stavinsky and Virginia with its beady black eyes.

'There, see that?' said Stavinsky. 'Even your squirrels are different. We have red ones in Russia, and I'm used to red ones. But what can you do about it? Do you know what my daughter used to say to me when we first arrived in America? "Daddy, the flowers here don't have any smell, the sun doesn't feel warm and the grass isn't soft. Take me back home, please." You see? But that was a long time ago. She can hardly speak any Russian now. As for me . . . No, the sun still doesn't feel warm to me . . . And that's why I've got to go back home to Russia.'

16

'All right, let's assume that Sadat's assassination has messed up some of their plans. It isn't certain that the Russians had anything to do with his death, of course, though it clearly plays into their hands. If I were in their position, I wouldn't want to increase international tension at the moment by getting Sadat assassinated *and* scaring Europe with my submarines. I would have postponed the date, too. But it's already 20 October, how long can we wait? Are you sure that it isn't possible to contact Yuryshev somehow and find out what's going on?'

Daniel J. Cooper rocked himself in his armchair and looked wistfully out of the window. The October rains were already lashing Washington, Sadat's murder had played right into the Soviets' hands, the White House was asking the CIA for precise information about the Russians' plans and he, Cooper, had already mentioned in the highest circles that he would soon be able to supply the President with some detailed information, but . . . Where, oh where was that damned submarine and this Colonel Yuryshev?

'I've already got through twice to Stevenson in Moscow,' said MacKerry, 'but he has no news as yet. And it's impossible for him to talk to Yuryshev. In fact, getting to see Yuryshev at all would be extremely dangerous and might mess up the whole operation. All we can do is wait for 7 November and the military parade on Red Square. Usually the whole general staff turns up to watch the parade, and if Yuryshev is among them, then Stévenson might be able to work his way into his presence. Then he'd have to take it from there . . . But if he's to do that, we'll have to summon him back home and give him instructions. And it would be more effective if you were to talk to him yourself.'

'Hm, yes,' said Cooper. 'It's a pretty thin chance, I must say. There's nothing worse than just waiting for things to happen. OK, I know the editor of the *Washington Herald*. I'll try persuading him to call Stevenson back home for a couple of days. And what about this émigré and his "wife"?'

'They're in the middle of a great love affair, I think,' said MacKerry with a broad smile. 'At any rate, they spend all their time together, and I'm afraid they may get married for real! If that happened, then either he'll refuse to go, or she'll also want to stay behind in Russia.'

'That's all we need! So now the CIA is to become a marriage bureau! How about it? Maybe we ought to shut up shop and start up a match-making business somewhere. It doesn't look as if this one is turning out too badly! Have they got their Soviet visas yet?'

'The real Dr Williams received them four days ago, and yesterday he left for his vacation in Florida. But I haven't said anything to Stavinsky and Miss Part yet about the visas coming. If I do, how will I be able to explain the delay in their departure?'

'All right, let's wait another five days, say. If there's no submarine by then, or if we haven't received a signal from Yuryshev, then Stavinsky and the girl will have to go back where they came from.'

'Well, Miss Part can always do that, of course. But what about Stavinsky? He's dead and buried, so to speak, so he can't reappear from the other world and visit his daughter. Especially with somebody else's face.'

'Hm, yes . . . Quite right. So what will he do?'

'I think we'll have to pay him at least a third of the money we promised him by way of compensation. After that he can look after himself.'

'But how will he get on in America? What name will he use? Besides, his Social Security number has been discontinued, and getting him another one will involve us in giving long explanations to the FBI. Christ, we've certainly landed ourselves in a mess!'

Cooper got up from his desk with a sigh and walked over to the window. It was a grey, rainy day outside. In Moscow the CIA had seven Soviet residents working under cover for them in various State organizations, and there were a handful of Russian diplomats and Foreign Ministry officials who weren't averse to taking bribes. But he wouldn't get *them* to make contact with Yuryshev. It was too risky. No, they'd have to wait. How did the Russian song go: 'You've only got to learn to wait, be steady, calm and firm . . .'

'All right,' he said. 'We'll wait until the 25th.'

17

Mark had rung Virginia several times to say that he was missing her and wanted to join her in Washington. Men were all the same, she thought. When she had been on the spot, he had been out day after day and some times all night, too. He couldn't stay at home with her. He had his own business, his own friends, and so on. And now he was missing her. Whenever he rang she would tell him irritably that she was busy filming every day, and was about to fly off on location at any moment. He would then say that in that case he was even more anxious to see her before she flew off. They hadn't seen each other for a month after all. Their final phone conversation was particularly painful, because Mark put on a cheerful voice and asked outright whether she hadn't found herself a lover in Washington. Virginia's answer was quite rude. She hadn't checked up when he used to go off with those Hollywood tarts he said were producers. Mark got angry, and Virginia hung up. She didn't know what was happening to her. Here she was, a grown woman, and her common sense told her that she mustn't fall in love with this Russian kamikaze. There was no future in it. He would remain in Russia, and that would be that. And even if he didn't get killed, it would make no difference to her; they would never see each other again. But another part of her made her wait on Stavinsky's every phone call, and she wanted to spend all her free time in his company. Why? Was it out of pity? Well, that could be part of it, but it wasn't the whole story. There was something else, besides, and she couldn't put a name to it. If you were to ask any woman whether she wanted to get to know a man who had made a conscious decision to risk his life – having a heart-transplant operation perhaps or taking a one-way flight to Venus – there was no doubt in Virginia's mind that the woman would agree. Perhaps Stone Age women loved their menfolk a lot more than women do these days, precisely because the man had to risk his life every day by hunting wild animals . . . And there was another feeling at work here too, a kind of unconscious envy – envy of Russia. Virginia considered herself to be an American, a real American, and so she was. Now she had suddenly met a man who in a sense was ready to exchange her country for another, who preferred cruel and distant Russia to her America. It was as if he was deserting her for another woman.

She wanted to show him her country. If she couldn't make him love it, then she would at least make him admire everything she had been proud of since she was a child. (Like most Americans she believed that nowhere in the whole world could be better or finer than America . . .) She bought a number of guide-books covering Washington DC and the surrounding area. Then she and Stavinsky went all over the place, visiting national parks and folk museums, as well as the capital's tourist high-spots. They went to Japanese, Chinese, French and Ukrainian restaurants. They went to concerts, they heard Rostropovich play, they visited the French ballet and the Japanese theatre. She wanted to prove to him that America contained everything. Everything and everybody came to her country, it was the 'roof of the world' – and yet he, Stavinsky, wanted to leave it.

Their relationship wasn't yet as MacKerry had described it to Daniel J. Cooper. They hadn't slept with each other. In fact, they hadn't even kissed, or 'accidentally' touched hands or exchanged 'meaningful' looks. Stavinsky's behaviour was entirely comradely and this had been enough to overcome Virginia's natural suspicion of a man who in one sense had a claim on her sexual independence. They were supposed to be 'husband and wife', after all, even if it was only a fiction . . . All the same, her feminine pride was wounded. After a whole day spent together in the romantic atmosphere of the national park, looking down on the roaring mists of the Potomac waterfall, wandering through the silent autumn woods, and then an evening spent at a concert bathed in the tranquil music of Saint-Saëns, he would just drive her back to her hotel, walk with her as far as the elevator and then say: 'Good night, Virginia. What plans have we got on for tomorrow?'

'I don't know yet. Perhaps we'll be hearing from Mr MacKerry in the morning.'

'OK, I'll be in touch. Sleep well.'

She would go off to her room, reviewing the day's events in her mind and unable to find the slightest trace of anything other than polite attention on his part. What was it? Hadn't he noticed that she was a woman? Or wasn't she capable of attracting a man any longer? His mind was so taken up with this Russia of his that all those waterfalls, parks, cliffs and romantic restaurants meant no more to him than a sightseeing tour. Well, let him go back to that damned Russia of his, and the sooner the better! In fact, why were those CIA guys so slow with arranging the whole trip? A month had gone by and here she was, still hanging about in Washington. Her month's 'contract' was practically over, and yet still she hadn't been to Russia and God knows when she would be going. She would finally tell them now that enough was enough. The month was up, and she had no more time to waste. And then go home. It was their business after all, not hers. They had asked her to stay for a month, and that month had gone by . . . Yes, that's what she'd do! The very next morning she'd ring MacKerry and tell him. Then let them pay her all the money they owed her for the last four weeks. It wasn't her fault if the trip to Russia hadn't worked out . . .

But come the next morning, Stavinsky would ring to say, in a cheerful and slightly ironic tone: 'Hello, Mrs Williams? This is your husband here. Did you sleep well, darling? I was wondering whether we couldn't drive out of town today. The weather is marvellous. It's sunny and warm . . .' And she would say to herself: OK, we'll give it one more day. But in fact she was deceiving herself because she was really hoping for something to happen between herself and Stavinsky that very day.

Stavinsky would drive up to her hotel in his white, rented Jaguar, looking spruce and freshly shaven, and sporting the stylish French suit which they had chosen together at Bloomingdale's. They would have a light breakfast at the hotel, and then they would be off again, racing down the highways and country lanes with Stavinsky laughing as he broke the speed limits. 'The CIA can see to any speeding fines later,' he said. 'They can always send them on to me in Russia, if need be!'

Unlike Virginia, Stavinsky knew very well what it was that attracted him to her. He had been in love with her from the moment he first met her in his room at the hospital. For him she was the kind of woman which every man searches for and which very few ever find – a woman resembling his mother. And it had to happen, he had to meet her when he'd already had plastic surgery, when he'd buried his old identity in a New Jersey cemetery and when there was no possibility of going back. He had to regain Russia now, and in so doing, he had to lose her. These days spent with her he now valued all the more, and he was more than happy to drive her all over the America she loved with its camping-sites, parks, hotels and restaurants. Nor did he begrudge the large amounts of money he was spending. It sometimes seemed to him that he was making up for everything that he hadn't managed to give his mother, when she was alive. After all, what boy doesn't think of giving his mother everything in the world – trips to far-away places, luxurious holidays abroad, concerts, exhibitions, expensive restaurants? Stavinsky knew that he was doing this for his mother's sake as well as Virginia's. And he was so impatient to get to Russia. Then he could show Virginia everything that he had intended to show his mother, when he was a child – Moscow and Leningrad, with their great concert halls, and theatres, Intourist hotels, exhibitions, the Pushkin Museum, the Hermitage, Nevsky Avenue, those fantastic Georgian restaurants in the environs of Moscow, Cinema House and Journalists' House. If you had money you could get to see everything. But his mother hadn't lived to see his success or his money. She was in a Saratov cemetery, and he had never even managed to show her Leningrad . . .

He already knew that he wouldn't betray the operation to the KGB. He couldn't take any risks with Virginia's safety. Damn this Russia, he thought, and damn himself! He wouldn't die, but even if he were to get killed, how long could he carry on as he was now, living on nothing but sorrow and bitterness? At least he would have seen a bit of life. Of course, the KGB would soon realize that something was amiss and start a nationwide search for the man who would have flown out of Russia in his place. That meant that photographs of his look-alike would be hanging in every police station throughout the Soviet Union, and no plastic surgery could help him then (where would you get plastic surgery in Russia anyway? They don't do such operations there.) Sooner or later, the KGB would catch up with him, and the noose would tighten around his neck. Well, what of it? he asked himself, putting on a brave face. He could always commit suicide by taking poison, but at least he would have *lived*. He would still manage to see life in Russia and he would still get to kiss this Virginia – over there, in Moscow . . .

To be perfectly honest, he was being a bit of a coward. He was simply afraid of touching Virginia, of betraying the desire, the passion that he felt for her. Who was he, as far as she was concerned after all? Just a loser who had failed to get to grips with life in her country, a has-been who hadn't managed to overcome the cultural barriers and become an American. That was all he was for her. She accepted his friendship now, because they were yoked together, because that was what their contracts with the CIA demanded. Being together with him for a time was what she was being paid for. And that was all. But what if he attempted something more? How would she react to that? Hit him round the face? Pour cold water on his feelings by a show of that terrible contempt which some Americans seem to have? Turn round and fly back to California? No, he couldn't afford to lose that woman. He would spend hour after hour telling her about Russia, about himself, his mother, his former wife, his daughter. He would tell her about Moscow television where he worked for twelve years, about Portland and his first few years in America. He would even tell her about Barbara from the 7-Eleven. And then he would take her back to her hotel, return to his own room at the Sheraton and pay for the services of some whore for an hour or so, to work off the passion which had built up over the day. But never would he so much as touch Virginia or betray his true feelings towards her, so as not to lose her before the appointed time.

. . . It was 27 October, and when Stavinsky and Virginia returned home that evening after a concert, they found MacKerry waiting for them in the hotel foyer. He had an official-looking, gloomy expression on his face.

18

MacKerry had flown back from Stockholm that morning and had an interview with Daniel J. Cooper after lunch. The editor of the *Washington Herald* hadn't summoned his Moscow correspondent back to Washington, and it was only with the greatest difficulty that Stevenson had been persuaded to travel as far as Stockholm, and even then only for a day and because he had a Swedish girlfriend in the city. But their conversation hadn't led to anything, as far as MacKerry was concerned. Stevenson flatly refused to go looking for this Yuryshev, and the suggestion that he might happen to meet him 'accidentally' during the military parade in Red Square elicited a very sceptical response.

'Now that Sadat has been assassinated the security precautions on Red Square will be so strict during the march-past, that you won't even be able to breathe, let alone meet anyone. And it's pointless even thinking of getting close to the rostrums where the top military brass will be standing. I've been given a white invitation card entitling me to sit on the journalists' platform, but that's three hundred yards from where the bigwigs will be standing. The most I could do would be photograph their stands with a telephoto lens. But what's the point? Even if Yuryshev is there, how will he know that I'm filming him from such a distance? He'll be standing there motionless, like the rest of them, with his arm raised in a salute – and that's all.'

So MacKerry flew back to America with nothing to show for his trouble, and he and his boss decided to abandon the whole show. In any case, it was pointless expecting the submarine to surface off Sweden tomorrow or the day after. It had had practically the whole of October to appear, and the fact that it hadn't, most likely meant that the Russians had cancelled the operation. They would have to come up with alternative ways of contacting Yuryshev. But that would take time, and meanwhile it was pointless to keep Virginia and Stavinsky hanging on in Washington indefinitely.

In the bar MacKerry ordered a ginger ale for Virginia and two screwdrivers for himself and Stavinsky.

'Unfortunately, our plans have changed,' said MacKerry, 'and the operation is cancelled . . . or at least indefinitely postponed. Miss Part, thank you for your co-operation. You will receive all the money due to you for this month. So let us say that the film is over. Tomorrow or the day after – it's up to you – you can fly back to Los Angeles. We've got you an open ticket. And here is your cheque. It doesn't say that it's from the CIA, don't worry. It's drawn on the account of a military film studio, so if you like, you can tell your friends that you've been making a film for the army.'

Virginia glanced at the cheque. MacKerry noticed the look of surprise and pleasure on her face when she saw the amount which she was being given: 7,500 dollars.

'Thank you once again,' he said with a smile. Then he turned to Stavinsky.

'As far as you are concerned, it's a little more difficult, Mr . . . er . . . I don't even know what to call you now. In any case, here's your cheque. It's for exactly one third of the amount which we agreed on. It's made out to the bearer and not to anyone in particular, so mind you don't lose it. You can change it for cash or traveller's cheques at the bank in the morning. As for what you do now . . . Looking as you do, we realize that you can't just return from the grave and go to see your daughter. But if you like, Dr Lawrence will change your face back to how it was. As for your death in the car accident, I think we can explain that away as an ordinary police mistake. You were set upon and robbed by some crooks. They stripped you of your clothes and then threw you out of the car, after which you spent a couple of weeks in hospital. One of the thieves hung on to your papers and was then killed in an automobile accident. And that's why the police informed your daughter of your death. Such things do happen. Dr Lawrence can give you a few scars, if you like. I hope that the money we're giving you will compensate you for your disappointment.'

He could see that Stavinsky was stunned by this news.

'What went wrong then? Didn't the Soviets give us our visas?' Stavinsky asked softly.

'No, the visas came all right. But as I said, it's just that our plans have changed, and I can't tell you why.'

'What if . . . what if I refuse your offer?'

'What do you mean?' asked MacKerry uncomprehendingly. 'What happens if you refuse the money, do you mean?'

'No,' replied Stavinsky, smiling, 'I'll keep the money. But I'm not so sure about changing my face back and turning up as Stavinsky again . . .'

'Well, I expected you to say that. But we can help you to change your name. Any citizen has the right to do so, if he wishes.'

'No, you don't get what I mean. I've already got a name. I'm Robert Williams. My passport and visa are made out in that name. What if I go to Russia myself, at my own expense?'

MacKerry certainly hadn't expected this. 'And what would you do there? Stay for a month and then come back?'

'No,' replied Stavinsky. 'I don't think so. If you give me the papers which you talked about, I don't think that I'll be coming back.'

'And what if we don't?'

'If you don't, well, I still won't be coming back. I'll think of something when I'm over there. You can even get hold of identity papers in Russia, provided you've got enough money.'

'Well, we'll have to think about it,' said MacKerry. It had suddenly dawned on him that Stavinsky might be able to make contact with this Yuryshev himself. He didn't know how or on what pretext, but they were details which could be tied up later. He even cheered up a little.

'Do you know what?' he said. 'I think that we will give you those Russian IDs. And one or two other things as well. When do you want to fly to Moscow?'

Stavinsky looked at Virginia. If she hadn't been so happy when she received the cheque and was told that she could fly back to California tomorrow, he might not have been so keen to rush back to Russia himself. If she had only said something or looked at him in some special way . . . But no. She had simply looked away, as if his fate and his decision were no concern of hers.

'Well . . .' he said with a sigh. He looked MacKerry straight in the eye. 'I could fly there tomorrow, if you like.'

'That's a bit early. Let's say that we'll meet somewhere tomorrow afternoon to talk everything over.' MacKerry needed time to discuss this new idea with Cooper.

Stavinsky looked at Virginia and asked what appeared to be a casual question: 'And how about you, Miss Part? When will you be flying back to LA?'

'In the morning, I expect,' she said. If he was ready to fly back to Russia at the drop of a hat, then let him. Let the links which had been forged between them over the last few weeks be cut for good.

'Yes, I'll be going back tomorrow,' she repeated more firmly.

'Will you let me accompany you to the airport?'

'What for? I'll take a taxi.'

'Well, it's up to you . . . In that case, let me wish you all the very best.'

'The same to you. I hope things turn out all right in Russia. Goodbye, Mr MacKerry. Thank you very much.'

She shook hands first with MacKerry, then with Stavinsky. And as for him . . . he didn't even hold on to her hand for more than half a second!

She turned around and walked quickly towards the elevator.

When she reached her room, she collapsed on to the bed and burst into tears.

19

The flight to Los Angeles was leaving at 11.30 a.m. Virginia had reserved her seat the night before and had now packed her case and ordered a taxi. There was one thing that she was keeping from herself, and that was a vague hope that Stavinsky would ring that morning or drive over to her hotel . . . But nothing happened. As she walked out of the hotel, she even looked furtively around just to see whether his white Jaguar was parked outside . . . But no, it wasn't. So what? It really was better that way. One stroke, and everything was over. Let him fly off to that Russia of his, let him disappear for ever . . . She had erased him from her memory. The film hadn't materialized, nor had the love affair between the two main actors. She smiled to herself with a mixture of bitterness and irony. She had failed to become an actress yet again – either in the movies or in real life. She really ought to give up and become a secretary, or even better – get married to some quiet, decent doctor or lawyer, have children and live a normal, human life. It was raining yet again in Washington, and it was cold and windy as well. At least in California she would be warm and comfortable in her own home. Yes, that's where she wanted to be. There's nowhere better than your own home, wherever it may be. But then Stavinsky was anxious to return home, too. Yes, perhaps she could understand him – now. Damn it, she was thinking of this Stavinsky again. She must forget him – forget him immediately, blot him out of her memory.

The taxi had arrived at the airport. Virginia settled up with the driver and got out of the car.

Stavinsky was standing in the main concourse next to the check-in desk, carrying an enormous bouquet of bright red carnations. She caught sight of him straight away. He looked tense and nervous with the red of the flowers reflected in his cheeks. She walked slowly over to the check-in desk, rolling her suitcase on wheels behind her.

He stood there motionless for a few seconds, looking into her eyes, and only then started walking towards her. And as he did so, and as she walked towards him, their eyes expressed any number of feelings – hesitation, joy, fear, hope, trust and sadness. A mass of half-conscious feelings and thoughts was eddying between them, and this emotional turmoil would decide in a matter of seconds the way they would greet one another and their whole approach to each other in the future. And so it did. They lifted their arms in such an embrace that you would have thought it was a hundred years since they had last seen each other rather than just a few hours.

'Shall we have a drink in the bar?' he asked.

'Yes, if you like,' she said, averting her gaze and cursing herself for the way she had betrayed her feelings, when she threw herself into his arms. What a fool she was! Why show him what she felt when he was about to fly off to Russia, whatever happened? It had been just like a scene from a film, although the movie side of it hadn't worked out. At least, not for her.

'It was just like in a movie,' she said with a smile, sipping her Manhattan cocktail, then she shook her head. Why was she pretending? Why was she lying to a man she was seeing for the last time in her life, the man she loved?

'No, I really am glad to see you,' she said and looked into his eyes.

'Thanks,' he replied.

'When do you intend leaving for Russia?'

'I don't know . . . that depends . . . In any case, nobody's rushing me, as far as I know. Will anyone be waiting for you in LA, Virginia?'

'Well,' she said uncertainly. She wasn't sure herself. Mark might be waiting for her, but then he might already have given her up. 'There's always somebody waiting for you somewhere . . .'

'Nobody's waiting for me,' he said.

'Why not? Perhaps somebody is.'

'Oh yes?' he said, looking into her eyes. 'Oh yes?'

'Yes,' she said softly.

'Well, listen to me then,' he said in a decisive voice. 'You're not going to Los Angeles, OK? In twenty minutes there's a flight to Florida. Why shouldn't you and I be on it? I'm rich. I've got thirty thousand dollars. I'll go and get the tickets right away.'

'What are you talking about?' she said. For some reason she suddenly felt scared.

'Quiet!' he ordered. And he even put a finger to his lips. 'Not a word to anybody. Let's go.' He threw a five-dollar bill on to the bar and started walking resolutely towards the ticket office.

'Wait a minute!' she shouted. 'What are you doing? I've already checked my case in on the Los Angeles flight.'

'So what? We'll get it back straight away. In any case, it doesn't matter if we don't. We can always buy you another.'

'You're out of your mind!'

'Of course I am! What have I got a mind for if not to go out of it and come back to it whenever I like! Give me your ticket to California.'

He took the ticket from her and marched up to the desk.

'Two tickets to Florida, please. For Dr and Mrs Williams.'

20

McKerry's suggestion that the CIA should send Stavinsky to Russia to make contact with Colonel Yuryshev was not greeted by Daniel J. Cooper with any great enthusiasm. It was one thing to use this émigré as a minor pawn but quite a different matter to entrust him with the whole operation. Even if he really were able to slip away in Russia as an American tourist, re-emerge somewhere in Siberia as some Ivanov, Petrov, Sidorov, or whatever, and then return to Moscow and find Yuryshev – they would still have to solve the problem of getting the colonel out to the West. No, if Stavinsky was so keen on going back to Russia, then let him sit it out in Portland for a while. He'd already waited six years. Another couple of months wouldn't make any difference. That would give one of the CIA's contacts in Moscow enough time to get in touch with Yuryshev. That wouldn't be so difficult after all. Their Soviet contact would only have to get to know one of the officials at the Novodevichy cemetery, bribe him with money or a bottle of vodka and gain access to the burial register. That would give him the address of Yuryshev's dead son and hence of Yuryshev himself. And if that didn't work out, there was another way of getting the information. One of the CIA's Russian agents could travel to this forester's place on the nature reserve near Kirov, spend a week or so there pretending to be a keen hunter and try to get the forester to tell him Yuryshev's address. And if the colonel confirmed that he still wanted to escape to the West, then Stavinsky could fly off to Russia, preferably accompanied by Virginia. Of course, it would be putting the Moscow agent at risk, but still . . . If everything were to be carried out slowly and carefully . . . And an Assistant Director of Strategic Planning at Soviet Army General Headquarters like Yuryshev was worth taking risks for. For the time being, all Stavinsky had to do was sit tight and wait. Meanwhile, Virginia could call the Soviet Embassy and ask them to extend the period of the visas for a month or two, because . . . Well, MacKerry could dream something up himself . . . Illness, an urgent movie assignment, or something like that. She was an actress, after all, and she was entitled to be capricious. Today she wants to go to Russia, tomorrow she changes her mind or is offered a part in a film.

MacKerry left the office and drove off to a telephone booth to ring Stavinsky at his hotel. But instead of Stavinsky the call was taken by a black chambermaid who was cleaning up the room. MacKerry recognized her accent as being from Alabama or Tennessee.

'That gentleman who's been staying here ain't here no

more. I's collecting up his things.'

'And where is he living now?'

'And how should I know that? The boss told me jus collect up his things and leave 'em downstairs in the foyer.'

MacKerry didn't prolong the conversation. Instead, he rang the hotel manager and managed to discover that Stavinsky had called up from Florida an hour before, asking for his things to be sent on to Room 67, Hotel Ambassador, Sarasota, Florida.

What about that! MacKerry thought to himself. Not bad! He sure can play some tricks! He gets the money and scoots straight off to Florida, without even letting us know.

He felt around in his pockets for change to call Florida. He needed a couple of dollars. But he didn't have it, so he had to give the operator his home number and get them to add it to his bill. It would work out more expensive that way, goddamnit! So what? The office would be paying for the call in any case.

But there was no reply from room 67. Stavinsky was out swimming, of course! As if he'd spend all day sitting in his hotel room! MacKerry left a message for him, asked the hotel telephonist to take a note of his home number and returned to the office. Stavinsky wouldn't be back in the hotel till nightfall, in any case. What other stunts was he going to pull? He said he was willing to fly off to Russia at a moment's notice, and then he goes off to Florida without a word to anyone. They'd have to think really hard before handing the whole mission over to him! In any case, MacKerry would need to talk it all over with Carroll.

Carroll hadn't been much involved in the operation over recent weeks, and MacKerry had been dealing with it himself. Not that there had been much to deal with! Meanwhile, Carroll was involved in preparing a report for Congress about the constraints which hampered the CIA in its work. Constraints! What a joke! All things considered, it was amazing that the CIA managed to get anything done at all! 'Employees of the CIA are forbidden to enter

Congressional buildings . . . the CIA is not allowed to carry out any operations within the United States . . . the CIA is forbidden to collaborate with the FBI . . . the CIA is not entitled . . .' etc. etc. So what *were* they allowed to do? You couldn't even make a phone call from your own office, if you wanted to do the job properly. But there weren't very many CIA employees who followed that particular rule. If you needed to make a phone call, who was going to traipse off to a different bar or subway station every time, just because the Russians had bugging equipment? If the government wasn't worried enough to kick up a fuss with the Soviets, and if they didn't tell them to get the hell out of it with their phone-tapping equipment, then why should anyone working for the CIA damn well worry about it? The result was that hundreds of potentially important operations were nipped in the bud, because the Russians found out about them after the first telephone conversation. Yet every damned time they had a meeting, they had the success of Soviet military intelligence and the KGB stuffed down their throats. They should see what kind of job the KGB would do if they were suddenly forbidden to enter government offices or use government telephones! MacKerry suddenly had a vivid vision of some KGB colonel rushing out of the Lubyanka on to the Garden Ring Road every time he wanted to call up one of his agents!

Smiling bitterly at these melancholy thoughts, MacKerry went off to find Carroll. But it turned out that he wasn't at the office at all. He was sitting in the Library of Congress, working away at his report. For want of anything better to do, MacKerry looked at the teleprinter. It was the same old routine stuff, not a word about any Soviet submarines . . .

No, today had certainly not been a success! MacKerry left the office, got into his Ford and drove off to the health-club. A dip in the swimming-pool and a good sauna, followed by another swim in the pool – and a stiff gin and martini – that was what he really needed now. After all, he was a human being, too. He would just take his salary every month and enjoy life, like every other CIA employee. If the rest of America wasn't worried by the Russian threat then why should he do all the worrying on their behalf?

The atmosphere at the health-club was calm and relaxing. In the changing-rooms a handful of men, stripped naked and wrapped in thick, fleecy towels were smoking and watching baseball on the television. There was nobody in the sauna at all. After he'd sweated it out a little, MacKerry dived into the marvellously cool swimming-pool. Of course, it wasn't quite the same as the ocean which Stavinsky was wallowing in, but it wasn't bad all the same. He came to the surface and swam with broad, elegant strokes to the other side of the pool. Little did he know that exactly ten hours later Daniel J. Cooper would be calling him up at home to give his sleepy subordinate the following piece of news: 'David! Russian submarine U-137 has gone aground off the Karlskrona archipelago . . .'

21

DECLARATION FROM THE SWEDISH GOVERNMENT TO THE GOVERNMENT OF THE SOVIET UNION

On 27 October 1981, it was discovered that a Soviet submarine bearing the number U-137 was inside Swedish territory. The submarine ran aground in Swedish territorial waters in the immediate vicinity of the restricted military zone at the entrance to the Karlskrona naval base.

On 28 October the Swedish Government summoned the Soviet ambassador and issued a firm condemnation of this flagrant violation of Swedish sovereignty.

On 29 Ocober the Government ordered the Commander-in-Chief of the Swedish armed forces to conduct an inquiry into the reasons and circumstances surrounding the Soviet submarine's incursion into Swedish territorial waters. During the course of this investigation the Swedish side interrogated the captain and navigator of the submarine and also carried out an inspection on board ship. This investigation revealed that navigational error could not have been the main reason for the submarine's appearance off Karlskrona.

As a result of this inquiry the Swedish Government has been forced to conclude that the Soviet crew entered Swedish territory with the express intention of engaging in prohibited activities. The Swedish Government has been both astonished and outraged to discover that the submarine was in all probability carrying one or more nuclear warheads on board. The investigation established almost beyond all possibility of doubt that the fore part of the ship contains the radioactive element Uranium-238.

In view of the urgency of the situation, the Swedish Government demanded an immediate reply from the Government of the USSR as to whether the submarine was carrying nuclear weapons or not. The Soviet Government ignored the Swedish Government's demands. The Government of Sweden is therefore obliged to assume that the Soviet Government is not able to deny the presence of nuclear weapons on board the said submarine.

The Government of Sweden wishes to protest vigorously to the Soviet Government about the violation of Swedish territorial integrity committed by the crew of Soviet submarine U-137. This violation is all the more unacceptable and serious for the fact that the submarine most likely penetrated Swedish territorial waters carrying nuclear weapons on board.

The Swedish Government demands that the Soviet Union refrain in future from committing such flagrant violations of Swedish sovereignty in direct contravention of the fundamental principles of international law.

Stockholm, 5 November 1981.

22

What does a thirty-year-old woman need to make her happy? Fame? The adulation of the public? The leading part in a Hollywood movie and her picture on advertisement hoardings all over the subway? Villas on the Mediterranean and in Mexico and Beverly Hills? Ten, fifty, or even a hundred lovers, each with his own airplane, Rolls-Royce and yacht?

Or, when the chips are down, does she just need *one* man, *her* man?

Virginia was curled up comfortably in bed and smiling at her own thoughts. She was radiating happiness, she felt just like the lights of a Christmas Tree. She had just had a wonderful dream in which she imagined that she had given birth to a son, a beautiful dark-eyed boy, who resembled both herself and Stavinsky. He was running all over some garden, laughing and talking a mixture of Russian and English. Virginia began to laugh so much herself, that she woke up with a start and was now lying there open-eyed and staring at Stavinsky, asleep next to her. His body exuded a masculine warmth and the wrinkles in his face had been smoothed out by sleep. Virginia tried to imagine what he had looked like before he had had plastic surgery. If they really were to have a baby, which Stavinsky would he resemble, the real one, as he was before he had the operation, or the one sleeping next to her now? He would be like the earlier one, of course. But during the last two nights, when Stavinsky had told her that he wouldn't be flying off to Russia now, but would get his old face back and take Virginia away from Hollywood to anywhere she wanted – Florida or even Alaska if she liked (he would buy a house and open up a dental laboratory there: he had enough money to start his own business), when he had said all this, she had immediately agreed. Except that he didn't need to change his face again. She liked the one he had at the moment. As for his daughter, well they could tell Olya that he had been so badly beaten up by the hoods that he had had to undergo plastic surgery. But no, she mustn't think about all the details now. That would only blur her dream, and she wanted to shut her eyes really tight and hold on to her son.

Virginia closed her eyes, but the bright southern sun peeping through the venetian blinds glowed pink through her eyelids. This and the gentle sound of the ocean lapping against the beach outside their bedroom window reminded her that it was time to get up and go swimming, before it got too hot. She didn't really feel like it, and it was a shame to wake Roman. He must be pretty tired, after all. They had hardly slept a wink all night.

The soft buzz of the telephone interrupted her thoughts. She was amazed. Who could be ringing them up at that early hour? Slowly and gingerly, so as not to awaken Stavinsky, she slid over to the side of the bed and lifted the phone.

'Hello?'

'I'm sorry,' said a familiar voice, 'but could I talk to Dr Williams?'

It was MacKerry. She recognized his voice. But now she felt confused. What should she say?

'Hello,' said the voice insistently. 'Can you hear me? Is that Dr Williams's room?'

Stavinsky opened his eyes. Virginia placed her hand over the receiver and said in a whisper: 'It's MacKerry.'

'Damn!' replied Stavinsky and took the phone. 'Hello. Yes, it's me. No, I can't. Listen, David, the operation is over, isn't it? And now I've changed my plans. I'm staying in America. Yes, she's here, but we're not going anywhere. No. Be seeing you!'

He almost hurled the phone down on to the table. Virginia looked at him inquiringly.

'Now they want us to fly to Russia instantly,' he said. 'Hard luck on them! Come here!' And he took Virginia in his arms, pressing her extra tightly to his chest.

23

Three hours later a taxi pulled up in front of the Hotel Ambassador in Sarasota. MacKerry settled up with the driver and went to find Stavinsky. The doorman said that Dr Williams and his wife would either be by the swimming-pool or on the beach, or they had maybe taken a walk somewhere. The sight of all those bronzed female bodies lying around the covered pool with their lascivious eyes and luscious thighs tormented MacKerry. There was actually a bar set up in the swimming-pool itself, so that you could drink a gin and tonic, or a cocktail or whatever you wanted without getting out of the water. Just imagine leaving a paradise like this to travel to a god-forsaken place like Russia, where it's as cold as hell and you've got the KGB and other treats awaiting you. Who would want to do it, especially if he'd got Stavinsky's kind of money and a woman like Virginia?

MacKerry looked really out of place, dressed as he was in a suit and collar and tie. Angry with himself for not going home to change, and with Stavinsky as well, MacKerry looked around at all the men and women relaxing comfortably on their sun-beds, soaking up the warmth. Neither Stavinsky, nor Virginia was among them, so he headed off for the beach. But the beach was empty. The midday sun was so hot that anybody there had either migrated to the swimming-pool or taken to the sea in a yacht. Swearing to himself, he started walking towards the marina. Dozens of private yachts were at anchor in that peaceful backwater, far removed from the political and economic rat-race of the world outside. Some families lived there the whole year round and managed to eke a living out of fishing, repairing the craft of wealthier yacht-owners, taking tourists for boat trips up and down the coast and manufacturing small souvenirs. They thrived in a setting of endless warmth, fresh air and spiritual isolation.

MacKerry found Stavinsky and Virginia at the very end

of the quay, seated beneath the awning of a tiny café. You could tell that they hadn't been here long by the colour of their skin.

'Hello,' said MacKerry, joining them at their table. 'Fantastic weather they get in Florida, don't they? I'll have a coke and some oysters,' he said to the waiter, and then turned to face Stavinsky and Virginia once again. Virginia looked embarrassed, while Stavinsky maintained a stony silence. MacKerry realized that this was going to be difficult and decided to take the bull by the horns.

'Well, this is how it is, friends. There's nothing worse than an uninvited guest, I know, and I certainly don't want to spoil your holiday. So I'll come clean with you right away. Exactly two months ago the Moscow correspondent of the *Washington Herald* happened to meet a very important Soviet military expert in the grounds of the Novodevichy Monastery. The meeting took place completely by chance. His name is Colonel Yuryshev and he's an Assistant Director of Strategic Planning at Soviet Army General Headquarters. He told the journalist that he wanted to escape to the West. In exchange for helping him get out of the USSR, he is willing to tell us what he knows about the plans of the Soviet military high command. And he even told us exactly when he wanted to escape. According to him, a Soviet submarine would run aground off the coast of Sweden, and when it did, he would go on vacation to a nature reserve somewhere in the Kirov Region of Russia and wait for a signal from us. That's why we were on tenterhooks all during the first half of October, waiting for news of this submarine. But nothing happened. So we decided that the plan had come unstuck and we told you that you could go home. But last night news of the submarine finally arrived. It's run aground off Sweden, as predicted. The captain says that it was an accident, that there was a fault in their navigational equipment, and so on. But we know all that is a bundle of lies. We had advance warning of their operation two months ago, although nobody here knows why they've done it. Yuryshev knows, of course, and he knows a lot more things about Soviet military planning, too. He is also the spit and image of you, Roman. Take a look at these.'

MacKerry pulled an envelope out of his coat pocket. It contained all the photographs which Stevenson had taken of Yuryshev at the Novodevichy that day. There was no doubt about it: it was Stavinsky's face looking out at them. There was the same grim determination, the same unyielding obstinacy.

'There's only one person alive in the world today who can get this Yuryshev out of Russia, and that's you, Roman,' said MacKerry. 'Everything is ready. We've got all the passports and visas ready, and we've already begun the count-down. We have exactly three weeks from today. That's when Yuryshev comes back from his vacation. And that's all there is to tell you. Of course, here you are, surrounded by the sea and the sun, and it's difficult to imagine going to Russia . . . But two months ago, you agreed to go of your own free will, and we haven't the time to look for a replacement now. The whole operation depends on you.'

'You're wasting your time, David,' said Stavinsky. 'The day before yesterday you said the operation was cancelled, and you even paid us off. I'm not obliged to do anything for your organization any longer. You'll tell me that only one day has gone by, but sometimes the thing that you've been waiting your whole life for can take place in a single day. And that is what's happened to me. I love this woman, and for her sake I'm going to stay in America. To be perfectly honest, I've loved her for a whole month, from the moment I first set eyes on her. But until the day before yesterday, I was in your hands. Then you cancelled our contract. And from that moment I was hers. I didn't walk out on you, while we had a contract, and I won't walk out on her. That's logical, isn't it?'

'Well, it may be logical,' said MacKerry, 'but there are

some things . . .'

'Listen,' said Stavinsky, interrupting him. 'I thought you wanted me to change places with somebody who was really important, some scientist like Sakharov who had the secret of a new bomb. I even thought it might be somebody like Brezhnev's son or possibly Raoul Wallenberg. Somebody whose defection would cause a real sensation, in other words. And who does it turn out to be? Some two-bit colonel with a few secrets from Soviet General HQ. Big deal! Listen, I'll tell you something. Whether you get to know this secret information or not, America has already lost to the Soviets. It makes no difference. They've already stripped you of half the world, and every day they grab more and more countries. And they don't even have to grab them: you hand them over to the Russkies on a plate. America acts like a rich man trying to get away from a beggar who accosts him on the street. If you toss him a few coins, perhaps he'll go away. But then the beggar gets bolder. First he asks for one dollar, then a hundred. Then he takes your coat, your house, your car, your wife and, finally, your children. And all you can do is give in, retreat further and further, hide yourself away, just like the people who live on those yachts. Anything to avoid awkward problems. Just as long as everything is OK *today*. Just as long as the Soviets don't send their tanks rolling down Broadway. And so it goes on, and for this you'll give the beggar your money, your grain, your wife and your mistress. You'll surrender Cuba and Israel, Europe and even Florida. And that's what I mean when I say you've already lost. You've lost, because you're rich, well-fed and too softened up by the easy life. You've got plenty enough to live on today, and you don't want to think about anything else. You ask any American whether he'd rather win a hundred dollars in a lottery today or have the chance of winning a million dollars in five years' time and he'll always say: let me have the hundred dollars today. Whereas in Russia people give everything they have to the State today in return for promises that in twenty, thirty or perhaps even a hundred years' time, they'll have a high standard of living as the US has got now. They were starving yesterday, they're starving today and they'll be starving tomorrow. And that's why they'll beat you, because the hungry are always stronger than the well-fed. That's a law of nature, isn't it? You Americans are doomed. You just wait. In ten years, fifteen at the most, there will be Russian soldiers swarming all over the White House. So what difference does it make whether you find out the Soviets' plans or not? As the rabbi said to the young girl before her wedding night: "It doesn't matter whether you get into bed naked or clothed. He'll end up screwing you all the same." And if you're so keen on finding out about the Russians' war plans, I can tell you them now without even leaving the spot. They want to Sovietize the whole world. And they want to grab your oil, your gold, your factories, your land, your rivers, your cities – the whole lot! Have you ever heard of a crook mugging a passer-by and not taking everything he's got? If you want to find out about their plans, just open up a volume of Lenin at any page. It was all expounded by him: the overthrow of capitalist governments throughout the whole world. That's all. Every schoolboy in Russia knows it. But if anybody mentions it to you Americans, you just brush it aside. You start talking about us Russian émigrés having a hate-complex about the Communists, and you accuse us of spreading propaganda. And meanwhile the Commies just carry on doing their own thing. Over the last sixty years they've managed to grab half the world, from China to Yugoslavia, from Vietnam to Nicaragua. And you're still wondering what their plans are! What a joke! That's why I'm not going anywhere. Eat your shrimps while you still can. When the Russians arrive, you won't be able to do that any more. But in the meantime . . . I'm a US citizen, too, and I want to enjoy life today to the full. Good health!'

Stavinsky poured some of the iced Italian wine into their glasses, but MacKerry pushed his away.

'Look, Roman,' he said. 'Everything you have just told me about the US may well be true. But don't forget that if the Russians do arrive here, as you say they will, then it's not just the Americans who will be finished. You and your daughter will be, too. You realize that the first people the Soviets will do away with will be former Russians, don't you? The best that could happen would be for you all to get sent to some labour camp in Alaska. If you really do love Virginia and want to get out of Russia again so as to be with her, we'll find a way of doing it. Getting a simple dental technician out is a thousand times easier than doing the same for a colonel at Soviet Army General HQ, and we'll have more time at our disposal, as well. But time is what we haven't got very much of at the moment. Remember, it was our country, the USA, which gave you citizenship when you left Russia. And it's the USA which has given your daughter her education and has now given you one of its prettiest women. Our country needs you, *you* – and it needs you today. You know what the Soviet threat represents. Think about it and ring me up in Washington tomorrow. Goodbye, Virginia. I'm sorry if I've spoilt your holiday.'

MacKerry got up and began to walk away down the long quayside, without turning to look round.

Stavinsky and Virginia stared after him. The Florida sun shimmered in MacKerry's half-empty wine glass.

24

For the rest of that day neither Stavinsky, nor Virginia made any mention of their conversation with MacKerry. They hired a yacht for a few hours ('Only forty dollars an hour, sir!'), then they ate in a Cuban restaurant ('The food's very spicy, Virginia, still what the hell!'), and finally spent the evening in a bar, with Stavinsky glued to the television. The news was on. 'Soviet troops in Angola . . . Soviet tanks in Afghanistan . . . Will Soviet forces invade Poland? . . . Is the Soviet submarine grounded off the coast of Sweden carrying nuclear weapons?'

Stavinsky waved to the barman and ordered himself a double vodka. He downed it without saying a word and then ordered another. After this third shot, Virginia stopped him.

'Roman, don't drink any more.'

He stared at her and then asked: 'Do you know what I've been thinking about all day?'

'Yes,' she said.

'I have to go.'

'I know,' she said. '*We* have to go.'

'Otherwise I'd never forgive myself for the rest of my life.'

'I know,' she said. 'We'll go together. But there's just one thing . . . I want you to let me have your child.'

'Wha-a-t?'

'I expect it will be a boy. I dreamed about him this morning. Please don't drink any more.'

He gazed at her for a long time and didn't know what to say. Only two months ago he had hated this country, hated it because it had beckoned to him from afar, but had then ruined his life. Youth had turned to old age, strength to weakness, vigour to impotence. And because of that he was willing to betray it. At the first opportunity he would have informed the KGB of the purpose of his mission, just to be shot of America. But he had already begun to pay for this potential betrayal. He had given up his daughter, changed his face and even buried his former existence in New Jersey. And all this because he wanted to *live* – *live*, and not vegetate. But this woman, who so resembled the mother he remembered as a child, this woman had turned his whole world upside down again. Of course, there was no question now of his betraying the CIA or of collaborating with the KGB. There were things in America now that he had to defend against Soviet tanks. There was his grown-up daughter, the woman he loved, and goddamnit, his unborn son! He had a whole family now. America was his country! He had something to fight for at last! And with any luck – and the help of the CIA – he would be able to return safely from Russia and sit on this same beach with Virginia again some time in the future.

'You know,' he said, 'I love you. I really do. And I want you terribly much.'

'And so do I – you,' she answered with a smile.

25

STRANDED SOVIET SUBMARINE – DIARY OF EVENTS

Stockholm, 6 November Reuter – Following is a chronology of the main events since Soviet submarine U-137 ran aground in a restricted military area inside Swedish waters:
27 Oct – A Soviet patrol submarine of the Whisky class ploughs into a mudbank among islands near the Baltic naval base at Karlskrona on Sweden's south coast.
28 Oct – Swedish fishing boat spots the submarine after it remained undetected by Swedish armed forces for twelve hours. Soviet ambassador is summoned twice to Foreign Ministry for protest against 'flagrant violation of Swedish territorial waters'. Soviet naval force heads towards area.
29 Oct – Sweden rejects claim by Soviet ambassador that vessel strayed into restricted zone because of navigational error in heavy fog. Government orders official inquiry and says submarine commander Pyotr Kushchin will be interrogated.
30 Oct – Kushchin refuses to leave submarine and says he will only face interrogation if Soviet diplomats are present. Two Soviet diplomats are dispatched to Karlskrona but are not allowed to enter the off-limits zone.

31 Oct – Submarine begins to list as weather worsens. Kushchin says he is awaiting fresh orders and continues to refuse to leave his vessel.
2 Nov – After approval from Moscow, Kushchin boards Swedish torpedo boat and is interrogated by Swedish navy experts. Weather worsens and Soviet crew send distress signals. Two Swedish tugs haul U-137 off rocks in near gale-force winds and tow it to safer berth.
4 Nov – Moscow reports for the first time that U-137 has run aground and blames faulty navigation. Swedish defence staff reveals secret trials of new anti-submarine torpedo, close to where U-137 ran aground.
5 Nov – Prime Minister Thorbjoern Faelldin charges that 'in all probability' the submarine had one or more nuclear weapons on board.

6 Nov – U-137 is towed out to international waters by Swedish tugs.

Part 2

A Russian Kamikaze

SECRET
PRIORITY

To: No 2, Moscow, Centre

Coded Telegram

In connection with your order No SS939/7 to ascertain the names of the patients of Dr Robert Williams of Potomac in the State of Maryland, I have to report:

Our agent, posing as a rival dentist to Dr Williams, managed to hire (for three hundred dollars) two criminals of Cuban extraction who penetrated the office of Dr Williams, which was closed during his absence on honeymoon, and removed his card-index. The card-index was photographed and returned to its place without evidence of theft. Examination of the card-index has revealed that Dr Robert Williams's clientele includes Senators S. McVayne and P. Jennison, Congressmen M. Walter, D. Parkson, and people of various ranks working in the State Department. Access to each of these people is of the greatest value to our intelligence.

I urgently request you take all possible measures to recruit Dr Williams. It is hard to exaggerate the significance of this operation.

Signed
No 4

Received by the Coding Section of the KGB from Washington, 4 November 1981, at 1305 hours

Resolution

To: Colonel Orlov, Head of Tourist Department

Take personal control of the recruiting of Dr Williams. On completion, report to me personally.

General Semyon Tsvigun,
First Deputy Chairman of the KGB

5 November 1981

1

Major Neznachny stood in the vestibule of the Moscow Theatrical Institute and looked angrily at the students walking past. What a bunch of trash! The bell went twenty minutes ago for the lecture, and these skivers were only now wandering into the Institute – they looked half-asleep, the girls were smoking, they were all wearing jeans, they chucked their jackets and coats on to the hooks without brushing the snow off first, and then dispersed to their lecture-halls wearing T-shirts covered on both sides with gaudy designs and slogans, and with their arms round each other. This style of putting their arms round each other – even the boys went in pairs: were they all queers around here? – annoyed Neznachny most of all. Neznachny had graduated from the Law Faculty of Moscow University ten years ago. That was a hard time for him; he went to lectures in patched trousers, for a time ate nothing but potatoes, and even then not enough to fill him, earned money on the side working as a loader at railway stations, and then in the summer all the students of Moscow State University were sent to collective farms to earth up potatoes by hand or to pick tomatoes, potatoes, cabbages . . . These punks here ought to be sent to the potato fields to drag thirty-kilo sacks through the black-earth mud in the rain. But the worst thing was that that wretch Olya Makhova wasn't here. Neznachny looked at his watch. 9.23! The whole day would be fouled up if she didn't appear. The Williamses were arriving in six hours, after taking a month to get ready, damned newly-weds! He had sent their visas through at the beginning of October, the whole operation was set to go. Neznachny, like the producer after the first night, had rehearsed every detail of the operation with all his regular and co-opted workes, and was waiting for their arrival from one day to the next, keyed up for the big occasion. He was on such a high at that time that he would have met them with flowers at the bottom of the gangway if he could. But they did not come. God knows why – you couldn't call up and ask! That was the trouble with his work – you prepared, you spent sleepless nights racking your brains for tricks and traps, you worked out every possible scenario with your assistants, you took busy people away from their work – painters, performing artists, doctors, scientists – and arranged for them to receive some Texas oil magnates and surround them with Russian hospitality, and then these damned magnates failed to arrive. And the whole show was spoiled, and all that laborious preparation, sometimes taking up to a month, went down the drain. And you went around fuming with rage, and at home you took it all out on your wife. And the boss couldn't care less that these Williamses, Smiths, or Joneses had decided to postpone their trip; the boss would just tell you to draw up a plan for recruiting new agents, or else no prize, no good progress report, no new star on your epaulette. And then suddenly – emergency, a coded message from Washington: these Williamses were on their way. It was a bad day for it, 5 November, just before the holiday. The whole KGB was mobilized to keep order during the October Revolution holiday, and tomorrow there would be as many KGB operatives in the centre of Moscow as militia – 6,200, one third of the Dzerzhinsky division. The authorities were all wound up – any crazy dissident or Jewish *refusenik* who had so far escaped being picked up could pull some trick, like take a placard out of his coat, or a bottle of gasoline so as to burn himself to death in front of the foreigners. Of course that wasn't Neznachny's concern, that came under completely different sections. All suspicious dissidents, Jewish *refuseniks*, Pentecostalists, and Volga Germans had been detained for the next few days, but you tell me what that long-hair with glasses over there has under his shirt. Maybe he would come to Red Square tomorrow with a bomb or with a 'Free Poland' sign, and these Williamses would happen to be right nearby! Hell, where was that bitch Makhova? The worst thing was that she didn't yet know the Williamses were on their way and the operation had started. Even Neznachny found out only the day before the Washington coded message came through, when Aeroflot sent the passenger lists for the Brussels–Moscow flight. And in these three days that girl hadn't spent one night in her own dormitory and hadn't been to the Institute. Neznachny had called and called the dean's office at the Acting Faculty and had left messages at the dormitory, but she had clean vanished! Knowing Makhova a year already, Neznachny had no doubt that she was shacking up with yet another painter or photographer. That thin, long-legged little creature with her narrow under-nourished hips, small breasts, flaxen shoulder-length hair and large blue eyes, with her childish face and innocently sinful little lips, had sex-appeal of almost magical force. There wasn't a fellow who could cast his eye over her little figure and then look away indifferently. It was as if there were a sort of pulse of sexuality beating inside that skinny little body, and Makhova herself was just the envelope round that demonic attractive force. Even Major Gasparyan, head of the French Section, had clicked his tongue when he saw Olya and offered Neznachny any exchange for Makhova – three, even five prostitutes working with the French. But Neznachny refused – she was his 'cadre', his personal find. A year ago in the Ukraine Hotel he had dragged this Makhova away from a thirty-year-old Canadian with his own hands; he had purposely not allowed her to get dressed and had brought her straight to the KGB in a van. Sobbing, she begged him not to report her to the Institute. Anything he wanted, only not to report her to the Institute. No wonder! To come from some Siberian backwoods like Bratsk and get into the best theatrical institute in the country without pulling any strings, where forty-seven people compete for every place and where the road leads straight to the cinema and the Moscow stage! And then suddenly, two weeks after the beginning of the course, the KGB removes you from a visiting Canadian in an Intourist hotel room. They would sling you out of the Institute in five minutes, and with such a note in your work record book that you wouldn't get a job even in a village club, let alone the theatre. Her whole life was ruined. So it did not take much to recruit this girl, make her an agent. He could have slept with her right then and there, and at any time after that – it was nothing to her, she would sometimes even tease him by hitching her skirt up and baring her little knees, or she would simply taunt him: 'You don't seem to have any feelings, Frol Yevseyich! Are you really married?' Never mind, one of these days he would show her if he had feelings, but meantime . . . he knew very well that if he once slept with this Makhova his power over her would be undermined and would disappear. She was already a scatterbrain, she might be late for an operation, or she might latch on to some other 'godson' and it would take days to prise them apart. Two months ago Michael Leonard, president of the biggest construction company in Toronto, postponed his departure from Moscow three times, paying for a new ticket each time in hard currency; he would have paid a fourth time too, if Olya's period had not begun. But the tickets were chicken-feed; this Leonard was already paying the KGB far more – and not in cash – for his Moscow pleasures, and far from grudging it, couldn't wait to get back to the Soviet Union again – a week ago his application arrived for a new visa. But now let him wait a little until Makhova had serviced Robert Williams. Anyway, where is she, the silly bitch? Neznachny swore under his breath. I'll screw her right out of the Institute! He walked anxiously up to lecture-hall two on the second floor, just in case Makhova had somehow slipped past him. Again and again he looked round the auditorium through the crack in the door: the students were rehearsing a scene from *A Street-Car Named Desire*, but, God, the way they did it! In the scene between Stanley Kowalski and his pregnant wife Stella when there is the scandal about her little sister Blanche being a prostitute, he lays his wife on the floor, lies down next to her, and then fondles her, tempts her, and works her up for sex while at the same time spelling out to her the fact that her sister is a slut. And poor Stella weeps away, frantic to sleep with her husband straight away and yet frantic not to know the truth about her little sister. So Kowalski, a pimply seventeen-year-old, quite openly puts one hand into her blouse and squeezes and presses her breast, while the other is already up her skirt. Not so bad, these drama classes! Neznachny would have been happy to spend his life going to classes like that; it was not like mugging up Roman law and the penal code by heart! What was more, Oleg Tabakov, People's Artist of the USSR, famous the world over for the film *Oblomov*, was even correcting this Kowalski: 'Not like that! You're the husband! You're supposed to stimulate her like a husband who knows exactly where to touch her so that she goes crazy with desire. And you're just pawing her! Come on, now, again!'

Satisfied that Makhova was not in the auditorium with the other students, Neznachny moved away from the door, lit a cigarette, and went down to the vestibule. What the hell was he to do? The lesson was half over, the Institute's vestibule and corridors were deserted, and that little wretch still wasn't here. And his whole day was planned down to the minute! He still had to get to the Tourist Department of Intourist that morning – that was the first thing; then he had to check that the listening equipment was all working in the hotel room where the Williamses would be staying; then to the producer Dmitry Lisadze; and even the stomatologist, Dr Semyon Bobrov, was expecting him at eleven.

A taxi, dusted with snow, drew up to the main entrance of

the Institute, and out jumped Olya Makhova, a black fur coat over her shoulders, a fur cap in one had, and a string bag with textbooks and notebooks in the other. Neznachny laughed without mirth – from the half-open, swollen lips, the almost transparent pallor of her face, and the straight, stiff walk he already knew he had guessed right – that wretch had spent several days and nights in yet another bed, and now she had come rushing to the Institute just because the acting workshop was on Fridays, with Tabakov himself in charge.

Sliding through the snow in her little slippers, Makhova ran into the vestibule, throwing off her coat as she went, and made straight for the cloakroom, looking about for an empty hook.

'Makhova!' Neznachny blocked her way out of the cloakroom.

She quickly turned her head towards him and immediately – what a little actress! – her eyes lit up with genuine delight: 'Oh, Frol! Hallo! Sorry darling, I must run, I have my acting workshop!'

'I'll give you "run" in a moment!' said Neznachny angrily.

'Why, what is it? What's happened?' asked Makhova innocently, and her little figure swayed in the air like the stem of an underwater plant. 'Frol, sweetie, the break is in fifteen minutes, and then we'll talk. Wait for me, won't you? Or Tabakov will kill me!'

'I'll kill you first. Stop! I don't have time to wait. Where have you been hanging around for the last three days?'

'I was staying with my aunt in the country. She got sick . . .'

'Liar,' said Neznachny calmly. 'Look at you. You can hardly stand up, and your eyes look "fucked"!'

'What did you say?' Olya's little blue eyes glanced at him slyly.

Seasoning one's Russian with American jargon was

considered bad taste in all the foreign sections of the KGB's Second Directorate; it was something that only young lieutenants did to show off, and people who had finished the special intensive English courses, which, incidentally, Olya Makhova had taken last year so as to be able to entertain the foreigners not only with sex but also with stories about the Soviet Union. But these courses had not done Olya much good – no matter how much Neznachny listened to her bedtime conversations with foreigners, they contained virtually no dialogue apart from words like 'once more' or 'have you come?'

'Now look,' Neznachny told her sternly. 'Your workshop ends at two. At 2.15 you are to be at the Hotel National. You will give your name to the manager and collect the key to a room on the twelfth floor. And remember – that's it, from now on you're on the job! And if you're just one minute late, this'll be your last day at the Institute, I give you my word as an officer!'

'Oh, all right, all right! But . . . Frol, I can't just move into the hotel without my things. I've got to go back to the dorm for a suitcase, and my stuff. And I've no money for a taxi. How long do I have to stay there? Who am I working with?'

'Robert Williams is arriving today, I told you about him.'

'Oh, him?! I'll screw him silly in two days! Only get rid of his wife for a couple of hours, can you?'

'We'll do all that. Only you have to get moved in before he does, is that clear?'

'Frol Yevseyich, last time you promised to get me an invitation to shoot for a film. And because of that I fucked that Canadian so hard he almost had a heart attack.'

'I will. You carry out this assignment, and I'll do everything.'

'Your word as a Communist?'

'Word of honour.'

'No, give me your Party word!' insisted Olya, and she

drew her little tongue so slowly and deliberately across her lips that Neznachny felt an ache in his chest and below his stomach.

'All right, my Party word,' he said reluctantly.

'That's it! 'Bye! I must dash! I'll be there at 2.15. Give me three roubles for lunch. Deduct it from my daily allowance.' And Olya impatiently snatched a five-rouble note from Neznachny, went up on tiptoes, and kissed him on the neck. Then she rushed upstairs to the second floor.

'Watch out, Olya!' Neznachny shouted after her. 'I shall be there at 2.15. If you don't get there . . .'

'I will! I will! I'm not an idiot!' Olya shouted from the stairs, and her beautifully chiselled legs, throwing her short little skirt up as she ran, were now right over Neznachny's head.

'Fool, you're not wearing any . . .' Neznachny yelled at her.

'I know, I didn't have time, it doesn't matter!' Makhova called back laughing, and disappeared.

Neznachny shook his head and sighed, exhausted. What a handful! Anyway, we've got some legs ready for Dr Williams – and what legs! Welcome, Dr Williams, enjoy yourself! Now we have to take care of your wife Virginia . . .

2

'Soviet airline Aeroflot announces the departure of its flight London–Brussels–Moscow. Passengers are requested to proceed to gate no five for boarding. I repeat . . .'

The velvety female voice floated across the Brussels air terminal, repeating the announcement in Russian with comic incorrect stresses and a non-Russian accent, but it was just this non-Russian accent that gripped Stavinsky's heart. That was it. The trap was closing. He was deliberately walking into the snare, into the trap. Of course, he had not forgotten MacKerry's final instructions. And the photograph of a Major Neznachny of the KGB who was involved in recruiting American tourists. And the photographs of his assistants of both sexes – before his departure MacKerry had spent several hours instructing him in the KGB's traps, since the head of the Russian Section of the CIA had given the order to show Stavinsky and Virginia everything they knew about the work of the American Section of the KGB's Tourist Department. And they knew quite a bit. On that secret map which Major Neznachny guarded so lovingly in his safe, by no means all the figures corresponded to reality – one or two of Neznachny's godsons had had the courage to go to the CIA on their return to the US and tell how they had been recruited in Moscow. And MacKerry laid out before Stavinsky and Virginia the entire collection of Neznachny's favourite techniques, including even a photograph of his 'trump' card – the tempting beauty Olya Makhova. Now two counter-intelligences were playing a new game of chess, in which the king and queen were Stavinsky and Virginia. The CIA were preparing Stavinsky as well as they could for the game, but you couldn't anticipate all the opponent's moves. The only thing Stavinsky could be almost a hundred per cent sure about was that what he had requested: two sets of Soviet documents, money to start out life in the USSR, and instructions on how to contact the CIA in case of emergency, would be waiting for him on 16 November in the automatic left-luggage office at Moscow's Yaroslavl Station, in box no 217 which opened to the combination 141516. And that was it. But oh Lord! There wouldn't be any more of this un-Russian cleanliness in the stations, these stewardesses and salesladies with their soft, quiet voices, these glittering, mirror-like shop windows which looked as if they had been washed in expensive shampoo and which contained everything, absolutely everything:

Japanese radio electronics, Chinese porcelain, Parisian cosmetics, Scottish wools, Italian footwear, Brazilian leather, Canadian fur, flowers and fruit from Israel, American cigarettes, Smirnov vodka, and hundreds of liqueurs, wines, cognacs, brandies, and whiskies from all over the world. No more.

Stavinsky and Virginia stood in the main concourse of Brussels Airport, a huge hall, but homely-looking with its flowers and Sky Shop windows. A few feet away from them was the soft, corrugated rubber travelator which took you from the main concourse to the departure lounge, but right now those few feet seemed to Stavinsky wider and longer than the Atlantic Ocean. At the other end of that travelator was the Tu-124, the Soviet plane, Stavinsky's trap. Just a few steps and you were already aboard the aircraft, you were in the belly of Soviet power, the power of another world. And what if he happened to bump into an air hostess he knew?

Nearby, a few feet away, was the doorway to Europe: the small customs desk; you just had to go up to it, show your American passport, and – 'Pass right through, please sir!' Pass right through to Sweden, to Denmark, to Australia and Japan, to New Zealand and even Jamaica! What an idiot he was not to have travelled to all those countries! MacKerry had given them just two days for Rome and three for Paris and Brussels, to give the Russians the impression that the Williamses were on their honeymoon . . .

Virginia touched his hand gently and looked questioningly into his eyes.

Stavinsky wanted to say, 'Let's go,' but merely winced from the pain in his throat. His throat really was sore, there was nothing phoney about it – the previous day, before leaving Paris for Brussels, he had eaten a whole carton of ice cream so as to give himself genuine swelling of the tonsils, and he did – his glands swelled up and became covered with an unpleasant whitish-yellow coating, so that he could neither speak nor swallow nor even inhale a cigarette. Now, even if he were tortured, he could not utter a single word properly in either English or Russian, he could only whisper inaudibly, and from a hiss like that no customs official would be able to catch him out speaking incorrect English.

Stavinsky adjusted the dressing on his throat – a hot compress tied round with a thick layer of bandages, then took Virginia by the hand, and together they took those few short paces that severed them from the West. The black travelator carried them towards the Soviet plane – away into the past floated the Sky Shop windows, their elegant salesladies, and the whole of His Excellency the West.

3

The fear that in the very first minute in the Soviet plane some air hostess or one of the Soviet passengers would exclaim in surprise, 'Hey, Stavinsky?! Long time no see!' – this purely hypothetical fear was nothing compared to what befell him the second he stepped from the gangway into the cabin of the plane. Not just some air hostess, but half the passengers of this plane were his former life, or to be exact – the dream of his former life in the USSR. The cream of the Soviet film industry – famous film stars, producers, script-writers, and cameramen, some with their wives and some without, were coming back on this flight from a tour of Europe. It was the London to Moscow flight, calling at Brussels on the way, and the Soviet passengers were not allowed off the plane at Brussels (not because of the Belgian authorities, of course, but because of their group leader Grisha Muryanov, Secretary of the Cinematographers' Union – why should he have to worry that someone would run away to the West at the last moment?).

And, stepping into the plane's cabin, Stavinsky came into

a totally Russian hubbub: 'Grisha, I've travelled halfway round the world and never run away! What's the matter with you – have you gone grazy? We're not the Bolshoi Theatre, you know!' the superb forty-year-old actress Iya Krasavina was saying to the sulky, gloomy Muryanov. 'I have some hard currency left, I wanted to buy some Chanel here!'

'You already bought some Chanel in London . . .' Muryanov muttered through his teeth, not looking her in the eye.

'Carrion!' said Krasavina indignantly. 'Just you wait!'

'Well I think we should write a collective letter to the Central Committee!' complained the producer Volodya Bolshov, who had recently received an Oscar. Seven years ago Stavinsky had interviewed him for TV about his first film, *Winnings*. Since then Bolshov had become very bald and very corpulent, but the Oscar had evidently boosted his self-confidence: 'It's a typical example of distrusting Soviet artists!' he said. 'The Party entrusts us with the education of the entire nation, and then Comrade Muryanov . . .'

'Comrades, quiet! It's embarrassing – there are foreigners getting on. We'll sort it out at home,' said Yakov Raiman, the doyen of Soviet film producers, in an attempt to pacify them all.

The noise subsided and the film folk turned, gloomy and disgruntled, to the windows beyond which lay the Brussels air terminal with its Sky Shops, French cosmetics and other wonders of Western civilization, now beyond their grasp.

The foreigners – about a dozen tourists and businessmen – moved down the aisle looking for their seats. Lowering his face, and expecting that at any moment one of these idols of Soviet cinema would chance to look up at him and recognize him, Stavinsky followed Virginia to the seventeenth row, his legs almost giving way under him. About twenty years ago he had dreamed of being among these people, for that reason he had left the Medical Institute during the third year and gone into TV journalism, and now – hey presto, he had landed up in their company! Out of the corner of his eye he noted the people he knew; the actress Lenochka Solovey from *Slave of Love*, the actor Aleksey Batalov from *The Cranes are Flying* and *Moscow Doesn't Believe in Tears*, Nikolay Burlyaev from *Rublyov*, with his wife Natasha Bondarchuk from *Solaris* . . . Of course, not all of them knew him, most likely none of them either knew or remembered some TV journalist who at one time had haunted the film studios, but he, Stavinsky, knew every one of them, he had written about them, had brief interviews with them during shootings, and even once had a beer with Volodya Bolshov at the restaurant of Cinema House. Half dead with fear, he slumped into his seat. A cold sweat had soaked his shirt and the cotton wool compress pressing against his neck was making it hard to breathe. He pulled the window blind down so that the light would not fall on his face and closed his eyes, realizing that this was – the end, the end! His hand was gripping the arm rest so tightly that it had gone white, and Virginia quietly covered it with her hand. Perhaps because of her gesture of sympathy, or because no one in fact was taking any notice of him, he began to feel slightly better. And anyway, how could they take any notice of me, he thought suddenly, if I've had plastic surgery! I'm different! Different! Maybe I look like some Stavinsky over there, but I'm sorry – where are the protruding ears, where's that hook nose, where are the puffy lips? A nervous, almost hysterical laughter began to rise in his sore throat, and if it had not been for the tonsillitis, had it not been too painful to laugh, he would have immediately burst out laughing for the whole plane to hear and would have ended up throwing a hysterical fit.

'Attention!' a woman's voice announced in Russian. 'The crew of our Tu-124 Soviet airliner welcomes you aboard the plane. In a few minutes we shall be taking off. May I request you to fasten your seat belts and to refrain from smoking.'

The Tu-124 taxied out on to the runway and came to a stop, the turbojets roared, causing the whole plane to shake with a sort of metallic shudder, and now, the entire craft with all its Soviet and foreign passengers, Stavinsky too, strapped to his seat, was caught in this shudder. The air hostess was walking down the aisle checking that everybody had their seat belts fastened.

The amazingly fat comic actor Yevgeny Mordunov said to the air hostesss: 'Darling, the straps won't reach across my stomach. You'll have to put your arms around me. Come here, honey . . .'

4

A coded radio message arrived that morning from submarine commander Kushchin. It was short – four lines:

SECRET

To: Oparkov, Head of General HQ

Mission accomplished. Today 6 November was escorted to international waters by Swedish naval vessels. Proceeding home to Baltiisk.

Captain Kushchin U-137

For Project EMMA this radio message signified the start of the effective encirclement of Europe with underwater energy transmission grids (Energy Matrices Mini-Attack) capable on a signal from central control of causing a direction-controlled earthquake up to a distance of 400 kilometres from a shaft on the sea-bed. For Colonel Sergey Ivanovich Yuryshev, an Assistant Director of Strategic Planning at Soviet Army General Headquarters, it meant a prize of 2,000 roubles, general's epaulettes, and twenty-four working days' leave. Colonel Yuryshev stood at the wide window that looked on to the Arbat from his office in General Headquarters, smoking and watching the snow swirling about Moscow. He loved this town. Possessing a phenomenal visual memory, he knew not only every street in the city, but almost every house. Now he looked at the snow-swept Arbat Square, at the people who, coat-collars raised and heads bent against the icy wind, were hurrying to the shops in the pre-holiday rush. As usual before the Revolution holiday, sausages, fruit, and even frozen beef had appeared in the Moscow shops. Yuryshev watched these people as they walked along with their bodies stooped forward towards the ground. Their arms and shoulders were weighed down with heavy shopping-bags full of packages. This was his country, his people, his life. Was it hard, was it painful for these people to live from day to day worrying about where they were going to get milk for the children, a piece of frozen meat, or a kilo of pickles? If it was, they went on living and did not complain. They just drank more and more. Even though the price of vodka had gone up, they carried on drinking cheap port wines, moonshine, home-brew, neat surgical spirit. For centuries Russia had drowned all her sorrows with vodka, thought Yuryshev, every grief was lightened and drowned in drunkenness. But he could not drink any more; he had tried, but was unable to quench even one drop of his troubles with alcohol. Three months previously his fifteen-year-old son Vitya, his only son whom he loved more than anything in the world, winner of young people's mathematics olympiads, a tall skinny boy who wrote chess problems and had never kissed a woman in his life apart from his mother, had arrived home a day earlier than expected from summer camp to find his mother, Yuryshev's wife, with a lover. And not in bed, not covered with a blanket or even a sheet, but on the floor, on the carpet, in a shamelessly perverted position. He leapt out of the apartment, and Galya threw on a bath robe and caught up with him out of doors, went down on her knees, and in floods of feigned tears begged him not to tell his father. And that evening, when Yuryshev returned from work as usual, she put on a great banquet to celebrate their son's return from camp and was amazingly tender, thoughtful, talkative, and accommodating. First she would snuggle up to her husband, then to her son – it was a fantastic family party, except for the fact that Vitya sat silent and pale, and Yuryshev made a passing joke that perhaps he had fallen in love with someone at the summer camp. Galya picked up the topic and said that it was high time Vitya got to know some girls, fell in love, and just became a man. In the middle of this harangue the boy got up and without saying anything went to his bedroom. A minute later a shot rang out. Yuryshev ran to the bedroom and was in time to see his son's body falling off the chair, face covered in blood, and his own officer's TT revolver in Vitya's white hand. In the other hand was a sheet of paper with some hurried writing on it: 'Dad, don't believe her. She's a slut, I saw *it* with my own eyes. I can't . . .' His son had not written anything else, but had simply held the gun two millimetres away from his right eye and pulled the trigger.

Yuryshev reported to the militia that his son had perished through careless handling of his father's gun, received a reprimand at work for not taking proper care of a personal firearm, and threw his wife out of the house, having first forced her to write down on a piece of paper in her own hand everything Vitya had seen that day. In their seventeen years of marriage he had never once been unfaithful to her. He loved her, and his son had seen all his life that his father loved his mother, and he loved her himself like a saint and was proud – Yuryshev had noted it more than once – that he had a beautiful young mother whom his father loved. It was all finished, everything was smashed and ruined in one day – family and fatherhood. And alcohol didn't help any more, nor did total immersion in work, nor did Tanya, the modest, quiet twenty-year-old waitress with whom he tried to forget about everything during his regular official trips to the submarine base at Baltiisk. Even Moscow was full of excruciatingly painful spots – there, Kropotkin Boulevard, he had walked with his son, there, the Moscow swimming-pool, he had taught him to swim, in that old chess club his son had come third in a young people's tournament, and right there on the Arbat they were caught in a downpour one spring, got soaked to the skin, called home to mother and laughed – two boys . . .

Yuryshev turned away from the window – he had neither the strength nor the desire to go on living in this city where every street assailed him with memories of his son. After cruel, sleepless nights he had come to the realization that he could not stand this life, that no amount of work, no amount of strategic military plans for the occupation of Europe in twenty-four hours, for the occupation of China in sixty-seven hours, for the seizure of Afghanistan, for breaking through to the Persian Gulf, or even for this Project EMMA – to shake up Europe with a seismic weapon which U-137 had already begun to instal in underwater shafts around Europe – no amount of war games could fully occupy his mind or his life. It used to have meaning – it was for the sake of the family, for his career, to establish himself in his own eyes and in the eyes of his beloved wife and son – yes, it had a meaning, and he always achieved what he set out to achieve – Assistant Director of Strategic Planning at forty, but now – what was the point, what was this life for? And with his clear analytical mind he realized that for him there would never be a single happy day as long as he continued to live in a world where every stone, every street, and every boy's face reminded him of his son. There was no future for him here, the future here was nothing but a wound flowing with blood and a heart gripped with despair. And anyway, what was keeping him here in this country? No sisters, no brothers, his father shot in 1937 when he was a year and a half, and a mother whom he had buried seven years ago. And on one of those sleepless nights a simple solution came and began to grow in him, taking possession of his thoughts – the West, America. No matter what he became there or what he ended up doing, it was a different world, different in every respect, from the faces around you – to the streets and the language. He began to take a passionate interest in American life, reading all the American literature, magazines, books, newspapers, that came to the library at General Headquarters. And his quick mind was easily able to separate out from the picture-postcard lives of Hollywood stars depicted in the gaudy magazines the grains of real American life with its unemployment, strikes, crime-rate, fierce competition, and daily fear for the morrow. Perhaps he was the only one of the hundreds of thousands of potential émigrés from the USSR who was looking as hard as he could for information about the negative aspects of American life. And when he found them he was glad. It was just that struggle for life, which he would have to start from the very beginning, that would absorb him and save him. Taxi-driver, stevedore, anything – just to dive head-first into that struggle and get rid of his exhausting insomnia . . .

But it was one thing to have daydreams about this and even to tell them to some American correspondent one happened to meet; it was quite another thing to go today, right now, to the Kirov nature reserve and wait for a signal from the CIA. He had hardly any doubt that the signal would come. Now that Kushchin had put his submarine aground near the Swedish naval base and the whole world was trying to guess why the Russians needed to do that, the CIA would be climbing the walls trying to get hold of him, Yuryshev. As long as that correspondent had passed his offer along to them . . .

It was already quarter to five; in ten minutes the secret section would close. It's now or never, Yuryshev, he told himself. He had to open the safe, pull out all the secret materials and maps, and take them to the safe disposal unit. Of course, it would not do any harm to have one more look at them, but even that was unnecessary – with his memory he could name by heart the exact co-ordination of the submarine shafts in which the energy transmission grids were to be installed around Europe, without even looking at the map. He could dictate from memory all the characteristics of the new seismic weapon that had been developed at the Marine Institute on the Highway of the Enthusiasts. It was too bad that there was no question of his taking out of the USSR the twenty-minute top secret film, *Project EMMA*, that had been made at the military film studio especially for the Central Committee's Politburo. Then the West would really have gasped: with their own eyes they would have seen, on a cloudless day 'x', a series of local earthquakes shattering NATO's coastal naval and air force bases and Europe's ports and capitals. Ballistic missile silos would collapse, concrete airfields would crack, naval quays would split open, water, gas, and sewage mains would burst, and the whole of Western Europe would find itself in the chaos of an elemental catastrophe – without any visible attack from the Soviet Union. And then, fulfilling its 'humane duty to help the suffering peoples of Western Europe', Soviet forces would enter these countries – without a single shot being fired, armed not with shells and rockets, but with repair equipment, medical supplies, mobile kitchens and electricity generators. A grateful Europe would welcome them with the flowers that had survived the earthquake . . .

Yuryshev's thoughts about the film that had called forth tumultuous rejoicing from all the members of the Politburo were interrupted by the telephone. Yuryshev walked away from the window and picked up the phone.

'Sergey Ivanovich, can you drop in and say goodbye before you go on leave?' asked the familiar, slightly hoarse voice of Marshal Nikolay Oparkov, Chief of General Staff.

Even privately Yuryshev did not want to admit that his decision to escape to the West was connected with this man – Marshal Oparkov was the father of his former wife Galina. It was to this family connection that Yuryshev owed his meteoric career, but after the death of his son, when he had thrown Galya out of the house, even a fool could have seen that it was goodbye to his career. True, the marshal thought it was a temporary family row made worse by a tragedy – their son's death. He did not know the real reason for the scandal, and Yuryshev could not tell him that his daughter was a slut and a murderess. The marshal was hoping to reconcile his daughter with Yuryshev, so now he would gently and cautiously ask Yuryshev to take Galya with him on leave . . . Well, once he was out of Russia the secret section would open up his safe and find a sealed envelope addressed, 'Marshal Oparkov, personal'. In that envelope were two sheets of exercise paper – Galina's confession and his son's note.

5

'Attention, please! Aeroflot flight twenty-four from Brussels has now landed. I repeat . . .'

It was a man's voice, and so deafeningly loud and distorted that Neznachny could not help wincing. Quite recently, only a year or so ago, a new terminal building had been built for Sheremetyevo International Airport by the Germans especially for the Moscow Olympics, a wonder of modern architecture, a blue-glass shrine to the twenty-first century that melted into the pine and birch forest that surrounded Moscow. The transparent walls doubled and tripled the sensation of space inside. Nickel counters and door handles gleamed brightly. Cleaners in snow-white imported overalls pushed noiseless imported vacuum cleaners through the halls, removing micro-particles of dust from the floor. And a soft, caressing female voice announced the arrival and departure of planes over the PA system in English, French, and German with a tone of non-Russian, almost heavenly ingratiation. And foreigners smelling of overseas cosmetics, with non-Russian suitcases on little wheels would pass through these halls, amazed to be met in Russia with European service. And in the buffets and bars their astonishment would reach its peak – black and red caviar was on sale there at fabulously low prices. And besides caviar there was salmon, goose-liver pâté, Finnish sausage, an abundance of vegetables, fruit, juices, wine, and vodka – and all at meaninglessly low prices, virtually free.

Even then, during the Olympics, Neznachny knew very well that this abundance and these ridiculous prices for caviar were just a trick to undermine the tourist's prejudice as soon as he stepped in from the West and to prove that all those rumours about food shortages in the USSR were just stupid anti-Soviet claptrap. He realized that as soon as the Olympics were over all this abundance would vanish. But now every time he came to Sheremetyevo to meet American tourists he felt bitter and annoyed. All right, so the buffets no longer sold caviar at seventy kopecks for fifty grammes, there was no more goose pâté and Finnish sausage, but what had happened to the soft, unearthly female voice on the radio? Why had it been replaced by this booming, rusty-iron masculine bark? And why were those fat-bottomed cleaners no longer wearing uniform white overalls, but going about, like the cleaners in all the Moscow stations, in a sort of grey sack-cloth? And why had the vacuum cleaners, once so noiseless, started to roar like airplane engines? And why on all the office doors, next to the blue glass and the nickel, had there appeared those monstrous warehouse locks?

'Oh, that Russian slovenliness of ours!' he said with a sigh to Lyuda Zvonaryova, the Intourist guide who, like Neznachny, had come to meet the Williamses. They were sitting in the cafeteria drinking tea and eating stale sandwiches – the day before yesterday's perhaps. Lyuda Zvonaryova was a pretty brunette of about forty – smallish, vivacious, cheerful, wearing foreign cosmetics and a smoke-coloured Canadian sheepskin jacket. She knew three foreign languages and was one of the best Intourist guides and KGB informers. Looking at this carefree, laughing woman with her mischievous, fun-loving eyes, this flirt and chatterbox with her constant stream of funny stories, not one foreign tourist could have guessed that at night Lyuda Zvonaryova wrote long, thorough reports for the KGB with detailed psychological character-sketches of her charges. From experience both Neznachny and Lyuda knew that they still had a few minutes between the plane's arrival and when the passengers came into the customs hall, and Lyuda said: 'You don't look so good, Comrade Major. Business is a bit slack right now – hardly any tourists . . . I mean valuable ones, useful ones . . .'

'That's it, all right,' replied Neznachny. 'When they had détente the tourists came in shoals and you could pick and choose. If one got off the hook it didn't matter, there were other candidates. But now there's a clamp-down and there are hardly any tourists, just old women, yet nobody has revised the recruiting plan. The planned economy! Kill yourself, but just produce the same norm we had three years ago with détente. That's why we've got to get this Williams into the pipeline from the very start. Anyway, he happens to be a figure of *special* interest.' Neznachny emphasized the word 'special', since Zvonaryova was not supposed to know any more than that, and got up. 'So let's go and cast the nets, Lyuda. Let's go and meet the newly-weds . . .'

'Well, I still have time while they go through customs,' she replied, staying to finish her tea. Neznachny made his way to the duty room which was concealed from the eyes of arriving passengers at the customs hall.

In the customs hall the Soviet film people who had arrived from Europe were noisily crowding round the baggage conveyer. They dragged off it huge cases crammed with Western stuff, apart from which they also had hand luggage, bags, hold-alls, shopping-bags, packages, boxes. To save on porters they dragged all this baggage by hand to the customs tables . . . Neznachny and three of his colleagues from the KGB's Belgian, French, and English Sections stood behind smoked glass in the duty room and, unseen from outside, were astonished to recognize faces famous throughout the land . . . Bondarchuk, Batalov, Burlyaev, Solovey, Mordunov, Krasavina. They did not even check their documents, let alone open their cases, and the film stars were convinced this was an example of the power of fame. Indeed, who does not know the famous comedian Mordunov? Amusing, Neznachny laughed to himself, he or one of his colleagues merely had to touch that red button on the special intercom panel and a red sign would light up, visible to the customs officer but not to the traveller and immediately any one of those film stars would get such a thorough search – every pair of jeans brought in from the West would be examined right down to the seams! But there were no orders to check out the film folk, and so, grabbing a suitcase and two bags in each hand and miraculously balancing a roll of imported carpet on one shoulder, fat Mordunov hurried towards the exit where his wife and grown-up children were waiting for him. But instead of embracing the head of the family on his arrival the children quickly seized his luggage and rushed outside to the car, dragging cases, bags and carpet with them. Only once they were sitting in the car speechless with happiness, thought Neznachny, would they believe their incredible luck – Dad managed to get an extra pair of jeans through and even four pairs of women's boots!

After the Soviet film-makers came the foreigners – a pro-Soviet Belgian writer (Vasya Sobinov of the KGB's Belgian Section pressed the white button, and the customs officer saw a white sign light up in front of him, meaning 'superficial search'), then two French businessmen, some English people, and finally, appearing at the end of the glass corridor, the long-awaited pair – the Williamses. As aways happens with foreigners arriving in the USSR for the first time, they were walking along the corridor with obvious caution and curiosity. Neznachny laughed. The handsome new European air terminal was thoroughly shaking their preconceptions about ending up in the sticks and finding barbed wire and the KGB everywhere. He was already reaching for the white button to signal to the customs officer to let them through without any hitches when he noticed that Robert Williams's neck was wrapped right round with a scarf from which a white gauze bandage was protruding. Having thought for a moment he pressed the blue button, and the officer immediately picked up the telephone: 'What's he got wound round his throat?' Neznachny said into the microphone.

And he heard the customs officer ask Williams in English, as he held their papers in his hand: 'What is the matter with your throat, Mr Williams?'

Williams opened his mouth and emitted a hoarse, unintelligible sound, but his wife immediately intervened and said with a laugh: 'You keep quiet, darling!' and turned to the customs officer: 'He's caught a cold. The weather in Brussels is ghastly, and he was even drinking Scotch on the rocks!'

Splendid, thought Neznachny, we shall treat you, Mr Williams; it will be a good excuse to introduce you to some of our doctors.

He pressed the button for the first aid room and gave an order to the doctor on duty: 'Olga Viktorovna to the customs hall immediately. See what's wrong with the

American's throat and make him think it's very serious. At the same time check that bandage in case he's bringing something in . . .'

Through the smoked glass he saw Virginia blanch as the doctor approached, and say: 'Oh, no! We don't need a doctor! It's an ordinary cold!'

'Do not worry,' answered Olga Viktorovna in poor English. 'Medical care is free here. Come along with me to the first aid room.'

At this point Lyuda Zvonaryova came running up and started twittering away gaily: 'Dr and Mrs Williams? Hello! I'm your Intourist interpreter and guide. The medical examination is a pure formality. But if the doctor says you need treatment, we have excellent facilities and all completely free.'

Robert Williams was happy to open his mouth in the first aid room and show the doctor his swollen glands with their white coating. And he did not exhibit the least anxiety when the nurse exchanged his gauze bandages for a new compress. Olga Viktorovna prescribed aspirin and a gargle for Dr Williams and told Lyuda Zvonaryova to take him to see the doctor at the polyclinic tomorrow without fail. He had a slight temperature (37.2) which might go up towards evening, and that was dangerous because it was below freezing in Moscow . . .

With that, the brief incident was over, and Lyuda Zvonaryova took the Williamses to the Intourist Volga. A porter followed, bringing their modest baggage – only two cases – on a trolley.

6

Even when you come home from a short trip you feel that something must have happened in town while you were away, and you cannot help looking around for signs of happenings.

Stavinsky had been away from Moscow for six years. For his first three years in emigration he had continued to visit it in his dreams; he had dreamed of its streets, squares, parks, the smell of the lilac outside his apartment window in Rostokinsky Street, the dry summer dust on Tverskoy Boulevard, the bustle of young people on Gorky Street. During the deep Portland nights his soul would traverse half the globe and wander along the Moscow streets. In his dreams Stavinsky would note everything that had formerly escaped his attention: a carved fence in a quiet side street, a shady gateway, a little old brick house . . .

Now Stavinsky was actually travelling through his past. Leningrad Avenue floated beneath the wheels of the Intourist Volga, swept with lightly drifting snow. From the front seat of the car the Intourist guide Lyuda Zvonaryova turned round to face the Williams couple and kept up a constant chatter in English, telling them how only twenty years ago there was just a wilderness where these handsome apartment blocks now stood.

Stavinsky hardly heard her chatter – before him lay Moscow, living Moscow, not a dream, but reality! Shop-signs shone in Russian letters, snow-clearing trucks devoured snowdrifts on the roadway, and in the stream of traffic there were trolley buses, something he had forgotten about in America. But there was already a second feeling welling up inside him – a feeling of shame at the poverty that was now so noticeable to his new eyes. A poverty of cars – nothing but Zhigulis and Volgas, Zhigulis and Volgas. A poverty of clothing – the grey, grey clothes people were wearing. Turning away from the driving wind and snow, bent beneath the weight of their bags and shopping-baskets, they were walking along in grey and black coats, with gloomy faces . . . And those queues at the shops, and above the queues, on the fronts of the buildings – the flags, posters, and portraits of Brezhnev, all new and fresh for the Revolution holiday . . . And on Gorky Street – the driving snow, a few scurrying pedestrians, short chilly queues outside the Sofia and Baku restaurants, and every hundred yards a detachment of militia.

'You're lucky,' Lyuda Zvonaryova was saying meanwhile. 'Your hotel windows look out on to the Manège and Red Square. You'll see the parade tomorrow! It's very interesting! But all the museums are closed tomorrow – I don't know how I shall amuse you. Perhaps we could just visit a famous painter. Would you like to? There'll be artists and writers there . . .'

Virginia looked into Stavinsky's eyes.

And suddenly Stavinsky realized in a flash of revelation that he did not need this Moscow or this Gorky Street that he had dreamed about for three years on end, and he certainly did not need some artist, probably Gladunov, a KGB collaborator. No, he didn't need snow-swept Russia or dreamlike America, he needed this woman right here who looked so like his mother. But it was precisely these two countries – America and Russia – that seemed to have conspired to take Virginia away from him. There were ten days left before their separation, and the first was already drawing to a close.

7

In his nine years' work with the KGB Neznachny had never seen tourists like these Williamses. They were not interested in museums, old Russian churches, a party with the fashionable painter Gladunov, theatres, ski-trips out of Moscow, excursions to the Moscow film studios, meetings with colleagues. In their de-luxe suite on the twelfth floor of the National, with its windows looking out on to the

Manège and Red Square, they were now in their third day of constant lovemaking. They effectively interrupted this occupation only a few times a day, for a brief sleep, for lunch, and for dinner. They even walked out of the Bolshoi after the first act of *Spartacus*, holding hands like children, and made straight for their bed.

Sitting in room 301, the special KGB room on the third floor of the National where the special service for the observation of foreigners conducted surveillance of all rooms in which foreign tourists were staying, Neznachny listened for hours on end to their bedtime tendernesses, heavy breathing, weak moans coming from Virginia, then a brief lull, the noise of the shower, and, after twenty minutes of quiet or television, fresh caresses. In vain Olya Makhova languished in inactivity on that same twelfth floor, in room 1214, which was specially equipped for secret photography and filming. In vain she would 'accidentally' appear in the café or restaurant, looking temptingly sexy, just as the Williamses were coming in. In vain Dmitry Lisadze, producer and unofficial KGB agent, came to the painter Gladunov's party. And in vain Lyuda Zvonaryova kept ringing through to the Williamses' room, suggesting the most enticing trips round Moscow, meetings with producers, artists, doctors. Virginia would come to the telephone and in a weak voice explain that her husband wasn't feeling too good and was afraid of getting really sick, and so they couldn't go anywhere out of the hotel. But that he didn't need a Soviet doctor since he was a doctor himself and had all the medicines with him. After that – Neznachny could hear it quite clearly – they would return to their embraces, caresses, and all the other rubbish that Neznachny found so frustrating. And the curious thing of all was that they hardly ever had any conversation. All right, thought Neznachny, so Robert has a bad throat, it's hard for him to talk, but that actress Virginia – why does she never utter a word apart from 'darling', 'honey', and 'I love you so much'? Surely all actresses are talkative. Or perhaps they whispered when the television was on? But however much he strained his ears Neznachny could not pick up a single phrase, whereas he could distinctly hear every squeak of their bed, every languid sigh, and the ardour of every skirmish. Even during the periods of lull he had the impression that they were not asleep but looking at each other, and sometimes he imagined he could hear Virginia crying – the concealed microphones picked up quiet female sobs which, to be sure, were immediately cut short by resounding kisses and a new outburst of matrimonial tenderness.

This ordeal of frustration was too much for Neznachny even on the very first day, 7 November. The military parade was moving down Gorky Street towards Red Square. Martial music was blaring from the military bands. Powerful loudspeakers mounted on the roofs of the National, the Central Telegraph, and the Hotel Moscow relayed from Red Square the stentorian calls of the famous radio announcer Levitan: 'Long live our own Communist Party!!! Long live our Soviet Government!!! Long live Soviet tank forces!!!' and so on. To each call the soldiers replied with an equally stentorian 'Hurrah!' while the commentator would repeat over television and radio: 'And now out on to Red Square, moving in perfect formation, here comes a column of our valiant missile forces that maintain a peace-loving watch to protect out Soviet skies!' And to these sacred and solemn words the devil knows what was going on up in room 1202 – Robert and Virginia Williams were tearing each other to bits in yet another amorous encounter. Their groans, their hurried breathing, and Virginia's little cries drove Neznachny to the point where he abandoned his control panel, tore off his headphones, took a healthy swig from a bottle of cognac, and rushed out of the duty room. The high-speed elevator carried him up to the twelfth floor, to room 1214 where Olya Makhova was wasting away with inactivity. From her room, too, one could see the huge carcases of missiles trundling up on to Red Square on their special trailers and moving slowly and sternly past the red slogans and the banners, past the members of the Government on top of Lenin's Mausoleum. The triumphant music of the military band thundered over Moscow. And to this music, with the military parade on Red Square as backdrop, Olya Makhova relieved Major Neznachny's tormented flesh . . .

On returning to the duty room he found his colleagues glued to his headphones. They were greedily listening to the Williamses' bedtime frolics. Aroused by what he heard, Captain Kozlov, who worked for the English Section, popped out of the duty room, avoiding Neznachny's eyes. A minute later Lieutenant Kulemin followed him, then Captain Zagoskin, and soon the duty room was completely deserted. Perplexed as to where his colleagues had got to, Neznachny almost intuitively pressed the button to room 1214. Now he understood it all – to the march of the military band and the challenges of Levitan, the unfailing Olya Makhova was simultaneously gratifying the English, French, and German Sections of the KGB. Swine! thought Neznachny wearily, and, taking advantage of the fact that he was alone in the duty room now, he switched on the concealed photographic and movie equipment in her room. Who knows, he thought, some day I could use these photos and films compromising Kozlov, Zagoskin, Kulemin, and all the rest.

Meanwhile, from the Williamses' room he could still hear the same quiet sounds of conjugal kisses . . .

Well, thought Neznachny, if the mountain won't go to Mohammed, Mohammed will have to go to the mountain . . .

8

The days of happiness imprisoned in the hotel room were running out. If the first three days had been filled with a hunger for lovemaking sharpened by the sense of danger (on the very first day Stavinsky had caught sight of Olya Makhova at breakfast in the cafeteria and had immediately recalled MacKerry's instructions), on the fourth day this hunger subsided; indeed they were both weary of lovemaking, and the approaching separation transformed their mood into a quiet, poignant sadness. In fact they had accomplished the first part of their mission – the day before yesterday Jacob Stevenson had visited them to ascertain that Stavinsky–Williams and Colonel Yuryshev really were alike as two peas, and Virginia had told Jacob that on 16 November she and Robert would be returning to Moscow on the Red Arrow express from a two-day trip to Leningrad. Now Stevenson had to book Yuryshev a compartment on the same train and send the tickets to him at the nature reserve on the Vyatka.

Stavinsky and Virginia spent most of their evenings now at the window – they would sit quietly and sadly on the window-seat watching the snow slowly falling on to the trees in the Alexander Park and the cars and trolley buses moving along the snow-covered Marx Avenue. Relentlessly the Kremlin chimes on the Spassky Tower counted the time away. Every half-hour the cobbles of Red Square rang out to the metallic stamp of soldiers marching to Lenin's Mausoleum for the guard of honour. And each time the Kremlin chimes died away on the frosty evening air it seemed to Stavinsky and Virginia that they heard the knell of their imminent separation being tolled. And each of them prayed mentally that Yuryshev would not receive those tickets or would miss the train – then they could both go back to America with a clear conscience . . .

A loud knock on the door interrupted their solitude.

Virginia looked at Stavinsky in alarm and went over to the door. Loud cheerful voices and gypsy singing could be heard outside the door.

'Who is it?' asked Virginia.

'It's me, Lyuda Zvonaryova!' came the resonant voice of their Intourist guide. 'I want to wish Robert a happy birthday!'

'One moment!' said Virginia. Lord, how could they have forgotten that today was Robert Williams's (the real Robert Williams's) birthday! It was on all the forms they had filled out just a month ago in Washington!

Virginia rushed to her wardrobe and hurriedly put on her best dress, and Stavinsky threw on a jacket, taking a quick look at his passport – quite right, Robert Williams was born today, 10 November 1935. But there was nothing on the table – no flowers, no champagne . . .

'Good heavens, Robert!' exclaimed Lyuda Zvonaryova, literally bursting into their room as soon as Virginia opened the door. 'How can you sit at home on a day like this!'

In her arms was a large bouquet of flowers which she immediately presented to Robert, while another seven people who had walked gaily into the room with her carrying champagne and a cake were already singing: 'Happy birthday to Robert! Happy birthday to you-u-u . . .'

Stavinsky smiled silently, Virginia put on a show of being moved and grateful: 'Thank you! Thank you!'

'My friends!' Zvonaryova presented her company. 'Three Intourist guides, they speak fluent English, two actresses from the gypsy theatre, Semyon Bobrov – stomatologist – your colleague, Robert, and a close friend of mine. Oleg, stop making eyes at Virginia, she's taken! And also another friend of mine – Dmitry Lisadze, film producer. Incidentally, it's my birthday today also, Robert. Guess how old I am. Seventeen of course! We've been feasting at a restaurant, the Aragvi, and now we're going to Dmitry's *dacha*. You're coming with us, and no arguments!

There'll be a sleigh there, a Russian troika! Have you ever been for a ride on a Russian troika? And with gypsy songs too! But first the champagne! Lord, where are your wine glasses, Virginia?'

With a drunken familiarity the company settled down in the room as if they owned it – they found three glasses, someone went along to the floor-lady for extra crockery – and now the champagne corks were popping, wine was being poured into glasses, the two gypsies were singing to the guitar and making comic advances to Stavinsky, and Lyuda Zvonaryova was chatting away non-stop: 'I don't want to hear about it! We'll wrap Robert up in a fur coat and he'll be quite safe from catching a cold! Robert, get dressed! Virginia, where's your coat? Dmitry, can you look after Virginia? Give her her coat and boots!'

('Pressure, pressure!' Neznachny had insisted to her twenty minutes ago. 'You burst into the room like a tornado and don't give them a second to think. Drag them out of the room, indulge them all evening, take them on the sleigh, give them champagne and caviar, con them, but the main thing is to break the ice, get friendly with them. Friendship, nothing more than friendship!')

And Lyuda Zvonaryova was executing her role with inspiration – a two-storey *dacha* was awaiting them that evening in Red Pakhra outside Moscow, with caviar, *shashlyks*, vodka, champagne, and even a sleigh with three horses, all at the KGB's expense. But if the Williamses did not come then the whole orgy was off. So it was not just Zvonaryova who was trying hard, but the whole company that had been hand-picked by Neznachny over the last three days . . .

But when the film producer Dmitry Lisadze, a handsome Georgian of about forty, handed Virginia her coat, she said: 'One moment!'

Then she opened the closet and got a precious bottle of Chanel No 5 out of her case which she had bought for herself three days ago in Paris.

'Lyuda,' she said to Zvonaryova. 'This is for you. Happy birthday, and I hope you will always stay seventeen! But we can't go anywhere with you . . .' and she put up her hand to stop the protesting voices: 'Today is a day of mourning for me. Ten years ago today my daughter died. She was seven months . . .' And in the sudden silence that ensued Virginia clung with tears in her eyes to Stavinsky's shoulder. Then she quickly wiped away her tears and turned to the guests. 'I'm sorry, Lyuda, I didn't want to spoil your birthday, but I had to tell you. That's why Robert and I are not celebrating his birthday . . . Forgive us . . .'

9

CONFIDENTIAL

To: General S. K. Tsvigun,
First Deputy Chairman of the KGB

REPORT

In connection with your instructions to take all possible measures to recruit the American tourist Robert Williams I have to report:

During the seven days of their stay in Moscow the married couple Robert and Virginia Williams have led an intensely withdrawn life, leaving their room effectively only for brief periods two or three times a day to take food; the rest of the time they have spent in bed like newly-weds on honeymoon. Throughout the whole seven days of their stay in Moscow they only met one American, Jacob Stevenson, correspondent for the *Washington Herald*, who spent twelve minutes with them in the hard-currency bar on the third floor of their hotel at 1300 hours on 9 November. Their conversation, which was monitored, indicates that this meeting was of the nature of a friendly get-together between Robert Williams and his friend from Washington. Nothing suspicious occurred during this meeting. Stevenson congratulated Williams on his marriage, advised them to visit some interesting exhibitions, suggested a walk round Moscow, and invited them back to his place at the American Embassy to a party. But Virginia declined the invitation, citing Robert's cold, and informed Stevenson about their two-day trip to Leningrad planned for 13 November by Intourist. Stevenson promised to see them off to Leningrad and meet them on their return.

All efforts to make friends with the Williamses by members of our American Section have proved fruitless.

Since only two days remain before the Williamses' departure from the USSR, and since these days will be spent by them in Leningrad, I request permission to mount a special operation requiring the participation of the Leningrad KGB.

Colonel P. T. Orlov,
Head of Tourist Department,
Main Directorate of the KGB

Moscow, 13 November 1981

General Tsvigun, brother-in-law of Leonid Ilyich Brezhnev, a fat sixty-year-old with a large head and eyes red from drinking brandy every day, read the report slowly, listened to the planned operation, then looked darkly at Orlov and Neznachny and asked: 'So? It turns out they came here just for intercourse?'

Orlov and Neznachny said nothing.

'What exactly have you been doing all this time?' the general asked Neznachny. 'Just listening to them having it off in their room?'

'Not at all, Comrade General!' Naznachny thrust his

whole body forward and rapidly sketched out for the general everything he had tried on these Williamses – Olya Makhova, the unsuccessful birthday party, and the final attempt: yesterday yet another agent – Lieutenant Sirotin – was sent to the Williamses posing as a plumber. He told the Williamses a melodramatic story about his love for an American girl who had come here last year to study Russian at the Pushkin Institute. He said the Soviet authorities took away this student's visa three days before their wedding and she had to leave, and her letters to him were not getting through. The Soviet censorship was stopping them. And he had been thrown out of the Institute because of his connections with a foreign girl. The plumber implored the Williamses to find his beloved in America and pass on to her a letter from him.

'I recruited that student back in the summer,' continued Neznachny. 'She is a virulent Communist. She could have got friendly with the Williamses in Washington and asked the doctor to introduce her to his patients in Congress – supposedly to rescue her fiancé. But even that didn't work. Do you know what that swine Virginia said to Lieutenant Sirotin? That they would have been happy to help him, except that when they got back to America they were going to be very busy selling their house in Potomac and moving to California.'

'Is this doctor planning to leave Washington?' asked the general.

'Rubbish!' said Colonel Orlov. 'What doctor would give up his clientele and go to California where nobody knows him and dentists are common as dirt?! It's just typical American callousness and cowardice. They've read up on the KGB and they're afraid of everything. It's high time we liquidated the odd Barron or Conquest so as to teach the rest of them to sling mud at us!'

'Well, that's debatable . . .' laughed the general. 'From one point of view it's mud, but on the other hand those books enhance our image abroad. But it's ridiculous that the legendary KGB hasn't been able to deal with a couple of newly-weds!' And he turned to Neznachny: 'Why do you think you'll succeed in Leningrad?'

'It's a tried and tested method, Comrade General,' answered Neznachny. 'I have used it more than once. First they are threatened with prison, they get interrogated harshly, and then I rescue them. And after their round-the-clock bedtime behaviour these Williamses are so weak that if you apply just the right pressure . . .'

'H-m, yes . . .' said Tsvigun. 'The strong-arm method . . . Psychological pressure . . . On the whole you used to work better before, Major, you were more talented, more productive . . .'

'But then there was a whole stream of tourists, Comrade General,' Colonel Orlov interceded for his subordinate.

'Forget it,' the general waved him away wearily. 'I've heard that line. All right,' he picked up one of the four telephones adorning his large desk and dialled a short number on the special line to Leningrad. 'Solomin,' he said into the receiver. 'This is Tsvigun. Tomorrow a Major Neznachny from our American Section will be coming to see you. He's conducting a special operation with two foreigners. Co-operate with him fully . . .'

10

Jacob Stevenson arrived at the station at 11.45 in the evening, ten minutes before the departure for Leningrad of the luxurious Red Arrow express. Nearby in a black Volga his eternal travelling companions and 'bodyguards', the KGB men, dropped anchor. Let them! Stevenson picked up the bunch of flowers for Virginia from the back seat of his Volvo and, stepping across the snowdrifts, walked nonchalantly into the station building. He slowed slightly as he went in case his 'guardian angels' should lose him in the crowd. Heaven forbid! He had no reason to hide from them now. On the contrary – let them see him presenting Virginia with a bouquet of tender pink carnations on the platform, chatting about this and that, and then going home. Everything plain and simple, with no conspiracy. And yet Stevenson was nervous. He felt as if he was taking part in a spy film, and from journalistic habit was already clothing everything he saw in the lines of his future novel. 'The platform of Moscow's Leningrad Station,' he wrote mentally, 'was full of foreign tourists and the cream of Moscow and Leningrad society; actors, actresses, painters, diplomats, high-ranking officials in expensive fleece jackets and coats, army colonels and generals in grey astrakhan hats, and the omnipresent KGB. Two agents were following hard on my heels, but I walked calmly past the red carriages to coach number five. The powdery Moscow snow fell softly on the bouquet of pale pink carnations which I was bringing for Virginia. My "bodyguards" had no idea that the key to the whole operation lay in this very bouquet: on a pretty card with meaningless good wishes for a happy journey were the two figures: 6 and 3 – the numbers of the carriage and compartment in which Colonel Yuryshev would be travelling from Leningrad. But five days earlier I had had quite a nerve-wracking time with my red-cheeked "guardian angels". I had driven in my Volvo to the large grocer's store on Smolensk Square, a corner building opening on to the Arbat on one side and the Garden Ring Road on the other. I walked into the grocer's in full view of my guards from the Arbat side, mixed with the crowd which was standing in three queues for sausages, pickles, and vodka, got into line for the pickles and having satisfied myself that my lazy "guardian angels" were sitting in their car near my Volvo, quickly walked out of the grocer's into the Garden Ring Road. Here my wife Lucy's Volkswagen was waiting for me. A bottle of Siberian vodka lay on the back seat. I stuffed it into my jacket pocket and three minutes later transferred to a taxi on Mayakovsky Square to be on the safe side, getting to the Leningrad Station for five roubles. I had to queue for seventeen minutes for tickets in the booking hall – that was probably my most nervous time. "A double compartment on the Arrow from Leningrad to Moscow for 15 November, please. Preferably coach six. Keep the change." I handed the woman forty-five roubles instead of the thirty-seven that the tickets cost, and that settled the matter straight away. Making sure once that I was not being tailed I bought an envelope and a stamp at the newspaper stand, wrote on the envelope, "Yuryshev, c/o Anikin, forester, Razboiny Bor Nature Reserve, Kirov Region," slipped the tickets into the envelope, and dropped the envelope into the mailbox. MacKerry and I agreed on this simple operation in Stockholm, but for the foreigner in Moscow even such a small thing as freedom of movement and freedom of correspondence can often became an almost insurmountable problem. Twelve minutes and two changes of taxis later I was back at Smolensk Square; I entered the grocer's from the Garden Ring Road direction and bumped right into my confused and angry "guardian angels" who had been scouring the whole store, wondering where I had got to. The bottle of vodka sticking out of my pocket reassured them – they concluded that I had been queueing for vodka and was now looking for the pickles queue. They were surprised of course – I can buy vodka and pickles and other food in the hard-currency Beriozka shop, which is forbidden to ordinary soviet citizens, without having to queue at all. So I took my notebook out of my pocket and began to interview the people standing near me in the pickles queue. "I am an American reporter. How many times a week do you have to queue for food?" I asked a tall old woman. The old woman recoiled in fright and didn't answer. I turned to a man in a rabbit-fur cap. Same question – same reaction. Soviet citizens are afraid to make contact with foreigners, let alone answer such "slippery" questions, especially in public. Beyond the people in the queue I saw my angry "guardian angels"; realizing that I was gathering material in this shop for another "slanderous" article on Soviet life they darted into the manager's office and a minute later the saleswoman announced from behind the counter: "That's it! The pickles are finished!" The queue started to protest: "What? Why didn't you announce it before?" but the sales woman took no notice of this mixture of shouting and cursing, she simply walked away from the counter and disappeared into the private part of the shop. The queue dispersed, swearing.

'When I came out of the shop to my car I saw that the two rear tyres had been let down, while my "guardian angels" were sitting in their black Volga laughing unkindly. The KGB had punctured my tyres to punish me for interviewing Soviet citizens in food queues. Now for two months I would have to prove my loyalty to them, otherwise "hooligans" would vandalize my car every night.'

Even so, I twiddled them round my finger, thought Stevenson proudly as he walked along the platform of the Leningrad Station, and if I manage to sell this story to Hollywood I'll have to begin this episode with an imaginary car-chase and other movie tricks . . .

'Now there are the Williamses – I can see them through the window of coach five. There's someone else in their compartment – a pretty brunette of about forty. She is standing in the doorway of their compartment and chatting gaily away to them about something. I knock on the window with the bunch of flowers, they notice me, and I motion to them to come out on to the platform. Let my "guardian angels", who have obstinately taken up positions only two paces away from me, not suspect that I am secretly trying to pass the Williamses anything except this bouquet. Still accompanied by this pretty brunette, Robert and Virginia come out of the train on to the platform and introduce me to their Intourist guide Lyuda. Robert has a scarf wrapped tightly round his neck, and both Robert and Virginia are pale, and Virginia's warm brown eyes stare sadly and anxiously out of her beautiful face with its fine skin . . . Yes, that was a wonderful idea of theirs, this illness of Robert's. But their voluntary seclusion in the hotel and Robert's tonsillitis have made them both become really pale and drawn, whereas Colonel Yuryshev is on holiday right now, in a nature reserve, in the fresh air, and he is certain to appear from the Kirov forests the day after tomorrow looking fresh and ruddy-cheeked . . . Hell, I suddenly realize how dangerous this is for the whole operation – in the space of one night on the Leningrad to Moscow train Robert Williams is going to be transformed from being pale and exhausted by his illness and his honeymoon with Virginia into a ruddy-cheeked and – Heaven forbid! – suntanned hunk. What can I do? How can I tell them about it when their Intourist guide is standing right there and my KGB men are six feet away?

'"Good heavens, Robert, you're terribly thin!" I say. "Virginia, you must make him walk and get some fresh air in Leningrad. You can't go home from Russia with a pale face like that! What will they say in Washington about Moscow, about Russia? That even foreign tourists don't get anything to eat? You'll let the whole of Russian Intourist down! Please, Virginia, you still have two days till your departure – feed him up! And fresh air, walks! Take trips out of town without fail – to Repino, to Peterhof, to Mikhailovskoye. And anyway, Leningrad is a beautiful city! Walk and eat! You can't go home from Russia with a pale face like that, isn't that true, Lyuda?" I turned to the Intourist guide as if for support, while my eyes were shouting, willing Robert and Virginia to understand me.

'"The Moscow–Leningrad train will depart in one minute," a voice announced over the loudspeaker. "Passengers are requested to take their seats, those not travelling are asked to vacate the train . . ."

'The Williamses got in, and Lyuda from Intourists and I were left on the platform. The train gently began to move, the red coach floated past my eyes, and when Robert's and Virginia's faces appeared in the window I motioned to them that they should eat, eat a lot and walk in the fresh air . . . God knows if they understood me or not . . .

'"Quite right," Lyuda from Intourist said to me. "They've been screwing each other so much this past week that they're not themselves any more!"

'If only she knew that it was not so much bad for their health as for their whole risky mission in the USSR . . .'

. . . Jacob Stevenson did not suspect, and the Williamses could not tell him, that apart from their week's imprisonment and lovemaking, their pallor was caused by the fact that in the corridor of the Red Arrow's coach five they had come face to face with that very Major Neznachny whose picture David MacKerry had shown them in Washington. Neznachny was travelling to Leningrad in the next compartment.

11

In Leningrad the Williamses surprised Neznachny for the second time.

Despite the fact that Robert Williams was still going about with his neck wrapped up, they ordered an Intourist car first thing in the morning and drove off to Peterhof for the whole day. There they wandered hand in hand up and down the snowy avenues of the former royal palace and lingered in each other's arms by some fountain that was switched off for the winter or at the far end of the deserted park. Even with a long-distance directional radio microphone it was impossible to catch what they were whispering, and Neznachny gave up these attempts to listen in to their conversations. He sat in his Leningrad KGB Volga nervously smoking and cursing the day when he bit this hook and even requested additional information on these Williamses from Washington. It was no joke. Now the case had come under the control of General Tsvigun himself, Andronov's Deputy Chairman at the KGB! How had he put it? 'You used to work better before, Major . . .' What was that? A threat? So, if he didn't sort things out with these Williamses – they might kick him out of his job as section head. Things are looking rough for you, Neznachny. He had played this dirty trick on himself, with his own hands. No! He had to break these Williamses, he had to!

The car from Leningrad Intourist that had been put at the Williamses' disposal was standing nearby at Peterhof Palace; inside the Intourist guide had been sitting dying of boredom for more than four hours, while the driver slept without a care in the world – both of them doubling as informers for the Leningrad KGB. And perhaps for the first time in his life Neznachny envied somebody else's profession. No plan for recruiting foreign tourists for you, no scoldings from the boss. Just do your driving, then sleep while the customers walk round all these Peterhofs, Pavlovsks, museums, and parks. And the best thing is, if you have a row with the boss, go somewhere else, drivers are always needed. But in the KGB you couldn't have a row with the boss. Of course you could quit and become a lawyer – it was not for nothing he graduated from the Law Faculty. But Neznachny also knew that of course he would never leave the KGB of his own accord. The KGB was a force, a power before which all became dumb – from the man in the street to the minister. It was enough to pull the little red booklet out of your pocket with its KGB initials and you could jump the queue at hospitals, garages, trading organizations, hotels, and restaurants at holiday resorts. At the sight of that little booklet the most pompous officials bowed like servants, shop managers would bustle about ingratiatingly, traffic-controllers would immediately turn the lights to green, and judges, prosecutors, and militia would obey your orders without protest. And to lose all that for the sake of some Williamses? No, Neznachny was not going to give up on them. He had never yet given up, he could wait till the last moment. Let's see how they will sing at the customs hall at Sheremetyevo Airport . . .

The next day, 15 November, the driver of the Leningrad

Volga allocated to the Williamses was given some instructions: on returning from a tour out of town to the famous spots where the painter Ilya Repin used to paint his landscapes, he was to stage a breakdown so that the Williamses would be forced to go the last three hundred yards to the Hotel Europe on foot. And the Intourist guide was supposed to get out of the car even before that, saying she had something to do or she didn't feel well . . .

And after the beauties of the Gulf of Finland, which was just beginning to freeze over, after the pine forest at Repin's house 'Penates' where the Williamses fed the red squirrels by hand with chocolates – after this whole romantic day, everything went off simply, prosaically, precisely according to Neznachny's plan. On the corner of Nevsky and Liteiny Avenues the driver stopped the car and in broken English mixed with Russian explained to his passengers that the car had broken down, something had happened to the engine, and therefore they would have to walk to the hotel – it was just nearby, only three blocks away. The Williamses got out of the car and began to walk along the Nevsky, and when they had gone one block three people approached them: a girl in a beige coat and young men in synthetic sports jackets.

'Hello, are you Americans?' the girl asked Virginia in English, and without waiting for a reply said very quickly: 'We are Soviet dissidents, you must help us in the name of freedom! Take this! It's a letter to the American President. And all the materials on the persecution of students. They don't let us study. They're chucking Jews out of the universities. Please take it . . .' She thrust a package into Virginia's hand and the two fellows tried to stuff some papers into Robert's pocket. Stavinsky knew perfectly well from their lascivious brazen faces that these were no students or dissidents, and Virginia also quickly realized that this was one of those provocations that MacKerry had warned them about. Afraid that Stavinsky would lose his temper and say something to them in Russian, Virginia, forgetting all her Russian words, started to wave her arms about angrily: 'Go away! Go away! Police!!! Help!'

But there were no militia about, and all the passers-by shied away from them. Only on the other side of the street, unseen by the Williamses, cameras were clicking and an 8mm movie camera was humming in a KGB pick-up.

Tearing themselves free from those people Virginia and Robert ran to the hotel. From her room Virginia immediately called Intourist, then the American Consulate, to report the incident. But it was already after six in the evening and both Intourist and the Consulate said they should not worry about such a little thing. They could make an official statement tomorrow at the American Embassy in Moscow.

Stavinsky sat silently at the table, teeth clenched. This incident was a bad sign. First Moscow, where he kept seeing that KGB beauty in the hotel and the guide Lyuda Zvonaryova kept calling to invite them on picnics and to meet the Moscow elite. Then the 'birthday', then the 'plumber', and then on the train Neznachny himself, head of the American Section. To any genuine foreigner that might have seemed insignificant, or a series of coincidences. But not to Stavinsky who had grown up in the USSR. He knew as well as anyone who had grown up in this country that an Intourist guide was not going to start inviting foreigners to picnics without the KGB's permission or even direct instructions. And then there was that suspicious 'plumber'. And finally, those 'dissidents'. There was something wrong here! Something wrong! Perhaps he ought to call up Stevenson and hint that the operation was off? But what could Stevenson do if he had already sent the tickets to Yuryshev and Yuryshev was right now somewhere in Leningrad waiting for the Red Arrow to depart and expecting Stavinsky that night to come to him in coach six, compartment three? On the other hand, if the KGB were making approaches to the Williamses, either through the Intourist guide or through the 'plumber' and the 'dissidents', it meant they still took them for Americans. And what in fact had happened? They had not bitten on one of Lyuda Zvonaryova's invitations or on the 'plumber's' yarns, and they had taken nothing from the 'dissidents'. They were clean.

Nevertheless, assuming that the KGB were listening in to their room right now, Stavinsky wrote the word 'Stevenson' with his finger on the tablecloth and with his eyes indicated the telephone to Virginia. She understood, and booked a long-distance call to Moscow. Calmly and without panic she explained what had happened to Jacob and asked him to come to the Leningrad Station in the morning and spend a few hours with them until their flight left Moscow. 'We don't want to have any more problems or incidents, Robert is feeling ill enough as it is.' Stevenson understood her. Certainly, if he was with them – Virginia and the surrogate Williams (Yuryshev), it would be harder for the KGB to try on some new provocation. 'Don't worry, I'll meet you in Moscow, at the Leningrad Station,' he said.

12

The privileged express Red Arrow crossed the snowy wastes of Russia. In its luxurious two-berth compartments passengers drank brandy and champagne, played cards, flirted with chance travelling companions and railway conductresses until three in the morning. A waiter from the restaurant car came through the coaches with a trolley loaded with wine, brandy, caviar and Finnish cold-cut sandwiches, chocolate, and cigarettes. By three o'clock at night the wandering up and down the coaches had died down. Major Neznachny was sleeping in his compartment with the feeling of a job well done. Yesterday, while the Williamses were having supper in the restaurant of the Hotel Europe, a cleaning woman had gone into their room on Neznachny's instructions, ripped open the lining of Robert and Virginia Williams' coats, and slipped in several sheets of fine cigarette paper closely typed with some text of an anti-Soviet nature. Now there was no way the Williamses could wriggle out of a charge of anti-Soviet activity at

Sheremetyevo Airport. In the neighbouring compartments generals and colonels were snoring, having taken their dose of brandy before bed, and so were the railway cheats, having cleaned yet another victim out of his last hundred roubles. And the lucky ones who had managed to get a travelling romance going were locked in their compartments with their alluring travelling companions and conductresses, and to the click of the wheels, with that unbridled avarice that characterizes all lightning romances, were giving themselves up to lovemaking on narrow, but very soft and springy train bunks. By five in the morning their ardour had died down and the whole train slept with that deep sleep that precedes the morning. The corridors were deserted apart from the occasional semi-clothed woman running along the narrow carpets to the toilet, and a young lieutenant who had had too much to drink and who was standing on the platform of coach three, vomiting on to the snowy sleepers as they rushed past beneath the train.

By six even these signs of life had subsided, and only three people on the whole train had not closed their eyes. In coach five, compartment seven Virginia and Stavinsky sat side by side, not even in each other's arms, but just holding hands. They were talking with their eyes. At ten past six Stavinsky got up with a sigh, and Virginia quickly got up also. They embraced and stood for another two minutes. The train wheels rattled below them. There was hesitation in Virginia's look, as though she wanted to say something important to Stavinsky but could not bring herself to. The whistle of the engine, like an internal signal, forced Virginia to thrust Stavinsky away from her. 'Go . . .' she told him soundlessly. Without a noise he opened the door into the corridor. He listened.

There was not a living soul in the corridor. One last glance at Virginia and . . . Just as a timid swimmer dives off a rock into the water while his beloved watches, Stavinsky took a deep breath and went out into the corridor. Through the cold platform to car six, past compartments one, two, three . . . He hesitated at compartment three and listened. But there was not a sound inside and he went on to car seven – the restaurant car. It was deserted except for a sleepy Georgian buffet attendant who was spreading red caviar on pieces of bread – making sandwiches. 'Tea!' Stavinsky said to him in English, and added in deliberately broken Russian: '*Chay* . . . Two, *dva* . . .' Then, holding in his hand two metal glass-holders with glasses of hot tea, Stavinsky went back to coach six. To anyone who met him now he would look like an ordinary sleepy passenger taking morning tea to his compartment. But even this little charade had no spectators – the corridor of the coach was absolutely empty. Stavinsky stopped in front of the door of compartment three. His heart was pounding louder than the train wheels. Stavinsky listened – still not a sound inside. Well, if Yuryshev wasn't in there he would just act the sleepy passenger making a mistake. And, hoping deep down that it would indeed not be Yuryshev at all in there, but some completely different people, Stavinsky slowly pressed the handle and pulled the door to the right. It gave obediently and slid back. It was dark in the compartment, but the light from the corridor lit up the empty top bunk and a clothed male figure on the bottom one. The man was lying with his eyes closed, but one look was enough for Stavinsky to recognize himself – Stavinsky. He entered the compartment, quietly closed the door behind him, felt for the switch, and turned on the light. In that light he met the hard, direct gaze of Yuryshev, but at that very moment the gaze turned to one of incomprehension and amazement – Yuryshev had recognized himself, Yuryshev. He was so amazed that he sat up on the bunk. He was dressed in a worn leather jacket with a fur lining, old hunting boots, and worn trousers. Under the table stood a knapsack stuffed full of things.

Stavinsky put the glass-holders on the table with the teaspoons tinkling in the glasses and said softly, almost in a whisper: 'Hello. We have two or three minutes for everything. Listen and remember. From this moment you become me, Robert Williams, American tourist and dentist from Washington. In coach five, compartment seven my wife, now your wife, Virginia is waiting for you. This morning you are flying to America with her on my documents. That's all. Change into my suit . . .' And Stavinsky began to get undressed. 'Yes! The most important thing – this,' he took the scarf and gauze dressing from his neck. 'You have tonsillitis, so you cannot say a word. Virginia will do all the talking, and you don't open your mouth. Do you know English?'

'I read fluently, but speak it badly – no practise . . .' replied Yuryshev huskily.

'What's the matter with your voice?' asked Stavinsky.

'Seven years ago I had a growth removed from vocal chords in the army hospital, and I've been hoarse ever since. What do you think, can they cure it in the West?'

'So far there's no cure for that anywhere. I tell you as a half-baked doctor,' laughed Stavinsky. 'So! Before leaving you must stuff a lot of ice to make your glands swell as if you had real tonsillitis. Because there may be a medical examination at the customs. There's ice in the hotel, in the refrigerator in our room. And here's my scarf and bandage – bandage up your throat like me . . .'

Without arguing Yuryshev changed clothes with him, right down to the socks. He winced when he put on the shoes.

'Do they pinch?' asked Stavinsky.

'A little . . .'

'Hang on a bit. In my suitcase Virginia has some shoes one size bigger – we anticipated that. That's it. Good luck in America!'

'And are you going to work at General HQ instead of me?' Yuryshev asked suddenly, and he stopped getting dressed.

'No. I'm mad, but not that mad. I shall take the first train out of Moscow in the morning. Get dressed! I think I've told you everything. You are Robert Williams with a bad throat, your wife Virginia is in coach five, compartment seven. Take this tea and walk along half-asleep. At the station in Moscow Stevenson will meet you. He'll stay with you till your departure. Oh, and one thing: don't even think of laying my wife – I'm coming back to her! Understand?'

'Do what you like with mine,' said Yuryshev huskily. 'I'm not returning to her, I threw her out because she's a slut. You don't need to know the details. So long!' Yuryshev offered Stavinsky his hand in parting.

'When will they start looking for you?' asked Stavinsky.

'I have twenty-four working days' leave. That means I have to be at work on 3 December. They won't worry about me for a couple of days, but after that . . . I told the forester Anikin that I had got a woman in Kirov and was going to see her. So they'll start looking for me in Kirov . . .'

'By that time I won't even look like you. Only don't start making any statements to the Western press, in fact lie low. Anyway, MacKerry can worry about that . . . Right! Off you go, the tea's getting cold. From now on you don't understand Russian and you don't even open your mouth in the compartment or in the hotel room alone with Virginia. Got it?'

Yuryshev nodded and picked up both glass-holders with the tea which was still hot. He went over to the door, grasped the handle in his other hand, but then turned to Stavinsky: 'You're a desperate man! We ought to drink to this! . . .'

'Shut your mouth!' replied Stavinsky roughly. 'You have a sore throat!'

'I know. If you want a drink – and you need one, you're shivering all over – there's some vodka in my knapsack.'

He adjusted the bandage and scarf on his throat. They were now both standing by the door in front of the long mirror on the door – amazing look-alikes,like twin brothers. And in the mirror they looked each other in the eye. Yuryshev pulled the door handle slightly to the left. They both listened. Not a sound came from the corridor through the crack in the door. Opening the door a little wider, Yuryshev slipped out of the compartment and closed the door behind him. Now he was Williams, Robert Williams taking tea to his wife Virginia. On the platform between coaches six and five he broke off a thick piece of icicle, pushed it into his mouth, and chewed and crunched it in his strong teeth. Then he walked on, to coach five.

The train wheels clicked over the rail joints; his heart thumped.

The empty corridor of coach five . . . The door of compartment seven was closed . . . Yuryshev pressed the handle and opened the door. In the compartment, on the top bunk, lay a strange woman, fully clothed and beautiful. From that moment – his wife. He saw that she was shivering and that there were tears running down her cheeks. Sitting up with a start and propping herself on her elbow, she looked at him with her big brown eyes and almost inaudibly breathed in English: 'Is it you?'

No matter how prepared Virginia was for the fact that the new Williams would be and must be like the former Williams, she was dreaming and praying that Stavinsky would come back . . . and had he?

Yuryshev closed his eyelids affirmatively.

With a burst of joy Virginia nearly fell off the bunk into his arms – Yuryshev dropped the glasses of tea as he caught her. She pressed her whole body against him, but a second later pushed him away again – he smelled different – of forests and sweat. Or had her heart guessed right?

She looked at him intently, then slowly shook her head and said with just her lips: 'I am sorry . . . Help me, please . . .'

He gave her his hand and she silently climbed back up on to the upper bunk where she lay on top of the covers, not looking at Yuryshev any more. She was no longer shivering, and there were no tears on her face. She simply lay with her eyes closed, not moving. And at that moment Yuryshev envied Stavinsky . . .

He picked up the empty glasses and glass-holders off the carpet and carefully placed them on the table, sat down on the lower bunk near the window, and drew back the heavy curtain very slightly. Outside the window lay dark, pre-dawn Russia with her snowy forests and villages . . .

Roman Stavinsky was also looking at this same Russia through the window of his compartment, greeting her. A bottle of Siberian vodka stood already broached on the table before him. On the floor next to him, half-unpacked, lay Yuryshev's knapsack, with several warm sweaters, padded trousers, a worn old military tunic, and all Yuryshev's documents – passport, officer's book, and the keys to his apartment. Stavinsky gazed out of the window at Russia, still asleep, forlorn, buried in snow, took large, silent swigs from the bottle of vodka, and in an involuntary gesture rubbed his neck where that bandage had been.

13

'The arrival of the Red Arrow from Leningrad is strikingly different from its departure,' Jacob Stevenson composed as he hurried through the stream of passengers towards the fifth coach. 'There is none of that nocturnal mystery, that holiday atmosphere of the journey to come. Passengers with worried, tired faces hurrying to taxis and metros, porters with baggage carts and coarse shouts of "Mind your backs!", the grey cold dawn. From coach five emerge generals in grey astrakhan hats, then the famous Soviet comic actor Yury Leonov, followed by a fidgety woman in a leather coat, then two musicians with violin and 'cello, finally – Robert and Virginia Williams. I hand Virginia another little bouquet of flowers and give her and Robert a friendly embrace. And only in that embrace do I feel how tense his whole frame is, every muscle of his strong trim body, and I realize that this is Yuryshev. So we've met up – two months after that meeting at the Novodevichy cemetery . . . But I cannot betray this with a word or a sign – my KGB "guardian angels" are standing just a few feet away staring right at us . . . And realizing that tenseness of the whole situation I stop looking at Yuryshev, call a porter over with his cart, while Virginia, clever Virginia, takes us both by the hand and starts chattering away like an actress on the stage: "I was charmed by Leningrad! It's delightful! Do you know, Jacob, we went to Peterhof and the Gulf of Finland. We fed the squirrels there with candy! Can you imagine, Jacob, Russia has red squirrels, and in Washington we have grey and black ones! Bob, darling, cover your throat with your scarf! But then there was this horrible affair with the dissidents! Why should we take papers from them? It's none of our business to interfere in internal Soviet affairs!"

'I listened to her pleasant chatter, obviously calculated both for my ears and those of my KGB men, and out of the corner of my eye I looked furtively around for the other Williams – the one who had stayed behind in coach six, compartment three in place of Yuryshev. But I didn't see him. I decided to turn round, and immediately met the gaze of a round-faced man with grey-blue eyes staring straight at us. I had the impression that while chatting away Virginia was also darting short searching glances from side to side. And to prevent her looking behind her and seeing yet another KGB face obviously following us I took her firmly by the elbow and, squeezing her arm, led them to my car . . .'

14

Stavinsky got out of his part of the train last. The sleepy attendant had collected the sheets and pillow-cases from all the compartments and was taking them in a big armful to her own compartment when Stavinsky, pretending he had slept through the train's arrival, put on Yuryshev's jacket, pulled his cap with its ear-flaps down over his eyes, and threw the straps of the cumbersome knapsack over his shoulders. And although Stavinsky really wanted to see Virginia one last time he did not allow himself to go out on to the platform until the stream of passengers had almost dried up. It wouldn't take much of a miracle to bump into that KGB Major Neznachny here!

'Overslept, dear? Shouldn't drink so much,' grumbled the attendant, coming into his compartment to get the sheets and seeing the unfinished bottle of vodka on the table.

In the old days when he was constantly travelling round Russia as a television journalist Stavinsky easily got into conversation with even the most casual acquaintances, and here too he wanted to come back at her with some sort of joke. But a sudden terror that he might say the simplest line wrong, or with some non-Russian accent, and give himself away – this terror rendered him tongue-tied. He had been silent for so long that now he was afraid to open his mouth. The one thing he remembered was that he ought to give her about a rouble tip. He felt around in Yuryshev's trouser pockets, found some notes, and pulled them out. There were tens, fives, and also a single. He offered it to the attendant.

'Thank you,' she softened immediately. 'And take your vodka, you'll need it . . .'

'M-hm . . .' growled Stavinsky, thrust the half-empty bottle of vodka into the pocket of the knapsack, and looked out into the corridor. It was empty, an icy wind was blowing down it from the open doors, the way was clear. Stavinsky pulled the cap down even lower and went down to the end of the corridor. A few feet away was the platform and the new, or rather old, life he had been yearning for until quite recently. But now these few feet came hard.

But then he stepped down on to the platform, which was empty and covered with a crust of trampled snow. His head bent down on his chest, he set off for the Yaroslavl Station afraid of everything – a shout, the looks of the idle porters, the figure of the militiaman on duty. He felt as though he were crossing a minefield, and if a child's pop gun had gone off near him he would have fallen down as if shot in the back. But no one paid any attention to him, no one was interested in this peasant in hunting boots with a knapsack on his back. He had become the same sort of grey Soviet citizen as the hundreds of others getting out of the suburban electric trains on the neighbouring platforms and hurrying to the metros and buses. The Yaroslavl Station was just over on the left, two hundred yards away, even more crowded than the Leningrad Station, and with its automatic left-luggage office where documents and money awaited Stavinsky. Trains went from this station to the depths of Russia – Zagorsk, Kostroma, Kirov – and from there every day suburban electric trains pull into its twelve platforms bringing fresh thousands of people dressed like Stavinsky in padded jackets, grey coats, and caps with ear-flaps. When they get out of the station these people – workers, students, housewives – hurry off, some to work, some – a good half of them – to the Moscow shops in search of meat, sausages, cereals, and vegetables.

Stavinsky mingled with this crowd surging across the square to the metro. He was pushed and sworn at: 'Hey, you! Stop shoving with that knapsack!' Someone stepped on his foot, but he was glad – he couldn't be tailed in a crush like this, you could have your own arm torn off and you'd never find it again. And he battered his way through this dense flow, all the time striking to the left towards the

Yaroslavl Station until finally he found himself in an oncoming stream surging from the metro to the platforms. Now he was carried backwards, and once again there was swearing and pushing and when at last he extracted himself and reached the building of the Yaroslavl Station some old lady said to him: 'Take a look, dear, your knapsack's been slashed . . .' Stavinsky looked over his shoulder and saw that the pocket where the bottle of vodka had been was neatly slit with a razor blade. He realized he was home.

On entering the station building he was satisfied that nothing had changed since he left his country – there was the same crush and stuffy atmosphere in the vast building, with people sitting on the benches and the floor with cases, bundles, hold-alls. Children were crying. Dense crowds surrounded the buffets. People slept or ate while waiting for their trains, mothers breast-fed their babies. It was quite normal for the Soviet transit passenger to spend half a day or even a whole day at the station. Stepping over people's feet and cases Stavinsky went to look for the left-luggage lockers. He was hungry and felt like smoking, but there were no cigarettes in Yuryshev's pockets. At the tobacco kiosk he held out five roubles and said his first Russian words: 'Tu-134 . . .'

Nothing terrible happened. The vendor threw a pack of cigarettes and the change on to the counter without even looking at him.

'And matches?' said Stavinsky, surprised that the vendor had not given him the matches with the cigarettes.

'Two kopecks!' demanded the vendor, and Stavinsky remembered that in the USSR matches also cost money. A mere nothing, two kopecks, but a trivial detail like that could blow the whole thing . . . Stavinsky took his box of matches, walked away from the kiosk, and saw the room with the automatic lockers. Long rows of metal boxes, and passengers with eagle eyes wandering up and down with their baggage looking for an empty one. He also walked down the rows, noticed No 217 some distance away, walked indifferently past it, and settled down on the floor by the wall next to a group of peasants.

That was what MacKerry had told him to do: take his time, observe the room and the passengers for about twenty minutes to make sure there was no one watching that box. Stavinsky pulled his cap down over his eyes, leaned back against his knapsack, and pretended to be dozing. To his right, under a sign, 'No Smoking. No Litter', people were sleeping on cases and bundles, and on his left a peasant with a broad Vologda accent was quietly reasoning with his wife: 'But how can we keep the cow? There's no fodder . . .'

'But Pete, how can we get by without the milk?' the woman was asking nervously.

'Somehow. Others do, so will we . . . There's nothing to feed her on . . .'

A wave of depression flooded Stavinsky's heart. Where had he come to? Why? A cold, frosty, hungry land where even Vologda – the butter capital of Russia – could not feed itself or its cows . . . And in three hours' time Virginia would be leaving Sheremetyevo Airport. Perhaps for ever . . . No, he must see, even from a distance! Just see her – and that was it, he would stay here and slowly claw his way out of the dung he had cast himself into and find a way to escape to the West. How or where – he would think of something, but right now he had to see Virginia, just see her. After all, she was still in Russia, in Moscow! Nothing would happen if he left Moscow in three hours instead of one, when he had seen her plane take off . . .

Spurred on by this sudden decision Stavinsky opened his eyes and looked around the room. Nothing suspicious. Right, let's risk it.

He got up. Unhurriedly, almost lazily, he went over to box 217, and, expecting to be arrested or pounced on or Heaven knows what else, began with trembling hand to dial the combination that MacKerry had given him: 1-4-1-

5-1-6. No one jumped on him, no one arrested him, just some country woman over there asked: 'Are you finished with it?'

'No,' he answered in a muffled voice, and she went away.

Without looking round Stavinsky threw open the locker door. Instead of a package of documents and money there was a small neat black leather case. With some diffidence Stavinsky drew this case out of the box and tried the lock. The catch flew back easily and Stavinsky lifted the lid slightly. There was clothing inside – a suit, shirts, a woollen sweater, and a tan-coloured Bulgarian sheepskin jacket. That was strange – there had been no agreement with MacKerry about any clothes.

The same old woman came up to him again and almost pleaded: 'Have you finished with the locker now?'

'No, it's taken,' replied Stavinsky gruffly, not knowing what he was supposed to do with this case.

The old woman gave a long deep sigh and dragged her bundles out of the room to the regular left-luggage office. Stavinsky thrust his hand into the case and felt under the things, under the sheepskin jacket until he found what he was looking for: a package. A fat, heavy package. He wiped the sweat from his brow with relief and even smiled – was MacKerry really so thoughtful that he not only supplied him with documents and money through his Moscow agent, but threw in clothing as well? And very handy! It would be absurd to travel to Sheremetyevo International Airport wearing these hunting boots, dirty trousers, and worn leather jacket. An international airport was not the Yaroslavl Station, you got a different public there. But where could he change? He glanced at his watch – he had inherited from Yuryshev a good, heavy Omega wristwatch. It was 8.30, nearly three hours until Virginia's flight. But where could he change, for Heaven's sake? In the toilet? It would look odd if anyone noticed – a real peasant type goes into the toilet and comes out in a sheepskin jacket looking like a fop. And where could he put Yuryshev's knapsack? It was dangerous to put it in this box; MacKerry had said he mustn't go back to the same locker twice. And there were no other vacant boxes, as luck would have it. Hell!

Stavinsky shut the locker, gave the knob a twist to muddle the combination, and trailed after the old woman to the regular left-luggage office. There was a long queue there and the same old woman gave Stavinsky a reproachful stare. Then she demonstratively spat on the floor and turned away in contempt.

Twenty minutes later, having handed in Yuryshev's knapsack at the left-luggage window and received a tag, Stavinsky walked out of the Yaroslavl Station into Komsomol Square and got into a taxi.

'To the baths at Krasnaya Presnya . . .' he told the driver.

'Or perhaps to the Sandunovsky Baths?' the driver asked.

The Sandunovsky Baths are the most famous in Moscow, but that was precisely why Stavinsky did not want to go there – he might bump into some old acquaintances or some of Yuryshev's. But the baths at Krasnaya Presnya were for the proletariat, the Moscow elite did not go there.

'No,' he answered the driver. 'You need to spend the whole day at Sandunovsky, but I just want a quick wash after my journey . . .'

'Where are you from?' asked the talkative driver. 'Yaroslavl?'

'U-huh,' grunted Stavinsky, not feeling like starting up a conversation with the driver . . .

Twenty minutes later he had emptied the contents of the leather case on to a marble bench in a private room in the Krasnaya Presnya Baths: a Hungarian suit, six new Indian shirts, two Czech sweaters, shoes and warm boots, a Neva electric razor, and finally the bulky package wrapped up in yesterday's *Pravda*. He unwrapped the package and found inside everything MacKerry had promised – two sets of Soviet documents: two passports, two work record books, two military service cards, and two trade union cards in the name of Boris Viktorovich Romanov, born in 1937 and Gennady Matveyevich Rozov, born in 1938. With the latter set of papers there was also a dentist's diploma, from which Stavinsky learned that Rozov graduated from the Saratov Medical Institute in 1960. All the documents – both Rozov's and Romanov's – bore his own picture, and in Romanov's passport it said that from 7 June 1977 to 9 June 1981 he had served a term of imprisonment under Article 104 of the Penal Code of the RSFSR in No B-672-OR corrective labour camp in the town of Salekhard in Khanty-Mansy National District. Stavinsky examined his new documents critically and began to count the money, still without having decided who he should become now – Rozov or Romanov. It came to 7,000 roubles. They could have given more, thought Stavinsky, and then recalled that seven was a lucky number. Counting the other 200 roubles that he had found in Yuryshev's pockets he had enough money to begin a new life in Russia without having to lie around on the stone floors of train stations. But where was the message about how to contact MacKerry in the future? Surely they hadn't just chucked him these papers, clothes, and money and abandoned him? He checked carefully through all the pockets inside the case, but found nothing. Once again he leafed through the documents and the money, even studied the scrap of *Pravda* that they were wrapped in – nothing. Swine! Swine! Swine! thought Stavinsky in despair. They've abandoned me in Russia . . . Naturally, why do they need me now? They know I can't go to the KGB now and sell Virginia out . . .

With bitterness in his soul Stavinsky walked barefoot across the cold stone floor into the shower, turned on the hot water, and only then remembered that he had no soap. He had forgotten to buy it from the attendant. The hell with it, he thought, I'll do without soap . . .

But ten minutes later, having dried himself with the

skimpy towel and put on the CIA's contemptible gift – the new Hungarian suit – he was just transferring his new documents and Yuryshev's documents into his jacket when he discovered in the inside pocket a worn postcard of Yalta. In a round female hand was written: 'Dearest! Darling nephew! Wherever you are, know that I remember you and love you and wait for your letters as always at the old address: Olya Nikanorovna Krylova, Poste Restante, Yalta. Your old, sick, but ever-loving aunt Olya.' Stavinsky read the message again and looked at the other side of the card. It was a view of Yalta – the sunny city on the Black Sea coast. Ships were lying at anchor and yachts were sailing away into the distance. Just like in Florida, at Sarasota . . .

15

'Metroliner announces the departure of its flight thirty-two from Moscow to Brussels. Passengers are requested to proceed to boarding . . .' said the same metallic booming voice in Russian, and then repeated it all in English.

Virginia took Yuryshev's arm and looked reassuringly into his eyes. 'That's it! Stop being so scared, Colonel!' her look pleaded. 'You look ghastly! But it's all over, it's all behind us! Baggage inspection, document check – it's all behind us, and there it is – the American Boeing! Along the travelator, through the glass gallery, across to the gangway, and then – home, America!'

But aloud she only said: 'Are you OK, darling?'

He nodded. He knew he had to get a grip on himself, smile in a carefree way, say goodbye to Stevenson who was standing behind the glass barrier waving to them. But something prevented him relaxing, a sort of inner soldier's presentiment of mortal danger. Just as one instant before a direct hit by an enemy shell you get one soldier who will leap out of the trench or the shelter. Yuryshev knew that feeling, and it had saved him more than once – on the Chinese border during the Sino–Soviet conflict, during surface-to-air missile tests when a live missile got jammed in its shaft in a nuclear submarine because some idiot of a technician had left his jacket in the shaft, and during the first trials of the test model of the 'energy matrix' in the Pamirs, when no controlled earthquake occurred and a mountain landslide engulfed the entire military and scientific expedition. And on a dozen other occasions he had detected this sensation in himself, while hunting wolves and bears, a sport which young officers indulged in in the forests along the Ussuri River. And always in such situations a split second before imminent death – the explosion or the leap of an animal on to his back – he almost unconsciously obeyed some inner instinct and saved himself and others. Even in the submarine, with the count-down already in progress, he managed by his own composure to persuade two technicians to go along with him into the shaft and literally two seconds before the firing of the rocket motors pulled that cursed jacket out of the jammed launch stopper . . .

But here, amongst this well-dressed foreign crowd, elderly American ladies with faces painted like dolls, the glass cleanliness of these rooms and the efficient bustle of the customs, he could not understand from which direction this sense of danger was approaching. After all, passport control and the customs inspection were indeed finished now, and here was the American plane, American territory, right nearby.

A string of Soviet and American passengers stretched to the plane's gangway. Yuryshev knew that he could now go into the safe belly of that Boeing, but some inner feeling of danger kept him rooted to the spot and would not allow him to step on to that black moving ribbon.

And the cause of all this anxiety in him was quite calm. Major Neznachny stood in the semi-opaque cabin at the end of the glass gallery and awaited his victim. In his hands was a folder with the photographs of the Williamses taken in Leningrad.

And there was yet another man in the Shermetyevo air terminal, unseen by both Neznachny and the Williamses. Stavinsky. He had had his way – he had seen Virginia walking arm in arm with Yuryshev and Stevenson as they followed the cart with their baggage into the customs hall, and now it was time to leave this dangerous place, take a taxi and rush to the Kazan Station so as to catch the first train to Siberia, but . . . He could not bring himself to leave. He stood on the balcony on the second floor watching the American Boeing through the window. The first passengers were already going up the gangway, heads bent against the icy wind. Baggage-handlers were loading cases into the hold. Stavinsky thought he caught a glimpse of his own two brown suitcases as they vanished into the Boeing's womb. America was right there – just the other side of this glass wall, but . . .

'Let's go,' Virginia said to Yuryshev, and they stepped on to the black ribbon of the travelator that carried the passengers to the plane's gangway.

And when they had passed the final check – a white Swedish arch that detected metal objects – beyond that arch, five yards away from the Boeing, Major Neznachny strode over to them from his cabin. A well-built border guard followed him with an automatic over his shoulder.

'Dr and Mrs Williams?' said Neznachny in tolerable English. 'My name is Neznachny, I am a major in the KGB. Please produce your documents,' and he took their passports out of Virginia's hand, but then, without even looking at them, opened his folder. Ten large black and white photographs recorded the different phases of yesterday's encounter between the Williamses and the Leningrad 'dissidents'.

'Do you recognize yourselves in these pictures?' asked Neznachny.

'Yes,' said Virginia. 'Some hooligans came and bothered us in Leningrad yesterday, and I called Intourist to protest about it.'

'Those people were State criminals. We have arrested one of them, the other two have gone into hiding. You will have to remain in Moscow to give evidence . . .'

'We can't stay,' answered Virginia, trying to remain polite and calm. 'This is our plane, we are leaving in a few minutes.'

'Unfortunately we are compelled to remove you from this flight. The arrested man testified that you took some illegal anti-Soviet letters from them.'

'We didn't take anything, I swear to you!' said Virginia, turning cold with horror.

'I believe you completely, Mrs Williams. Only you will have to confront this criminal, and we shall have to check your clothing. You can see for yourself from these photographs that Mr Williams is putting some papers into his pocket . . .'

'We can't stay, my husband is sick! You have no right to arrest us, we are American citizens!'

'Who came to the USSR for a special purpose – to make contact with anti-Soviet conspirators . . .' Neznachny continued her sentence politely. He knew quite well what would happen next: a minor scandal, indignation, tears from Virginia, and a demand from her husband to contact the American Embassy immediately. But the documents retrieved from their clothing would be incontrovertible proof of their anti-Soviet activity. They would spend a couple of days apart in cells at the Lubyanka prison waiting for the arrested 'conspirator' to be brought from Leningrad, then – the confrontations, lengthy interrogations during which all the other interrogators would treat them roughly and threaten them with jail, and only he, Neznachny, would 'believe' that they were not guilty of anything and offer them a deal: co-operation with the KGB in exchange for freedom. Oh, nothing very special, and certainly not now, but some time in the future, and basically it was a pure formality – just sign a couple of meaningless documents. Otherwise he simply wouldn't be able to persuade the authorities to let them go and close this case. Oh, he would become their best friend as well! This Virginia would look ingratiatingly into his eyes, and he would tell her that he helped them to get free only for the sake of her beautiful eyes and their meeting 'some time in the future'. And they would even thank him for saving them, as had happened more than once with other godchildren . . .

'Please follow me,' he told Virginia and Robert with a smile.

But what happened a second later came as a complete surprise to both Neznachny and Virginia. At the very beginning of this conversation Yuryshev had become calm – as always in moments of mortal danger. And while Virginia was talking to Neznachny Yuryshev's cold officer's mind was calculating the options for escape. He could not remain even half an hour in Moscow because his very un-American pronunciation would give him away completely at the first interrogation. And then . . . He had read somewhere that he only had to step on board an American airplane and he was on American soil, under the protection of the American flag. And even if that was not so, there was still only one means of escape – that plane. A few Soviet diplomats who had already gone ahead into the plane could be his hostages if the Soviet authorities forbade the plane to take off. He needed a weapon. He did not know if this KGB major had a gun under his coat, but right next to him was another weapon – a Kalashnikov automatic over the border guard's shoulder with thirty rounds in its magazine. And it wouldn't be a bad idea to pull the major himself into the plane as a hostage . . . What else? How else could he escape?

No, there was no other way out. It was either the KGB torture-chambers or . . .

Keep calm. Two meek, obedient steps after this major,

Virginia's look of despair, a sharp turn towards the border guard marching behind them, and – that time-honoured technique of hand-to-hand combat acquired back in officer's training school: his foot in the soldier's groin, and his hand had already grabbed the automatic from his shoulder.

Virginia gasped, Neznachny turned round in amazement. There was the familiar click of the bolt in Yuryshev's professional hand, and without knowing himself why he said it in German, he shouted at Neznachny: '*Halt!*'

Perhaps because that is what he shouted as a child when he used to play partisans and fascists with the other kids.

'You're out of your mind!' Neznachny rushed at him, realizing that no American tourist would ever shoot, and exultant at this new turn of events – now he really had this Williams in his hands! And how! Assaulting a Soviet border guard!

But that was Neznachny's last thought and the last mistake of his life. Hardly had he put out his hand to snatch the automatic out of this idiotic American's hand when Yuryshev squeezed the trigger. A short burst of automatic fire stitched Neznachny's greatcoat and little fountains of blood spurted out of his back; but it was not so much pain as surprise that was written across Neznachny's face as he fell.

Seizing Virginia by the shoulder Yuryshev dragged her to the gangway, while frightened passengers and an air hostess dived inside the plane. Several officers and border guards rushed out of the air terminal and froze under the steady aim of Yuryshev's automatic.

But what Yuryshev did not see at that moment was visible through the glass wall of the air terminal to his look-alike Stavinsky and hundreds of passengers and other people drawn by the sound of shooting. To the side of the gangway near the plane's hold they saw one of the 'baggage-handlers' draw a pistol out of his overalls, calmly take aim, and shoot Yuryshev as he was already on the gangway, two paces from the door. He was a good shot, the bullet hit Yuryshev in the head. Yuryshev dropped the automatic and fell down the gangway stairs still clasping Virginia's fur coat and dragging her with him. At the bottom, on the ground, KGB officers and border guards ran up and had picked up Yuryshev's body and Virginia. Virginia swung at someone's face and kept trying to reach Yuryshev's automatic, but her arms were immediately pinned behind her back and she was led, dragged inside the air terminal.

Behind her the soldiers carried the body of the hapless Major Neznachny who simply wanted to fulfil his plan for the recruiting of foreign tourists, and the body of the American tourist Robert Williams who for some unknown reason had suddenly become so aggressive . . .

And in the air terminal itself Aeroflot staff were running along the walls chasing passengers and others away from the windows.

Stavinsky sat down in an armchair in a cold sweat. He needed to clear out of here before it was too late, as fast as his legs could carry him; but those legs right now were numb with fear for himself and for Virginia . . .

Part 3

Trapped

1

Embassy of the United States of America,
19–23 Tchaikovsky Street,
Moscow

To: USSR Ministry of Foreign Affairs,
First Deputy Foreign Minister,
Mr Viktor Afanasyevich Kozlov

The United States Embassy presents its compliments to the USSR Ministry of Foreign Affairs and would like to draw its attention to the fact that on 16 November 1981 two citizens, Robert and Virginia Williams, were detained at the Moscow International Airport at Sheremetyevo, as they were about to leave after a tourist visit to the USSR. According to the eye-witness reports of passengers on flight number thirty-two from Moscow to New York, the said Robert Williams was killed while being arrested, and his wife, Mrs Virginia Williams, was detained by members of the KGB.

Despite the rules of conduct established by the Consular Convention between our respective Governments and in defiance of the norms of Soviet justice and generally accepted international practice, members of the US Consular Department have still not been able to interview Mrs Williams three days after the incident took place, nor even to ascertain her present whereabouts and the reasons for her arrest. Numerous appeals for information to the appropriate authorities have gone unanswered.

The United States Embassy is confident that the Soviet side will provide it with a detailed account of the incident forthwith and also explain the reasons for the attempt to arrest Dr and Mrs Williams, which led to the death of a United States citizen. At the same time the United States Embassy demands that its Consular officials be given immediate access to Mrs Virginia Williams with a view to procuring her release from detention.

Respectfully yours,
Counsellor at the United States Embassy,
Hubert N. Green

18 November 1981

On Friday, 20 November a meeting was held between Assistant Secretary of State Richard Malvick and the head of the CIA's Russian Section, Daniel J. Cooper. Cooper had requested this meeting himself, although the two men had disliked each other from their time spent as students together at Princeton University. But Yuryshev's death and the arrest of Virginia Part-'Williams' had placed the CIA in a difficult position. It wasn't just that an operation of emormous importance had foundered. But the newpapers had got on to the story and knew about Mrs Williams's arrest and her 'husband's' demise. Thank God that the only journalist who really knew what the whole affair was about, the *Washington Herald* correspondent, Jacob Stevenson, had acted decently and confined himself to a short, formal account of the incident, without going into sensational details about how this was yet another defeat for the CIA etc. In fact, it would have been dangerous for him to do otherwise, because he had been mixed up in the operation himself, and had he described it in the newspapers, the Russians would almost certainly have put him behind bars for engaging in anti-Soviet activity. But the twenty lines that did appear in the newspapers about the incident had been enough to make the real Dr Robert Williams, the stomatologist from Potomac, put in an appearance at CIA Headquarters the previous day, armed with a copy of a newspaper announcing his decease in Moscow. They had had to pay him hefty compensation and persuade him to take another urgent month-long vacation in somewhere like Hawaii or the Bermudas – also at the CIA's expense, of course. He agreed to this only when MacKerry had shown him a photograph of Virginia and explained that, if the real reasons for her journey to Moscow should ever leak through to the press, then this charming-looking woman would have to spend years and years in a Soviet prison, sentenced for being an American spy.

Robert Williams was a forty-six-year-old bachelor with an eye for the women, and seeing these photographs of Virginia made him think twice. A beautiful actress-turned-spy returning from the Soviet Union would cause a sensation in the newspapers, of course, and here was a chance for him not only to make the headlines along with her, but also – you never know – to make it with the woman, too! It was worth losing a few patients for a chance like that – especially if the CIA was willing to pay compensation. As they dispatched him to the Bermudas, both Daniel J. Cooper and David MacKerry swore to him that, as soon as Virginia was released from Russia – and the CIA 'will do everything it can to make sure that that takes place within the next couple of weeks, Dr Williams, there's a lot at stake here for us, you see' – he would be called back from his vacation to accompany the two of them, when they went to meet her off the plane at Kennedy Airport. But Daniel J. Cooper wasn't nearly so sure himself that they would succeed in getting Virginia out so quickly. A lot would depend on how she behaved at any interrogations, of course. If she didn't reveal that the dead man wasn't Williams at all, but a colonel from Soviet Army Headquarters, then they were still in with a chance. MacKerry was convinced that she would keep quiet about it, if only to save Stavinsky and not to put the KGB on his tail . . .

But this conversation with the Assistant Secretary of

State hardly took place at all. No sooner had Cooper opened his mouth to say that the CIA was 'for certain reasons extremely concerned that urgent and active steps should be taken by the State Department and the US Embassy in Moscow to bring about the release of an illegally detained US citizen, Mrs Virginia Williams', than Richard Malvick handed him a photostat copy of the following document which had been received from Moscow that very day.

USSR Ministry of Foreign Affairs,
32–34 Smolenskaya-Sennaya Square,
Moscow

To: Mr Hubert N. Green,
Counsellor at the United States Embassy

The USSR Ministry of Foreign Affairs presents its compliments to the Embassy of the United States of America and, on behalf of the Soviet Government would like to draw its attention to the following.

On 16 November 1981 at the Moscow International Airport at Sheremetyevo, KGB Major F. E. Neznachny detained US citizens Robert and Virginia Williams as they were about to board a plane for America. The reason for their detention was the discovery of incontrovertible evidence linking Dr and Mrs Williams with criminal, anti-Soviet elements within the country. On the previous day the Williamses had been in Leningrad, where they met three individuals who passed illegal printed materials and letters on to them for distribution in the West. Photographs of this meeting and the testimony of witnesses and of the criminals themselves, since charged with anti-Soviet activity, provided documentary evidence of these facts.

When detaining them, Major Neznachny showed these incriminating photographs to the Williamses and asked for an explanation, since what they had done constituted a flagrant violation of the tourist agreement existing between our two countries and inadmissible interference in the internal affairs of the Soviet Union.

While they were being questioned by the steps leading to the American aircraft, Dr Robert Williams suddenly attacked a Soviet border guard, seized his sub-machine-gun and used it to kill Major Neznachny. He and his wife, who also attempted to resist Soviet officials, causing them bodily harm, then attempted to climb on board the American plane. In order to put an end to these terrorist actions and also to protect the lives of American and Soviet passengers, members of the KGB stationed at Sheremetyevo Airport were obliged to resort to armed force. As a result of the exchange of fire that followed, Dr Robert Williams was killed and his wife, Virginia Williams, was placed under arrest.

Subsequent examination revealed that the anti-Soviet materials in question had been sewn into the lining of Dr Williams's overcoat and Mrs Williams's fur jacket, a discovery which tells us the real reasons for the Williamses' journey to the Soviet Union and why they offered armed resistance when being apprehended.

Mrs Virginia Williams, née Part, born 1948 and an actress by profession, will shortly be brought before a Soviet court of law, charged with terrorism and anti-Soviet activity. In connection with the above incident, the Government of the USSR has instructed the Soviet Ministry of Foreign Affairs to register a strong protest with the American side and hopes that the US Government will take whatever measures it can to prevent individuals who are hostile to the Soviet Union and the Soviet Government from arriving in our country under the guise of tourists.

Respectfully yours,
First Deputy Minister of Foreign Affairs,
V. A. Kozlov

19 November 1981

'Your interest in this affair,' Malvick told Cooper drily, 'only confirms the correctness of what the Soviets say. If these Williamses travelled to Russia at your instigation, then my advice to you would be to keep right out of it now. As I see it, up to now the Russians have regarded her as nothing but an eccentric actress who received some illegal documents from a group of Soviet dissidents. As for her husband, they think that he was some idiot who imagined he was James Bond. Quietly and without applying any pressure, we'll ask them to show leniency towards the woman. But it'll take a long time . . .'

'But they didn't take any illegal documents,' shouted Cooper angrily. 'It was nothing but a put-up job on the KGB's part. They planted those documents on the Williamses . . .'

'Now why should the KGB go planting anti-Soviet propaganda on American tourists?' asked Malvick coldly. 'Besides, if you insist that it was a KGB provocation, then the CIA ought to provide us with a report on the affair. But if you do that, I can't guarantee that it won't find its way into the newspapers. And if that happens, the consequences could be awkward not just for your agent, but for you personally. I'm telling you this as a friend, Dan, in memory of our student days together . . .'

Cooper left the State Department swearing under his breath. You just try competing with the KGB, when even the US Government can't succeed in keeping anything secret from the press . . .

2

You are taken up three flights of stairs leading from the cellar of the special KGB prison on the Lubyanka – through the snow-covered prison courtyard. You taste a mouthful of fresh, frosty air and then you are back inside again. Only this time it's into the KGB Headquarters itself and the corridors are covered with red carpets. Then the guard takes you by elevator to the third floor. What a change from the damp solitary confinement cell where Virginia had spent the last few days! She would never forget the concrete floor, the thick, windowless walls and the bed which folds back into the wall and is kept locked from six in the morning till ten at night, leaving you only a tiny metal seat to perch on fixed into the other wall. Nor would she forget the daily interrogation lasting for hours on end at which she would repeat one thing and one thing only: 'I am a US citizen and I demand an interview with officials from the US Embassy.' And the repulsive food! If you could call it food, that is, that watery pea soup or oatmeal porridge served with tea and a hunk of sticky black bread. The guards would pass it in through the tiny food hatch in the metal door. But now, after four days of absolute hell, she suddenly found herself in a luxurious warm office furnished with soft leather fittings and broad, light windows looking out over the busy square commemorating Felix Dzerzhinsky, the founder of the KGB. The walls of this office were covered from top to bottom with bookshelves, and Virginia's sharp eyes soon made out a whole series of English volumes: *The Red Terror*, *The KGB*, *Gorky Park*, *Lolita*, *Airport*, *Wheels*, *The Joy of Sex* . . . Above the bookshelves in a couple of places were framed portraits of Lenin and Brezhnev. The desk and coffee-table were strewn with American and English newspapers and magazines, including the *Sunday Times*, the *Washington Post*, *Newsweek*, *Playboy*, the *Wall Street Journal*, and the *Washington Herald*.

The man whose office this was, the boss as we shall call him, was seated at the desk. He resembled Marlon Brando in the film of *The Godfather*, except that he was balder than Brando and his eyes were hidden behind glasses. He had Virginia's case-file in his hands and was immersed in reading it. Apart from him, there were four other people in the room – his deputy, General Tsvigun, a solidly built and even rather stout man, aged about sixty with bloated features and red veins in his eyes, and another, rather imposing, dark-haired man aged about fifty. That was Colonel Orlov, whom Virginia had already seen at her interrogations. Finally, there were two young journalists aged about thirty-five, who were sitting there, notebooks at the ready. With the exception of the boss, they all stared at Virginia with unconcealed curiosity, and for the first time in days she gave some thought to her outward appearance. Her dress was creased from her nights spent lying on the prison bed, and one stocking was torn at the knee. She had no make-up on, of course, and her hair was completely tangled and uncombed (her hair-pins and comb had been taken away from her, like everything else, as soon as she had arrived at the prison). But the main thing was that she had gone for four days without a shower! In the fresh air of this office, where you could hear the sound of traffic coming up from the street below, she suddenly became aware of the acrid smell of her own unwashed body. Only twice a day, when they allowed her to use the prison latrine, was she allowed to sluice her face in icy water straight from a tap in the wall. She suddenly remembered the tramps who live in the New York subway. She must look like them and smell the same . . .

Meanwhile, the boss, without even bothering to look up from the file of documents that he was reading, dismissed the guard and secretary with a leisurely movement of the hand and then said to Virginia in English: 'Sit down.'

He nodded towards an armchair placed in front of his desk.

'I demand an interview with officials from the US Embassy,' she said, without moving from the spot.

He looked up at her calmly. His eyes looked weary, but immensely self-confident.

'Demand what you like,' he said slowly and deliberately. He had the deep, slightly muffled voice of a heavy smoker. 'But you might as well do it sitting down . . . Would you like something to eat?'

Without waiting for her to answer, he turned slightly towards the intercom on his desk and pressed a button. 'Bring some tea and sandwiches,' he ordered in Russian.

Then he switched back to English again. 'Do you smoke?' he asked in a noticeably British accent.

'No, I don't.'

'It would still be better if you were to sit down,' he said in perfect English. 'Otherwise, we'll all have to stand up, as you are a woman.'

'Not any more,' Virginia said defiantly. 'If you know English, then you will probably have noticed from the books you have read that a woman needs to take a shower at least once a day. But being in your prison has turned me into an animal. So there's no point in playing the gentleman with me. I demand to see somebody from the US Embassy.'

He listened to her in silence, his head bowed slightly. Then he pressed the button on his desk once again. A moment later his secretary appeared at the door – an impressive young major carrying a tray. He put it down on the edge of the desk. On it was a glass of strong tea in a silver glass-holder, a tiny dish with sugar and lemon and a plateful of open sandwiches with red and black caviar.

'Take Mrs Williams to my personal shower,' he ordered, still speaking in English. Virginia stared at him in astonishment. He smiled.

'You really do need to take a shower,' he said. 'Please go ahead. Or don't you want to?'

'I . . . I . . .' she mumbled. She couldn't resist the temptation of having a shower, and why should she have done? Her period was nine days overdue now. For the first five days she had thought nothing of it and hadn't told Stavinsky. Then she had been arrested, thrown into a cell and placed in solitary confinement. Then one night, when she was lying in despair on her straw mattress, she had suddenly felt a nagging pain in her breast, and she realized with horror that her dream had come true – she was pregnant. But God! Why did this have to happen here and now in this God-forsaken country?

'Please follow me,' said the major, and walked towards a side door behind the boss's desk. Virginia went after him in confusion. She found herself in a second room containing armchairs and settees, a small dining-table, a colour television and a Grundig music-centre. Beyond this was yet another room – a smaller one on this occasion with a bed and a bedside table. Next door to it were a toilet and bathroom. As she entered the bathroom, she halted in amazement.

For a second she thought that she was in the luxurious apartment of some movie star in Beverly Hills. There was an enormous bath, the size of a miniature swimming-pool, made out of black marble, there was a mirror the length of the wall, a shower, the familiar scent of Lancôme soap, under-floor heating, gigantic bath-towels, a hair-dryer and even a bidet.

'What would he be wanting a bidet for?' wondered Virginia.

'Here you are . . .' said the major in a toneless voice. He turned on the taps to fill the bath and then left the room, shutting the door behind him.

Left on her own, Virginia slowly approached the mirror. For four days she hadn't caught sight of herself. Not a long time, but God! How she had changed! What had they done to her? Tears burst from her eyes and she collapsed on to the warm tiles of the floor. For the first time she lost control of herself, and only the sound of the running water drowned out the sound of her sobbing . . .

Meanwhile the boss was dictating the following instructions to a couple of journalists.

'The main point of your article must be this. Our country is always in favour of developing friendly relations with the West. But in recent years the Imperialists and particularly the new American Government have been stirring up anti-Soviet hysteria throughout the world. And there is no shortage of hotheads in the West who fall under the influence of this propaganda and even commit anti-Soviet acts. They bring into our country, printed materials which have been provided by the CIA and various émigré and Zionist organizations. Customs officials at Sheremetyevo are always finding books by such renegades as Solzhenitsyn, Voinovich and Bukovsky in their suitcases, not to mention journals like *Posev*, *Kontinent* and *Grani* which openly advocate the overthrow of Soviet power. During the Moscow Olympics dozens of these so-called "tourists" tried to bring leaflets into the Soviet Union as well as thousands of fake copies of *Pravda*, printed in Italy and containing articles which were anti-Soviet in character. They were intending to distribute these leaflets and newspapers at the Olympic Stadiums and on the streets of Moscow. This incident with the Williams couple shows you just how far these anti-Soviet hotheads are willing to go. No government in the world would allow into the country foreign tourists who were bent upon stirring up anti-government feeling and were even ready to murder members of that country's security forces. We consider that the just sentence about to be passed on Virginia Williams by a Soviet court will be a good example to any other so-called "tourists" who are about to stuff their suitcases with anti-Soviet and Zionist materials, provided by the CIA and other doubtful sources . . .'

All this was delivered in an unhurried, even voice, without any hesitation. It was obviously something that the speaker had made his mind up about a long time before. The two journalists tried to copy down his every word.

'That's all,' he said. 'That's what I want you to say. When you've written the article, let me see it.'

'Of course we will,' said one of the journalists. 'But could we ask her a few questions?' he continued, nodding towards the door which led to the bathroom.

'What questions?' came the calm reply.

'Well, for example, why should a Hollywood actress have decided to take part in anti-Soviet activity?' said one of them.

'How did she come into contact with these criminal, dissident elements?' asked the other.

'You don't need to ask her any questions. You can go now,' he said, motioning the two journalists towards the door. But then he added, softening his tone a little: 'You've seen her, and that's enough. As to what she would say in reply to your questions, you can invent that yourself . . .'

When the journalists had gone, he turned to General Tsvigun and Colonel Orlov, and said pensively: 'Now we have to decide what camp to send her to. That's the first thing. We don't have any camps for foreign women, and we can scarcely build one just for her . . .'

'Let her go to an ordinary camp,' said Colonel Orlov. 'We've had cases like that in the past . . .' Then he suddenly stopped short. The boss didn't like being interrupted. He didn't give a damn for the opinions of his underlings, in any case. The most confidence which he would show in them was thinking out loud in their presence. That was all.

'The second thing is this,' he continued, paying so little heed to Orlov's remark, that you might have thought the colonel wasn't even present in the room. 'I cannot understand why this Williams reacted so violently to being arrested. He didn't know that anti-Soviet materials had been sewn into the lining of his overcoat, after all . . .'

He stopped talking and peered through his glasses at Orlov and Tsvigun. Now they had an opportunity to speak.

'Most likely he was simply a lunatic . . .' said General Tsvigun.

'I don't know . . . I'm not so sure about that,' came the reply. 'In any case, we'll have to increase the combat training of our officer class. Even agents in the field have begun to look bloated, I notice . . .'

He suddenly stopped talking, when he realized that Virginia had entered the room.

Even without make-up on she was beautiful. The shower had restored the freshness to her cheeks. Her clean, blow-dried hair hung magnificently around her shoulders and her creased dress only served to emphasize the contrast between her beauty and the clothes she was wearing. She was obviously in need of different apparel . . .

But this sudden silence was the only indication that the speaker had noticed Virginia's presence. The imperturbable expression on his face did not alter. He tapped the glass of tea and said to Virginia in English, in the same even voice: 'Your tea is still warm. Sit down and drink it. And do eat some sandwiches. The KGB isn't as fearsome an organization as some people write in the West. We simply have our job to do, defending the interests of our country. Sit down.'

Whether it was the quiet authority which his voice exuded and the conviction that she would eventually submit, or whether the refreshing shower had made her famished, Virginia silently edged forward on her chair and began to consume the tea and sandwiches.

Meanwhile, nobody said a word. They watched her eat, and although Virginia did her best to persuade herself to eat slowly, the combined effect of hunger and the fresh air made her head spin, and in order to stop this giddiness, she had to eat with more speed and enthusiasm than she thought was desirable. At the same time she felt humiliated by this unseemly haste, and she couldn't help looking up occasionally at the men as she ate. General Tsvigun had lit up a cigarette and moved over towards the open ventilation-window.

The boss pressed the button on his intercom once again and said in Russian: 'Bring in some more sandwiches and tea.'

Virginia had scarcely finished the first glass of tea, when the door opened and in walked the major once again, carrying a new plate of sandwiches and some more tea. But now that she had overcome the first pangs of hunger, Virginia took herself in hand. Overcoming temptation, she pushed away the second plate of sandwiches and took only a couple of sips at the tea.

'Thank you very much,' she said. 'I still insist on seeing a representative from the US Embassy.'

He smiled, and Colonel Orlov and General Tsvigun laughed openly – the sight of this voluptuous woman looking as cosy as a household cat, actually 'insisting' on something was too incongruous!

'Very well,' said the boss. 'I have taken note of your demand. And now will you tell me why your husband murdered one of our officers? After all, he only wanted to detain you for a couple of hours so as to get answers to a few questions.'

Virginia gave him a hard stare. Colonel Orlov and the other investigators had already asked her this question dozens of times at the interrogations. She had never given any reply, preferring to repeat over and over again the same phrase: 'I insist on seeing a representative from the United States Embassy.' But lying alone at night on her hard straw mattress, she knew that she would eventually have to give some kind of explanation for Yuryshev's – 'Williams's' wild behaviour. Until they came up with the right answer themselves, that is. And wouldn't the US Consular official put the same question to her, anyway? As she listened to the sound of her body at night, she went over everything that had happened to them in Moscow and finally found a peg for her story. Now, as she stared at this well-fed, self-confident individual dressed in a smart French suit, she could feel his eyes calmly staring back at her and weighing her up.

'Robert was very unbalanced,' she said. 'We didn't mention in the visa application the fact that he had fought in the Vietnam war and got shell-shocked. We were afraid that we wouldn't be given visas to enter Russia. And when we arrived here, Robert immediately noticed that this major was following us . . .'

General Tsvigun and Colonel Orlov looked at her in

amazement, but their boss's face remained as impassive as ever, and only a slight whitening of the skin above the cheekbones indicated his anger. Virginia knew very well that she was bluffing and playing with fire, but it wasn't as if the dead Major Neznachny could contradict what she was saying, was it? And wasn't he the one that had sent that ravishing beauty to tempt Robert, *and* the gypsies on Robert's birthday, *and* the plumber? And, last but not least, wasn't he the one who had accompanied them to Leningrad in the next compartment?

'Yes,' she said. 'He kept an eye on us in the hotel and even travelled to Leningrad with us. We saw him in the train! And this made Robert terribly nervous. And besides, he was ill. He had a high temperature at the time, and he kept on imagining that we would get arrested for something, because he'd fought against the Communists in Vietnam, or something like that. Otherwise, why should anyone have been tailing us? Robert was afraid even to leave the hotel, and only in Leningrad did we decide to do a bit of sightseeing. But when we were approached by some hooligans on the street, Robert told me immediately that it was a provocation, and that if they tried to arrest us, he wouldn't give himself up alive. And that's why things went as they did at the airport . . .'

The man seated at the desk pressed the button to summon his secretary. When the major appeared, he nodded in Virginia's direction and said: 'Take her away.'

'Follow me,' ordered the major in English.

Virginia stood up and looked at her questioner in some confusion. 'Will I get to meet an official from the US Embassy?'

'What you will get is a minimum of three years' prison for complicity in the murder of a Soviet officer,' he replied. 'Go now . . . and you can take the rest of these sandwiches with you to your cell.'

Virginia felt as if she had been struck in the face with a whip. He had spoken to her as if she were some contemptible beggar appealing for alms.

'You just listen to me!' she shouted. 'If I was able to puke up everything I've just eaten all over your desk, I would do it with pleasure.'

The major grabbed her elbow in alarm and began to drag her out of the room, but not before she had time to turn round again and shout: 'And you like to give yourself airs as a gentleman!'

The major pushed her out into the reception room, where a prison guard was waiting for her.

Meanwhile, behind the quilted leather door leading to the office, the occupant of that room was drumming his open palm against the top of his desk and speaking to Colonel Orlov.

'What's going on in your department? Have you got a bunch of utter lunatics working for you, or what? Some wretched dentist from Washington realizes he's being shadowed the very first day he arrives!'

He was interrupted by a voice over the intercom. 'May I speak to you, Comrade General?'

'Who is it?' came the angry reply.

'Brusko, the head of Classified Records.'

'What do you want?'

'When examining the contents of Major Neznachny's safe, I came across a strange map of North America, Comrade General. In my opinion, Neznachny used this map to mark the locations of all the tourists he dealt with over the last few years.'

The boss let out a silent sigh and shook his head in sorrow! God! What cretins he had to work with! 'And why did he mark them on a map, do you suppose?' he asked wearily.

'God alone knows, Comrade General. Perhaps he wanted to sell the map to the Americans. Shall I look into it?'

'Hm, yes . . .' he mumbled apathetically. 'Look into it . . .'

3

Two hours later US Embassy representative Larry Kugel was sitting in the office of the Lubyanka prison-governor. Worn carpets covered the floor. Colonel Orlov was showing him documents connected with the accusations against Virginia Williams. The grey file contained photographs of the Williamses' meeting with Leningrad 'dissidents' on Nevsky Avenue, the 'full and frank' confessions made by those same 'dissidents' about the materials which they handed over, and finally photographs of Robert Williams's overcoat and Virginia's fur jacket, their linings ripped open and the 'anti-Soviet' materials found inside them displayed side by side.

As he examined the contents of the file, it occurred to Larry Kugel that the Williamses were obviously guilty, and that all he could do was attempt to get the whole affair soft-pedalled and appeal to the Soviets to show leniency to Virginia, because she was a woman. It ought to be possible to lay all the blame firmly at Robert Williams's door, and he was dead, after all . . .

'When will I get to see Mrs Williams?' he asked.

'You can talk to her now, if you like,' replied Orlov. 'Have the prisoner brought up,' he said, turning to the governor.

A few minutes later Virginia was led in. Neither Colonel Orlov nor the prison-governor made any move to leave the room, and Kugel didn't insist that they did. His conversation with Virginia would be overheard and recorded on a hidden tape-recorder in any case. He stared at the woman. She didn't look at all bad, despite the four days she had spent in prison. It was difficult to believe, that this gentle, sensuous-looking woman could have been involved in killing someone.

'Sit down,' said Colonel Orlov. 'You asked us to arrange a meeting with a representative from the US Embassy. Here he is. As you can see, we observe the law.'

Kugel introduced himself, showed Virginia his credentials, and then asked: 'Do you want to make any statement?'

'I certainly do,' replied Virginia. 'I maintain that neither Robert Williams nor I took any documents from these dissidents, and that we had no idea that anything was to be found in the linings of our clothes. I think that these so-called "anti-Soviet materials" must have been put there after our arrest. In any case, I wasn't present when they were "found". Anything could have been planted on us. Diamonds, atomic secrets, whatever you like . . .'

Hm . . . Kugel thought to himself. She hadn't chosen the best way of going about it. But he didn't say so out loud, of course.

'Why did Robert attack the KGB officer, if he didn't know about all these documents?'

'I've already explained that to them today. Robert was shell-shocked when he was fighting in Vietnam. We didn't mention that in the visa applications, as we were afraid the Russians would refuse us permission to come here. But I'm sure you'll be able to confirm to them that he really did get shell-shocked in Vietnam.' Her eyes were almost screaming at Kugel to do so. 'But when we arrived here, we immediately noticed that we were being followed. Robert wanted to go back straight away, but he was afraid that that would look even more suspicious. Besides, he was ill and had a high temperature. And when they arranged this provocation in Leningrad, he said to me that if they tried to arrest us, he wouldn't surrender himself alive. I'm sure that if you ask Washington, they will send documents confirming that Robert was shell-shocked in the Vietnam war, and you can show them to the Russians . . .'

Once again her eyes flared up, almost ordering him to do as she said.

Yes, she's a strange woman, thought Kugel. And she's choosing a strange form of defence. After all, *she* is going to be on trial, not her dead husband. And even if this Robert Williams did fight in Vietnam, why should the Russians have planted anti-Soviet materials in his clothing? It doesn't make sense! Most probably Robert Williams got into contact with these dissidents himself, especially if it was a Russian grenade or shell that made him suffer in Vietnam. He wanted to get his own back on the Soviets, that's obvious. But that's one of the disadvantages of our freedom, he thought. Just imagine an ordinary Soviet citizen arriving in a foreign country and stirring up anti-government feeling off his own bat, without being ordered to do so by the KGB. Yet US citizens can fly wherever they like, do whatever they like. And then you have to come up with ways of getting them out of Turkish prisons, Soviet prisons, or whatever! Just like this Virginia here. Still, I'll have to think of something for her to say, suggest another version of events to her somehow. But how?

'I don't think you knew your husband well enough, Virginia,' he said. 'You only met fairly recently, didn't you? If he fought in Vietnam, that may mean that he had some old scores to settle with the Russians, something which you knew nothing about. And it can't be ruled out that he really did take some anti-Soviet materials from these dissidents and sew them into the linings of your coats, without your knowing anything about it. See what I mean?'

Now it was his turn to cast meaningful looks at her in an attempt to persuade her to accept his version of events. She didn't know anything; her husband had been responsible for everything. 'It's very noble of you to try to defend him now,' that was what his eyes were trying to tell her, 'but he's dead anyway. He was afraid of being found out and acted too hastily, especially when you take his shell-shock into account. But you didn't know anything about these documents, get me?'

Virginia stared at his eyes. She knew what he was getting at. It looked as if they wouldn't be able to say anything else to each other while Colonel Orlov and the prison-governor were present. And she couldn't even mention the names of David MacKerry and Daniel J. Cooper.

'In any case,' Kugel went on, 'you mustn't despair. The

United States Government will do everything it can to secure your release. We are certain that the Soviet side will not be too hard on a woman who was the victim of her husband's unbalanced behaviour.'

'I was told earlier today that I would be imprisoned for a minimum of three years.'

'You must be patient, Virginia. We will do everything in our power to get the sentence reduced and we will insist that one of our lawyers defend you. I don't think the Soviet side will refuse us that,' he added, turning to the colonel. 'What do you think, Mr Orlov?'

But the latter didn't take the bait. 'That's not my decision,' he replied, knowing full well that no foreign barrister had ever been allowed to defend his client in a Soviet court, let alone an American lawyer. Otherwise, what kind of trial would it be? thought the colonel with a smile.

Kugel stood up and was obviously about to say goodbye. Then he asked one final question. 'Virginia, do you have any requests? I've brought you a parcel of food from the Embassy. They'll examine it, of course, but I think they'll let you have it. What would you like me to bring you next time?'

She shrugged her shoulders. 'I don't know. Something nourishing. I think . . . I think, I'm pregnant,' she added with some embarrassment.

Colonel Orlov turned suspiciously towards her, but Kugel literally beamed.

'Ah! but that makes all the difference!' he said. 'That's fantastic! Why didn't you tell me that in the first place, Virginia? I'm sure the Soviet side will show leniency to a pregnant woman. This changes everything.'

When she got back to her cell, Virginia sank on to the floor and burst into tears – for the second time that day. Immediately the tiny hatch on the cell door opened and she heard the guard shout: 'Stand up! Lying on the floor is forbidden! Here, take your food parcel.'

Thereupon the guard threw Larry Kugel's food parcel in

through the hatch. As it fell on to the concrete floor, it burst open and milk streamed out all over the place along with a pile of Florida oranges, ghosts from what seemed now to be her distant past.

Virginia wiped her tears and picked up one of the oranges. But at that moment the door burst open and in rushed two burly guards. They picked her up under the arms and frog-marched her down the corridor and then up some stairs, leading not to one of the interrogation rooms, but to the prison hospital. There a gynaecologist summoned by Orlov examined Virginia in the colonel's presence. The doctor insisted that it was impossible to diagnose pregnancy so early on without carrying out a urine analysis, and that to do that he would need a supply of the scarce German chemical Gravimun.

'OK, damnit!' said the colonel. 'We'll do without the analysis!'

4

The train was heading south towards Yalta. This was the fourth day that Stavinsky had spent wandering up and down the railways of Russia, constantly changing trains and carriages. At first what had driven him from Moscow was simply animal fear, fear for his life, and he had travelled in nothing but second-class coaches, filled with workers and peasants. Everywhere smelt of sweat, soldiers' rough leather boots and unwashed linen. In the open carriages there were children perched on potties, with their parents sitting next to them eating salted herring with fried potatoes and onion. It was only when surrounded by people like this that Stavinsky felt relatively safe. The KGB would hardly be likely to look for him in this part of the train. They would concentrate their search on the first-class coaches which had individual compartments. On the other hand, if they really did start looking for him in earnest, then they would leave no stone unturned. Nothing would help him then, not even the modest stubble which had begun to sprout on his chin, nor the sleeveless quilted jacket which he had bought off somebody at one of the stations. The smart Bulgarian sheepskin which he had been wearing to begin with would have betrayed him immediately. All the same, lying on the top bunk in a second-class coach, covered by a dusty quilt and a grey sheet, your head resting on a padded railway pillow, was preferable to sitting in an individual compartment with fear gnawing constantly away at you, body and soul. You still felt afraid, of course, but talking to the other passengers on the lower bunks helped ease it a little. Over the last four days Stavinsky had found out more about the state of the country than he would have done by spending a whole year in Moscow. Workers from Siberia and the Arctic regions were heading south for their holidays, in search of the warm sun, and they were only too happy to tell their fellow passengers about the enormous salaries which they earned up there in the north. Even so the money just disappeared, because vodka had doubled in price, and even surgical spirit no longer cost the five roubles ninety-eight kopecks it did a few years ago, but twelve roubles a litre! There was no meat to be had, and all you could get anywhere was frozen venison. One family from the Urals were taking their partially blind daughter to get treatment at the famous Filatov clinic in Odessa, and they described how they had had a ration system in their area for the past five years. All food was rationed and you weren't allowed more than one and a half kilos of frozen beef per person per month, just like it was in the war. There was no fresh fruit or vegetables to be had, and the lack of vitamins meant that people's teeth fell out. You could see young people walking about who had two, three or four metal teeth in their mouth. To get vitamin pills you had to stand in line at the chemists' shops, and you just look at the length of the queues when the things were put on sale! Of course, the Poles and Jews were to blame for it all! The Jews did nothing but rob the country, and when there was nothing left to plunder, they simply flew off to Israel or America. And as for the Poles, they were even worse. It was enough that we had to save them from Hitler and the fascists, and then feed them for the next thirty years. Now they had to go on strike as well! Thirty million Poles had already been on strike for a year, and who do you think had been feeding them all that time? Why – us, of course! They spent their time doing bugger-all, or organizing something called 'Solidarity', while we sent them our meat, our butter and our bread. How much longer were we going to carry on feeding them? They all deserved it in the neck! Yes, it was a pity Stalin wasn't around! He'd soon teach them to strike, the scum!

Conversations like these, accompanied by vodka and fried potatoes, soon reminded Stavinsky of life in the Russia which he had forgotten. More often than not, the tables would be adorned with bottles of cheap Algerian wine, which because of its dark colour and sweet aroma, people simply referred to as 'ink'. Vodka had doubled in price and even then was difficult to get hold of, while 'ink' was plentiful as yet, as were potatoes – so long live Mother Russia! She'd survive!

'Drink up, friends! While we've still got something to drink, we'll see them all into the grave, the Chinese and the Poles, fuck them!'

Generous-hearted Russia! Frank, good-hearted souls! If you buy them a bottle of vodka or 'ink', you're a good companion, and they'll pour their hearts out to you. They'll tell you everything that has ever happened to them. Ah, Russia! thought Stavinsky. If you could only get half a glimpse of what America has to offer! He thought of all those supermarkets crammed full of meat and poultry, cheese and sausages, vegetables and fruit, juice and foreign foods. He remembered walking around Vienna with his daughter six years earlier, staring into every shop window filled with smoked sausages and other delicacies that the

Russian language didn't even have words for. Eating meat till you've had your fill. It sounds so simple, yet in Russia it's an impossible dream! Stavinsky remembered from the history he had been taught at school that there had once been meat riots in the Volga basin. Today there was still no meat, and yet the riots didn't happen. The Bolsheviks certainly knew how to pacify Russia! What a fool he was! Why had he come back? The home-sickness of the last six years had been nothing but an irresponsible whim! Just one day spent in a second-class coach, somewhere in Russia, with the sickening smell of sweat and fried potatoes in his nostrils, and that damn home-sickness of his had disappeared in a puff of smoke! What an absolute imbecile! He had dreamed of restoring his youth, of returning to himself as he had been ten years earlier. And he'd done it! His dream had come true! And what was the result? He was trapped! And the best way of getting out of it would be this very minute simply to walk along to the platform connecting the two coaches and throw himself under the wheels of the train . . . What a brave adventurer! And what a coward! thought Stavinsky, pillorying himself more and more. At least make up your mind! Who needs your life now? You buried yourself once, when you settled down as an ordinary dental technician in Portland. Then you buried yourself again, at the cemetery in New Jersey. Why not bury yourself for a third time – here in Russia. And do it properly this time!

Well, he didn't throw himself under the train, of course. Stavinsky was just an ordinary human being, no more of a coward or a hero than anybody else. And the greatest punishment he could devise for himself was simply to lock himself in the lavatory and hit his head against the wall of the carriage (but not too hard), weeping and calling himself a half-wit and a moron . . .

But after three days spent travelling, the fear of being arrested began to ease and he stopped leaping down from his bunk, impatient to leave the train at the nearest station and board another one heading in a different direction. Not that he had suddenly got any braver or said farewell to his fear. It was just that he had become accustomed to it, as a man gets used to an illness, even a fatal one, or a wounded soldier gets used to the piece of shrapnel embedded in his spine.

Then he decided to travel to Yalta, to visit this 'Aunt Olga' of his who had 'always loved him' and whom he knew to be connected with David MacKerry. Let them smuggle him out of the country right away, let them hide him in the hold of some foreign ship, even if he had to stay hidden for a week or a month, until it steamed out through the Dardanelles . . . He'd put up with anything! Yes, Yalta, that was where he must go! And right away, before he got caught, before he got arrested and recognized.

So before he reached the Urals, Stavinsky got off the Khabarovsk train and transferred to another one going to Simferopol. Now he was heading for the south, the sun, the sea and 'Aunt Olga'. But the less he was bothered by fear, the more he was assailed by thoughts of Virginia. What had happened to her? Would the KGB be torturing her? And would she already have betrayed his real identity? Or perhaps she had pretended to the KGB that they really had killed her husband, Robert Williams? In that case, they might have apologized and let her go. She might already be in America. In that case, he was saved, or almost saved . . . But how could he find out? Of course! 'Aunt Olga' would tell him. She might not be very pleased to see him roll up in Yalta out of the blue, but he had to find out whether the Soviets thought he was still alive or not . . .

Dear Virginia! Of course, they would already have let her go. There would have been an enormous international outcry! They had killed an American tourist! The US Government had probably already lodged a protest with the Soviet Union. Perhaps Reagan had even made a personal phone call to Brezhnev. What would it cost him to do that, after all? What a fool he was! Here he had been, shaking with fear for the last four days, travelling about in these stinking railway carriages, while Virginia was most likely already back in America. The KGB wouldn't be searching for anybody, either Yuryshev, who was supposedly still on vacation, or himself, Stavinsky, who left the USSR with his daughter six years ago and had since been living in the USA. So things weren't that bad as yet, Stavinsky said to himself. Everything was OK so far. If the KGB had really been searching for him, they would have found him a long time ago. And as they hadn't, that meant that it hadn't occurred to them to start looking for him! You're alive, Stavinsky, alive! First you were buried in New Jersey, and then you got a bullet in your head at Sheremetyevo. But now you are sitting in the dirty restaurant car of the train travelling from Irkutsk to Simferopol, drinking watered-down Zhigulovskoye beer and stuffing yourself with cold macaroni. But the point is: you are alive! And that means that you'll stay alive, goddamnit!

Thus Stavinsky's mood see-sawed between fear and hope, and back again as he crossed Russia on those lumbering long-distance trains. Through the windows he could see the gloomy, snow-covered forests and bleak plains of Russia, leaden snow-laden skies and sometimes a red sun, devoid of heat. Spending hour after hour in these second-class coaches was more like living in an army barracks or some mobile prison camp, rolling around the immense expanses of Russia from west to east, from one barbed-wire fence to another. People spent their time sleeping and drinking, telling each other jokes and quietly cursing the Government and collective farms. In the spaces between the coaches you would find soldiers on leave pressing spotty young girls tight up against the wall. But when the train stopped at a station, all the second-class passengers would unite in their silent hatred of the occupants of the two first-class coaches. They would stare resentfully at these men in their fashionable imported clothes who paraded up and down the platform, giving the eye to any pretty young girls who happened to be sitting in one of our coaches and inviting her along to theirs.

All Stavinsky's meditations while lying on his bunk or sitting at the table in the restaurant car had convinced him that his home-sickness for Russia had been nothing other than an ex-con's nostalgia for his former prison camp, except that, in Stavinsky's case, the camp had been Russia as a whole, and far from being an ordinary convict, he had possessed extraordinary privileges. And all because he hadn't had to work in a factory or on a collective farm. He had been in television, a camp freelance, so to speak. Privilege – that was all your home-sickness amounted to, Stavinsky, he said to himself contemptuously.

Meanwhile, some beer had been loaded on to the train at Bursak, and the restaurant car was suddenly invaded by a group of tipsy young rustics. One of the lads was carrying a Spidola transistor radio, which was blaring out jazz obviously from a foreign radio station. Stavinsky wasn't pleased at having to move over towards the window to let the boys occupy the spare seats at his table. They took over the table in front of him and behind him too. He knew in advance what they would get up to. They would buy two crates of beer among seven, then, when the waiter wasn't looking, they would fill their glasses with home-made vodka, sprinkle a bit of beer in it to give it colour and proceed to drink it to the accompaniment of much shouting and swearing, until they reached the next station. Then they would get off, board a train back to Bursak and do the same thing again in that restaurant car. And after they had got off, another group of 'beer-enthusiasts' would probably get on to take their place . . .

He suddenly heard a voice speaking in English at the table behind him. It was the radio. Stavinsky was certain that they would switch it off straight away, now that the jazz had finished. But the lads paid no attention to what the radio was saying. They carried on with their own conversation (one of them was telling the story of a fight in their village). Meanwhile, the announcer carried on speaking in that free-and-easy manner, which Stavinsky had grown accustomed to, while being in the West. 'Nobody gives you as much music as your favourite radio station. But now it's time for the latest news. The American newspaper the *Baltimore Evening Sun* has reported that the father of John Hinckley, the man who shot at President Reagan, is about to take the US Government to court, because, he says, his son doesn't feel very well in prison and is tired of being constantly interrogated. John Hinckley has been question over several months now, and, according to his father: "That is enough to wear anybody out." In Vienna a member of the Austrian police has been arrested, accused of spying for Romania. Four days ago a KGB officer named Neznachny and an American tourist called Robert Williams from Maryland were killed at the Sheremetyevo International Airport in Moscow. Robert Williams was spending his honeymoon in Moscow with Hollywood actress, Virginia Part. UPI reported today that Miss Part, who tried to defend her husband, will be put on trial by the Soviet authorities, accused of taking part in the murder of a KGB officer. Rumour has it that the Russians intend to sentence her to three years' imprisonment and send her to one of their labour camps. An American lawyer has been refused permission to defend her at the trial. You might well ask what on earth could have persuaded Mr and Mrs Williams to spend their honeymoon in Russia when United Airlines can offer all newly-weds the holiday of a lifetime on the wonderful islands of the Caribbean for only $650 per week! Just $650 all-inclusive, with a hired car thrown-in and no KGB agents hanging around your neck! Fly United Airlines! And now we're going to play a current favourite: "Meet me at the corner" . . .'

The music started up again and the boys increased the volume. But Stavinsky wasn't listening any more. He was sitting there, completely stunned. Virginia was in prison! And she hadn't betrayed him!

5

Stavinsky didn't travel as far as Yalta after all. The next morning he got off the train in Krasnodar, the chief town of the Kuban Region. The weather was fairly warm, plus eight centrigrade, and the empty station square was bathed in light from the mild autumn sun.

In the station lavatory, Stavinsky shaved himself with his electric razor and put on the clean shirt and suit which he had been 'given' by the luggage locker at the Yaroslavl Station in Moscow. As for the quilted jacket which he had bought himself, he had no need of it any more, so he stuffed it into a rubbish-bin as far as it would go. After handing his suitcase in at the left-luggage office, he walked out on to the station forecourt. The quiet and sleepy southern town lay at his feet. Dozing on the benches while they waited for the next local train were a few collective farm women, wearing printed cotton shawls, and with shopping-bags full of bread pressed tightly in between their feet. A man selling roasted sunflower seeds was standing in front of the closed beer kiosk.

Stavinsky got on a trolley bus and travelled as far as the city centre. He had been in Krasnodar about ten years earlier and vaguely remembered having seen a big multiple store with a radio department somewhere in the middle of the town. Every big city had such a store, in any case. On the way to the centre, the trolley bus filled up, mainly with women who caught his attention immediately because of their massive hairstyles. Every one of them had her hair piled up high in a mass of ash-blonde curls. Even the woman driving the trolley bus, a big-breasted Kuban cossack, had her hair dyed and styled in the same way. When the conductress called out Lenin Avenue, Stavinsky suddenly saw the local department store on the other side of the street and quickly got off. The wide road was divided into two by an avenue of tall Kuban poplars and rows of flowerbeds with bright autumn flowers. The benches in between were occupied by grandmothers with prams and students reading books. Every hundred yards there were hoardings with portraits of Brezhnev and exhortations like: 'Let Us Give Our Country One Million Tonnes of Rice,' 'Let Us Complete the Five-Year Plan in Four Years,' 'Forward to the Victory of Communism!' and so on.

On the ground floor of the department store there was a long queue of people standing noisily in line for enamel saucepans. But the radio department on the next floor was empty. The shelves were full of Ruby and Tempo colour televisions as well as heavy Riga-10 radio sets.

'You haven't got any Spidolas, I suppose?' Stavinsky said to the sleepy shop assistant.

'You must be joking!' she replied.

The Spidola is a small, compactly built transistor radio and is always in short supply. That hasn't changed in six years! thought Stavinsky.

'Does the Riga-10 have short wave?'

'Yes it does. Are you going to buy one?'

'Yes.'

'That'll be 144 roubles. Pay at the cash-desk.'

Holding the ten- or eleven-pound radio set by its handle, Stavinsky left the shop. Half an hour later another trolley bus had taken him to the Park of Culture on the outskirts of the town. In the park the paths were all covered with autumn leaves, which crushed beneath his feet. The benches were full of courting couples, most of them locked in a motionless embrace and with radios or tape-recorders blaring out foreign pop music. Carrying a transistor radio about with you has become as fashionable with Soviet youth as it is with the blacks on 42nd Street in New York, he thought with a smile. Knowing no English, many of the youngsters couldn't tell the difference between an advertisement for jeans or hamburgers and modern jazz or pop music. Walking among these courting couples was like going from one radio station to another.

In the depths of the park he caught sight of the grey-looking waters of the sluggish River Kuban. Stavinsky found a bench in a place where it was open and there were no people around. If anybody were to approach him, he would have time to retune the radio . . .

He switched on his Riga-10 and began to look for the Voice of America, the BBC, Deutsche Welle or Radio Liberty. These radio stations broadcast in Russian, Ukrainian and other languages, specially for listeners in the Soviet Union, and they usually carry more news to do with the USSR than most of the other Western stations. Half an hour later Stavinsky was fully conversant with whatever had been going on in the world. Lech Walesa had called on all trade unions in the free world to support Solidarity and to increase their emergency food supplies to the striking Polish workers; in England a former Deputy Chief of British Naval Intelligence, John Moore, had published a book, arguing that the Soviet Union now possessed the largest fleet of submarines and mine-laying ships in the world; Brezhnev was about to visit Bonn; the West German Government had announced that the contract to supply West Germany with Soviet gas would strengthen economic ties between the two countries; during the following week the Central Committee of the Polish Communist Party was intending to discuss measures designed to put an end to industrial chaos in the country and save the economy.

Ah, at last!

'The trial took place in Moscow today of US citizen, Virginia Williams. The Soviet authorities have accused Mrs Williams of attempting to smuggle *samizdat* materials out of the Soviet Union and also of affording armed resistance to KGB officials when they tried to examine their luggage at Sheremetyevo Airport. As we reported earlier, one KGB officer was killed during this incident, along with Mrs Williams's husband, the American dentist Robert Williams. During a meeting with a representative of the US Embassy in Moscow, Mrs Williams informed him that she was pregnant. In spite of this, an American lawyer was refused permission to defend this American citizen at her trial. The trial took place *in camera*, and no foreign journalists were allowed in to report the proceedings. According to an announcement issued by the US Embassy in Moscow, the court sentenced Mrs Virginia Williams to three years' imprisonment. Western experts interpret this trial as a warning to foreign tourists, many of whom, when they arrive in the USSR, attempt to make contact with dissidents and Jewish activists. Merano. At the World Chess Championship in Merano Viktor Korchnoi has lost the eighteenth game to Anatoly Karpov. As a result Anatoly Karpov has retained the title of world champion . . .'

Stavinsky switched off the radio. Virginia was pregnant. His wife and his child were now in a Soviet jail! He knew what that would mean! As soon as she gave birth, the child would be taken from her and placed in a children's home. No! Anything but that! Anything but that!! Of course, the US Embassy would beg the Kremlin authorities to give a pregnant woman early release, but a fat lot of difference such requests would make to the Kremlin. They knew very well that the White House wouldn't make a great deal of fuss about some Hollywood extra. At best some Western feminist organization would send Brezhnev a tearful or threatening petition. And that would be the end of it. Carter hadn't even managed to get the American hostages out of Teheran, until Khomeini was ready to give them up himself. Anyway, it wasn't even worth thinking about it! One of the things that had most shocked Stavinsky in the United States was the discovery that he had made within a week of arriving there. The Americans were afraid of the Soviets! The great United States, the bugbear of every Soviet boy and girl, the country whose inevitable decision to attack the Soviet Union has been used by every Soviet leader from Stalin to Khrushchev and Brezhnev as a justification for building up Russia's armed forces – the mighty and wealthy United States turned out to have a manic fear of the Soviet Union! So how could he expect the

Americans to quarrel with the Russians just because of some woman called Virginia Williams, even if she was pregnant? No, thought Stavinsky. A drowning man must save himself.

He looked around. It was quiet and there was nobody about. The grey river rippled slowly past the sloping, leaf-strewn banks. You could hear the sound of frogs croaking. The mild autumn sun was reflected in the water. But his wife and his child were far away – in a Moscow jail.

Stavinsky stood up, holding the radio set which was of no further use to him. He took a decision. Yes! A drowning man must save himself! He swung his arm and hurled the radio into the river. It made a splash and sank immediately.

An hour later Stavinsky was sitting in the Krasnodar Public Library. In the medical section he found what he wanted – information about retrograde amnesia from the *Transactions of the Moscow Psychoneurological Institute*. Those three years that his mother forced him to spend at the Medical Institute would come in handy after all!

In an article written by one Leonid Dondysh, MD, entitled 'Concussion and Its After-Effects', he read the following: 'Concussion of the brain may lead to a breakdown in the functioning of the nervous system. In the majority of cases a partial or total loss of consciousness occurs for a short time . . . When the patient recovers consciouness, he may experience headaches, nausea, vomiting, vertigo and retrograde amnesia, that is to say, loss of memory. The patient is unable to remember what happened or the circumstances which caused the injury. Often he may forget many of the episodes in his life which preceded the injury. His sense of time and space may be dislocated. Depending on the degree and seriousness of the injury, his memory may return to him immediately, or in a few hours or days. On the other hand, it may not return for years. Unfortunately, medical science throughout the world has not yet come up with a means of determining the degree of retrograde amnesia or of curing it. Even if electroencephalograms and X-ray photographs of the head and internal organs together with analyses of the blood fail to reveal any serious injury to the brain, the patient may nevertheless suffer amnesia for months. In that case, the task of medical personnel must be to create the conditions necessary for the patient's general recovery, e.g. the bringing in of close friends and relatives who, by reminding the patient of his past life, may be able to trigger off the process of memory recovery within him. Treatment: to dispel headaches – intravenous injections of glucose and calcium chloride, and magnesium sulphate, together with intravenous and intra-muscular injections of vitamins B1 and B6. Further reading: D. Fedotov, "Psychoses Resulting from Injuries to the Brain"; B. Shefer, "Curing Brain Injury" . . .'

Stavinsky sat in the library until evening, reading books on retrograde amnesia and textbooks on clinical otorhinolaryngology: 'In order to treat tumours on the vocal chords,' he read, 'surgical intervention is necessary. However, surgery will alter the length of the vocal chords, which in its turn may bring about local or partial voice distortion and hoarseness . . .'

That same evening Stavinsky boarded a train for Moscow.

When he arrived back at the Yaroslavl Station, he retrieved Yuryshev's knapsack from the left-luggage locker and left for Kirov.

The next morning Stavinsky's train thundered over the bridge across the frozen River Vyatka. Through the carriage windows he could see lots of men and boys sitting along the river bank, fishing through holes in the ice. Behind them he could see smoke coming from the bonfires which they had made.

6

Department of State,
Washington DC, 20520

To: Mr Daniel J. Cooper,
Head of Russian Section,
CIA,
Washington DC

Dear Mr Cooper,

In view of your interest in the trial of US citizen Mrs Virginia Williams in Moscow, I am sending you a copy of the report which we have received from our Embassy official, Mr Larry Kugel, who represented the US Embassy at Mrs Williams's trial in Moscow yesterday.

I assume that the speed with which the trial was arranged, was the result of the Soviet side's customary unwillingness to allow a US lawyer to travel to Moscow to defend the accused or to present in court documentary material relating to Dr Robert Williams's military service in the Vietnam war (about which Mrs Williams was so insistent during her first meeting with Mr Kugel). Personally I am surprised that she should have been so insistent about producing materials, since Robert Williams's name does not appear in lists of Vietnam war-participants.

If the Williamses' trip to Moscow was in any way connected with the work of the CIA in the Soviet Union, then you ought to send an appropriate report about it to the State Department immediately.

Yours,
Richard Malvick,
Assistant Secretary of State

Enclosure: text of Mr Larry Kugel's report on the trial of Mrs Virginia Williams, held in Moscow on 21 November 1981.
22 November 1981

From Mr L. Kugel's Report

. . . At 9.00 a.m. on 21 November 1981 Mr A. Vlasov, an official of the Soviet Foreign Ministry, informed me by telephone that the trial of US citizen, Mrs Virginia Williams, would take place that same day at noon at the Moscow City Court and that I, or any other representative of the US Embassy, might attend as observers.

When I asked whether the US Embassy could send its own lawyer or legal consultant to defend Mrs Williams, Mr Vlasov informed me that the court had already nominated a Soviet lawyer, Mrs Lyudmila Borisovna Lidina, to defend Mrs Williams.

When I arrived at the Moscow City Court just before midday, I discovered that the building was being guarded by the militia. The correspondent of the *Washington Herald*, Jacob Stevenson; the Associated Press, Jennifer Ronalds; and Reuter's, Morris Inger, tried to enter the court building, but they were prevented from doing so. I myself was allowed in only after a long and painstaking examination of my credentials.

Before the proceedings began, I was allowed to talk to Mrs Williams's lawyer, Mrs Lidina, a member of the Moscow Bar. I informed her that her client was pregnant and that she should take account of that fact when presenting her defence. However, it turned out that there was scarcely anything for us to discuss. This is what the lawyer said to me: 'This lady of yours is feigning pregnancy, but she won't get away with that sort of thing in our courts! In my opinion, her guilt is already fully proved, and the only thing she can rely on is the leniency which may be shown her by a Soviet court of law.' It transpired that Mrs Lidina met her client for the first time when the latter was already in the court room. She spoke to her for five minutes at the maximum in the presence of the guard which had conducted Mrs Williams from prison.

The actual trial was obviously a put-up job and lasted exactly seventeen minutes. Judge Petrukhina read out the indictment and, as none of the prosecution witnesses had appeared in court, declared that their affidavits had been placed on file and taken into account by the bench. After this, public prosecutor Ksanchuk declared that US citizen Mrs Virginia Williams stood accused of crimes under Articles 17-66, 70 and 193 of the RSFSR Criminal Code, and that her guilt was fully proved by the material evidence and affidavits, already painstakingly examined by the court. In particular, Mrs Williams was accused of aiding and abetting an act of terrorism committed by her now deceased husband Robert Williams, as well as of engaging in anti-Soviet agitation and propaganda by receiving and concealing anti-Soviet materials, with a view to smuggling them out of the country. She was also accused of affording violent resistance to Soviet officials at Sheremetyevo Airport, when they were attempting to put an end to her criminal activities. And although these charges, when taken together, could add up to the death penalty, the prosecutor said that he would ask the court to show this US citizen an example of Soviet leniency by sentencing her to three years' imprisonment in a 'hard regime' corrective labour colony.

Speaking on behalf of the defence, Mrs Lidina thanked the public prosecutor for the lenient attitude which he had shown towards her client and emphasized that, as a Soviet citizen herself, she was appalled by the crimes which Mrs Williams had committed, although the later had not admitted her guilt. Mrs Lidina asked the court not to go beyond the punishment proposed by the prosecution and begged forgiveness on behalf of her client who, according to her, had not realized that the way to get the court to show clemency was not to deny what she had done, but to make a full and frank confession.

In view of the fact that Mrs Williams had a poor command of Russian and that the court could not understand English, Judge Petrukhina deprived Mrs Williams of the right to say anything in her own defence. My offer to act as interpreter was turned down by the judge on the grounds that the court would be unable to judge the adequacy of my translation.

After this the judge and people's assessors left the court room to deliberate amongst themselves, returning four minutes later with the verdict. Judge Petrukhina passed the sentence which the prosecution had requested.

Despite my insistence, the court refused me permission to meet Mrs Williams after the trial. She was escorted from the building under guard and transported to the Moscow Transit prison at Krasnaya Presnya.

7

In Kirov the weather was already freezing – it was twelve centigrade below. The low, snow-covered buildings of the town made it look more like a barracks than ever. The food shops were absolutely empty. There was no meat, no sausages, no milk, no cheese. The only things available were loaves of damp black bread, more like the sort of thing you get in prison, macaroni and cheap tinned fish . . . cod and bullheads in tomato sauce. And all you could get in the wine and spirit shops were cheap port and expensive Streletskaya vodka at eight roubles a time. Stavinsky bought a bottle of vodka, two tins of fish and a loaf of bread. In another shop, he bought himself an axe, a fishing rod and a few fish-hooks.

Before leaving the train he had changed back into Yuryshev's clothes – his worn leather jacket, sweater, quilted trousers and fur hunting boots. As a result, there was little to distinguish him from all the other fishermen seated along the river bank, fishing not so much for the pleasure of it as in an attempt somehow or other to get something for their families to eat.

Stavinsky walked down snow-covered Sovetskaya Street towards the river. Many horse-drawn sledges and carts went past him, as did lorries. Rime-covered horses, steam coming from their nostrils, trudged on up the street, urged on by the loud shouts and curses of their drivers. The local boys, with skates attached to their felt boots, would scatter as they passed, some attempting to hitch a lift off the sledges by catching long wire hooks on the back of them and careering on up the steep road. The others would hurtle down towards the river under their own steam, on skates or on sledges, whooping and whistling, rolling on down the steep bank towards the ice-covered river at top speed.

Slipping and sliding, Stavinsky reached the river's edge himself and walked on down a ready-made path in the snow, past all the fishermen sitting with their backs towards him, past their camp fires, deeper and deeper into the undergrowth and trees. At last he found what he wanted – a secluded spot near an abandoned ice-hole which was already beginning to freeze over again. Nearby were the remains of an old camp fire, not used for a day or two and half covered with a sprinkling of fresh snow. Stavinsky opened up the ice-hole again with his axe, dropped his empty fishing line into it, secured it to the ground with Yuryshev's knapsack and an ice-covered stone, and then set about the main task of the day. He gathered a few dry branches together and kindled a fire on the old ashes. Anybody looking at him from a distance would have taken him for a real fisherman, just like the dozens of others seated along the bank. The only difference was that periodically he would look cautiously around and then remove some objects from the suitcase which he was sitting on next to the camp fire. These were the things which he had retrieved from the left-luggage locker and he was burning them to ashes. First of all he disposed of all the forged documents made out in the name of Romanov and Rozov: two passports, two work record books, two military service books and a diploma from the Saratov Medical Institute. He had to stir the ashes very carefully, breaking them up with a dry stick, because the various identity booklets retained their shape, even when completely burnt. Once he had done this, Stavinsky took a breather and had a slug of vodka. It was all over. There was no turning back. Now he was Sergey Ivanovich Yuryshev, an Assistant Director of Strategic Planning at Soviet Army General HQ. All he had to do now was burn the money, the imported Hungarian suit, Yuryshev's shirts and the sheepskin coat, and – most important of all: 'lose' Yuryshev's memory and all his expert knowledge. Then he would have to get concussion and amnesia. He would be able to imitate Yuryshev's hoarse voice without undergoing surgery on his vocal chords, however.

8

REPORT

To: Chief of the Moscow–Gorky Railway Militia,
Colonel I. R. Gorbunkov

At 19.30 hours on 25 November 1981 Citizen Sergey Ivanovich Yuryshev caused a disturbance in the restaurant car of train No 78, bound from Kirov to Moscow, on the stretch between Kirov and Kotelnich, not very far from the station Bystryaga. Being already in a drunken state, Yuryshev asked the waiter for beer and champagne, neither of which were available in the restaurant car. He then went on to shout abuse at a group of soldiers going home on leave, who were attempting to calm him down. A fight ensued as a result of which Citizen Kvinikhidze, the director of the restaurant car, forbade the bartender to sell Yuryshev any vodka. Threatening to find vodka in any case, Citizen Yuryshev opened the door of carriage number six and jumped from the moving train. This forced the guard, Comrade P. O. Timofeyev, to stop the train at 19.52 hours. The crew and passengers found Citizen Yuryshev lying next to the track in an unconscious state. He was carried back to the train and delivered to the first aid post at Kotelnich Station. Comrade Timofeyev searched the victim's pockets in the presence of the other passengers and found a passport, military service book and other official identity papers in the name of Sergey Ivanovich Yuryshev, a colonel at Soviet Army General Headquarters, as well as money to the sum of 218 roubles. In view of the victim's important position, he was immediately transferred to the surgical ward at Kotelnich Municipal Hospital No 1. I immediately informed the Kotelnich Military Commander, Major D. M. Krivorukov, of what had happened.

Head of the Kotelnich Station Militia
Captain P. C. Zarubin

Kotelnich, 25 November 1981
22.15 hours

PRIORITY
BY SPECIAL MILITARY TELEGRAPH

To: Duty Officer,
General Headquarters,
Major-General L. T. Ovcharenko

Telegram

In connection with your order, received in telegram No

217-S, I have to report the following:

Colonel S. I. Yuryshev has been transferred to a private room in the surgical ward at Kotelnich Municipal Hospital No 1. The doctors have come to the conclusion that, although the colonel is no longer unconscious, he is suffering from retrograde amnesia or complete loss of memory, as a result of concussion caused by his fall from the train. Despite this, I have carried out your order to ensure the safety of any State or military secrets known to Yuryshev, by placing an armed guard outside his room twenty-four hours a day. In view of the patient's serious condition (vomiting, headaches, vertigo, fracture of the right arm and injury to the lower jaw), the doctors are of the opinion that he cannot be transported to Moscow for another two or three days.

Military Commander, Kotelnich,
Major D. M. Krivorukov

Kotelnich, 26 November 1981
00.55 hours

To: Head of the USSR Defence Ministry Central Medical Directorate, General F. I. Komarov

Order No 89/762

In connection with the injuries suffered by Assistant Director of Strategic Planning at General HQ, Colonel S. I. Yuryshev, when he fell from a train, I command that:

Colonel S. I. Yuryshev be immediately transported from Kotelnich Municipal Hospital No 1 and transferred to a military hospital in Moscow. The doctors there are to take whatever measures may be necessary to restore Colonel Yuryshev to health in the shortest possible time.

First Deputy Chief of Staff,
General S. F. Akhromeyev

Moscow, General HQ
26 November 1981

Handwritten postscript
Fyodor Ivanovich! We need to do all we can to get Yuryshev back to normal health. He's one of our best and most talented officers. Family troubles – the death of his son and his separation from his wife – have knocked him off balance. Keep an eye on the course of his recovery yourself. Whatever you ask us for, will be provided. Do you need any special medicines from abroad? Let me know when Yuryshev can be visited by Marshal Oparkov and other officers from General HQ.

Yours,
Akhromeyev

To: First Deputy Chief of Staff
General S. F. Akhromeyev

Report on the Execution of Order No 89/762
In accordance with order No 89/762 of 26 November 1981, Colonel Sergey Ivanovich Yuryshev was transferred today from Kotelnich to Military Hospital No 214/67 near Moscow. Because of his fractured arm and the damage to his jaw, he has been placed in a surgical ward. His condition is satisfactory. Doctors at the hospital are doing all they can to dispel the headaches and other after-effects of concussion. The electroencephalograms and X-rays taken of his head and internal organs immediately after he arrived in hospital have revealed no serious damage to his vital organs, which gives us reason to hope that the patient will make a full recovery. However, neither Soviet nor foreign medical science has yet invented drugs which will cure retrograde amnesia. For this reason, the most important factor in restoring Colonel Yuryshev's memory may well be regular visits from his relatives and colleagues at work. I imagine that it will be possible to begin such visits in a few days' time, when the patient's headaches have ceased.

I have informed both Colonel B. R. Levitsky, the

director of the hospital, and Colonel L. P. Tarusov, in charge of the surgical department, that Marshal Oparkov is personally interested in Colonel Yuryshev's recovery in the shortest possible time.

Head of the Defence Ministry Central Medical Directorate,

General F. I. Komarov

28 November, 1981

9

Military Hospital No 214/67 is situated on the outskirts of Moscow, beyond Sokolniki, and stands in its own grounds, surrounded by a high brick wall. It is a long, white, six-storey building, with large windows and warm, spacious wards. For the first week or so, Stavinsky-Yuryshev continued to simulate headaches, vertigo and nausea, as he was afraid of meeting Yuryshev's former friends and fellow officers. But he refused to have a special room to himself right from the beginning, saying that he was afraid of being left alone. After all, the main purpose of this risky undertaking was precisely to put himself in Yuryshev's shoes and at least find something out about officers' manners and customs. They put him in a ward with five other officers, where he listened avidly to the endless conversations of young lieutenants and captains, wounded in Afghanistan and now on the mend. They were all grateful to have got out of Afghanistan with nothing but bullet-wounds or shell-shock to show for it. And they didn't bother to conceal their rejoicing either. On the next floor down were patients who had fared infinitely worse. The first floor contained wards for soldiers and officers who had fallen foul of the Soviet Army's own chemical weapons and gas attacks. In fact, among themselves the other patients referred to this floor unofficially as the 'gas chamber', and they were strictly forbidden to enter it. And they weren't the only ones. The ordinary hospital staff had nothing to do with what went on in those wards, either. New patients arrived only at night, which was when they took away the corpses, too. Even to talk about the place had been strictly forbidden by the hospital authorities. All the same, everybody in the hospital knew that the 'gas chamber' contained soldiers who were paralysed, their skin completely discoloured and rotting from the effects of the poison gas. Accidents like this would happen when the winds blowing through the Afghan mountain passes suddenly changed direction, just as the Soviet soldiers were mounting a routine gas attack on Afghan villages or partisan detachments, and a cloud of the greenish-yellow gas would blow back on to the attackers. This led to paralysis and cutaneous irritation, followed by incurable rotting of the skin. There were only two ways out of the 'gas chamber': either straight to the mortuary, or, at least to begin with, to a closed convalescent asylum.

That was why all the other patients outside these wards were, more often than not, astonishingly cheerful, considering what they had gone through. They knew that once they were discharged from hospital, there would be no sending them back to Afghanistan. They would either be invalided out or sent to garrisons on the 'home front', that was how they put it. For them the occupation of Afghanistan was a real war, and soldiers serving anywhere in the Soviet Union itself were safely 'behind the lines'. Phrases like these, along with 'auto-pilot', 'bunker', 'arms-dump', 'homing device', 'strike capability', and any amount of military slang, Stavinsky would eagerly imbibe. Then, with his eyes closed beneath his gauze bandage, he would repeat them silently to himself several times, so as to learn them off by heart.

Strangely enough, the officers hardly ever talked about the Afghan war itself. Instead they would tell stories and jokes about officers' training schools, barrack life and, of course, women. Only at night would these twenty-five-year-old lads have unquiet dreams, and then they would start gnashing their teeth and screaming 'Fire!' or 'Mother!'. Once Stavinsky was standing in the lavatory, which also served the patients as a smoking-room. Wincing with the pain from his broken jaw, he asked one of these young officers, Lieutenant Lavrov it was, a question.

'You spent half the night shouting "Fire!" What were you dreaming about?' Lavrov's grey eyes stared at him through silky young eyelashes.

'You're lucky to be suffering with what you've got, Comrade Colonel,' he said to him quietly. 'If only I could lose my memory, like you . . .'

Then gloomily, he stamped out his unfinished cigarette and returned to the ward.

But that very night Stavinsky discovered what it was these officers dreamed about. In the early hours of the morning there was a sudden commotion in the ward next door. Second Lieutenant Vasilevsky, a burly helicopter pilot who had suffered shell-shock and multiple burns, suddenly came crawling out of the room, shouting and tearing the dressings from his wounds. A week before, Vasilevsky's helicopter had been shot down by Afghan rebels near Kandahar. The plane had caught fire, and it was only a miracle and the protection afforded by the snow on the mountain slope where the 'copter had ditched, that enabled Vasilevsky to escape with his life. Now, in the middle of the night, the lieutenant had crawled out of his ward, scaring the duty nurse half to death as he did so. There he was, wildly climbing up the fire-escape on all fours and heading for the roof. Some medical orderlies finally caught up with him, when he was already up there, covered with snow. They tied him up and dragged him back down to the ward. But smeared all over with pus and blood from his half-healed wounds, he managed to get away from them and started to scream. 'They've come to get me! They've come to get me!'

The duty doctor appeared and gave Vasilevsky an

injection. That calmed him down, and he burst into tears. 'Children, it wasn't me who killed you . . .' he whispered. 'Children, it wasn't me who killed you . . . I was made to do it!'

Twenty minutes later an ambulance arrived to take Vasilevsky away to a psychiatric hospital. The doctors and nurses made everybody go back to their beds, but there was no more sleep for any of the officers in Stavinsky's ward that night. Although it was strictly forbidden, they spent their time chain-smoking, not saying a word to each other. Two of the more mobile ones, Lavrov and Captain Sysoyev, stood over by the window with the ventilation-hatch open, and stared outside at the falling snow. When the duty doctor entered the ward, he winced at the smell of tobacco smoke but said nothing.

'Comrades,' he said finally, 'won't you take a sedative?'

Captain Sysoyev spun round on his one leg and crutches to face the doctor. 'We don't need sedatives. They won't help. Now a bottle of spirit . . .'

'I'm not allowed to,' said the doctor.

'And what if I go off my rocker, too?' asked Sysoyev quietly, gripping his crutches so tightly that you could see that his knuckles were white. 'Or do you think that the rest of us don't dream about children gassed or crushed by tanks in Bagrāme, Kunduz and Panjshir? Shall I carry on?'

The doctor stared at him. Then he turned round sharply and walked out of the ward. A few moments later he was back again with a litre retort more than two thirds full of pure surgical spirit.

'This is all I could find,' he said. 'But the refectory is closed, and there's nothing to eat . . .'

'We'll manage,' Sysoyev replied. He poured the spirit into tumblers, and then looked at Stavinsky hesitantly. 'Will you be drinking with us, Comrade Colonel?' he asked.

'No,' said Stavinsky, well aware of the insatiable looks of the other officers. 'I don't have any dreams. There's no need to pour any out for me.'

There were no toasts or clinking of glasses. They each downed the alcohol at one gulp and in silence. Eventually they all fell into a dreamless sleep. Or at least they had no nightmares.

10

After a week or so, Stavinsky had become accustomed to hospital life and responded automatically to 'Comrade Colonel', 'Yuryshev' or 'Sergey Ivanovich'. The officers returned to swapping stories and jokes all day long, studiously avoiding any talk of the war in Afghanistan and the episode with Vasilevsky. They just laughed a little louder than was absolutely necessary and they made even more effort to chat up the young nurses. They were particularly assiduous in playing practical jokes on new patients in the ordinary soldiers' wards, too, lads who would arrive in hospital, not from Afghanistan, but from the 'home front', diagnosed as having inflammation of the gall-bladder, stomach ulcers, diabetes, hypertonia and other 'trifling' complaints. Both the doctors and the 'real' patients, i.e. those who had been wounded in Afghanistan, believed that many of these new arrivals were merely feigning illness, in order to get invalided out of the army or officers' training schools. (And in many cases they were right.) Some of those who complained of hypertonia would swallow enormous amounts of caffeine and codeine, and you could simulate the symptoms of a stomach ulcer by swallowing chloride of lime wrapped up in tiny balls of bread. One Ukrainian lad called Zhmenya tried proving to the doctors that he had diabetes, because of the way he had to drink at least a dozen jugs of water each day, to slake his thirst. Two pranks were particular favourites of the officers: 'perspiration analysis' and the 'enema treatment'. Whenever a new patient arrived at the hospital, the nurse would place two jars on his bedside table, one marked 'Urine Analysis', the other marked 'Faeces Analysis'. This was the crucial moment. Somebody had to divert the attention of nurse and patient so that another jar, marked 'Perspiration Analysis' this time, could be placed next to the other two. Now, when the new arrival noticed these three containers next to his bed, he would often ask his fellow patients for advice.

'Listen, lads. I understand about urine, but how do I give them any sweat for analysis?'

The officers would do their best to keep a straight face and tell him in a fairly off-hand manner that he would have to lie down on his bed, cover himself with several blankets, or preferably two or three mattresses, and start sweating. He'd then have to collect up the sweat with a bit of cotton wool and squeeze it into the jar. After that, they carefully helped him heave a few mattresses on top of himself. Then they would invite friends and acquaintances from all over the hospital to come and watch the poor fool sweat away and try to squeeze the damp cotton wool into the glass container. It was strictly forbidden for anybody to laugh while this was going on, but the other soldiers were allowed to offer the new lad various pieces of advice.

'Where are you getting the sweat from? Under your armpits? Don't be an idiot! You'll never get the jar filled by tomorrow at that rate. Under the balls is where you should get it from! That's the sweatiest place!'

'Have you drunk any tea? No? How are you going to do it then? There's nothing for you to sweat out! Hey, lads, why didn't you give him any tea to drink? He'd better have six cups right away, then he'll have something to sweat . . .'

The 'enema treatment' was reserved for patients said to be suffering from stomach ulcers, cystitis and other internal complaints. A stomach X-ray was compulsory and this had to be preceded by an enema. Just as the nurse was squeezing three or four pints of warm soapy water into the patient's backside, all those in the ward who could walk, would casually wander along to the lavatory and occupy all the cubicles. A few seconds later the victim would rush into the latrines, clutching his buttocks for all he was worth, and try to push open the cubicle doors which were all occupied and locked from the inside.

Then some of the other soldiers, who were standing around smoking, would suddenly growl at him: 'And where do you think you're going? Can't you see there's a queue?'

'But I haven't got time to wait! I've just had an enema,' he would squeak beseechingly, pressing his legs together in desperation.

'Are you just about to have an X-ray, or what?' one of the soldiers would ask in a friendly voice.

'Yes!'

'Well, you're not supposed to go to the lavatory straight after an enema. The water has to pass right through your stomach and intestine. Otherwise, the X-ray won't show anything up. You ask the lieutenant here. He's had to be X-rayed six times, and all because his stomach didn't get cleaned out properly . . .'

'What do I do about it? What's the best way to work the water round?'

'Do a dozen press-ups. Come on, start now. One . . . two . . . That's right, lad! Stomach off the ground. Three . . .'

By the fourth or fifth press-up, the poor sod couldn't hold out any longer, and . . .

After a week or so, Stavinsky began to feel better, although his arm was still in plaster and his broken jaw was all bandaged up. In fact, when he had leaped from the train, he hadn't expected to injure himself at all. He had kicked up all that fuss in the restaurant car on purpose, of course, so as to have some witnesses around, and when he actually jumped from the train, his main concern had been to avoid crashing into one of the telegraph poles dotted along the railway track. He jumped into the snow, thinking that it would soften his fall (when he was a boy, in Saratov, he'd learned to jump from trains with no trouble: that was a trick which all the local lads could perform). After that, he thought it would simply be a matter of feigning concussion, amnesia and a hoarse voice like Yuryshev's. Although he wasn't a qualified doctor, he had enough medical training to know that it was practically impossible to disprove concussion, if the 'patient' knew how to feign all the right symptoms.

Well, fortunately for him, he didn't hit one of the telegraph poles, but the snow turned out not to be very deep. More important, it was hard and somewhat glazed. Even so, he hadn't felt any pain when he fractured his arm. What he had felt, was the hard snow scratching and tearing at his face. The most important thing had been to fool the railway crew and the soldiers, who would be jumping off the train to find him. He had to put on all the symptoms of concussion – loss of consciousness and vomiting. He managed this brilliantly, but not because he'd practised it in advance in Krasnodar. It was just that when he was lying at the bottom of the railway embankment, he saw the train stop and various people jump down from the carriages, including the soldiers and staff from the restaurant car, whom he had just been insulting. He knew full well that he was about to get beaten up, both for riling them and for stopping the train. The best way of avoiding that, was to shut his eyes and pretend to be unconscious. You don't kick somebody when he's down – that's an old custom in Russia. But the first one to arrive was the guard, and he had no such scruples. He booted Stavinsky right in the ribs, then again and again. There's a lot of pent-up anger in Russia, Stavinsky thought later, if people are willing to beat somebody up at the drop of a hat, just to give vent to their own feelings . . . The fur coat he was wearing didn't do much to soften the blows, but Stavinsky just gritted his teeth and willed himself to keep silent. The main thing was not to cry out or groan. 'Stop! Perhaps he's dead!' somebody shouted. And that was the last thing Stavinsky remembered. At that moment a boot kicked him in the jaw, and he really did lose consciousness. He never found out whether he had broken his arm when falling from the train, or whether another person's 'solicitous' hobnailed boot had landed him one three inches below the elbow.

When he came to in the train, there was no need for him to dissemble. The vomiting, giddiness and headaches were perfectly natural, and he'd lost two bottom front teeth. He spat them out when vomiting blood. Two more teeth were hanging by a thread, and his jaw had been cut to the bone. But there was no way he could complain to the police about being beaten up. He had 'lost consciousness' after all. In any case, didn't he have reason to be grateful to the people who had given him such a drubbing? They had given him real concussion after all, and fracturing his right arm suited his purpose very well. You might lose your memory, but none of the medical textbooks mentioned forgetting your own handwriting. Losing his teeth would mean he would lisp for some time, too, which would be handy for imitating Yuryshev's voice.

All the same, Stavinsky was very nervous the day before he was due to be visited by Marshall Oparkov, the Chief of Staff, and some of 'his' erstwhile colleagues at General HQ. Because of the marshal's visit, all the floors and windows at the hospital were scrubbed spotlessly clean and Stavinsky was moved into a separate room.

That night he opened the window in the lavatory, grabbed some snow from the sill and ate it. By the morning he had a sore throat and a temperature of 37.6°.

At nine o'clock in the morning the daily papers arrived. Stavinsky came across the following article in *Izvestiya* headlined 'A Just Punishment': 'Foreign tourists come to our country with various aims in mind. Some of them are attracted by the very strangeness of visiting Russia, others are interested in our culture and art. Some come to look at our medieval architecture, others to examine the treasures contained in the Hermitage and the Tretyakov Gallery. Yet others are anxious to get a close view of that strange beast called Socialism, which breeds free medical treatment and full employment, and where ordinary people are spared the worst terror of capitalism – fear of what tomorrow will bring. And we greet these tourists with the joy and hospitality for which the Russian people are so well known. Look at us and learn! we say. But amongst the many thousands of visitors who arrive here each year, there are some "guests" who pretend to be tourists, but whose intentions are anything but friendly. Some try to smuggle anti-Soviet and Zionist literature into the USSR. Others try to make contact with so-called "dissidents" and other renegades.

'So it was that two newly-weds, Robert and Virginia Williams, arrived in Moscow recently from Potomac in the American State of Maryland. Intourist met them with their customary friendliness, providing them with a de-luxe suite at the Hotel National, getting them tickets for the best performances at the Bolshoi and other theatres, arranging for them to spend a couple of days in Leningrad, etc. But these particular newly-weds turned out not to be interested in Russian culture or Russian art at all. Dr Williams and his young actress-wife scarcely left their hotel room for a whole week. They didn't visit the Tretyakov or the Pushkin Museum, and even left a performance of *Spartacus* at the Bolshoi Theatre after the first act. Well, so what? you may ask. It's all a matter of taste. After all, perhaps there was nowhere in distant America for the young couple to spend their honeymoon and so they decided to spend it in our country at the Hotel National. People do have their whims, as you know.

'But the real reason behind this particular "whim" soon became perfectly clear. The "young couple's" peculiar behaviour came to the attention of the security organs, who discovered that, despite their extraordinary passion for one another, the true reason for the Williamses' ten-day visit to the Soviet Union wasn't at all because they wanted to spend their honeymoon in an exotic place. When they were in Leningrad, the Williamses arranged a secret meeting with three so-called "dissidents", who attempted to pass themselves off as being representative of Soviet youth. These hooligans handed some anti-Soviet literature on to the American couple – some illiterate appeal to the US President to send troops to the USSR and free our country from the "Communist tyranny". After sewing these treasonable "documents" into the linings of their coats, Dr and Mrs Williams attempted to smuggle them out of the Soviet Union. When they were detained at Sheremetyevo Airport, they attempted to resist arrest, however, and even killed a Soviet officer.

'Mrs Virginia Williams recently appeared before the Moscow City Court, charged with aiding and abetting an act of terrorism. She was found guilty. The court dealt very leniently with her however, sentencing her to three years' imprisonment in a Soviet corrective labour institution . . .'

The rest of the article was about the humane character of Soviet justice and about how this story would serve as a firm lesson and warning to anybody else who was contemplating visiting the Soviet Union as a terrorist, when they really had other 'secret' aims in mind . . .

Stavinsky screwed up the newspaper. The bastards! What an idiot he was! What a fool he had been to agree to this whole senseless venture! But he'd get her out of prison – Virginia and the child!

Suddenly the duty nurse rushed into the room.

'Colonel Yuryshev! Marshal Oparkov is here to see you!'

11

'Take your clothes off!'

'Undo your hair!'

'Spread out your fingers and toes!'

'Open your mouth! Stand with your legs apart!'

Virginia was standing in the reception section of the

Moscow Transit Prison at Krasnaya Presnya. She was entirely at the mercy of these brisk stone-faced women warders. The room was cold and sparsely furnished, with a long wooden table running down the middle. She had to get undressed and place all her clothes and belongings on the table. The warders spoke no English, but Virginia knew enough Russian to understand their simple commands, especially as she could copy the actions of two other women prisoners who were standing next to her. One was a forty-year-old prostitute with a black eye, the other a gypsy, no older than twenty, who had been arrested for theft.

'Take everything off, you scum!' shouted one of the warders, a corpulent woman who tried to pull Virginia's bra and pants off her. 'Open your mouth!' she barked, and pushed her dirty fingers into Virginia's mouth, feeling her cheeks and under her tongue. 'OK! Stand with your legs apart! Wider! Bend down!'

She pressed Virginia down towards the floor and probed her anus and vagina. Virginia gave a loud scream and burst into tears.

'No screaming!' said the warder. 'I'll teach you to shout!'

Then she started to poke around roughly in Virginia's hair, looking for fleas.

'OK! Get dressed! No, wait! Let me look at your bra. Huh! American stuff, eh? A pity it's not my size!' She tore the tiny hook and gave the bra back to Virginia. Then she examined the pants, and tried them up against herself for size. Her enormous behind bulged absurdly behind the small garment and she let out a sigh of disappointment. 'Oh, take them back . . . I'd never get them on,' she said crossly, flinging the pants at Virginia.

Outside in the corridor the other two prisoners went one way, while Virginia was led up an iron staircase to the first floor and past a row of cell doors. They came to a halt at the end of the corridor outside cell No 147. The warder drew the bolt, and the heavy door swung open. Virginia's nostrils were immediately assailed by a musty smell, an unpleasant mixture of sweat, menstrual discharge and rotten teeth. She instinctively stepped back, but the warder gave her a violent push into the cell. There the feeble light from a barred window high in the wall revealed twenty or so women, sitting or lying down on their bunks.

'Here's the American for you!' said the warder, and slammed the door behind her with a smile.

Virginia stood by the door. The heavy stench made her giddy, and her stomach heaved. Twenty pairs of female eyes looked at her expectantly.

'What are you – a professional?' said one of them in a deep voice. She was a tall, beefy-looking woman with a greyish moustache.

'Of course she is, Vasily,' said a thin, flighty-looking girl, pressing close to the deep-voiced woman whom she addressed by the man's name, Vasily. 'If she's nicknamed the "American", then it stands to reason.'

'Nobody's asking *you*,' said Vasily suddenly. 'Well?' she asked, staring insistently at Virginia.

'I . . . I . . . don't speak much Russian,' came the reply. 'I'm a foreigner, from America.'

'How do you like that?' shouted somebody else. 'They've sent us a head-case, the bastards!'

Vasily lowered herself down heavily from her bunk and went over to where Virginia was standing.

'So that's how it is,' she said grimly. 'Well we don't like schizos here, they get their eyes scratched out. What's your name?'

'Virginia Williams. I'm an American . . .'

A sudden blow to the head hurled her against the door. About to faint, Virginia began to sink to the floor, until Vasily grabbed her savagely by the hair and brought her fist close to her face.

'Any more tricks like that, and I'll teach you!'

The door opened with a loud clanking noise, and the warder looked in, grinning all over her face.

'Stop that, Vlasova! She really is an American. Can't you

tell she is from her teeth? So you just treat her carefully, or else there'll be an international incident. In fact, you should say thank you. It's not often you have a chance to try a real American . . .'

With a dirty wink, the warder slammed the door again and drew the bolt.

Vasily put her fingers in between Virginia's lips, full of curiosity. Right enough, this new prisoner did have unusually white and even teeth.

'Hmm!' said Vasily and let go of Virginia's hair. Then she helped her stand up and lean against the wall. 'Well, say something in your language, in American.'

'I want to lie down,' Virginia said in an almost soundless whisper. Then she translated it into Russian: '*Ya . . . khochu . . . lezhat.*'

'Not bad!' said Vasily, full of admiration. 'Make way, girls! She can sleep with me!'

'And where will I go?' asked the thin, flighty-looking girl with indignation . . .

'You can go to hell! Sleep under the bunk, if you like,' said Vasily imperiously.

12

Marshal Oparkov turned out to be a short, thick-set, brawny fellow about sixty years old with a rotund, good-natured face, lively brown eyes and close-cropped grey hair.

After dismissing the doctors, he sat on a chair next to Stavinsky's bed and said: 'Listen, Sergey, are you sure you really can't remember anything?'

Stavinsky shrugged his shoulders helplessly. A fresh gauze bandage covered the lower half of his face; he had more bandages around his neck, and his right arm was in plaster. He waved his left hand weakly in the direction of his jaw, as if to say: 'Look, it's really difficult for me to speak.'

'Well, it's an ill wind,' said the marshal. 'There was a lot you needed to forget, if you were to carry on living. Just look at the way you were behaving before your accident. You'd taken to drink, then you caused a fight and fell out of a train. And Galya has been having a terrible time. She told me that she was to blame for everything between you. She is my only daughter, after all, and I love you like a son, so I want the two of you to come together again and make it up. Believe me, I'd do anything for you, if only . . . I've been talking to the doctors. Not the ones in this place,' he added, nodding towards the door, 'but to Chazov and Schmidt at the Kremlin hospital, who look after the whole Politburo. They said that a person's memory can gradually be restored. And I'm going to do everything I can to help. Everything. So what, if you've forgotten some of your expert knowledge? I don't give a damn. You know the old saying. All a boss needs to know is the name of his secretary and where the official stamp is kept. I'll hush up this little drinking bout of yours, and as for Project EMMA, you'll get your general's epaulettes for that. Can you remember anything about EMMA?'

Stavinsky shook his head. So that was the way of things! Yuryshev had been married to Marshal Oparkov's daughter! He must avoid meeting her at all costs! He might fool most people, but not Yuryshev's wife. The moment they got into bed together she'd realize that something was wrong! On the other hand, leaving hospital as a general was a very attractive proposition. Stavinsky was bound to make some pretty stupid mistakes to begin with, and Oparkov would explain them all away . . .

'Well, if you can't remember anything about EMMA, it doesn't matter,' said the marshal. 'We'll show you a film about it, and you'll remember everything, I assure you! If you like, I can arrange for the project-leader, Benzher, to show you the film in your room tomorrow. Do you remember Benzher?'

Stavinsky shook his head once again.

'Never mind! You'll remember him when you see him! I beg you, Sergey . . . Galya is only thirty-seven years old. You can still have children. Please allow her to come and see you. She's in a terrible state . . .'

Stavinsky threw his head back on to the pillow almost as if he was afraid of the prospect.

'All right! Not today!' said Oparkov rapidly. 'How about in a week's time, or a fortnight? Or when you leave the hospital? But please give her something to hope for, I beg you . . . She loves you, I swear it!'

Stavinsky closed his eyes as if to show agreement.

'Is that all right then?' asked Oparkov, jumping up with pleasure. 'Are we agreed? May I tell her? Sergey, let me shake your hand! I knew you were a good man. To be quite honest, when all this happened, it was as if I had lost all my children at one go – you, Galya and Vitya. But now everything is going to be all right, I'm sure of it. When can she come to see you?'

The combined effort of sore throat, broken teeth and gauze bandage led to a hoarse, scarcely audible whisper: 'Later . . . Afterwards . . .'

'I understand. OK. But don't you worry about remembering! We'll soon get your memory back. We'll move heaven and earth to do it. In any case, you'll be concentrating on EMMA from now on. EMMA is your most important task and the Politburo has set us an almost impossible timetable. But you just carry on resting for now, and getting better . . .'

When he'd left the room, Stavinsky closed his eyes out of sheer exhaustion. He could feel beads of sweat over his whole body. Enough there to fill a jar of 'perspiration analysis'!

13

The endless, snow-covered Arctic wastes were being swept by a greyish blizzard. Every now and then the watery polar sun would peep through the clouds and shine on enormous ice-ridges, dotted here and there with telegraph poles and wooden mock-ups of military installations – anti-aircraft batteries and missile launching platforms.

Meanwhile, in the control room of a nuclear submarine, a count-down was in progress: 'Six . . . five . . . four . . . three . . .' A group of military and civilian personnel were standing or sitting by the control panel. One of them was Colonel Yuryshev. 'Two . . . one . . . zero . . .' he intoned authoritatively. Standing next to him was a dark-haired, hook-nosed man aged about forty, whose slender, nervous fingers then pressed the white button marked 'Attack'.

The tundra suddenly shook, and the snow-covered earth twisted and turned. The dummy anti-aircraft and rocket installations swayed from side to side and finally came crashing to the ground, along with huge lumps of ice thrown up by the quake. It was as if a subterranean storm were bending and buckling the tundra, spewing up rock through the cracks in the earth and hurling great ice-blocks and boulders down into oblivion along with the entire dummy missile site.

In Stavinsky's room the cine-projector crackled away, as it churned out the rest of the film. The scene switched to the forests along the Ussuri River. The camera showed a clump of age-old cedars with their gigantic roots embedded firmly in the ground and then panned to a small river, meandering quietly and smoothly into the Ussuri itself. The river bank was dotted with military installations, just like those in the tundra.

Meanwhile, in the Sea of Okhotsk, Colonel Yuryshev had started the count-down from the same submarine: 'Four . . . three . . . two . . . one . . . zero . . .' And once again the dark-haired man pressed the button.

This time it was the forests which shook from the earthquake. Great cracks appeared in the earth's surface, churning up the river and sending the centuries-old cedars crashing to the ground, disappearing roots and all into the abyss along with the rocket installations . . .

After this Colonel Yuryshev's face appeared on the small screen.

'This new seismic weapon,' he was saying, 'will allow us to produce controlled, localized earthquakes at a distance of four hundred kilometres from the energy transmission grids. Without appearing to enter enemy territory, we are able, with the help of submarines, to instal energy matrices containing explosive material off the coasts of foreign powers. These matrices can be activated by radio from command points in Murmansk, Klaipeda or Severodvinsk. In principle, all the technical problems have already been overcome. We have the submarines, equipped with special drilling equipment . . .'

Then a series of photographs and technical diagrams came up on the screen, accompanied by a running commentary from Colonel Yuryshev: 'The submarine descends to the sea-bed at a predetermined point. It takes between six and ten days to drill one shaft for the energy grid, depending on the nature of the rock. It is absolutely essential to select places where the drilling equipment will not encounter granite or any other very hard rocks. After this the so-called "energy matrix" can be installed in the bore-hole. Eight of these matrices, installed in eight different shafts, together form an arc, which is able to cause an earthquake over an area of between 150 and 200 square kilometres at a distance of 400 kilometres from the arc itself. Look at this model of Europe. Practically every NATO base is within range of EMMA . . .'

A crude relief model of Europe appeared on the screen, showing Scandinavia, Germany, France, Spain, England, Italy, Greece with their mountains, rivers, ports, NATO bases, electric power stations. A hand presses the 'Attack' button and a series of earthquakes suddenly rends the model in all directions. Towns, NATO bases, airports, guided missile silos, power stations, railway lines and motorways – everything is engulfed.

Then Colonel Yuryshev's face appeared on the screen again. 'Of course, developing this fundamentally new form of weapon will not be cheap. We need a factory to produce the energy matrices. We need to develop better and quieter drilling equipment to drill shafts in the sea-bed. We need groups of highly qualified submarine drilling teams. And we need a fleet of submarines involved in simultaneous drilling around the territories chosen for attack. It might be Europe, China, the oil-producing countries of the Arab world or the United States. But one thing is clear. In order to increase our country's defence capability, the group of scientists from the Marine and Power Engineering Institutes led by Academician Benzher have produced a weapon unknown to the West. Look again at the havoc which this weapon is able to wreak . . .'

The camera flashed back to the tundra, and then to the Ussuri River . . .

'Well, how about it?' somebody asked Stavinsky. It was Benzher, the middle-aged man with the dark hair and hooked nose, who had appeared in the film. 'Can you remember it? But we've got a great problem at the moment. Kushchin's trial journey to the Swedish coast proved that it is possible to drill and instal the energy grids right under the enemy's nose. But this has got its advantages and disadvantages. The main disadvantage is that the Government has decided that everything is going well. They insist that we rush on with the programme as fast as possible. But you know yourself, we have to muddle along, making everything by hand. We need a factory to mass-produce the grids, and we need new drilling equipment. I won't be able to prove this to them without you . . .'

'I'd like to look at the film a second time,' said Stavinsky. The only thing he needed was to copy Yuryshev's manner of speaking, his intonations, and also the habit he had of inclining his head slightly to the left before putting forward a new suggestion.

14

At ten o'clock in the evening it was 'lights out' in the cell, and the only illumination came from a dull lamp, protected by a grille, high up in the stone ceiling. Virginia was lying on one of the upper bunks, between Vasily and the wall. The bunks themselves were rough-hewn planks stretching continuously down one wall and taking up about half the area of the cell. Ten people could fit on the upper row, and ten below. In order to make a little more space for the American, Vasily had evicted another couple of women to the lower bunks. This Vasily was generally very solicitous on Virginia's behalf. During the day she had used her position as cell 'monitor' to ask the guard for a jug of water and would give Virginia a drink, like a child, whenever the stuffiness of the cell made her feel queasy. And then she excused her the invariable duty of all new-comers – changing the close-stool. That evening, when the warder pushed the soup-ration and tea through the hatch in the door, Vasily gave Virginia *her* sugar, and then just before lights out produced a comb from under her mattress and proceeded to comb the American's hair. During the four hours which Virginia had been in the cell, she had had time to realize that most of the prisoners weren't professional criminals at all, but ordinary women who had been arrested for black-marketeering, petty fraud of for murdering their husbands or lovers in a fit of jealousy. As she lay there in the dark, next to this protectress of hers, the mannish and extremely malodorous Vasily, Virginia knew that all the attention she was receiving was not for nothing. Something was going to happen and she had a rough idea what it was. What should she do? Jump down and hammer on the door, shouting for the guard to bring the Investigator, and then tell him whatever he wanted to know – even about Yuryshev and Stavinsky? But what good would that do her? It would only highlight the fact that she had come to the Soviet Union as a CIA spy, charged with arranging the defection of a colonel from General Headquarters. In fact, she would appear to be the linch-pin in the whole operation, arriving with one husband and intending to leave with another. There would be more interrogations, another trial, and at the end of it, she would receive a worse sentence than the one she had already been given. And what would await Stavinsky when they eventually found him, as find him they would? Whereas now she only had a three-year sentence to serve, and according to Larry Kugel, the US Embassy would do all it could to press for her early release. Perhaps they would exchange her for some Soviet spy arrested in the West. The CIA had to come up with something in the end. Perhaps they had already made a couple of arrests in the States and were about to offer the Soviets a deal. So for now she had to put up with this cell and the awful smell of sweat and menstruation and the stench coming from the close-stool. Above all, she had to put up with Vasily, whose hand was already on her chest. Virginia removed it and said, with as much firmness as she could muster: 'No.'

'Ssh! Don't make a noise,' said Vasily, moving up close against her and putting the palm of her hand over Virginia's mouth. Then she rolled over on to her, body, smell, and all.

'*Nyet!* No!' said Virginia in a muffled cry of terror, biting the slippery palm and trying to escape from this heavy body and the rough hand, that was already scrabbling away between her legs.

But Vasily had already worked herself up into a frenzy of desire. One hand was crushing Virginia's mouth, and the other was trying to drill its way in between her legs, while the rest of her heavy, sweaty body rubbed up against Virginia, contorted with sexual pleasure.

A convulsive pain spread through Virginia's body. She lost consciousness and didn't hear the cell door opening or see the warders rush in and remove the frenzied Vasily from on top of her . . .

When Virginia came to, she was lying in complete darkness on the icy metal floor of a bumpy lorry. She was frozen to the bone. Her blood-stained dress had stuck to the floor. She managed with great difficulty to get to her feet, only to fall down again, when the lorry made a sharp turn and came to a halt. Then she heard the sound of heavy footsteps crunching through the snow outside. The door suddenly opened with a loud clank and an icy blast of fresh, forest air swept into the lorry. In the darkness somebody's hands roughly picked her up off the floor and humped her out of the lorry. She glimpsed a dark, single-storey building, surrounded by a high stone wall and trees. A hefty soldier dragged her away from the lorry over to the entrance of the house, where two guard dogs tried to thrust their muzzles under the hem of her blood-stained skirt. A loud shout from the soldier and a kick from his boot drove them away. Then he dragged Virginia into the house, picked her up in his arms, so she wouldn't get blood-stains on the carpet, and took her down a brightly lit corridor, still carrying her, through the magnificently furnished vestibule and into a bathroom. There was nobody else around. He sat Virginia down on the edge of a huge black marble bath, filled with enticingly warm, blue water and smelling of pine extract. Then he walked out of the room and shut the door behind him. Virginia looked around for a few seconds and was absolutely amazed. It was just like the bathroom she had seen before on Dzerzhinsky Square, the one that belonged to the head of the KGB. So now she knew whom she had been taken to see, and why. Without touching the water, she slid slowly down on to the warm, tiled floor. She was shivering all over, but there were no tears.

The door opened, and there in the entrance stood a tall, corpulent-looking man, aged about sixty and with a bald patch. It was the same person who had offered her the caviar sandwiches at KGB headquarters. His greyish-blue eyes stared at her through thin horn-rimmed spectacles. He was carrying a glass and a bottle of Johnnie Walker. He looked at Virginia for a few moments, then placed the glass and bottle on the floor next to her and left the room.

He didn't shut the door after him, however, and Virginia could hear the sound of his heavy footsteps die away, as he entered another room. Then she heard the characteristic click of a tape-recorder being switched on, followed by the sound of Liza Minnelli singing: 'If I can make it there, I'll make it anyway, It's up to you, New York, New York . . .'

Virginia burst into tears. Somewhere far away, in a life that was no longer hers, were New York, Broadway, Carnegie Hall, Greenwich Village, cafés, restaurants, Liza Minnelli. It all still existed. And yet here was she, in a filthy state, bruised all over and half-raped by a dirty, old lesbian prisoner . . . God! If her mother could only see her now! But she had died long since – in Colorado in 1961. Virginia crawled over to where the bottle of Johnnie Walker was standing and poured herself nearly a glassful. The neat whisky burned her throat and empty stomach, but it restored her strength. She got to her feet and drank another. Then, clutching the bottle and smiling, she started walking towards the sound of Liza Minnelli's voice.

The owner of the *dacha* was sitting in a spacious living-room, in front of an open fire and reading the *Washington Post*. He was dressed informally, with a dark-brown dressing-gown over trousers and a white shirt. On a nearby coffee-table were copies of *Pravda*, as well as the *New York Times*, the *Sunday Times* and *Playboy*. There was yet another bottle of Johnnie Walker, some smaller bottles of soda water and a large silver dish filled with grapes, apples, oranges and bananas. The birch twigs in the fire crackled merrily.

'Sit down,' he said, without looking up from his newspaper. Then he leaned across to the music-centre and turned down the volume slightly.

'What do you want from me?' asked Virginia, continuing to stand there.

'I want you to sit down.'

'I'll spoil your furniture,' she said with a smile.

'You could have taken a bath and changed your clothes.'

'Convicted prisoners are not supposed to have baths or wear towelling dressing-gowns. What do you want from me?'

'Not what you think,' he replied. Then at last he looked in her direction and took off his glasses. His eyes looked weary, as if there was something wrong with them. He rubbed his eyebrows and the bridge of his nose. 'You think that I want to get this dirt washed off and then get into bed with you. But you're wrong. There are lots of beautiful Russian women, and they're younger than you, and not only Russian women, either. There are Lithuanians, Uzbeks, Georgians, Jews, not to mention Poles, Hungarians, Turks, if you like that kind of thing. So there's no shortage of women. Sit down, or else you'll fall. And don't drink any more. Have some fruit.'

Virginia sat down in the soft leather armchair. He was quite right. She really didn't have the strength to keep standing any more. But she made no attempt to touch the fruit and tried not to look at it.

Her host emitted a sigh.

'It's about your case,' he said. 'Everything that I'm going to suggest is for your own benefit. You are a beautiful young woman, but you won't survive prison for very long, especially in your condition. What you really need at the moment are vitamins, a high-calorie diet and plenty of rest. Perhaps you are thinking that today or tomorrow the Americans will exchange you for one of our spies. Forget it. What good is a spy once he's been detected? He would cause us more trouble than you, because we would need to keep an eye on him for the rest of his life. Who could guarantee that he hadn't been recruited by the CIA? Do you know anything about this organization?'

This was a shot in the dark, as far as the speaker was concerned. A few hours ago a file had been laid on the desk in his study, which compromised this cretinous Major Neznachny more than the fact that he had been noticed by an ordinary Washington dentist. The file had contained photographs showing Neznachny in bed with his own agent Olga Makhova, photographs which had been taken by a concealed camera in one of the rooms at the Hotel National. The prudent Lieutenant Kozlov had done to Neznachny, what Neznachny then went on to do to Kozlov and the other KGB officers. Apart from that, the file also contained the testimony of the woman who cleaned Neznachny's office. She revealed that the major had more than once locked himself in his room with his secretary, Katya Kunyayeva. There was also a transcript of Kunyayeva's interrogation, where she admitted to having lived with Neznachny. In other words, if Robert Williams had cleansed KGB ranks of an imbecile and possible future traitor like Neznachny, he had in fact done the Soviet security organs a signal service . . .

The owner of the *dacha* smiled at the thought. Then he carried on speaking to Virginia, who had been silent all this time.

'OK, let's talk about you. So you're not going to be exchanged for any Soviet spy either today or tomorrow. You'll have to spend your three years in prison, or even longer. Don't look so surprised. We can extend your sentence for infringing prison regulations. Take that fight which you started today in your cell, when you attempted to violate prisoner Vlasova . . .'

'She was trying to rape me!' Virginia shouted.

'Who can tell?' he asked with a smile, staring into her eyes. 'Vlasova will write a complaint, maintaining that you tried to rape her, and all the other prisoners will be prepared to back up her story. Then the People's Court would impose a new sentence upon you for sexual offences. And what guarantee is there that you won't try to seduce a soldier on your way from here back to prison? Now can you understand what I'm talking about? We can keep you in prison for as long as we please, and no American President will be able to save you. And I can't guarantee that you won't get raped by more lesbians or by guards in prison or in the camps. Cattle behave like cattle after all. But one thing I am sure of: you won't even survive the three years you have been sentenced to. The filth, the hard labour, the lousy camp food – you'll be an old woman before the year is out. And if you really are pregnant, then what about the child?'

'What is it you want from me?'

'I want you to co-operate with us . . . Wait a minute! Don't interrupt me. It's not as bad as it sounds. We need people like you for work which is quite unstrenuous, e.g. training agents destined to settle in the West. You're an actress. You know what life in America is like, you know the latest slang. But that's just one possibility. There are others. I've been studying your visa application. You lost both parents when you were young, so you've been alone for most of your life. And let's be honest about it: your life hasn't been very successful. You haven't been in many films. Or to be more exact: you haven't really been in any films at all. You got married three or four months ago, but I guess that was because you were already thirty-four years old and you were thinking it was time to begin raising a family. What I'm saying is that this wonderful America of yours hasn't given you a career, or made you happy. But everything you dreamed about *there*, can be yours *here*, in Russia. Just one word from you, and you'll have everything you ever wanted: a luxurious flat, money, a car, admirers, you name it. And after that . . . who knows? A Russian husband perhaps, and the lead roles in some of our films. Remember one thing: we can do whatever we like! Well, what do you think? Or do you prefer a children's home for your child, and common soldiers, lesbians and prison for yourself?'

'That's blackmail,' said Virginia.

'No, it's business,' he replied.

'I must have time to think . . .'

'Where? In prison, or here?' he asked with a smile.

'Is there nowhere else on offer?'

'All right,' he said. 'For a woman like you we can make a

small exception. Only not for long. Let's say we'll give you two weeks. You'll be living in more or less tolerable conditions. But I warn you. In two weeks it'll either be back to the criminals in prison, or . . . Would you like to dine with me? Or take a bath first?'

'But you've just given me two weeks to consider.'

'Well, having dinner won't commit you to anything.'

'All the same, I think it would be better to postpone it,' said Virginia, realizing full well that if she stayed here for as long as another half-hour, he would be sure to win. And not in two weeks' time, but that very night.

15

This was the third night that Stavinsky had dreamed about Yuryshev. Not that there was anything strange about that. For Stavinsky the whole of the last week had been filled with Yuryshev, morning, noon and night. The energetic Benzher had given him a detailed account of Project EMMA, while Yuryshev's former colleagues at General HQ, acting on Marshal Oparkov's instructions, had taken turns to remind him about events in his past life, while secretly smuggling bottles of Yuryshev's favourite Ararat cognac into the hospital, as well. Moreover, Pyotr Kushchin, the commander of submarine U-137, had arrived from the Baltiisk naval base to tell him about his voyage to Sweden. His men had succeeded in drilling three holes in the bed of the narrow Swedish fjords and installing the vertical energy matrices into them. And just as Benzher, Yuryshev and the seismologists had planned, the fourth bore-hole was sited within direct view of the Swedish naval base at Karlskrona.

'We drilled the bore-hole during the first night, before the fishermen found us the next morning and raised the alarm,' said Kushchin, smiling into his dark moustache. 'After that, the Swedes dragged me off for questioning, but the crew carried on doing the job, installing the matrix into the bore-hole and sealing it with special mud and screening mortar, so that not even a bloodhound could sniff it out. It was the devil of a job, I tell you! The Swedes detected traces of Uranium-238 and tried to enter the forward part of the ship. Like hell! I didn't let any of them through, even though I was more or less under arrest myself. Only I tell you, Comrade Colonel, I wouldn't advise anybody to get into a mess like that a second time! You need drilling equipment which can deal with any kind of rock, even granite, otherwise you'll get stuck on those sandbanks . . .'

'There you are! What did I tell you?' Benzher said to Stavinsky. 'OK, let's say we position two more matrices somewhere off Musko Island, so as to complete the Swedish arc and get the Lenin Prize. But that's all. After that, we have to stop all this messing about and insist that the Government provide us with the money to start mass-producing the matrices, as well as manufacturing a new design of diamond drilling bits. Whatever happens, the most important thing will be to get the first few million roubles and spend it quickly. After that, you just mark my words! They'll give us all the money we need. But we're having a visit from the Defence Industry Commission at the Institute tomorrow, Sergey Ivanovich, and there's no way I can receive them, unless you're there!'

'But tomorrow is Sunday. Nobody works then,' said Stavinsky in surprise.

'Every day is a working day for the Institute. And for the Government, too.'

'But my arm is still in plaster . . .'

'Rubbish! You can walk, can't you?! We'll take them around the stands and show them a couple of hand-made matrices, moaning on all the time that it's impossible to carry on working this way. We'll put on a double act: you begin and I'll carry on. The main thing is not to pause and to say everything as simply as possible. They won't understand anything to do with the technical side, anyway . . .'

'And I haven't shaved in weeks . . .' said Stavinsky, running his hand over his cheeks. Because of the large, irregular scar on his chin, he had stopped shaving, preferring to cultivate a moustache and beard. A few outward alterations like that, he thought, would catch the attention of anybody who had known Yuryshev before and prevent them from taking too much notice of any other changes that he couldn't do anything about. In any case, you would expect changes in somebody who had had concussion to the cerebral cortex, leading to amnesia. Alterations in muscular co-ordination were also very much on the cards, things like the way he walked and moved, even his handwriting. But Stavinsky kept on complaining about pain in his jaw, thereby putting off the day when he would have to have new teeth put in. Lisping he found a great asset, because it enabled him to conceal possible errors in the way he imitated Yuryshev's rasping voice. Stavinsky could see that everything had gone very well so far, perhaps because it never occurred to anybody that he could be anyone other than who he said he was. He had arrived in hospital with the colonel's papers, and had immediately received the treatment appropriate to the son-in-law of the Chief of Staff. The first officer from General HQ to see him had been Marshal Oparkov's adjutant, Major Ryazantsev, and he had been immediately taken in by Stavinsky's appearance. 'Well, I'll be damned! You're growing a beard, old lad! It suits you, too.' Everybody was excessively considerate with him, pretending that there was nothing wrong with him and not noticing the bandage around his face or the scar on his chin. People in that situation pay more attention to their own behaviour than they do to the patient's.

Yes, everything had gone smoothly so far, but that didn't stop Stavinsky pacing up and down his room torn between anxiety and excitement, once Benzher and Kushchin had gone. He would be taking over practically all Yuryshev's responsibilities the very next day, beginning with a visit from the Defence Industry Commission. Not bad! He couldn't refuse. Before Benzher and Kushchin had even left the hospital, Marshal Oparkov had sent his adjutant over with his son-in-law's new general's uniform. Colonel Yuryshev had been promoted for the successful part he had played in helping develop Project EMMA. So there it was, as brought over by Major Ryazantsev, a brand-new, khaki general's uniform complete with oak-leaves on the sleeves and collar, gold epaulettes and a major-general's star, a red stripe down the seams of the trousers, a wide ceremonial belt made of plaited gold thread and semi-circular yarn, a long greatcoat made of fine grey cloth with a huge turn-down collar adorned with more gold oak-leaves on the tabs and yet another gold belt, not to mention the tall, grey astrakhan hat with its gold cockade and red silk lining, the light-coloured khaki shirt and finally the soft leather, laceless boots reaching halfway to the knee. Nor did Major Ryazantsev forget Marshal Oparkov's request to mention that Yuryshev's wife, Galya, had had this uniform and greatcoat made specially at the Soviet Army Generals' Outfitter's, visiting the workshop on three separate occasions to make sure that the clothes were tailored perfectly to Yuryshev's measurements.

Now all these general's accoutrements were on hangers in Stavinsky's room at the hospital, and he kept on looking at them out of the corner of his eye. He realized that Project EMMA wasn't the only reason for his promotion. After his encounter with the Defence Industry Commission the next day, he would finally have to meet Marshal Oparkov's daughter and Colonel Yuryshev's former wife, Galya. On the way back from Leningrad Yuryshev had told him that he had kicked her out for being a tart. So what was he to do? How should he act towards her? The simplest thing would be to continue in Yuryshev's role as the outraged husband, but that would mean forfeiting the patronage of her father . . .

That night Stavinsky dreamed about Yuryshev again, except that this time the colonel was in bed with Virginia.

Stavinsky couldn't for the life of him make out in the dream whether Virginia had realized that it was Yuryshev in the bed with her, and not Stavinsky. Then he dreamed of Major Neznachny, trying to rape Virginia . . .

When Stavinsky woke up, he was covered in cold sweat. So he'd dreamed about two dead men. Could that be an omen?

He got up out of bed, gave himself a quick wash and donned the general's uniform.

16

Somebody else woke up that morning long before dawn, too. It was Yuryshev's wife, Galya. To be thirty-seven years old and to lose your son, your husband and the comfortable life you have been living for years, all in one day, was no joke, and it had come as a shattering blow. Her father didn't know the real reason for her break with Yuryshev, but for some reason he blamed his daughter for it all the same. Perhaps he did so, because he really had loved Yuryshev like a son, always emphasizing that he wanted to advance his career, not because he was married to his daughter, but because Yuryshev was genuinely talented. And, because they had worked together every day for years, Galya's father and Yuryshev had developed a really firm friendship. The death of his grandson and the break-up with Galya had destroyed this friendship, and the father firmly blamed the daughter for this. Galya blamed herself, too. Who else was at fault? She loved Yuryshev, and these chance affairs which she had on the side could do nothing to alter that. On the contrary, when she stopped seeing her latest student or researcher (they were mainly from the Library Institute, where Galya taught French; like the overwhelming majority of daughters belonging to the Moscow Party and military elite, Galya Oparkova had graduated from the Institute of

Foreign Languages), when her latest affair came to its rapid and inevitable end, Galya always returned to her husband, uplifted by her feelings of love for him, her son and her family. How could she even compare her talented, calm and loving husband – who was a colonel, a huntsman and a father to boot – with some snotty-nosed student? Forever busy with his work and trips to other parts of the country, Yuryshev never noticed her comings and goings, and Galya didn't feel guilty about her infidelities. What woman in her thirties doesn't feel flattered by the attentions of young men with their trembling hands, embarrassed blushes and timid, worshipping eyes? Life was slipping past, after all, and in a few years' time she would be forty. That prospect frightened her, and every new lover was ammunition in her battle with that hated age. No, she wasn't forty yet, nor even thirty! To look at her, nobody would have thought that she was more than thirty. She had a good figure, blonde hair, big green eyes, large, sensuous lips, small, but firm, compact breasts, and long legs. Many of her eighteen-year-old students envied her figure, and nearly all of them coveted the fashionable, imported clothes which she was able to buy in the foreign currency shops or at the special department at GUM, reserved for members of the Government and their families. Fur coats, sheepskin coats, women's jackets, dresses, boots: she had whatever those younger women could possibly have desired, not to mention French perfume and, of course, her own export model Lada. A beautiful, fashionably dressed woman in Moscow seated behind the wheel of her own car isn't much different from Anouk Aimée on the Champs-Élysées or Liza Minnelli on Madison Avenue. That, at least, was what Galya thought, not suspecting that what attracted all these young students to her, quite apart from her manifest feminine charms, was the certainty that she, as a French language teacher, must know infinitely more about *sex* than any ordinary Russian woman. That is to say, she must know something about sex *à la française*. And this longing of the typical young Russian male to try a bit of sex '*à la française*' made her admirers so romantically persistent that even the most straitlaced of puritans would have found it difficult to resist. And when she did give in, whether her empty light-blue Lada could be seen languishing deep in the snow of some Moscow side street or waiting at the edge of a green birch wood on the Minsk Highway, whether her resistance had crumbled in the comfort of a friend's flat, borrowed for a few hours, or in the prickly grass of a forest glade, the result was totally unlike those modest games she played in bed with her husband. Not one of her ardent lovers was content to indulge in a straightforward screw. Each of them, depending on how he imagined the French in terms of subtlety, refinement – would invent something bizarre, some fantastic position or a unique deviation. In practice it was not Galya who taught and corrupted them, but vice versa. Meanwhile, she interpreted their studlike behaviour as genuinely ardent love for herself. It was while she was in the middle of one of these so-called 'French' extravagances, that her son Vitya returned a day early from his summer camp, and caught her *in flagrante delicto*. At that point everything collapsed and died – her son, her husband and even her father. At the same time all her admirers disappeared as well, perhaps because her face no longer embodied that seductive combination of success, levity and mystery. All that had been replaced by the usual Soviet air of depression and low spirits . . . And although, straight after the break-up with her husband, she moved in with her father, who lived in a luxurious multi-roomed apartment in one of those blocks built specially for the government elite on the Frunze Embankment, his housekeeper, Aunt Klara, wouldn't even allow her to help with domestic chores, and so her life became totally inactive. Her father hardly spoke to her. Indeed, he seemed almost to avoid her, spending more and more time in his office at General Headquarters, although this may not have been his fault. Whatever it was, Galya suddenly found herself left alone, aged thirty-seven, with her useless knowledge of French and the Lada, which gave her no more joy. She tried drowning her sorrows in drink or in some new love affair . . . But nothing helped. Her inner buoyancy was gone, her flair, her mood. Yuryshev! How she needed a man like him *now* – calm, self-assured, strong and able to protect her from any misfortune. But there weren't any more like him around, and if there were, then they had long ago been snapped up by other women. There was no way you'd get a man like that out of his wife's clutches, just as there was no way anybody had been able to get Yuryshev away from her during the seventeen years of their marriage. And women had tried, she knew that very well.

But when her father had told her that Yuryshev had fallen out of a train in a drunken stupor, broken some bones and lost his memory, a modicum of hope returned. What if he had forgotten that fateful day, the twenty-eighth of June? She rushed along to see the psychiatrists. Slowly and cautiously she tried to ascertain from them, whether he would recover his memory at all, and if he did, how long there might continue to be gaps in it, with regard to individual objects and events. What she discovered was that all these learned specialists, the so-called stars of their profession, didn't know the slightest thing about it. They could guarantee nothing, except that there was no way of controlling the process of recovery. If the memory returned at all, it would happen over a number of weeks, months or even years. This was a source both of hope and despair. Sometimes she imagined that the very sight of her would send everything flooding back into Yuryshev's mind – his son, that fateful summer day and the confession which she had written in her own hand, while he threatened her with his revolver. So she kept on putting off the moment when she would have to see him, and was overjoyed when her father told her that she needn't visit Yuryshev in hospital. But now the day had arrived. Yuryshev was leaving hospital today. He had a meeting in the Marine Institute at twelve o'clock, and then . . .

When it comes to it, I'll nurse him like a nanny, she thought, or a mother, or whatever he likes – if only he forgives me, if only he forgets, if only a part of our former life together can be recovered and this awful emptiness filled. These had been Galya's thoughts and prayers that morning, uttered with all the devoutness of a repentant sinner. The fact that he's ill, with a broken arm and a faulty memory is all to the good. It means that God has forgiven me and is giving me another chance. But Lord! How am I supposed to greet him? How can I look him in the eyes? How can I be alone with him when there is *this* between us?

Suddenly a new thought hurled her out of bed. Those two pieces of paper, her son's suicide note, and her confession . . . They must be lying around in their old flat somewhere. Even if he doesn't remember anything at their first meeting, by the time he gets home and sees his son's things lying around . . . Now where could they be? Probably in his desk . . .

She dressed quickly and then, forgetting that she had an appointment at nine o'clock with the most fashionable hairdresser in Moscow, Rosa from the 'Enchantress' hair-salon on Kalinin Avenue, Galya quietly slipped out of the flat, taking care not to disturb her father, who was a light sleeper, like most old people. With her fur jacket thrown loosely over her shoulders and clutching her fur hat, she ran over the freshly fallen snow to the car. She got in, after hurriedly wiping the snow off the windscreen with her mittens, and then, without even waiting for the engine to warm up, she headed quickly down the dark empty streets towards their old apartment on Lenin Avenue.

By the time she got there, her heart was pounding. She put the key in the lock and entered the flat, switching on the light as she did so. She felt afraid of something, although she didn't know what. Perhaps she was scared of finding another woman there, or at least discovering that one had been there. It was only when she actually entered the flat and switched on the light, that she realized what it was: she was afraid of her son's picture. There was a large portrait of the boy, blown up from a smaller photograph, hanging in the living-room. Vitya had been four years old then, a smiling youngster dressed in a sailor's cap and staring out at her with his father's serious-looking eyes. She didn't even go up to the picture. She froze in the middle of the room and then slowly sank to her knees.

'Forgive me, Vitenka,' she whispered. 'Forgive me . . .'

Like all new religious converts, she was willing to pray and weep endlessly.

But after a few minutes, she got to her feet, removed her son's picture from the wall and hid it in her bedroom, at the bottom of the chest of drawers. In passing she stuffed the family picture album in her bag, and then went over to Yuryshev's desk, pulling out all the drawers on to the floor one by one. But neither they, nor the suitcases in the store cupboard, nor any of the books in the book-case seemed to contain those two sheets of paper, which Vitya had torn out of one of his school exercise books . . .

Suddenly the telephone rang, and she gave a start. Should she answer it, or not? She walked hesitantly over towards the phone. Who could be ringing Yuryshev so early in the morning? She plucked up her courage and answered it.

'Hello . . .'

'Is that you?' It was her father's voice.

'Yes . . .'

'Are you clearing up the flat?'

'Yes . . .'

'Good. Clever girl.' It was the first time in months that her father had said anything kind to her. 'Don't go away,' he went on. 'I'm sending the chauffeur over with some food, and then you can go over to the car showrooms with him to get your new Volga. It's already paid for. Then you can drive it to General Headquarters for five o'clock.'

'A Volga?' she said in total amazement.

'Yes. General Yuryshev can't travel about in a clapped-out old Lada. Only don't tell him that it's from me. Don't forget that he doesn't remember whether he's got a car or not. I'll be interested to hear what he says.'

'Papa, you've . . . you've got a heart of gold!'

But he'd already hung up.

She burst into tears again. Could it be that life was really starting up again?

17

About ten miles south-east of Moscow, on the busy Highway of the Enthusiasts, is a long, eight-storey building built in the 1950s, the so-called 'Marine Institute'. In fact, the building doesn't even have a sign outside bearing this name. For the last twelve years the term 'Marine Institute' has been a convenient mailing address for the country's main centre for research and development of new kinds of secret weapons. Year after year the Institute has expanded, occupying more and more land behind the original building. It already has its own branch-line leading to the main Kursk railway track and its own bus service ferrying engineers and scientists between the different workshops. Otherwise, it would take you an hour to walk all round the place from one end to the other and back again. Of course, the people who live in the surrounding streets, workers for the nearby cable and car engine factories mainly, have no idea what really goes on behind the walls screening off the inner buildings of this 'Institute'. Little do they know that those great concrete boxes, as large as aircraft hangers, conceal segments of the latest nuclear submarines and missiles. The scientists and engineers who work at the Institute fit these missiles with the latest computers, which are able to direct rockets to their destinations some six or seven thousand miles away from their launching silos. The scientists here are in constant competition with their defence industry counterparts in America. The latest Western technology of submarine missile construction always finds its way to this Institute. These were the people who created the first Soviet long-range missiles with multiple warheads and who copied the Americans to produce nuclear submarines with vertical missile shafts, filling a single submarine first with nine, then with sixteen, and finally with twenty-four missiles, all of them capable of reaching Japan or the USA from the Arctic Ocean in forty minutes. And these same scientists invented the so-called 'goldfish' submarines with hulls made of a special alloy able to foil radar and any other detection equipment . . .

The Government was generous in rewarding the Institute's achievements. Triple salaries were the order of the day, along with off-the-record Lenin and State prizes, academic degrees, the title of Hero of Socialist Labour, military decorations, new apartments, access to special food supplies, vouchers enabling the holder to buy the most up to date cars without having to wait years for the opportunity, and various other inducements designed to stimulate scientific and technological creativity. The Defence Minister, the Politburo and even Leonid Ilyich Brezhnev himself were constant visitors to the Institute, as was Brezhnev's son, Yury, a particularly close friend of the Institute's fifty-three-year-old director, academician Ashot Gaikazyants . . .

In 1978 one of the buildings at the very back of the Institute became the centre for work of the highest secrecy – the research and development of Project EMMA. It was the place where the very first 'energy transmission grids' and 'energy matrices' were hand-produced.

Today the Institute was awaiting the arrival of the Defence Industry Commission, a special organization set up under the direct control of the Party Central Committee to oversee the technical equipping of the Soviet Army. However, nobody expected Brezhnev to come with them as well. News of his arrival caused a certain amount of commotion throughout the Institute, as nobody knew which particular workshop he would decide to visit.

The Secretary-General's black armour-plated limousine passed through the reinforced military guard at the Institute's main gates, followed by a posse of similar black-painted Government cars. Brezhnev's chauffeur then drove across the courtyard, past sections of new missiles and nuclear submarines, all parcelled up and ready for dispatch, past the snow-covered swimming-pool and volley-ball pitch, past the wreckage of Israeli and other Western planes, shot down in the Near East, Angola, and so on, and drove straight up to academician Benzher's establishment, a four-storey concrete hangar. The heavy metal doors heaved open, and the cars drove right into the workshop.

Brezhnev's chief bodyguard helped him get out of the car. Dressed in a fur hat and a heavy winter coat with a fur collar, Brezhnev shuffled slowly over to the stands, where two half-completed 'energy matrices' ten yards high were exhibited. Without their protective cylindrical covering, they looked like two gigantic metal candles, criss-crossed with energy pulsators.

Leonid Ilyich was accompanied by other members of the Defence Industry Commission, including the Defence Minister himself, Marshal Ustinov, and Marshal Oparkov. They all shook hands with Ashot Gaikazyants, the Institute Director, and with Benzher and Stavinsky, who, dressed in Yuryshev's general's uniform, offered Brezhnev his left hand instead of his right, which was hanging loosely from a sling.

'What's happened to you?' asked Brezhnev, nodding towards his right arm.

'A little accident, Leonid Ilyich,' replied Stavinsky hoarsely.

'And your voice is even rougher than it used to be. Have you taken to drink, or what?' asked Brezhnev in a querulous growl, speaking slowly because of his own speech defects. 'Drinking, not shaving . . .' he continued.

'He's got a cold, Leonid Ilyich,' said Benzher, intervening on Stavinsky's behalf. 'This place is full of draughts. And as for shaving, we all work two shifts a day, so there's no time for eating, let alone drinking and shaving.'

'Why two shifts? Why not three?' asked Brezhnev. 'When did you promise us these "grids" of yours would be ready?'

'By New Year, Leonid Ilyich.'

'And will they?' he asked.

'These two will, Leonid Ilyich, but it's tough work. We have to make them all by hand. What we need to do is get a mass-production programme under way as quickly as possible. We need a factory, Leonid Ilyich.'

Benzher looked quickly at Stavinsky for support.

'Apart from that,' said Stavinsky, 'our submarines can't do the work with the drilling equipment they've got at present, Leonid Ilyich. What we need is portable and noiseless drilling equipment for working in difficult geological formations.'

'"We need!", "We need!",' said Brezhnev, obviously enjoying mimicking the nasal sounds of somebody with a worse enunciation than his own. 'Everybody "needs" something from me!'

The other members of the Commission put on their prepared smiles, and Brezhnev carried on, drawing inspiration from himself.

'No, it's true! Wherever I go, all I hear is "Give me, give me." Give me money! Give me meat! Give me missiles! And nobody says "Here you are." Here's meat for *you*, Leonid Ilyich! Here's a good harvest for *you*, Leonid Ilyich! Here's a seismic weapon for you to trounce those Imperialist sods with and those Poles, Leonid Ilyich! That's what you never hear! Instead of that, I'm treated like a milch-cow. That bloody business in Kar . . . in Kar . . . How the hell do you pronounce it?'

'Karlskrona,' said Gaikazyants.

'That's right, that's right . . . That bloody business cost us 170,000 dollars in compensation to the Swedes. Did you really have to do your drilling just there? Couldn't you have found somewhere else?'

All the other members of the Commission immediately put on well-rehearsed expressions of disapproval. Brezhnev was displeased. The chorus appeared likewise.

'Sweden is a neutral country, Leonid Ilyich,' said Benzher, turning pale. He still had the courage to tell Brezhnev that the Secretary-General had approved the choice of Sweden himself. The trick was to remind him of it as anonymously as possible. 'If you remember, we didn't want to go for a NATO base immediately. Besides, if war should break out, Sweden would be able to box in our entire Baltic Fleet, so that's why . . .'

'I'm not talking about that,' said Brezhnev, interrupting him. 'Why did you have to run the ship aground near this Kar . . . Kar . . . however you bloody pronounce it!'

'It was a question of completing the arc, Leonid Ilyich,' replied Benzher. He could see that Brezhnev really had got worked up, not so much over the submarine business, but because of the fact that he couldn't get his tongue around the word 'Karlskrona'. 'You see, in order for EMMA to work, we had to instal a grid at that point. Of course, when we switch over to EMBA, Energy Matrix Big Attack . . .'

'And when will we?' snapped Brezhnev.

'As soon as we get a factory,' replied Benzher doggedly.

'And newly designed drilling equipment,' added Stavinsky.

'There you are, you're off again,' muttered Brezhnev, frowning at Stavinsky. 'Give me this! Give me that! You've rehearsed your whole act! And what guarantee do I have that we really will be able to use this weapon to set up earthquakes in Sweden, England, Japan or America?'

'Well, you've seen the film, Leonid Ilyich,' replied Benzher.

'The film indeed!' said Brezhnev, with a smile. 'You can make a mock-up of anything in a film. I saw a film called *Deep Throat* about five years ago. It showed this woman who was able to take it right down her throat . . .'

The rest of the Commission burst into peals of instant

laughter at this dirty joke. Brezhnev looked at them and smiled with pleasure. He considered himself to be enormously witty and liked to see the fact confirmed by others.

Stavinsky realized that he had to build on his wave of laughter. 'But that's exactly the kind of drilling equipment we need, Leonid Ilyich,' he said. 'So as to drill deep boreholes from a submarine and stuff these grids down it.'

'Is that so?' said Brezhnev with a crafty look. 'In that case, you can call this new project "Deep Throat" or else you'll use another Jewish name like EMMA! OK, we won't begrudge you a bit of money for "Deep Throat". We're not peasants, are we? But you can shave off that beard. There's no need to overdo the hard work angle. I can see the job is going all right.'

'May I keep the moustache, Leonid Ilyich?' asked Stavinsky with a smile.

'You'd better ask your wife about that!' said Brezhnev.

Then he turned to Ustinov and the other members of the Defence Industry Commission. 'Let the two of them go by plane tomorrow and spend the next week inspecting a dozen factories or so. Then they can choose one. There's no time to build a new one. Let them make do with one we've already got. That's the first thing. And the second thing is to get Andronov to snoop about in America and Israel for the latest drilling technology . . .'

'They haven't developed the kind of technology we need, Leonid Ilyich,' said Gaikazyants.

'Are you sure?' asked Brezhnev.

'We receive all their technical literature. They have fantastic equipment for drilling in the open sea, but none suitable for use from submarines . . .'

'So you need a design office as well?! You'll take every last kopeck from me! OK, as it's "Deep Throat", we'll have to throw in a design office, too! When was it the Americans dropped an atomic bomb on Hiroshima?' he suddenly asked, screwing up his eyes.

'In 1945, Leonid Ilyich . . .'

'Well, we'll give them their own Hiroshima now! It's about time we got even with them . . .'

When Brezhnev had left, Stavinsky received congratulations from all sides.

'Listen! Why didn't you get amnesia before?' said Benzher, laughing loudly and thumping him on the back. Then he opened a bottle of pink champagne by smashing it against the stand containing the 'energy grid'. 'You just carry on being as hoarse as you like, until we get the project finished!'

An hour later Stavinsky was at General Headquarters, where Marshal Oparkov had driven him. The duty officer handed him the keys to 'his' office along with the key to Yuryshev's safe and various secret papers, which the colonel had handed in before going on leave. Although it was a Sunday, General Headquarters was full of people and nervous bustle. When Stavinsky opened the safe to deposit the secret documents, he discovered a large white envelope marked 'Marshal Oparkov, Personal'. He turned it over in his hands and then opened it. It contained two sheets of paper torn from an exercise book, and a short note, written in Yuryshev's hand.

The note ran as follows: 'Dear Nikolai Petrovich. What you are about to read was written by your daughter when she was in her right mind and fully in control of her faculties. All my subsequent actions follow naturally from her words. Farewell. Yuryshev.'

Stavinsky locked his door and began to read the testimony of Galya Yurysheva.

'I, the undersigned Galina Yurysheva-Oparkova, confess to having systematically betrayed my husband over the last six years of our marriage. Today my son, Vitya, caught me in the act of sexual intercourse with . . .' There then followed a detailed, perhaps even a sadistically detailed description of that sexual act and the three that had preceded it. Galya wrote that she had brought her lover, a young student from the Library Institute, to her flat at ten o'clock in the morning, straight after Yuryshev had left for work. Stavinsky could tell from the jerky writing and the tear-stained paper what it must have cost Galina Yurysheva to write those detailed descriptions of her philanderings that day. 'I confess that the death of my son was caused by the mental shock of catching me unawares with my lover. I confess that the boy committed suicide that day because of me. Signed: Galina Yurysheva. Dated: 28 June 1981.'

The second sheet of paper contained two lines only: 'Dad, don't believe her. She's a slut. I saw *it* with my own eyes. I can't . . .'

Stavinsky sat staring at these sheets of paper for a long time. Should he burn them? Or . . . He was already holding a lighted match near to the envelope. He extinguished it firmly.

18

The new white Volga sped along the Garden Ring Road. The treads of the new rubber tyres left firm marks in the snow. In her rear-view mirror Galina could see the orange disc of the sun, sinking below the horizon. She was listening to a summary of the daily papers coming over the radio:

'The leaders of Solidarity, while hating one another, share a single aim: to undermine the entire Socialist system and see a capitalist Government set up in Poland. By gloating over and exploiting the errors made by the previous Polish Government, by mouthing pseudo-democratic catch-words and stirring up hatred amongst ordinary people, the leaders of Solidarity have succeeded in creating chaos throughout the country and in paralysing the Polish economy. Their chief support is to be found amongst elements of Polish youth with fascist leanings. But the great mass of Polish workers remain firmly committed to the ideas of Socialism and the Socialist system. The new

Government of the country headed by General Wojciech Jaruzelski has announced that the period of warning and rational persuasion cannot last indefinitely. The people's patience is at an end. There is a limit to the Polish people's indulgence and their willingness to forgive the criminal actions of political adventurers and enemies. This should be realized by those who have exploited failures in the economy as a weapon to bring about the overthrow of . . .'

Galya switched off the radio. She had been feeling miserable enough about her own personal life, and now this business with Poland had to come along! Perhaps this was the reason why her father spent so much time hanging about at work, not coming home till two in the morning, his eyes red with exhaustion. The Voice of America and French radio, which she listened to in the evenings, having nothing better to do, were constantly announcing that the Soviet Union was moving more and more divisions up towards the Polish border. Of course, her father would be in charge of all this – who else? But whenever she said something to him like: 'Well, papa, is it time for us to be invading Warsaw again? It won't be the first time that you've . . .', he would rudely interrupt her and tell her to mind her own business. Something was wrong in the upper echelons. They were obviously waiting for something to happen, or perhaps they were simply afraid that Poland would turn into a second Afghanistan. But then perhaps this Jaruzelski would succeed in restoring order by himself. Galina had met him a few years before at a reception held at the General Staff Academy. He had an unpleasant, frog-like face, in her opinion, with moist lips and a sweaty hand, which he'd offered her when they were introduced. Even now the thought of it made her shudder. She hated men with moist lips. Anyway, those Poles could go to hell! Did they have such a bad life? We have meat rationed in some parts of Russia. Milk is only for children, and even then it's watered down. People queue for hours on end at the chemists' just to get vitamin pills. Yet even so, nobody in Russia goes on strike! The Poles could go to hell! It made her sick just to think about them!

At Vosstanie Square Galya made a right turn, enjoying the sensation of driving a powerful car. As she was passing a theatre, she saw the famous young actor Boyarsky getting into his Lada. He looked just like d'Artagnan from *The Three Musketeers*. His large brown eyes met Galya's and then followed her progress down the street. She smiled to herself. Everything was still OK. In fact everything was *very* OK! A good-looking, shapely brunette dressed in a mink jacket and seated at the wheel of a new, white Volga . . . General Yuryshev's wife, no less! This was Life, with a capital L! True, Galya's hairdresser, Rosa, had tried to dissuade her from going brunette, but she had insisted. The less she resembled her old self, the more chance there was that Yuryshev wouldn't remember her infidelities . . .

All the same, as she approached the massive edifice of General Headquarters on the other side of Arbat Square, she felt more and more worried. She looked at her watch. It was registering 4.47, 12 December.

A few seconds later she skirted Arbat Square and drove along Frunze Street, as far as the main entrance to General Headquarters. The area had been cleared of snow. Parked in front of the stone steps were a dozen or so black limousines. The usual soldiers on guard at the entrance doors had been reinforced by a detachment of sub-machine-gunners dressed in thick army jackets. Down on the pavement there were two police majors, armed with megaphones, impatiently ordering passing motorists to drive past as quickly as they could: 'Drive on quickly! No stopping!'

But Galina needed to stop just here. No sooner had she braked by the kerb than one of the majors rushed over to her and struck the roof of the car with his iron truncheon.

'Drive on! Who do you think you are?'

Galina lowered the car window and was about to say something, but the major forestalled her. 'I'll smash in your headlights! Drive on, you scum! Who do you think you are?' And with that, he hit the roof of the car again.

'Scum yourself!' screamed Galya, beside herself with fury. 'You'll pay for what you've just said!'

'Whaaat?' said the major, bending down towards her and giving her a threatening look.

'I am the daughter of Marshal Oparkov! And I've come here to meet my father and husband.'

Galina stared him in the eye and watched the major suddenly go pale, with a feeling of vindictive satisfaction. He looked completely crushed.

'I . . . I'm s . . . sorry . . .' he stammered. 'F . . . forgive m . . . me. I d . . . didn't know . . . N . . . nobody is allowed to p . . . park here . . .'

'Bugger off!' said Galina, who had just caught sight of her father and Yuryshev coming down the steps. Her father had his marshal's greatcoat thrown over his shoulders, while Yuryshev was wearing his, with the empty right arm tucked into a side pocket. He had a moustache and the obvious beginnings of a beard. Damn that major! He hadn't even given her time to collect her thoughts!

Her father and Yuryshev crossed the road and headed towards the car. Her father bent down towards the open window.

'I'm sorry, Galya, but I won't be able to come with you. I've got to stay here . . .'

'But I've ordered a table for three at the Aragvi restaurant!' She was afraid of being left with her husband from the very beginning, and even avoided looking at him. 'You promised! Sergey has been let out of hospital, and he's just been promoted. We have to celebrate it!'

'Galya, I'm sorry, but there are more important things. Tomorrow martial law will be declared in Poland.'

She stared at the two of them, wide-eyed with fear.

'Does this mean war?'

Her father gave an angry frown.

'Not yet. So far it's nothing more than martial law. After that, we'll have to see. But it's got nothing to do with you.

Go to the restaurant without me, and have a good time this evening. I'll give you a ring later . . .'

And with that, he left, stooping more than usual.

Galya froze. She watched as Yuryshev walked around to the other side of the car, opened the door with his good hand and sat silently next to her in the wide passenger's seat. For a few seconds neither of them said a word, not even looking at each other. Galya didn't have the strength to turn round and look him in the eye.

At last she said the first thing that came into her head: 'Have you . . . decided to grow a beard?'

He shrugged his shoulders evasively.

'Where shall we go, Sergey?'

He coughed and then he said hoarsely: 'I'd like to visit Vitya's grave.'

Her heart sank. So he did remember . . . Everything!

She placed her hand obediently on the gear lever and drove slowly off. The Novodevichy cemetery, where their son was buried, was no more than ten minutes' drive away.

19

The 'more or less tolerable conditions' that Virginia's interrogator had in mind were those at Camp No 821-OR, a special establishment for female juvenile delinquents, situated in a former monastery twelve miles from Moscow on the shore of Lake Glubokoye. The ancient stone wall surrounding the monastery was reinforced by three rows of barbed wire and six look-out towers spread at intervals around it. The monastery church, which had long since lost its cross and gilded cupola, now housed a workshop for producing army sheepskin coats and mittens. Where the altar had been, there was now a dirty cinema screen. Once a week the inmates were shown old patriotic and educational films. The rooms at the back of the church and in a brick-built extension adjacent to it, contained classrooms, a refectory and the office of Colonel Yemelyanova, the camp commandant. The little cemetery attached to the church had long since been abandoned, of course, but there were still a few gravestones there, most of them defaced with obscene words and drawings, scrawled in indelible paint. The male sexual organs were the most popular design, usually accompanied by such phrases as: 'What wouldn't I give for a really big, hot prick!' You could see such inscriptions all over the camp in enormous quantities – in the latrines, in the former monks' cells each of which now slept nine or ten young girls aged between fourteen and eighteen years. Graffiti adorned the corridors and walls side by side with red calico banners and posters, bearing such slogans as: 'Shock Working and a First-Class Education are the Way to Freedom,' 'Preserve Your Honour from the Time You are Born' and 'Through Honest Labour We will Requite the Motherland's Trust in Us.' The camp authorities were constantly on the look-out for these anonymous artists, but it seemed that this was an accomplishment of which all the girls could boast. The banner 'Preserve Your Honour from the Time You are Born' was their especial favourite. *What* you didn't find written and drawn around that particular motto! During the two weeks which Virginia spent at the camp, these graffiti were enough to teach her the whole gamut of Russian abuse from A to Z.

As a teacher of English and yet a prisoner herself, Virginia really was in a special situation. The other people who taught in the camp school – there were six of them in all – used to arrive by train from Moscow at three o'clock every day, and from then until seven in the evening this assorted collection of under-age thieves, prostitutes, alcoholics and hooligans would receive lessons in Russian language and literature, arithmetic, geography and history, although lessons might not be exactly the right word for what went on during the class-hours. No other subjects were taught, as it was difficult to find teachers to work in such a school. After working from seven in the morning till one o'clock in the afternoon, the girls had an hour's lunch and were then allowed to walk around the monastery courtyard. By the time lessons started at three, they would be feeling fairly sleepy. Thin, under-developed, vicious and with a tendency to hysteria, all the girls were dressed in the same grey flannel uniform and heavy, rough leather boots, that nobody referred to by any other name except 'shitcrushers'. Unkempt and badly washed (they were only allowed a bath once every ten days), it was hardly surprising that the only things to hold their attention in class were fights and arguments. And in fact fights occurred all the time, usually for no reason at all, and always ended up in a general mêlée, interspersed with the vilest gutter-language. The only person who could pacify them when that happened, was the camp commandant, Yemelyanova herself, who had a fist as strong and hard as a man's, an asset which she put to use more often than shutting the girls up in the cooler.

At seven o'clock in the evening the civilian teachers used to rush out of the camp to catch the electric train back to Moscow. They might have been leaving Dante's Inferno! But Virginia remained. She had her own room – a tiny monastic cell with a narrow, barred window. The first night she spent there, after arriving straight from her interrogator's *dacha*, Virginia had felt positively happy. It was a far cry from what she had had to endure in the transit prison. Here she had an iron-framed bed with a real mattress and pillow, a bedside table, a wash-basin and no heavy bolt on the door. All the cells gave on to a long corridor, guarded night and day by 'wardens' – coarse individuals dressed in military uniform, who looked more like men than women. The next morning Colonel Yemelyanova informed her of her daily routine. From seven till one she was to work alongside the other prisoners, making quilted army jackets, and after lunch from three till seven she was to teach English to the rest of the girls. Virginia was amazed. What kind of teacher was she, when she could scarcely understand

Russian? How was she to explain grammar and the meaning of the words to the other inmates? 'That is your business,' said Yemelyanova. 'I've received my orders, that's all.' Then she took Virginia into the workshop, where sewing machines were rattling away like machine-guns and clouds of cotton wool dust hung in the air. This dust got everywhere, in your ears, nose, throat, and it made your eyes water. Virginia was given the messiest job – dragging the tightly packed rolls of cotton wool out of the sacks in which they arrived, unrolling one of them on a wide wooden table, placing a cardboard pattern on top of it and cutting out the shape of the back and sleeves with huge scissors. After an hour of this, her fingers were a mass of blisters and her eyes were streaming from the dust.

After a lunch consisting of pea soup, sticky black bread, oatmeal porridge and weak tea, Yemelyanova conducted Virginia to the classroom and informed the forty-five girls sitting there that they would now be learning English, as happens in ordinary schools. To make sure that Virginia didn't start preaching any bourgeois propaganda, Yemelyanova would always sit in on her classes herself or get one of her wardens to do so. Strangely enough, Virginia's lessons went very well, perhaps because the presence of Yemelyanova or one of the other women guards made the girls behave. Or perhaps it was because they felt a certain solidarity with her as a fellow prisoner, or again because Virginia, as an American, was like a creature from another planet, and this exercised a certain fascination over the girls. Particularly when Virginia put her English textbook to one side and said that she was going to teach them some children's songs. 'Oh! not children's songs!' they all shouted. 'Teach us some love songs!' Yemelyanova gave a frown, but said nothing as love songs were hardly likely to contain any capitalist propaganda. Ten minutes later the whole class was singing one of the songs from *West Side Story* with great relish. And so she became very popular in the camp. For the sake of being taught English and

American songs, even the more inveterate trouble-makers were willing to join together and repeat English irregular verbs after their teacher. And in the workshop they even presented her with a delicate silk glove so that the scissors wouldn't cause any more blisters or callouses on her hand.

But these songs soon led to an emergency. Four or five days after Virginia had arrived, the girls began to make something in the snow during their free time after lunch. The warden on duty assumed that they were busy making an ordinary snowman and so went into the office to keep warm. However, ten minutes later the sound of loud singing from the girls as well as laughter from the sentries in the watch-towers, made Yemelyanova and her wardens look out of the window. There, made of snow and ice, was an enormous phallus with dozens of girls cavorting around it, screaming out the song which Virginia had taught them a day or two before, and dancing to the rhythm as if they were at a disco. In the heat of the moment a few of them had thrown their prison uniforms on the ground and were prancing around half-naked, teasing the soldiers on sentry-go in the towers by wiggling their breasts and bottoms provocatively.

Because of the 'corrupt influence of bourgeois culture', Colonel Yemelyanova forbade Virginia to teach the prisoners any more English or American songs . . .

And so the time passed. Virginia soon became accustomed to life in the camp and viewed the end of her two-week period there with considerable alarm. Should she return to the transit prison and the company of Vasily and the other adult prisoners? Never! But as for agreeing to collaborate with the KGB and indeed *work* for the KGB . . .

She realized full well that she *would* give in and agree to work for them, of course, though not for herself, she argued, or out of fear of Vasily, but for the sake of her child . . .

But while Virginia was torturing herself with these doubts and fears, those at the top of the KGB, where her fate was decided, were in no doubt that she would agree, and like grandmasters in chess, were already looking several moves ahead. That was why, on 12 December, Virginia was called away from the workshop by Colonel Yemelyanova. Ten minutes later she was sitting under armed guard in the back of a lorry once again, and an hour after that she was arriving outside the gates of that very prison at Krasnaya Presnya, which she had left two weeks before, unconscious, after being raped by Vasily.

When she saw the prison gates she became hysterical. 'No! No!' she cried, trying to escape from the hands of the wardress who had grabbed her by the elbow. 'I want to see the Investigator. I want to tell him that I agree . . .' But the guard brutally kicked her into the cell and drew the heavy bolt loudly behind her.

She was immediately hit by the foul stench that she remembered so well. That moist, glutinous smell made her gasp for breath. A sudden silence had descended on the cell, and then she saw the smiling figure of Vasily gradually descending from the upper bunk.

'You've come back, my darling,' she said, 'my American, my beautiful one . . .'

Her dirty, pudgy hands stretched out to touch Virginia, who could see nothing but that lecherous face and those thick, hairy lips. She could already smell that horrid mouth, opening to kiss her. Virginia lost control of herself and stuck her dirty nails deep into that face for all she was worth . . .

. . . An hour later, covered in blood and bruises from head to toe, with a split lip and a black eye, Virginia awoke to find herself in the prison's medical wing. To spare herself any more pain and shock, she willingly let the duty doctor place a gas mask over her face and administer a general anaesthetic.

20

The dining-room table at General Yuryshev's spotlessly clean, three-room apartment on Lenin Avenue was bright with flowers. A bottle of champagne and another of brandy were placed carefully on it, along with a delicious-looking cream cake, as yet untouched. That morning Galya had decided that she and Yuryshev would make up in the restaurant and then come home to be greeted by flowers, dessert, his favourite Ararat cognac and all the domestic comforts that could be thought up by a loving wife. But instead of going to a restaurant, they drove to the Novodevichy cemetery. There she showed Yuryshev where Vitya was buried, and he spent a long time standing silently and sorrowfully by the snow-covered grave. There was some rubbish around, including an empty brandy bottle which was actually lying alongside the gravestone. Galya took this as yet another reproach to herself. She hadn't been to the cemetery once since Vitya had died, and there had been no one to tend the grave. And now she suddenly remembered and rushed to remove the muddy old shreds of frozen newspaper, some tin or other and, of course, the brandy bottle. But a look from Yuryshev was enough to make her stop. Suddenly, with the rubbish still in her hands, she fell on her knees in front of him, in the deep, hard, icy snow.

'Well, kill me! Go on! Kill me!'

It was dark, and in the frosty half-light she could scarcely make out his features. Still without saying anything, he turned around and began walking towards the exit and the car. She got off her knees and trudged after him. The nightwatchman was already shutting the gates and was shooing off a couple of beggars. The two women held out their hands towards Stavinsky for alms. Both were wearing tattered old gloves. Without looking what he was doing, Stavinsky produced a couple of notes from his pockets, giving a rouble to one and five roubles to the other.

'Say a prayer for God's servant, Vitya . . .'

'We will, my dear, we will, with all our hearts . . .' they said, so overjoyed that they looked ready to begin their lamentations on the spot. But then they noticed Galya coming, and new hope was kindled in their hearts. Dropping the rubbish and empty bottle on the ground, Galya quickly opened her handbag and gave them everything she had – nearly fifty roubles.

'Who is it for? Who shall we pray for, my dear?' asked one old woman, almost in alarm.

'For God's sinner, Galina . . .' she said, bursting into tears. Then she walked past them, bending her head in an attempt to hide her tears.

The old women shouted something after her, and then one of them picked up the bottle which Galya had dropped. She could get some money for that, too. They give you twenty kopecks a time for any empties you return to the shop.

Stavinsky was already sitting in the passenger's seat. He leaned over and opened the other door.

'Where are we going?' she asked, without looking at her husband.

'Home,' he replied.

And now they were back at the spotlessly clean apartment, with the flowers, brandy, champagne and cake waiting festively on the table. A low standard lamp provided what little light there was in the room, concealing the patch on the wallpaper, where Vitya's picture had hung. Galya stood by the darkened window, exhausted and smoking nervously.

Stavinsky went over to the table and half-filled one of the champagne glasses with Yuryshev's favourite Ararat brandy. This woman was his most dangerous inquisitor, but what he knew about her gave him great power over her. And this power he would have to hold on to for as long as he could. So that meant: no intimacy. He'd have to delay that for as long as possible. He went over to Galya, stood behind her back and passed the glassful of brandy over her shoulder.

She turned her tear-stained face towards him. He could

see that she was about to fall on her knees again, crying and begging him for forgiveness, so he said hoarsely: 'Drink it, drink it, and give me a little more time . . .'

'All right. Of course, I will. Thank you, Sergey . . .' She took the glass and looked at her husband with such gratitude that he could stand it no longer. He turned around quickly and went into the bedroom. There he opened the chest of drawers, found some sheets and carried them into the room which had once belonged to Stavinsky's dead son, Vitya.

Galya could see that it was difficult for him to carry the sheets in one hand, so she rushed to help.

'Are you going to sleep in Vitya's room?'

He nodded.

'All right. I'll make the bed up for you,' she said submissively.

Later on, when he had closed the bedroom door, Stavinsky undressed and got into bed.

He could hear Galya nervously wandering about in the living-room, and then he heard the sound of a bath being run. A thin ray of light was coming in through a crack in the door, and Stavinsky couldn't wait for her to finish, turn out the light and go to bed. But he fell asleep without noticing it, no doubt because of everything he had had to drink during the course of the day.

He woke up an hour or two later. It was still the middle of the night. He could feel somebody touching his right arm, which was encased in plaster.

Galya, drunk, with no clothes on, and with a nearly empty bottle of brandy in her left hand, was sitting next to him and stroking his plaster cast.

When she noticed that he was awake, she started sobbing. Then, still holding on to his right arm, she said softly: 'It's all *my* fault! God, what did you do to yourself because of me? I'm a shit, a swine!'

Here's one of those beautiful women you so often dreamed about in Portland, Oregon, Stavinsky thought to himself. She's drunk now, so you could sleep with her and enjoy all the pleasures of sex. She's drunk, so she won't notice that you're not the husband she had. Whereas the next time . . .

'Galya,' he said hoarsely. His hoarseness came naturally this time, as if he was a bad actor who can't forget about playing a part, even in real life. 'Galya, go back to bed, and sleep now. Everything's going to be all right. But you'll have to wait . . . and . . . not in this room . . .'

She recoiled, as if somebody had struck her with a whip. What a bastard I am! Stavinsky thought to himself. What a bastard I am!

21

The next morning, 13 December, two reports were lying on Daniel J. Cooper's desk at CIA Headquarters, awaiting his arrival. One was an account of the declaration of martial law in Poland, the other was a short coded message from one of their agents in Moscow, employed as a tailor at the Soviet Army Generals' Outfitters. What he had to report was that his workshop had just dispatched a general's uniform and greatcoat to Army Hospital No 214/67. It had been specially made for the son-in-law of Marshal Oparkov, Major-General Sergey Ivanovich Yuryshev.

Part 4

Avenue of the Americas

1

Even before opening her eyes Virginia could feel the freshness of the sheet, evidently not a prison sheet, and that the blankets were not just plain cloth, but fleecy. Her battered body was still covered with traces of cuts and bruises, but the clean, warm, comfortable bed seemed to take away the nagging pain. Where had they brought her – to a civilian hospital? But it did not smell of hospitals – that particular smell of carbolic and medicines was missing. The air was fresh, and the pillow under her head was not a straw one like the ones used in prison and camps for female juvenile criminals, but a gorgeous downy pillow that she just didn't want to take her head away from.

Don't move! Don't open your eyes and don't stir, otherwise you'll give away the fact that you've woken up. Just steal five more little minutes from this latest encounter with damned Russia, the KGB, the prison officers. Curl up small as you used to do in Mummy's bed when you were a child . . .

Afraid of everything – a sudden blow, torture, another rape – Virginia slowly began to open her eyes. The room where she was lying was small and dark, but coloured patches of light came through the open window from the street. Virginia slowly began to sit up, unable to believe her eyes – there were no bars on the window! And next to the bed on the floor, on the soft, deep-pile carpet, lay her suitcase, half-open with her things hanging out of it untidily – dress, tights, sweater. Her coat and shoes were on an armchair nearby. So-o, she thought to herself, I'm back at that KGB chief's *dacha.* Carpets, clean bed, television, comfortable chair, door into the bathroom, standard lamp, but my God, what poor taste – like a typical room in some Holiday Inn. Even the windows didn't open outwards like

Russian windows, but in a typically American way – upwards. This KGB chief was a real admirer of the West, that's all you could say. Cheap stuff! Fixes up his *dacha* with American furniture, reads American books and newspapers, and drinks Johnnie Walker! Even so it was strange there were no bars on the window. Of course you couldn't actually get away from this *dacha*, for even if you climbed out of the open window there were guard dogs outside and a protective fence. And yet . . . What were those coloured patches of light flickering through the window? Surely there wasn't a Christmas tree out there?

Pulling on some tights and her favourite black sweater and hurriedly thrusting her feet into her black shoes, Virginia walked over to the window, full of curiosity.

What she saw made her feel weak inside.

Before her very eyes coloured neon signs flashed from the opposite side of the street: 'Hairdressing Salon', '7-Eleven', 'Lucky Casino', 'Video Games'. Through the wide glass window of the games hall someone was jerking the handle of a one-armed bandit. The window of the 7-Eleven was stocked with brightly coloured magazines and books. A police car drove slowly down the snowy street.

Virginia's throat felt dry. She was in America. They had got her out of Russia, exchanged her for some Russian spy! Oh Lord, but when? How? Why didn't she remember anything? What was today's date?

Virginia rushed over to the television – yes, it was a genuine American Zenith TV. She turned it on, but it didn't seem to be working. My God, this was some sort of a trip, a mirage, a dream! But no – she could see herself there in the mirror, she still had a bruise under her eye and it hurt to touch it . . .

With shaking knees Virginia went over to the door. A key was sticking out of the keyhole, a key with a plastic hotel tag and the number thirty-three! Virginia put her ear to the door and listened, but it was completely quiet outside the door. Summoning up her courage she cautiously turned the key to the left and the lock opened. So, an American lock – in the hotels where Virginia had stayed in Moscow and Leningrad the locks always opened to the right. Virginia carefully opened the door a little and stealthily looked about her. Right across from her door were some stairs, and the stair carpet also ran along the corridor with its numerous doors, as in any other hotel. A standard sign hung on the wall: 'No Smoking. No Spitting under Penalty of Law.' It was that sign that really convinced Virginia she was not dreaming and not mad. You don't dream signs like that! she thought feverishly, rushing back into the room to her case and frantically pulling out a dress, a blouse, a skirt, and all the time telling herself: You don't dream signs like that! You don't dream them!

She simply could not think what to put on. Oh, who cared? She grabbed a narrow white skirt and with trembling hands zipped it up. There you go! she thought in passing. This skirt used to be snug, and now it's hanging loose round my waist and on my hips! And yet it was strange that she could remember nothing – neither crossing the border, nor the flight. When all was said and done, it was an eleven-hour flight from Moscow to America, she couldn't have slept the whole time! And how did she get through customs at Kennedy Airport? No, it was delirium, she was going crazy! But – here was the open door, the corridor, the stairs . . .

Slowly, one stair at a time, Virginia began to go cautiously down. After one flight she found herself in an exactly similar corridor with the same red carpet. There was no one here either, and once again the same sign was hanging on the wall: 'No smoking. No Spitting under Penalty of Law.' Virginia touched the sign – a real glass sign. She stroked it lovingly and would even have kissed it if at that moment she had not heard music downstairs and a voice that she could have recognized among a thousand others – Stevie Wonder was singing about fateful love. Drawn by this music Virginia took a few more steps down the stairs and saw the hotel foyer – the typical foyer of any middle-class American hotel: armchairs, porter's desk, Christmas tree in the corner, magazine table with advertising brochures. A girl in glasses sat at the porter's desk reading a thriller by Ed McBain. Trying to walk so that this girl would not hear her footsteps, Virginia moved slowly towards the hotel's revolving glass doors. She did not know herself why she was afraid to go up to this girl – perhaps so as not to shatter the mirage, or perhaps because this whole hotel might turn out to be the Soviet Embassy or Consulate in the USA. She was within a few feet of the door when there was a sudden sharp ring of the telephone on the girl's desk. Virginia's spine turned cold, she made a dash for the door, and ran out into the street.

The cold air chilled her burning face.

The street proved to be real. Not only that, from some window in the hotel, which did indeed have a Holiday Inn sign hanging on it, Virginia caught a familiar sound: the breathless hysterical patter of a Crazy Eddie ad: 'Nobody's-got-prices-cheaper-than-Crazy-Eddie! Go-to-any-store-find-out-the-price-of-any-article! But-don't-buy-it! Don't-buy-anything-from-anyone! Bring-that-price-to-a-Crazy-Eddie-store! And-Crazy-Eddie-will-SMASH-that-price! Crazy-Eddie-will-sell-it-to-you-even-cheaper! Only-buy-at-Crazy-Eddie!'

Virginia leaned against the wall of the hotel, closed her eyes, and silent tears of happiness rolled down her cheeks.

God, she was *home*! Never in her life had she so loved that Crazy Eddie, that 7-Eleven, and all of America as she did now!

Two well-dressed men were walking along the sidewalk of the deserted street straight towards Virginia, and one of them was complaining to the other in perfect New York slang: 'His lectures make me puke! Where did they dig up an idiot like that?'

They were obviously about to go into the hotel, but Virginia blocked their path: 'Excuse me, sirs, but what town is this?'

They both stopped and stared in amazement at Virginia who was now shivering in the cold.

'What's the name of this town? What state?' Virginia repeated, looking from one to the other.

But there was a sort of barrier of alienation in their eyes. Silently, without uttering a word, they walked round her as one would walk round an explosive object or a lunatic and quickly vanished through the revolving doors of the hotel. And once again Virginia thought it was all a dream. It's only in a dream that you talk to someone and they don't understand you, don't see you, don't answer you. And it was a dream when she saw an elderly Negro in a sheepskin jacket coming out of the 7-Eleven with a package in his hand. He crossed the street and headed for the hotel too. Seeing Virginia he stopped.

'Miss, I don't think you're dressed for this weather. You could catch cold. This isn't Florida, you know.'

'Well, where is it?' Virginia raised her face to him, her heart flooded once again with hope and despair. He had spoken to her; she heard his voice with its typical southern, Negro, Alabama accent. 'What town is this, sir?'

The Negro's good-natured face suddenly closed up, and he muttered through his teeth: 'Have you had too much to drink or something? Let me take you into the hotel . . .' and he took her firmly by the elbow.

But Virginia wrenched her elbow free and shouted into his face: 'I'm not drunk! I just want to know what town this is!'

'OK, quit kidding around!' said the Negro. 'Where do you live?'

'In Los Angeles. Lake Street, Altadena . . .'

'Got you,' replied the Negro scornfully. 'I'm sorry, miss, but this is a different state . . .' and he went into the hotel, obviously considering Virginia to be either drunk or insane.

Feeling that she was freezing and really losing her sanity, Virginia ran across the street to the 7-Eleven and pulled on the door handle. Immediately a little bell tinkled inside the shop to announce her entry. That familiar sound sent another pang of joy through Virginia's heart – home, she was home after all! She had never heard bells like that in Russia!

Inside, the store was crammed with products she had known since childhood – Apple Jacks, paper cartons of milk labelled 'American Farms, Inc', Lipton tea, Welch's fruit juices, cans of Manischewitz kosher food, Sanka coffee, and so on; a man of about forty sat behind the high counter chewing on a pipe and reading *Penthouse*. Looking up at Virginia he threw out the usual phrase: 'Can I help you, lady?'

Virginia looked round her like a hunted animal. No, she had not gone mad, there was American Budweiser beer, sliced bread for toasting, Kent, Winston, and Marlboro cigarettes, and finally, on the wall, an American telephone.

Virginia ran over to the phone, grabbed it off the hook, and dialled 'O'.

'Operator. Can I help you?' said a woman's voice immediately.

'I want to make a collect call to Altadena, California, please. The number is 797 0330,' Virginia blurted out. The shop assistant took his pipe out of his mouth and looked at Virginia in astonishment.

'Where are you calling?' the voice at the other end asked in surprise.

'California. Altadena, in Los Angeles,' and Virginia repeated the number of her hotel in Altadena. If only Mark could be home . . .

There was a long pause at the other end, then the operator's voice said sternly: 'Quit playing the fool, hang up!' and Virginia heard the dial tone.

Shattered, she hung up the phone and met the shop assistant's gaze.

'Have you been in our town long, lady?' he asked with a very slight British accent, and his hand slipped slowly, almost casually, under the counter.

'You want to call the police, sir?' said Virginia joyfully. 'I would be so glad if you did!'

'I already did,' he said and immediately pulled out a pistol from under the counter and aimed it at Virginia. 'Don't move!'

Behind Virginia's back the little bell rang softly again. She looked round. A well-built policeman stood in the doorway. Hanging from his belt, as normal, were a bunch of keys, a wooden night stick, handcuffs, a gun-holster, and a few other objects. A police badge adorned the chest of his uniform jacket.

'Willy,' the shop assistant said to the policeman. 'She wanted to make a collect call . . .'

'Put your gun away,' the policeman interrupted him. 'She's new. Slipped out of the hotel without Mickey noticing . . .' And he ordered Virginia: 'Follow me, miss!'

This policeman also had an accent, but Virginia could not quite make out what – was it Arizona? She felt as if she was taking part in the shooting of some surrealistic film. Suddenly there would be the order: 'Cut!' The street lights would go out, and the producer would say: 'Hopeless! It's all hopeless! One more take!'

But nobody shouted 'Cut!' and the policeman took her across the street frowning.

'Sir, where am I?' she asked him.

'You'll find out in a moment, miss . . .' He let her go ahead of him through the glass doors of the hotel, then led her past the hostile glances of the girl behind the desk, along the ground-floor corridor to door eleven, where he stopped and knocked.

'Come in!' said a voice inside.

The policeman opened the door, and the first thing Virginia saw was a large portrait of Lenin on the wall of a tastefully furnished office. A small plump man sat at the desk looking like a kindly country gentleman, a little old man in the uniform of a Soviet colonel smoking a fragrant Havana cigar. As soon as Virginia entered he got up from his chair and in a beautiful Oxford accent said in a kind, almost fatherly way: 'Please sit down in this chair, Mrs Williams. I see you are completely recovered. That's splendid! You look wonderful! Sit down, sit down, my dear! We won't get anywhere standing up. Sit down, we have a lot to talk about. Would you like some tea? Coffee? Or something a little stronger?'

The combination of the portrait of Lenin and the refined English, the cigars and the Soviet uniform, all seemed to fit in with the idiocy of this dream.

'Who are you?' said Virginia to the colonel, gripping the arms of her chair till it hurt her hands.

'My name is Stanley.' The old man leaned back in his chair and observed Virginia's uncomprehending face with a smile. 'Actually though, my name is Stanislav Vasilyevich, but *here*,' and he emphasized the word 'here', 'here I'm called Stanley.'

'What do you mean, "here"?' asked Virginia. 'Where are we?'

The old man's eyes lit up merrily. He sprang to life, drawing himself up to his desk again and leaning his round little tummy against it.

'And where do *you* think we are? Well, guess!'

Virginia looked out of the window at the flashing signs on the casino and the gambling hall which for some reason had not disappeared as they were supposed to in dreams, then at the portrait of Lenin in this office. And she said: 'I don't know . . .'

'You don't know?' the old man was surprised, even perhaps a little hurt. 'All the things you have seen, don't you recognize them?'

'America?' said Virginia, the hope rising in her once again.

'Right!' said the old man with delight, and Virginia felt as if she were at an exam and had received top marks for her answer. 'You had me quite worried. I had come to the conclusion our efforts had been in vain, building all this. Or that we had missed something. Of course it's America! The most genuine possible America!' Suddenly he asked: 'And what State do you think this is?'

Virginia shrugged her shoulders helplessly.

The old man sighed: 'Hm, yes . . . It's hard to say, isn't it? Because everyone's talking in different accents, right? And that's where you will help me, my dear. You are going to correct their American pronunciation. Well don't look at me as though you'd seen a ghost!' He was clearly enjoying Virginia's completely bewildered face. 'This town is an artificial mini-America quite close to Moscow. To put it crudely, it is a *dacha*, or if you like, a branch, of our intelligence school. Our students come here in batches to do a month's practical in natural American living. You know, you don't want to make a fool of yourself over there on some trivial detail. Like one time in Chicago back in 1939 I had a public embarrassment. I didn't know which way to go through revolving doors and started to push the wrong side . . .'

Slowly Virginia was returning from her dream to reality, from America to Russia. Her shoulders drooped and she only half-listened to the kind, cheerful voice: 'We have everything in this town: bank, bar, casino, supermarket, hotel, even dope – in limited quantities of course. But then we do have our own policeman. And you are a real find for us! Apart from the American accent you will act out situations from everyday American life with the students.' Then, seeing Virginia make a small gesture of protest, he raised his hand: 'You have a gift for teaching, we've checked that. You completely won those juvenile delinquents over with your English lessons! And here you're going to do even better work! You realize that once you have been brought here . . .'

'I'll never get home again . . .' said Virginia gloomily.

The colonel shrugged his shoulders, and then, leaning across the desk, said confidentially, as if he were speaking to his little daughter: 'Listen, Virginia. You would never have got home from the camp either. You simply wouldn't have lasted out there! I did six years under Stalin and came out more dead than alive, and I'm a Russian, I'm a Siberian! But here it will be like living in the bosom of Christ, believe me!'

2

Galina Yurysheva had come to a strange period in her life. She had not seen her husband for weeks. On 13 December he had flown off with Benzher and a group of engineers to select a factory for the mass production of some 'energy transmission grids'. The very fact that before his departure he had casually mentioned these energy transmission grids to her testified to a discernible thaw in their relationship. He had never previously confided in her over the details of his secret work, and this aloofness, Galina thought that morning, had been one of the reasons, if not the reason, for her infidelity to her husband. But now everything would be different. Of course, she had to give him time, and of course she had to surround him with affection, be patient over his eccentricities, over the fact that he had not noticed the new car and did not ask about the old one, that he drank sweet tea for breakfast even though in the past he couldn't stand sweet tea. And he lisped in a funny way from having his teeth knocked out, and had become more taciturn. But in the end what had happened to him was her fault. It was because of her he started to drink and even jumped out of the train. But now everything would be different. They would be together, they would be husband and wife in the full sense of the word, without fail! She wondered if he had had any women during their separation. Oh, she would soon knock those women out of his memory, let him just receive her back in his bed! She would show him everything her young lovers had taught her and he would not regret coming back together with her. She wouldn't just be a wife to him, she would be a lover like he'd never had before!

And as she fell asleep at nights in her lonely bed, she would think about that first night when her husband would come back to the nuptial bed, and her body would be drawn out with anticipated pleasure. She noticed that she had regained her former confidence in her own attractiveness. Her step had once more become springy, the languid look that excited the men had returned to her eyes. Young students were once again being drawn to her, and even some young tailor from the Soviet Army Generals' Outfitters, where she had been ordering her husband a general's uniform, was now calling her almost every day to say that some fantastic English cloth had arrived (wouldn't she like to order her husband another greatcoat?), and a really luxurious tweed, and some beautiful Italian wool (she could order suits for herself and for her husband) and finally – 'What about some Chinese silk, Galina Nikolayevna? We have some incredible silk for an evening dress . . .'

Naturally this twenty-five-year-old tailor – a slim, stylish young man with brown hair and vivacious eyes – had amorous designs on her. But to hell with those plans. You've had your innings, girl, Galina told herself. It caused your son's death and your husband's brain damage. But why not order her husband a new suit, and at the same time one for her father who was having sleepless nights just now over this Polish business; God knows what was going on in Gdansk and Silesia – any day now they would have to bring the troops into Poland – why not order them each a suit, and an evening dress for herself – such a temptation, of course, Galya could never withstand. And when she arrived at the tailor's her eyes just popped out of her head – the cloths which this sprightly young tailor laid out before her could not be found in a single shop.

She ordered two suits each for her husband and her father, and for herself – three evening dresses in Chinese silk and fine Italian wool and also a skirt in cherry-pink velours. Yes, that's what it meant to be a general's wife – you went straight into a different category of special supplies, and not at all, as it turned out, because the young tailor was trying to make advances on you (on the contrary, he wasn't making advances, but behaving very modestly), but simply because all this was now something you were *entitled* to. Not through influence, because your father was a marshal, but because you were a general's wife. As long as she was a colonel's wife she was not entitled, but as soon as she became a general's wife – at your service!

And Galya was already imagining how she would present her husband with two new suits made at the tailor's from the measurements of his old uniform, when the tailor said: 'And when can your husband come in for a fitting?'

'No, I want it to be a surprise – two *ready-made* suits. You made him a uniform without his coming in.'

The tailor faltered: 'You understand, a suit is not the same as a uniform. The cloth is different, and the style has to fit the person, the figure . . . I can probably make your father a suit without his coming in, I don't think it's so important to him whether the lapel is broad or narrow. On the whole older people like a conservative style. But for your husband I think the suit needs to fit the figure, and be done beautifully. Have him call in, it'll only take five minutes. Or if you want I can drop in and take his measurements.'

'No, thank you, he's on a trip just now.'

'For long?'

She shrugged her shoulders.

'How annoying,' said the tailor, measuring Galya's waist, bust, and hips and calling out the measurements to his assistant. 'I would make him a suit in three days. Would you like the skirt down to the calf, or lower, to the ankle? Anyway, when your husband gets back have him call me and drop in for five minutes. I work here till late every day. My name is an easy one to remember – Volodya Ivanov. How shall we make the sleeve, straight or gathered?'

But on first returning from his trip her husband did not have time to get measured up for his suit. They all – her husband, Benzher, and three other engineers, colleagues of Benzher's – drove straight from the airfield to Yuryshev's apartment. Without telephoning, without any warning (He's checking up on me, thought Galina bitterly, wants to catch me unawares . . .), Sergey walked into the apartment and called to her from the threshold: 'Galya, let's go to a restaurant. Benzher and three others are down below in the car, so let's get a move on . . .'

She was hurt that he did not come up to her and kiss her – they had not seen each other for a week, and *she* had been thinking about him every day, waiting for him . . . But sitting in the Sofia with new Bulgarian wine, export vodka, lamb and mushrooms, but above all the abundance of male attention (she was the only woman among five men), Galya's mood improved. She noticed that her husband was glancing at her with a masculine interest and refilling her glass. And a hot wave of hope, that tonight there would be a full, total reconciliation, caused her to drink freely, laugh, and listen absentmindedly to the men's idiotic business talk. Oh, these Russian men! Even at a restaurant, even in bed with a woman, they talked about nothing but their work. And that was just how it was now: they'd been travelling for a week, inspecting some factories in the Urals, along the Volga, in the Ukraine, and now look: they still couldn't stop talking about it!

'Best of all would be if the factory were in Moscow,' said Benzher, a sharp-eyed man with brown hair. 'We have to try and push that through, Sergey Ivanovich.'

Galya looked at her husband. He inclined his head slightly to the left, just the way he always did before uttering some sentence, then said: 'No, it won't work in Moscow, but somewhere near Moscow. We might be able to take over the old electrical factory at Shatura and convert it to our own use in a couple of months . . .'

They got home about one in the morning, but in spite of Galya's hopes her husband once again went to bed in their son's room, and early the next morning went off on another trip.

3

Stavinsky sometimes felt he could no longer stand this insane tension, this balancing on a knife-edge. The conversion of the Shatura factory did not demand his constant presence, of course, Benzher's assistants coped with that perfectly. But the desire to keep his distance from Yuryshev's wife, from General Headquarters and 'his' father-in-law Marshal Oparkov, forced him either to hang around in Shatura or to think up trips for himself to Baku where the design office of the Azerbaidzhan Institute of Oil-Drilling Equipment was working on a new design for a machine that would drill holes from a submarine. In practice his work boiled down to chivvying up other people and to being able to make a single authoritative telephone call and obtain an immediate consignment of Yakut industrial diamonds for the new design of diamond drill, some 'teflon pulsators' which were a mystery even to him, or titanium for the 'Benzher batteries'. He was managing the job brilliantly because, like it or not, he was devoting all his working hours and his spare time to it. The result was that, having been sent to Russia by the CIA to extract from the Russians the secret of the EMMA project, he was in fact vigorously pushing that project forward towards mass production. Benzher was absolutely delighted with his supervisor's energy. Several times he had tried to explain the 'Benzher effect' to Stavinsky over a bottle of brandy, that is, he had tried to remind Yuryshev of it – the discovery that underlay the whole organization of the new seismic weapon.

'To tell you the truth,' Benzher said to Stavinsky

confidentially, 'it's all based on the discovery of an eccentric geologist from Ashkhabad called Odekov who spends his time predicting earthquakes and who spent seventeen years establishing that vertical and horizontal tectonic movements in the earth's crust are unrelated, and even discovered new tectonic movements which he has called seismo-generating . . .'

But the mysteries of tectonic geology, seismology, and generation mechanisms were beyond Stavinsky's comprehension.

'Sweden is situated at the boundaries of the Baltic Shield of the East European Platform and the structures of the Caledonian Fold Belt that surround it. The structure of the Shield contains proterozoic metamorphic complexes of Svecofennides, Karelides, Gothian, and Dalslandian as well as non-metamorphosed sequences of Sub-Jotnian, Jotnian, Sparagmites . . .' – now what is the ordinary person supposed to get out of all that? After talking to Benzher one thing was clear to Stavinsky – Oparkov, Benzher, and that Yuryshev whom he was now impersonating had selected Sweden to be a new Hiroshima for a number of reasons. First, Sweden was not a member of NATO, and her own anti-submarine naval forces were laughable. But even though she was very weak by modern military standards, Sweden had two naval bases that were crucial for the Baltic – Horsfjord in the Stockholm skerries and Karlskrona – and one on the west coast – Götteborg. The first two of these bases kept the entire Soviet Baltic Fleet under observation. The Stockholm skerries and thousands of other Swedish fjords afforded naval vessels excellent cover even in the event of a nuclear attack. And rather than smoke these ships and submarines one by one out of the fjords and skerries, it was easier to eliminate them with one seismic pre-emptive strike, in which moreover no one would suspect the Soviet Union of anything. That old lady Sweden would be shaken by an earthquake, an elemental disaster that would bring down the coastal cliffs and naval shelters where the fleet was, and destroy her military bases . . .

In other words, in case of war Soviet strategic planning had prepared for neutral Sweden the same fate as for 'neutral' Afghanistan, and Marshal Oparkov was hurrying Benzher and Stavinsky to complete the encirclement of Sweden with the seismic arc. Several submarines had been sent into Swedish waters to clarify the sea-bed tectonics in the Stockholm skerries and near Götteborg.

Of course, amidst this daily round of military production activity, when Stavinsky either had to rush around General Headquarters, or fly to the submarine base at Baltiisk, or take part in the first sea-trials of the new drilling rig at Oil Rocks in Baku, or speed up the conversion of the factory at Shatura (and the whole time behave like Yuryshev, feeling day and night as if he were at an oral exam answering questions from someone else's question slip or being prompted) – amid all this tension Stavinsky did of course have other moments. These were the moments he had once dreamed about in America, moments when he was able to enjoy his prestige, enjoy being a member of the elite and belonging to the elect caste. A young general flies around the country in the first-class section of a Tu-124 accompanied by four talented engineers, staying at the best hotels. Past the ticket queues at airports, straight to the reservation desk, and from there straight on board the plane to the first-class section where no ordinary mortal would ever get a ticket at any booking office, only Party members, Government officials, generals, deputies of the Supreme Soviet of the USSR, and so on. Even his new teeth were fitted for him without waiting on line, and for nothing, at the military clinic in Baku. A moustache, a neat little beard, and a slight huskiness made this young general even more impressive. He gradually reduced the huskiness, making it less coarse and thick – after all, who would remember the voice of the real Yuryshev seven years ago, before the operation on his vocal chords?

Then in Baltiisk a completely different memento of the

real Yuryshev suddenly visited Stavinsky – in that closed naval town a hundred kilometres from Kaliningrad where the submarine base for the Baltic Fleet is located.

After flying into Baltiisk Stavinsky spent the whole day at the dock where the U-137 was being overhauled. Like the other docks along the shores of the Kursk–Neringa Spit it was disguised to look like an ordinary house from the outside. But inside these 'houses' overhanging the water were hangars and workshops for the winter overhaul of submarines. Their hulls covered with thick tank rubber, the submarines were hoisted up on slings by the repair men. The rubber, damaged during long tours of duty at sea, was cut from the vessel with circular saws, the hull was scraped clean of rust, painted with red lead, and once again encased in a thick layer of rubber containing polyurethane balls for extra strength. The painters were painting out the pennant number U-137 and putting on a new number: U-300 . . .

After spending the whole day in the dock Stavinsky went to the Ocean Hotel in the centre of Baltiisk with the commander of the U-137, Pyotr Kushchin, and his political deputy Vasily Danov.

It was a small, quiet town with buildings not more than four storeys high, dusted with snow and surrounded by beautiful pine forests where Hitler and Goering once had *dachas*, and where now members of the Politburo sometimes hunted elk, deer, and wild boar . . . The town would have had a completely ordinary, sleepy, tranquil air about it if it had not been for the dark naval greatcoats of the submariners that one kept meeting. But the hotel was particularly striking for its abundance of sailors, especially the large restaurant on the first floor. A band blared away on the small stage, and to this ear-splitting music visiting naval engineers, naval supplies staff, and resident submarine officers drank every evening a huge quantity of vodka, brandy, and champagne and danced with the local female contingent which was clearly not enough to go round them all.

Stavinsky, Kushchin, and Danov sat wearily having supper in a corner of the restaurant at a table that had been reserved since that morning. They washed a tough piece of tongue down with a bottle of vodka, but Stavinsky pleaded tiredness and refused a second bottle. As he moved towards the door a waitress from the other side of the room – a large blonde of about twenty with big doe-eyes – casually came over to him.

'Congratulations,' she smiled, indicating his general's epaulettes.

'Thank you . . .' he answered with Yuryshev's huskiness.

'You've grown a beard,' she drawled and even stroked his cheek . . .

'Tanya!!' someone shouted from one of the tables. 'Where's the mineral water? How long do we have to wait?'

'Coming . . .' replied the waitress, drawling again, and went unhurriedly into the kitchen.

At twelve-thirty the noise of the band beneath Stavinsky's window finally ceased, in another fifteen minutes Stavinsky was asleep, and at exactly one in the morning he was awoken by a short tap on the door.

'Who is it?' he asked with irritation, quite sure that it was some drunk trying to get into the wrong room.

'It's me, Tanya,' came the soft, singsong voice of the waitress.

Stavinsky pulled on his uniform trousers and opened the door.

'Are you alone?' Tanya marched into the room as if she owned it. There was a large shopping-bag in her hand. She took out a bottle of Soviet champagne, a half-empty bottle of Armenian cognac and some snacks, caviar, lettuce, pastries. She put it all on the table and without saying a word went into the bathroom. Stavinsky heard the noise of the shower. He realized that this Tanya must have come to Colonel Yuryshev's room in this unceremonious fashion when he came up to Baltiisk on official business. Now Stavinsky had 'inherited' this Tanya. It could have been quite an interesting little situation, if only Stavinsky were not afraid of being discovered. So he undressed again, got into bed, and pulled up the cover, and when Tanya came out of the bathroom completely naked, her hair down over her shoulders and her ample breasts, he mastered his growing desire and said: 'I'm very tired tonight, you know . . .'

'I know, you always are,' she answered calmly, sitting down at the table. 'I'm exhausted too, I've been on duty since morning . . .'

She poured herself a full glass of cognac, drank it down in one, slowly ate two caviar sandwiches, had another drink, then turned off the light and silently got into bed with Stavinsky.

He automatically moved away towards the wall, but she passed a soft strong arm under his head and he felt her strong body against him, swelling like a young apple. He froze. And Tanya also lay quietly, not moving, her eyes closed, resting from a long, hard day's work. Her breathing became more and more regular, her full lips opened slightly, and it seemed as if she was falling asleep. And indeed she did fall asleep – quickly, almost immediately. But he merely had to stir, and she turned towards him sleepily, and her whole warm, soft body clung to him from shoulders to feet. And by an erotic reflex that was beyond his control his hand reached for her breast. When she felt this she gave a little gasp, became very still, and opened a large green eye. This eye stared at him expectantly.

'Wait . . .' he breathed out and very slightly pushed her away from him. 'You know . . . You know I was in an accident . . . And I . . . I . . . How can I put it simply? Well anyway, I had concussion and I forgot a few things . . .'

'What did you forget?' she said in surprise.

'Well . . . I forget how we used to do it . . . How you like it . . .'

She laughed: 'Hm . . . As if that ever interested you! Just lie still. I'll do everything as usual. I'll do everything the way you like it . . . Silly! Just keep holding my breast, all right? . . .'

. . . That night he discovered things about Yuryshev that no amount of former friends or documents could have told him.

At dawn next morning a tousled Benzher came bursting into his room without knocking.

'Old man, a great idea!' he began in the doorway without even shaking the snow off his jacket, but seeing Tanya in Stavinsky's bed he stopped short. 'Oh, hell!' he said in annoyance. 'Good morning . . .' and he began nervously pacing up and down the room, saying to Stavinsky: 'Get up quickly! Let's go, I have something to tell you . . . I had an idea in the night, so I got on a plane and came straight here . . .'

. . . A few minutes later on the dark snowy street Benzher was striding along the icy pavement waving his arms and heatedly explaining to Stavinsky: 'I'm an idiot! An utter moron! If I'd had this idea six months ago we wouldn't have had to put the U-137 aground at Karlskrona. And we don't need any drilling equipment for laying EMMA! Imagine a minute submarine. Well, about the size of that bus, only on tracks and remote-controlled. The whole EMMA is packed inside it. The mother submarine delivers this little bag of tricks to the required area and lowers it to the bottom about five miles from, say, Stockholm or this Karlskrona. And this midget submarine crawls by itself to the exact spot and buries itself in a skerry, under the rocks, in a crevice in the sea bed. Do you understand? And it just lies there quietly until the right moment, until we press the button in Moscow. Can you imagine? The longer it lies there the more it gets covered with slime, mud, seaweed. In six months' time it will be indistinguishable from some boulder. Or even better: it would be draped from the very start with a sort of net covered with seaweed and shells. Ha! Superb! A sort of gigantic remote-controlled flea on tracks, with the whole of EMMA inside. Well? Can you imagine that?'

Stavinsky understood Benzher's idea very easily. This

Benzher might be an adventurer, but he was a genius.

'It's so simple!' continued Benzher with inspiration. 'Such midget submarines can be assembled right at the factory, mass-produced like cars. And like underwater fleas they'll crawl into all the NATO naval bases – in Sweden, Norway, Italy, and even America. And then – a word of command over the radio, and all the NATO bases are wiped off the face of the earth by an earthquake! Well? Nice?'

Stavinsky said nothing. Benzher's idea was simple and irrefutable, like everything born of genius. But he had to think up some way to hold up this plan and stop this brilliant madman. Kill him perhaps? Right now on this dark and snowy street, with nobody to see or hear anything . . .

'Look,' Benzher squatted down and with his glove began to draw in the snow the hull of a submarine with a tiny midget submarine attached to it . . .

Stavinsky looked about him and saw a heavy-looking rock near at hand. If he gave Benzher one on the back of the head with this rock . . .

'You see,' Benzher was saying. 'Last night I was watching the American news with my assistants. And when I saw how those Americans had attached their Columbia to the outside of a Boeing and the Boeing took off with it, I said to them: "Fellows! A submarine could do that too! It's exactly what Leonid Ilyich has been asking us for – cheap and original!" . . .'

Too late to kill him, thought Stavinsky, but not to stop this . . .

Stavinsky took a deep breath and said: 'If we suggest this idea now there will be a scandal. The new drilling rig has already been developed in Baku, and the factory in Shatura is nearly ready to begin production of the energy transmission matrices. And are we to stop all that now? They'll have our heads for squandering Government money. What it means in practice is that Academician Benzher put into production an idea that was not fully thought out, the Government spent millions of roubles on it, and now, just because another idea has come to him in the middle of the night . . . and what if tomorrow he gets a new idea?'

'M-yes . . .' sighed Benzher. 'It's always like that: the good idea comes too late. No, we're not going to halt anything. Because I still don't know how to pack EMMA into this mini-sub. And then, when would they instal remote control? In other words, it would be about a year from the idea to the test model, no less. No, we won't halt anything. But we can begin work on the mini-subs at the same time . . .'

Stavinsky sighed with relief to himself. Within a year he would somehow get out of the USSR and inform the world about these mini-subs with their seismic weapon. In actual fact they were delayed-action mines, mines on tracks . . .

'The main thing is to convince Oparkov of the brilliance of this idea,' said Benzher. 'And that's your job, old man. In some family setting when the marshal is in a good mood. Understand?'

So that's why you flew out to see me from Moscow in the middle of the night, thought Stavinsky scornfully. To get me to push your idea through with Oparkov! But it seemed that was not all.

'American surgeons have a brilliant piece of equipment,' continued Benzher. 'A TV eye is inserted into the patient's digestive tract, and this TV eye crawls around in total darkness, but the doctor sees everything on a screen and even controls the movement of the TV eye. What if we bought that equipment in America and converted it for the remote control of the mini-sub? Well?'

You son of a bitch, thought Stavinsky in admiration, you son of a bitch! That TV device can be found these days in an American hospital, it would be easy to buy it, no FBI is going to object to supplying the USSR with medical equipment. One would just need the permission of the State Planning Authority for the outlay of hard currency . . .

That afternoon, having promised Benzher he would pick the right moment to tell Oparkov about the midget submarines, Stavinsky flew to Baku to see the designers of the underwater drilling equipment. And he deliberately extended his stay in Baku, wasting a day in the drawing office and, as an important visitor from Moscow, being taken around in the evenings to various *shashlyk* restaurants out of town that were closed to ordinary people and where they served superb *shashlyks* of fresh young lamb and sturgeon. At night, like the rest of the Soviet elite, he listened to Voice of America and the BBC in his hotel room. The only difference was that everyone was interested in Poland at the time, but Stavinsky was hoping for a news flash about Virginia – that she had been released or exchanged for some Soviet spy in the US.

But the story of Virginia had sunk into oblivion and had long been overtaken by other sensations and other news – martial law in Poland, the Siberian gas pipeline to Europe, Reagan's sanctions, and the Christmas rush in America and Europe . . .

4

Meanwhile in Moscow, three days before the New Year of 1982, the Marine Institute completed the assembly of two new energy transmission grids, as they had promised Brezhnev. The engineers in Baku were promising from one week to the next to submit the first test model of the new drilling rig. This meant that Captain Kushchin could once again move in towards the Swedish coast in order to complete the 'Swedish arc', and it was only the high tension of events in Poland and the scandal in the Kremlin hierarchy that delayed this operation. Ustinov, the Minister of Defence, said as much to Marshal Oparkov when the latter laid on his desk Benzher's report that the operation was ready.

'Fuck Sweden!' he said testily. 'Let's sort Poland out

first. And anyway I can't ratify an operation like this without Leonid Ilyich, and he's ill right now . . .'

Soon Brezhnev's 'illness' took on a new colouring. First vague rumours went round General Headquarters and the Marine Institute about connections between Brezhnev's family and big-time dealers on the unofficial economy, and about wholesale arrests of these dealers. Then suddenly, on 19 January, General Semyon Tsvigun, the brother-in-law of Brezhnev and first deputy to Andronov, Chairman of the KGB, had either died or shot himself in extremely mysterious circumstances; and then five days later Mikhail Suslov, the chief ideologist of the Communist Party and Secretary of the Central Committee, died, and the wave of arrests even reached Brezhnev's family: his daughter's lover, the gypsy artist Buryatsky, was arrested over some machinations with diamonds, and they even pulled in his daughter for questioning . . . In other words, just now Brezhnev was not feeling up to Poland, or up to Afghanistan, and certainly not up to Project EMMA. Moscow was full of rumours about an impending change of Government, and right after Suslov's funeral Stavinsky even overheard a joke in the factory smoking room at Shatura: 'Hey, fellows!' said a young blue-eyed fitter to his friends, quite loudly and unafraid. 'At Suslov's funeral Brezhnev goes up on to the mausoleum, takes a piece of paper out of his jacket pocket, and reads: "Comrades!" – here the lad did a very good imitation of Brezhnev's speech impediment – "Today . . . our Party and the whole Soviet nation has suffered a great loss . . . Our dear, much-loved Leonid Ilyich Brezhnev has died! Hey, what am I reading? Oh, shit! I've put on Andronov's jacket again!" . . .'

Meanwhile the delay over completing installation of the 'Swedish arc' was annoying Marshal Oparkov. A career officer and professional soldier, he could not stand the military illiteracy of his immediate superiors – Marshal Ustinov, Minister of Defence, and Marshal Brezhnev, Chairman of the Defence Council. The mere fact that these

Party workers had given themselves the rank of marshal – the same rank that he had – infuriated the Chief of General Staff. But it was not just that they had given themselves the highest military rank, it was that, although they understood nothing about military strategy and were less literate than any little lieutenant, they still poked their noses into army plans, jumbled up military projects, and postponed the most important operations.

And realizing that any day now a far more decisive and powerful personality would come to power in place of Brezhnev, Marshal Oparkov watched everything that was going on in the Kremlin as if he were sitting in a trench shelter rather than General Headquarters. The campaign to discredit Brezhnev's name had failed, but Andronov had skilfully got out of the affair and was even staking a claim to be made Secretary of the Central Committee in place of Suslov who had died. But Brezhnev had survived too, he was alive, damn him, and nobody yet knew who would topple whom after Brezhnev's death, Chernenko – Andronov or the other way round. Yes, everything was vague at the moment, he needed to keep on the sidelines, but also stay on guard, and strengthen the army constantly. Whoever came to power, if he, Oparkov, presented the new Soviet leader with the most powerful army in the world, he would stay in charge of the army, and might even become minister.

And in order to let this future successor to Brezhnev know of his concern for the army, Marshal Oparkov decided at short notice to write a pamphlet about his military doctrine. Let Brezhnev write memoirs and enjoy literary fame, awarding himself prizes for literature – he, Marshal Oparkov, would use the printed word to far more important ends.

Summoning his assistants, the marshal began to dictate the main theses of his pamphlet. Looking ahead it must be said that this seventy-page pamphlet, *Always Ready to Defend the Fatherland*, was put out by the military publishing house Voyenizdat very quickly, as early as March 1982, and circulated in millions of copies to all sections of the Soviet Army, but more important than that for Oparkov, it was written about in the Western press and broadcast on Voice of America. That meant that even if Brezhnev's future successor had not taken the trouble to read the pamphlet right through, he could not help finding out what had attracted the West's attention in it, namely: '"The Soviet Union," writes Marshal Oparkov in his pamphlet, "cannot afford to fall behind in the technical achievements of modern military science, especially since at the present time the arsenal of basic weapons systems in the Western armies is being completely renewed over a period of ten to twelve years. Under such conditions any delay in the renewal of strategic military ideas, any manifestation of feet-dragging in the development and introduction of new concepts of military construction, is fraught with the most serious consequences . . ."' Marshal Oparkov spent a long time with Stavinsky working on this last sentence and editing it – so that the allusion to the criminality of delaying Project EMMA would be understood by those who were guilty of that delay and were postponing the operation, and yet would not be understood over there, in the West . . .

5

'Couldn't you perhaps stop by the tailor's for a fitting for my birthday, so as to be wearing the new suit on 6 February?' Galya asked Stavinsky nervously on one of his lightning visits to Moscow.

Stavinsky could see that Galya was extremely tense and that he could not postpone the 'fulfilment of marital obligations' any longer. There is nothing more frightening and more dangerous than a frustrated woman. But by now he was in a sense twice as prepared for this operation: in Baku, the city where you can buy anything you want under the counter, even imported contraceptives, he had bought some heroin from some underground pushers. Barbara from the 7-Eleven in Portland had flirted with heroin for a time, and on those nights she completely lost her head. It would be no great problem now to get Galya drinking the next time they had dinner out at a restaurant and then to tip some heroin into her glass of mineral water before going to bed. That night was perhaps a night such as neither he nor she had ever experienced before. Whether it was because Galya was starved of sex or because under the influence of the drug she completely lost her head, she demonstrated in bed all the most piquant things she had learned during her infidelities to her husband. At the same time she kept laughing and assuring him: 'Listen, you've grown, honestly!' Stavinsky told her it just seemed that way because she was drunk, but she could not stop kissing him, exclaiming drunkenly: 'I love it, I love it, you're driving me crazy!' And this in turn aroused Stavinsky . . .

He even regretted that this had not happened on the very first night he had spent in Yuryshev's apartment. Over-insurance as usual, he laughed to himself, but in this instance over-insurance turned out to be an advantage . . .

'You know, it wouldn't be a bad idea to invite Yury Churbanov to your birthday party,' he told her during a moment of rest. Yury Churbanov, Brezhnev's son-in-law, was the Deputy Minister of Internal Affairs of the USSR and would undoubtedly know in which camp foreign prisoners were held. This opportunity meant that becoming General Yuryshev had finally paid off!

Galya put her own interpretation on his idea. Right! The young General Yuryshev needs to move into the highest circles. And in that case he needed to get in not only with Brezhnev's set. That day they had shown Brezhnev on TV at Suslov's funeral. She had never seen such a frightful sight – Brezhnev was a total wreck, he had one foot in the grave. No, if she was going to kill herself to impress someone at her birthday party, it was not Churbanov they needed to invite, but Ilya Andronov, the son of the Chairman of KGB, one of the country's leading experts on America. One had to look ahead, into the future, one had to get connections with the future master of the country.

The next morning they went to the tailor's for a fitting for his two new suits. When he saw Galina with her husband, the general, the young tailor Volodya Ivanov threw out his arms: 'Well, at last! I was about to put your suits into mothballs as my Auntie Olya does in the sunny city of Yalta! Please step into the cubicle so I can measure you up, Comrade General . . .'

Stavinsky paid no attention to the tailor's flourish about his auntie from Yalta. He went into the fitting-room, undressed, and waited for the tailor to bring the half-finished suits. Galya sat in the hall looking at fashion magazines. At last the tailor appeared with two genuinely beautiful suits which were almost complete and fitted Stavinsky perfectly. But the tailor was not satisfied and kept twirling Stavinsky this way and that, stabbing invisible wrinkles and folds with pins and jabbering away non-stop: 'As my Auntie Olya in Yalta would say, the suit feels at home on you! Lift up your arm, Comrade General. Is it too tight under the arm? Splendid! Oh, if my Aunt Olya from Yalta could see who I'm making suits for!' And the tailor looked merrily into Stavinsky's face, giving him a meaningful look, and the words 'Yalta' and 'Aunt Olya' suddenly hit him like an electric shock.

'Keep still, Comrade General, don't fidget or you'll get pricked,' the tailor smiled. 'My Auntie Olga Nikanorovna – she's a sick old woman now – but when she was young she once got so badly pricked that she ended up pregnant . . .'

'What's your aunt's surname?' asked Stavinsky quietly.

'Krylova,' said the tailor equally quietly and added even more softly, looking round at the fitting-room door beyond which Galina Yuryshev and other customers were sitting: 'Aunt sends you greetings. Order yourself some trousers or a jacket so that you can come for another fitting. And come tomorrow after eight in the evening. There won't be anyone here, we can talk . . .' and he called loudly through the door: 'Galina Nikolayevna! Come and see how the suit looks on your husband.'

6

More than a month had passed since Virginia had found herself in the strange town of Mini-America, the country residence of the KGB's intelligence school. For the first week she was left alone. She caught up on lost sleep, got up late, wandered idly up and down the town's two streets – Avenue of the Americas and 7th Street – and examined the signs and shop windows, some of which were artificial, but more of which were genuine. She spent a long time in the 7-Eleven browsing through the American goods – cosmetics, shampoos, food. Touching these things with their little labels saying 'Made in USA' caused her both pleasure and pain, like reading old letters. The two little streets of this town, with their typically American flat-roofed buildings, were deserted in the mornings; these snow-covered streets ended abruptly at the edge of a large snowy field beyond which was a dense pine forest, and watch-towers. Virginia did not know whether the field round this little town was surrounded with barbed wire, but she realized there was no point in thinking about escape, and quite frankly thoughts of running away never entered her head. She was weary of everything – tired from what she had been through with Stavinsky in Washington and Moscow, from the Lubyanka prison and the interrogations, from the Russian women criminals and juvenile delinquents. Her heart was now filled with a quiet feeling of submission to fate and with thoughts about her future child. When it came down to it this gilded cage was far better than a prison cell. On the first evening old Colonel Stanley had issued her with fifty dollars for the week ('When you begin work you'll get more,' he had said), and now she could plan her own expenditure – six dollars a day went on breakfast, lunch, and supper in the hotel restaurant, and she could spend the rest of the money on afternoon coffee or cosmetics. The first thing she did, of course, was to buy Lancôme cream, soap and deodorant. To her surprise these things cost much less than in the US. Then on one of the shelves in the store she discovered some children's toys and decided to buy them immediately, however much they cost. But the shop assistant – the same forty-year-old with brown hair and the pipe who had called the police – said to her: 'You can have those toys for free. Some idiot brought them here, I don't know who! We don't have any kids in our town and I don't suppose we ever will . . .'

But Virginia did not want to think about the future.

A little plastic doll and an inflatable rubber penguin adorned the bedside table in the hotel room. Really, if you could detach yourself from the fact that you were in Russia and forgot that there were watch-towers in the forest clearing, you could almost pretend you were at home in this little town, almost like being in a hotel room in Altadena, Los Angeles. Or more precisely, like being on a filming expedition when the artists have built a set out in the open and thewhole group just lives in the set.

At two in the afternoon the residents of this small town poured out into the streets after their morning classes at the Holiday Inn. Now, during the second half of the day they were obliged to lead an active 'American' life – move four private cars from one side of the street to the other under the sign that said, 'No Parking 8 a.m.–2 p.m.', sit in the café, play poker, pool, use the gambling machines, make purchases in the stores, read American newspapers, argue about baseball, check their bank accounts, and date the few women on this intake – three students from the intelligence school – and the hotel manageress Mickey and the waitress at the restaurant, Gloria. Of course this flirtation was also more put on than serious: everyone knew that Mickey was Colonel Stanley's daughter and Gloria was the wife of one of the teachers at the intelligence school, the Spaniard Rodriguez. So Virginia, who was 'free', immediately became the focus of general male interest.

But to begin with Virginia held herself aloof and after two in the afternoon preferred to sit in her room with a book – especially as the hotel library was Colonel Stanley's pride and joy; he had amassed a vast quantity of cheap sentimental American best-sellers. But at breakfast, lunch and supper in the restaurant, even though she sat at Stanley's table and was under his care, she could not avoid the interested male glances and the occasional remarks that were made about her.

And she herself began to look at these 'students'. There were about thirty of them – of varying ages, but mostly about thirty years old, of varying nationalities – Bulgarians, Armenians, even Koreans, but Russians for the most part. These people, thought Virginia, would in the course of time go to America and live there on forged or genuine documents, open their own stores, firms, and perhaps even newspapers and banks, they would drive along American roads in American cars, sleep with American women and even father American children, and all for the purpose of spying and destroying her country.

But strange as it seemed, she could not find it in her heart to hate these people. Perhaps because she envied them, envied the fact that every one of them would be able to live in America as she wished. And even more because she felt abandoned and forgotten by the very people these 'students' were going to work against – Daniel J. Cooper, David MacKerry, and Carroll. Although she was soft and kind by nature, Virginia felt perhaps for the first time in her life a strange, unfamiliar joy of revenge – the CIA, that Daniel J. Cooper – such a smooth, conceited Washington dandy – they had persuaded her to come to this damned country, promising her God knows what – money, a wonderful trip, a leading role in a film, then this Stavinsky had swept her off her feet and even given her a child, and now they had chucked her, forgotten her, they couldn't give a rip for what she had been through in the Russian jail and what she would have had to go through in the camps if she hadn't ended up here in this odd Mini-America. They had abandoned her here and forgotten her, and not one radio station even mentioned her name any more! So – these 'students' of the Russian intelligence school would punish the CIA for their stupidity, treachery, and deception . . . But more often than not she realized she was being unfair, and she tried to justify herself for what she was doing. After all, if she didn't teach these students a Californian accent or some detail of behaviour typical for real Americans, then someone else would – Colonel Stanley and the three others – Garcia Rodriguez, a Spaniard of American extraction, the Negro Louis Norton, and the American Hungarian Martin Koren – all in charge of the practical course at the town . . .

Of course she could see that the fat little colonel was surreptitiously trying to draw her into the work. Each day at supper he would question her about any small discrepancies that had struck her during the day between the town and normal American life. Virginia would list these discrepancies: there were no sales notices in the stores, no coupons, one of the standard toys that all Americans grow up with, like Miss Piggy and Superman, no paper cups in the café, and in the movie theatre where the students were shown old American films, no one was putting their feet up on the backs of the seats in front of them, and the movie theatre didn't sell popcorn.

'And apart from all that I don't have an American Express card,' joked Virginia.

And then a few days later she noticed that nearly every one of her comments had been noted by the colonel: large signs appeared in the 7-Eleven saying, 'Sale', '30% Discount', holes appeared in the pages of the *New York Times* and *Washington Post* where coupons had been cut out offering discounts on toothpaste and men's underwear, the café introduced paper cups, in the movie theatre they started to give out free popcorn to everyone in the audience so as to get them used to this American custom.

A week later Colonel Stanley gave her eighty dollars instead of fifty, saying with a laugh: 'My child, you've already earned yourself a raise!'

Virginia looked at him in surprise – what for? And he said: 'What's more, I shall introduce a regular increase to keep pace with inflation. By the way, I want you to come to my class at nine tomorrow. Don't be afraid, you're not going to do anything terrible, you'll just sit and watch. It will be held in the café.'

But 'just sit and watch' was of course an empty phrase. When Virginia arrived next morning at the Now Café the whole group was already there – eight people, with Colonel Stanley dressed in a civilian suit with his eternal Havana cigar in his mouth, sitting in front of them at the bar on a high revolving stool and holding a book in his hand – *How to Pick up a Girl*.

'Today we're having a practical on how to recruit an American girl. A week ago I gave you this book to read, and I expect you have studied it by now, so now we shall get down to the practical. Virginia, my child, come over here and sit next to me.' He pointed to a high revolving stool at the bar, and when she had sat down he turned to the group: 'Well, who's feeling brave? Who wants to come up and recruit this corker?'

Colonel Stanley spoke such classy English, playfully inserting bits of everyday slang in just the right places, that Virginia forgot she was in Russia as she listened to him. And in fact this lesson, like all subsequent ones, was just like a class in drama school, rehearsing by that same Stanislavsky method – 'act the part whatever the circumstances' – which Virginia had been so fond of during her younger acting days. And to see this book. *How to Pick up a Girl* (it had been a best-seller in America five or six years ago) in the hands of the fat little Stanley, a KGB colonel using it as a teaching aid in a KGB school, just made Virginia laugh. She recalled the furore that this book had caused in the papers: a shy reserved little fellow simply had not been able to find himself a girlfriend or even get to know any girl or woman, so he got a tape-recorder and went out into the streets like a reporter and began asking women that very question: what was the best way to get to know them? After a few months he collected all his interviews together into a book and became a millionaire. But she wondered what he would think if he knew that this book had become a teaching aid in a Moscow intelligence school . . .

Virginia sat up at the bar, ordered a Pepsi, and quickly sent the first student packing – a good-looking and rather forward young man from the Caucasus – either a Turk or an Armenian. This Caucasian sat down at the bar two seats away from Virginia and quite skilfully offered her his lighter when she took a cigarette, acting out a bored American in a café. Virginia listened quite favourably to his first routine phrases, but as soon as he moved to the stool next to her and said: 'May I get you a drink?' she turned away from him sharply and shook her head at Stanley.

'What's the matter?' asked the colonel.

'In the first place, he doesn't know what he's supposed to be,' she explained. 'What is he – a clerk? A businessman? A plumber? In any case he smells like a plumber, even worse in fact. To be quite frank, he smells of sweat. No American woman is going to start talking to a man with BO like that.'

For the first time Virginia saw Colonel Stanley, who so resembled a fat, kind little old gentleman, grow so purple with rage that even his neck darkened.

'Well done . . .' he said to Virginia through his teeth, and turned to his students. After that Virginia heard such a stream of American obscenities as you don't often hear even in Harlem. 'How many times have I told you to use expensive soap, expensive shampoo, and deodorant! You're skimping, you bunch of crap! You're skimping on the soap so as to get an extra slug of brandy! I'm going to come round the rooms today and check who's got what soap! How many of you rinsed your mouths out with Fresh Start this morning?' Nobody put his hand up, but this honesty calmed Stanley a little. 'So-o,' he grumbled, already appeased. 'At least you admit it! You're letting the school down in front of Miss America . . . Next!'

He had called Virginia Miss America and the name stuck – not just at that lesson, but for good. In a couple of days Stanley's whole group smelled of Chloe and Cavalier, everyone had beautifully manicured nails, and nobody scratched the back of his head while talking to Virginia. And Virginia found it more and more difficult to get rid of these cavaliers, not just during classes but afterwards, in the evenings. Because these men turned out to be very well educated, with an excellent knowledge of American and English classical and modern literature and music. Graduates of foreign language institutes in Moscow and the provinces, and also of the highest military interpreters' school and the KGB school, each one of them had studied English for no less than ten or twelve years, sitting round the clock in language laboratories, according to them, working on their British or American pronunciation; they had read mountains of books and learned by heart whole pages of Shakespeare, Whitman, Salinger, Bradbury, Updike, and other writers that Virginia had never even heard of. But of course no language stands still, it flows like a river, assimilating new words and nuances, new turns of phrase. Virginia noticed that some of the words these students were bandying about were old-fashioned or were not quite pronounced the same as they used to be, and she picked up these unwanted items in their speech and corrected them; sometimes she herself could not even understand certain words or ancient proverbs dredged out of some old English textbook . . .

On the whole she settled down quickly in Mini-America. Her lessons on the American way of life became more and more like fun play rehearsals and students from other groups began to be drawn towards them. Colonel Stanley quietly started to hand the whole course over to her and go about his own work, since he was already up to the eyes in other things in the little town.

From the third week on, Virginia began to receive 100 dollars a week – not at all bad for a small town where there was really not much to spend one's money on apart from food and toiletries.

At the New Year's party in the hotel restaurant the students presented Virginia with gifts, attention, and very persistent courting. And then at one of the classes, 'How to Behave at a Disco', with the disco music crashing about her, flushed from dancing, stimulated by her work (she could never get these men to relax, they danced in a stiff, wooden sort of way), in the middle of all this noise, laughter, and general excitement Virginia suddenly saw the students go completely quiet and still. She continued to show them dance steps to the music, and went on dancing, but then, following their gaze, she turned round to the door and . . .

In the doorway stood Colonel Stanley and a tall elderly general with a tired face wearing horn-rimmed glasses – the very one who had given her caviar sandwiches in his office on Dzerzhinsky Square and Johnnie Walker at his *dacha*. The same general who had decided her fate and sent her here from the prison. But this was the first time Virginia had seen him in his general's uniform.

She was confused and embarrassed, not knowing how long they had been standing watching her, and she hastily switched off the record-player which was still pumping out crazy disco music.

'No, no,' said the general. 'Go on.'

And he walked out of the class with Colonel Stanley.

Virginia made a hash of the rest of the lesson, and before lunch Colonel Stanley's daughter Mickey came up to her and said: 'Daddy would like you to go and see him in his office,' and she winked knowingly: 'Go put a pretty dress on.'

Virginia went to her room and for a long time could not decide what to wear. Of course that general would be in Stanley's office. How should she behave with him? It was his people who killed Yuryshev at the airport, it was his people who threw her into jail, interrogated her, fed her on some ghastly watery soup, and shoved her in the cell with 'Vasily'. But on the other hand, had she not come to their country of her own free will as a spy, to steal Yuryshev who knew some Russian secrets? They had caught her and put her in prison – wasn't that what they did in America to Russian spies? Wasn't the famous Russian spy Abel in an American jail? It was just that the prisons they had here – God help you! You wouldn't want to go back into one for love or money! But wasn't it this general who had pulled her out of that frightful prison and transferred her here, to human life?

And Virginia put on the same dark-purple dress with the high neck that she had worn when she came to the restaurant of the Capitol Hilton for her first meeting with Daniel J. Cooper. And she gathered her hair in the same way in a modest bun at the back. That was her little female revenge on the CIA and on Cooper personally as head of the Russian Section, because they had abandoned her and forgotten her.

The table in Colonel Stanley's office was set for three. It was adorned with a bucket of French champagne. The general and Colonel Stanley stood up as Virginia entered, and Stanley politely helped her into her seat, then banished the awkwardness of the first minute by cracking a few jokes. The first toast he proposed to Virginia, or, as he said, 'To Miss America, to the Hollywood star who has honoured our small provincial American town with her presence and has become a full member of our local community!' After that he praised Virginia's teaching talent to the skies and began with comic exaggeration to recount to the general amusing details of the lessons on 'how to pick up an American woman' and other incidents from the life of their little town.

Virginia blushed and got embarrassed when he praised her, and noticed the general's tired pale blue eyes resting on her attentively. After lunch the general said: 'I would like to invite you to come for a ride with me. Would you object?'

Virginia said nothing. Could she object to a man who could consign her and the whole town to a prison camp, hard labour with a mere gesture, let alone a word! But he was polite, courteous, and even asked her permission!

A long black Government limousine with a chauffeur stood in the street outside the hotel, as well as a black Volga with the general's bodyguards. No sooner had the general and Virginia emerged from the hotel than one of them ran over to the limousine and opened the door for his boss and his lady.

The limousine glided off, quickly left the town, passed the fields, and without stopping at the control points and barriers, which obligingly opened a hundred yards before the car reached them, plunged into the pine forest. The bodyguards' Volga followed along behind politely.

The general and Virginia sat silently in the back seat separated from the driver by a dark glass partition. A fairy-tale Russian forest floated past the windows, its white and lilac snow-caps shining in the sun. The icy orange disc of the sun glinted through the trees as if it was chasing the car.

The general took Virginia's hand. She looked at him with shy, anxious eyes. He moved his arm across her shoulder and gently pulled her towards himself. And Virginia leaned against his general's uniform as obediently as a kitten, noting almost unconsciously that he smelled of good soap and exquisite male cologne.

7

'. . . According to our information the Main Directorate for Corrective Labour Institutions at the Ministry of Internal Affairs of the USSR has one special camp in the USSR for foreign prisoners. The camp is located in the town of Potma, 280 miles north-east of Moscow. The U-2 pilot Garry Powers served his prison sentence in this camp, as did the Americans Gerald Amster, Paul Brawer, and Dennis Burn, all accused of drug trafficking in the USSR. At the time they were in the camp, in 1976, there were only men there, about 110 from various countries. The prisoners are made to work at the camp factory making crystal chandeliers and television cabinets. They wear a flannel uniform bearing their names – no numbers! – printed on the front and back. The food is very poor, the daily ration containing not more than 2,500 calories. It is possible that since that time a women's camp or women's barracks for foreign women prisoners has been organized at the camp or nearby, although in 1977 one foreign female prisoner from Singapore served her sentence in a regular women's colony owing to the lack of such a camp.

'Unfortunately this is all the information we have at our disposal on the maintenance of foreign prisoners in the USSR. We recommend that in searching for Virginia you do not make contact with KGB workers, but get to know those in charge of the Corrective Labour Institutions' Directorate, in particular the head of the Directorate, Lieutenant-General Ivan Bogatyryov.

'We request you pass on without delay through our resident all materials concerning the submarine U-137 and the reasons for its penetrating Swedish waters. We are also vitally interested in all other secret information to which you have access . . .'

'Only in exchange for their getting Virginia and me out of the USSR,' Stavinsky stated to the tailor Volodya Ivanov, and burned the coded message from MacKerry and Daniel

J. Cooper in an ashtray. The coded message also contained Cooper's and MacKerry's mild surprise that Stavinsky had risked taking the place of Yuryshev. 'Full of admiration for your courage and praying for your success and Virginia's health,' they wrote from Washington.

'They're praying!' said Stavinsky grimly. 'Virginia's already in her third month, she needs a high-calorie diet, fresh air, walks. And they're praying! No, I shall hand over all the secret materials only when they get me and her out of the USSR. And as to how they do it – that's their problem!'

'But we don't even know which prison she's in! And besides, think – why would American intelligence want to get you out of the USSR when you're occupying such an important position?!' said Volodya Ivanov.

'That's precisely why I shan't say anything till they get me out,' said Stavinsky. 'Just tell them it is indeed about a new super-powerful strategic weapon that can shake up any continent. And let them bear in mind that the encirclement of Europe with this weapon began with the cruise of the U-137. It will resume in the next few weeks. But I'm not going to tell them any more, not a word.'

'Strange,' said Volodya. 'If you have such important information in your hands how can you sit on it? If something were to happen to you, God forbid, it would mean the weapon would remain in the hands of the Kremlin and those swine would bring the whole world to its knees. Right?'

'And if I give you the materials on this weapon today, then in a week's time it will be in the American papers, and a day later I will be bumped off by the KGB. So tell Washington my conditions: the drawings of the new weapon in exchange for Virginia's and my freedom . . .'

On receiving the tailor's coded report Daniel J. Cooper said to David MacKerry: 'Fucking hell! It gets harder every minute! Now what are we to do – find look-alikes for both Stavinsky and Virginia? Or organize a raid on all Russian prisons and Soviet Army HQ?'

'If the Russians organized the Pope's assassin's escape from a Turkish jail . . .' said MacKerry.

'How can you compare, David!' Daniel J. Cooper interrupted him nervously. 'If I had Andronov's facilities we wouldn't need either this Stavinsky or even Yuryshev. I would have put a stop to the leakage of American technical information twenty years ago, and the Russians would have had neither intercontinental missiles nor nuclear submarines. But now we have to steal our own technical secrets back from the Russians. I wouldn't be surprised if it turned out that this new Russian weapon had also been stolen from somewhere in Silicon Valley. But we've got to do something! It's a ridiculous situation! On the one hand we have to warn the Pentagon and our NATO allies of a new Soviet threat, and on the other hand we haven't a clue what they've cooked up over there . . .'

8

PRIORITY
SECRET

To: Marshal N. V. Oparkov,
Chief of General Staff

It is reported by our special service in Norway that the day before yesterday, 3 February, Daniel J. Cooper, Head of the American Section at the CIA arrived in Oslo for the conference of NATO chiefs and on the same day met with the American General Peter N. Scott, Chief of Combined Staff NATO Forces. It was announced in Oslo today, 5 February, that large-scale NATO exercises would take place in northern Norway under the code name Ella Express 82, and would involve about 15,000 servicemen, warships, and aircraft from the USA, Canada,

West Germany, Britain, Italy, Holland, Luxembourg, and Norway. At the same time as the NATO exercises, Sweden will be conducting a large-scale training exercise of her armed forces involving 24,000 servicemen, air force, and navy.

This report will be published in tomorrow's newspapers.

General B. Krasnopolsky,
Head of Main Intelligence Directorate, Soviet Army Moscow, 5 February 1982.

Reading this report in Marshal Oparkov's office, Stavinsky felt as if his legs were giving way under him. Cretin! He knew perfectly well that as long as he was here in Russia the Americans simply must not be given any information at all! They had received the coded message from the tailor about Europe being surrounded by some new weapon, and so, if you please – off goes Cooper to see the NATO Chief of Staff. But the KGB undoubtedly had its own agents in the CIA and at NATO Headquarters. And if the KGB found out the reason for Cooper's trip to Oslo! Finished! A complete cock-up! No more meetings with that tailor Ivanov! What the hell had induced him to go sounding off to the tailor about a new weapon? Just trying to boost his own price, idiot! It was time to tell Oparkov about this new idea, because Benzher kept nagging him every day wanting to know if he had told Oparkov about the mini-subs or not. And it was dangerous to delay the report any longer, because Benzher might go to the marshal himself . . .

'I think these NATO exercises are a delayed response to our concentration of forces on the Polish border,' Marshal Oparkov was telling him meanwhile, and he nodded at the huge map of Poland hanging on the office wall to his left. This whole map of Poland was slashed with powerful arrows indicating tank strikes and landings, the main strike being aimed at the Polish ports – Gdansk, Gdynia, Szczecin. 'They understand very well in NATO,' said Oparkov, 'that unless Jaruzelski deals with Solidarity himself we shall go into Poland. So they're doing a bit of sabre-rattling, trying to scare us. But it's too late – our navy has already blockaded Gdansk and Gdynia.' He leaned back in his chair wearily and took a sip of strong tea from his glass before continuing: 'However, Kushchin's cruise will have to be postponed for a couple of months. There's no point in pushing in there when there are manoeuvres going on, we'll wait. They'll buzz around for two or three weeks doing their little exercises and then as usual spend six months recovering from them. Incidentally,' he screwed up his pale blue eyes and threw the reddish grey forelock back off his forehead, 'while all the NATO forces are in the north, how about sounding out the bottom down south, somewhere around Italy? Italy is our next one after Sweden, isn't she?' He leaned over to the intercom, pressed the button, and said: 'Commander of the Fleet Gorchakov. Gorchakov? It's Oparkov. Listen, General Yuryshev is going to give you some points on the sea-bed near Italy in about an hour's time. You'll send a sub to these points to take samples of the bottom . . . Yes, it's for Project Deep Throat. He'll give you the details personally. Goodbye.' Oparkov switched off the intercom and looked at Stavinsky: 'There we are. By the way, it would be nice to put on that film *Deep Throat* for the guests at Galya's birthday party . . .'

Oparkov's face was tired but kind. Now that after many sleepless nights he had got Poland blockaded all round by Warsaw Pact forces, he could afford to rest and relax.

With a push of a button he summoned his adjutant, Major Ryazantsev: 'Kolya,' he said to the major. 'Call Statefilm and ask for *Deep Throat* for tomorrow.'

'They've already given us *All That Jazz*, Comrade Marshal,' replied the major.

'Never mind, they can give us *Deep Throat* too, they won't go broke.'

Stavinsky felt the colour returning to his face and his legs recovering from their numbness. When he read that secret intelligence report a minute ago it seemed to him as though that piece of paper brushed against his heart like the wing of Madam Death. But it had passed! He must quickly give Gorchakov all the details so that he could send a submarine to Italy, and not only that . . .

'Nikolay Viktorovich, I don't think we've quite finished the Kushchin story,' he said to Oparkov.

Oparkov looked inquiringly at him.

'No one in the West believes that Kushchin ended up in the Karlskrona Bay through a navigational error. And Western intelligence is almost certainly trying to find out what he was doing there. In other words, their interest right now is focused on Baltiisk, the U-137, and on everything connected with it. And we have a constantly growing circle of people involved in the project – designers in Baku, a factory in Shatura. So it would be very surprising if Western intelligence lost interest in Kushchin and his sub. How about putting Kushchin in prison for this Swedish affair? Not actually in prison of course, but let that story leak out to the West . . .'

'I understand,' said Oparkov. 'Not a bad idea. We'll discuss it tomorrow with General Krasnopolsky. Will he be at Galya's birthday party?'

Stavinsky shrugged his shoulders.

'Better invite him,' said Oparkov.

'I thought it would be better if the information didn't come from our intelligence, from the KGB, but from the camp or prison where Kushchin was supposed to be,' said Stavinsky. 'So that if we contacted the Directorate of Camps and Prisons, General Bogatyryov . . .'

'We need to discuss it with intelligence first, with Krasnopolsky,' Oparkov remarked, and asked: 'By the way, have you bought Galya a present yet?'

'Not yet,' answered Stavinsky, cursing to himself: he just wanted to use Oparkov to get into contact with General Bogatyryov, and now the whole thing had fallen apart. (It had turned out that Brezhnev's son-in-law Yury Churbanov,

Deputy Minister of Internal Affairs, would not be able to come to Galya's party, he was busy, but if he could just get hold of Bogatyryov he could take it from there.) Meanwhile Stavinsky said aloud: 'I can't think what to get Galya. Shall we take a spin round the shops?'

'Going round the shops would be pretty useless!' laughed Oparkov. 'But I could give the head of Army Stores a buzz.'

He was already reaching for the telephone, but Stavinsky said: 'I have one other question, Comrade Marshal. Academician Benzher asked me to report to you about a new idea of his.' Stavinsky briefly expounded to Oparkov the idea of making remote-controlled midget submarines for delivering EMMA to the required points. Then he pulled several sheets of Benzher's drawings out of his briefcase . . .

Oparkov heard Stavinsky out. Like Stavinsky, Oparkov in his turn needed only a few moments to grasp the essence of the new project and realize all its potential. And without even looking properly at Benzher's drawings Oparkov got up out of his chair and began pacing the room excitedly.

'Incredible!' he said as he went. 'It's just brilliant! When do you think we could make these submarines?'

'In a year, I should think . . .'

'Hell!' said Oparkov in disappointment. 'Today's when we need them, today! No, we're not going to postpone surrounding Sweden with the seismic weapon for a year. She's got me by the throat, that Sweden, she's got my whole Baltic Fleet bottled up. So we're going to have to work in Sweden as before, drilling as we did earlier. But those mini-subs – if we had a couple of hundred boats like that now that could quietly creep into all the NATO naval bases and sit there until the right time! We would immediately offer the USA general disarmament, withdrawal of missiles and tanks from Europe! Then they would really begin to sing!'

He went over to his desk, thinking to call Ustinov immediately, and had already placed his hand on the red Kremlin telephone, but checked himself at the last moment.

No, Ustinov wouldn't take one step without Brezhnev's permission, and Brezhnev was not up to midget submarines just now. Hell, then who could he call? Dmitriyev, Chairman of the Central Committee Defence Industry Commission? But Dmitriyev would not take any decisions without Brezhnev either. No, mini-subs with seismic matrices were a weapon of the future, a weapon for the one who got into power after Brezhnev. But who would? Chernenko? Kirilenko? Andronov? Grishin? Hell, one wrong move and you could be backing the wrong horse – and then you would blow your whole career.

Oparkov sighed. That Brezhnev, he was so gaga it took months to get through to him with any new project. He would have to wait and wait . . . If only someone more decisive and energetic could take power soon . . .

And instead of the Kremlin telephone Oparkov picked up the regular black one and said to the operator: 'Give me the head of Army Stores . . .'

9

The working day of General Georgy Andronov, Chairman of the KGB, began early – two hours before it began at the Committee. This time the general devoted to English. Three times a week – Monday, Tuesday, and Friday – at 6.45 a.m. his official limousine would be standing outside 119, Vernadksy Avenue, and Innessa Petrovna Goryunova, a large, tall woman of forty with a round Russian face, full arms and a large bust – Professor of Foreign Languages at Moscow University, one of the best English teachers in the USSR, if not the best – would dive into the warm car, shivering from the chill of an early summer morning or from the winter's frost.

As soon as she got into the car it would move off softly through the dark streets of Moscow, its bullet-proof tyres swishing softly through the snow, and speed towards the building on Kutuzovsky Avenue where Leonid Brezhnev, General Andronov, Chairman of the KGB, and Nikolay Shcholokov, Minister of Internal Affairs, lived, each of them occupying two floors. After greeting the guard at the entrance Innessa Petrovna would take the elevator up to General Andronov's apartment, accompanied by one of his bodyguards. He would be already waiting for her by the open door and would take her silently into his study so as not to wake his wife. From that moment and for the next two hours Russian was banned from use. Innessa Petrovna, a pupil of the Bulgarian Professor Lobanov and an enthusiastic believer in the game-playing method of learning foreign languages, not only forbade Russian to be spoken in her presence, but thought up English names for herself and the general. During the lessons her name was Susanne, and he was George. The cheerful, energetic Susanne adopted a high-pressure tempo of language study that was infectious. She would make the general learn off huge chunks of text that she had composed herself using an English frequency dictionary. And not just learn it by heart – no, he had to repeat the text after her first in a drawl, then in a whisper, then in a rapid patter, then with melodramatic intonations, then in a drawl again. This technique helped him to assimilate new words, intonations, and English pronunciation without any difficulties, as in a game. Then they read English and American newspapers and chatted about various abstract subjects, and at the end of the lesson there was always some new English or American song which they would sing in harmony.

These classes got the general primed for the day. Innessa Petrovna had trained him to read *The Times* and the *Washington Post* every day, and in recent years he was deriving more and more pleasure from seeing his own picture and name in these papers. Every time there was a rumour that Brezhnev was ill, Western journalists would efficiently and unashamedly discuss who was going to seize power in the Politburo in the 'post-Brezhnev era'. The name of General Andronov was featuring more and more often as one of the top three or four on whom Western Sovietologists and journalists were putting their money. Admittedly, they kept giving preference either to the Ukrainian Kirilenko, Secretary of the Central Committee, or to Brezhnev's new favourite, the Ukrainian Chernenko, not realizing that the moderate democratization of Party power brought about by Khrushchev had greatly strengthened the Russian nucleus within the Party machine. Khrushchev and Brezhnev, the Ukrainian Party mafias' henchmen, had been forced to play along with the Russian Party mafias and promote the Communist bosses of Siberia, the Urals, and the Volga region to leading positions. And General Andronov was himself surreptitiously encouraging this movement and the Russophile tendencies in the intelligentsia. He forgave film producers, theatrical producers, writers and painters all their modernistic pranks and even turned a blind eye to their disaffection towards Soviet power, even though it clearly smacked of dissidence, provided they preached Russophilism in their films, books, plays and pictures, a rebirth of the Russian spirit. Some painters, realizing which way the wind was blowing, were beginning to collaborate openly with the KGB, others had not the faintest idea why they were being permitted to do things that hundreds of others were forbidden to do. And only Andronov saw the whole picture: by means of this Russophilism he was surreptitiously impressing upon the country the fact that after the Georgian Stalin, after the Ukrainian henchmen Khrushchev and Brezhnev, Russia, the Russian Party machine no longer had the right to admit yet another Ukrainian to power like Kirilenko or Chernenko, or some Belorussian like Mazurov.

To be frank, Leonid Brezhnev had outstayed his time in the Kremlin – for seventeen years he had held power. But the years were also slipping by for the one who was waiting his moment, sizing up all his rivals, plugging and plugging at his English so as to become a new type of leader, the first ruler of the Russian Empire since Nicholas II capable of conversing with ambassadors and heads of state without any interpreters or translators.

This thought flattered the general's vanity – he knew that his moment would come, but he felt a constant urge to hasten it and bring it closer. What if Brezhnev was planning on living to a hundred? No, his little heart would have to be given one more shake-up, and that would perhaps take care of him; for example, a public scandal over his daughter's lover or the exposure of his brother-in-law's and son's bribe-taking . . .

But Brezhnev survived everything – the death of his brother-in-law Tsvigun, the death of Mikhail Suslov, the Secretary of the Central Committee, and the public scandal over his daughter's amorous escapades and speculation in diamonds. This forced General Andronov to sink his hands into his pockets and once again play the waiting game. Of course he knew now for certain that he would not have long to wait. The old man had perhaps lived on but he had barely survived two heart attacks and the KGB medical experts were convinced that he was on his last legs.

But the general's own health was already giving out warning signals. The doctors insisted that he should take a holiday, spend a month on a strict diet and above all, relax. But the general considered all his doctors to be idiots. They did not understand the simple fact that a soldier in combat does not fall ill. In spite of mud in the trenches, pouring rain, intense heat, frosts or snow, soldiers can sleep out in the open for weeks without so much as a cold or any other ailment. The nervous system is stronger than any armour. But what would happen when he won his war? After any war the number of illnesses in the army increases dramatically – that also is a statistic. The nervous system becomes weaker and you cannot deceive it with any old trick. For this reason he had to hurry, to kick Brezhnev out quickly before his own nervous system exhausted all its resources.

Everything was ready for a coup. His chief Russian rivals – Grishin and Romanov – had long ago been neutralized, and even Chernenko seemed to understand that he was not going to be able to skip into the Secretary General's chair now that the Russian faction had gained such strength within the Communist Party. That was why he had been currying favour with Andronov over the last few months, trying to please him by being the first to nominate him in place of Suslov at the Politburo meeting – crafty little Ukrainian, he knew, he could only hold on in Moscow by switching allegiance to the new boss in good time.

Eighteen years of working in the KGB had trained the general to stay completely calm in this most dangerous and complicated of games, both abroad and at home, and he knew that on the eve of the final push he needed to relax slightly, to have some distraction, to ease the tension in his muscles and nerves as a good sportsman does before a decisive Olympic race.

Virginia Williams had become the general's relaxation.

Once or twice a week the car brought Virginia to his *dacha* to the east of Moscow – sometimes for a few hours, sometimes for whole days. Virginia's submissiveness flattered the general's vanity even more sometimes than his photograph in the *Washington Post* or *Time* magazine. Having made her his lover chiefly from old man's vanity and male ambition – he had never had American women before that in his life – after the first night the general began to feel a particular, even non-carnal attraction for her. Thus did the ancient warring kings give preference in their harems, not to local concubines, but to conquered foreigners and, as history loves to gossip, would even fall in love with them. In such cases the writers of antiquity would add that 'the general's victory became his defeat', but in the given instance there was no defeat. The general just liked to spend time with Virginia, talking for hours with her about America. He had never been there and for that very reason, despite his agents' most accurate and detailed reports, it teased him from afar with its elusive beauty.

Virginia was the first swallow of the future submission of the whole of America to the will of this ageing but still strong general. There was no point at all in destroying that country with nuclear strikes or seismic weapons, there was no point in occupying her gigantic territory and driving her farmers into collective farms – no, he would have a different power over America. The power that he already secretly wielded in populating America with his agents, planting his people in all social and administrative levels of American society, starting newspapers, banks, radio stations, engineering firms and insurance companies in America. And with thousands of his agents already in that country picking up the tiniest noises in the American organism like little electrodes, he would talk to her as she had talked to Russia until quite recently – from a position of strength. The Russian tsars, and Lenin, and Stalin, and Khrushchev, and Brezhnev, had dreamed of talking like that to America and to the rest of the world, and now it was becoming a possibility, a reality. The new seismic weapon would give them the trump card. The seismic weapon would be known as the 'Andronov absolute weapon' and would go down in history as such. But before putting on some exemplary Hiroshimas in Sweden one could use this weapon for a little bit of quiet fighting – in small wars like Afghanistan, Angola, Yemen, San Salvador. And when the whole of South America and all the rest of the world had been prised away from America by these different means, revolutions, coups d'état, military putsches, and seismic weapons, *then* that arrogant country with her decrepit virgin the Statue of Liberty would become as submissive as Virginia. But that was in the future. For now . . .

The general felt he had strayed into that banal phenomenon known as senile love. Accustomed to analysing coldly other people's passions and to playing on other people's human weaknesses, he did not doubt that he himself was immune to such wordly stupidity, to the vulgarity of romantic attractions. Now the general found that even during the day, during working hours – at the emergency Politburo meeting over the death of Suslov and even at Suslov's funeral, as he was standing in the guard of honour at the grave of his party protector and co-author in many international intrigues and actions, even at these moments he was thinking of Virginia. She had been so thrillingly fresh, pretty, excited when she turned to look at him during the American disco lesson. And so bewitchingly shy in the swimming-pool and sauna at his *dacha* to the east of town . . . And so enthusiastically interested in everything Russian when he drove her round Moscow in his limousine visiting old parts of town, museums, and picture galleries.

There had only been two such sorties so far – on one night he had had the Tretyakov Gallery opened and had taken her through the rooms showing her pictures by the greatest Russian artists and dreaming of how one night he would take her to the Kremlin and show her the treasures of the Granovitaya Palace; and then he would take her to the Pushkin Museum, the Hermitage, and Kizhi where the wooden buildings are held together without a single nail. He derived enormous pleasure from these excursions. Particularly when he and Virginia stood together on Lenin Hills, formerly Sparrow Hills, looking down over Moscow from the garden of the Soviet Government's official guest house. Covered with white snow, Moscow lay at their feet, lit by night illuminations and garlands of street lights. Monumental and tall, erect in his long general's greatcoat, he stood above his city, his country – for the moment in control behind the scenes, but soon to become the official master of the whole Soviet empire.

Of course such power has its burdensome aspects too. He could not just go for a walk with the woman he loved down the favourite Arbat side streets of his youth, he could not go to a restaurant or the Bolshoi with her. And he could only go to the out-of-town Arkhangelskoye restaurant, with her or without her, if his guard cleared it of all other guests. This was burdensome.

'I'm like the Balzac skinflint who only opens up his gold chest at night,' he once said to Virginia. But he did not tell Virginia that the vanity of Balzac's moneylender flattered his vanity also.

That morning, 6 February, they went to Zagorsk. The prickly-cold misty air of a late winter dawn hung over the empty Yaroslavl highway that had been cleared of all traffic. Forewarned over the radio that a Government cortège was on its way, the traffic controllers had chased the occasional trucks and private cars that were out on this non-working Saturday morning off the road into the gutters ten kilometres ahead of the general's limousine. The land across which its future master sped, seemed empty, dead, buried in snow. (And only when the orange-yellow rim of the sun rose over the sparsely wooded snowscape and began to chase the general's car and the escort's two Volgas did Virginia catch sight of the humble settlements with their smoking chimneys and churches perched on hillocks, mostly without crosses. Pushkino, Pravdinsky, Zagoryanka . . .)

The general stretched out his long legs in their warm socks, half sitting and half lying in the limousine's spacious saloon, drank strong tea out of a glass in a silver glass-holder, and read *Gorky Park*, carping from time to time at each inaccuracy in the descriptions of Moscow or the Russian way of life. Virginia sat next to him on the seat with her legs tucked up under her, looking out of the window and drinking tea too. The strange turn her life had taken no longer alarmed her or caused her to wake up in terror in the middle of the night. Now that she had begun to feel the weak stirrings of another, new life in her body, the instinct to preserve not only her own, but also this second life, caused her actor's nature in her dealings with the general to look for those colours and details which captivated and charmed her omnipotent lover and protector. Not at all through cunning, but through her instinct as an actress, she was able to guess what reaction her partner was expecting from her and how important it was to be thrilled with everything he showed her. She really did like Russia, she really was thrilled with the pictures at the Tretyakov Gallery, she was overwhelmed by 'Ivan the Terrible Killing His Son', bewitched by 'The Appearance of Christ to the People', she was really taken by the sight of Moscow at night from the top of Lenin Hills, but with all this, as an actress she intuitively wrapped her feelings up in a typical gaudy American wrapping: 'Great! Wonderful! Exciting! Fantastic! Unbelievable!' Not being deceitful, but just slightly laying on the enthusiasm for Russian scenery and Russian art (just as in their intimate moments she would lay on the surprise at the general's sexual powers), Virginia was, without realizing it, capturing the general's heart in the simplest, tritest, most banal, yet most effective way – through flattery.

After an hour's drive, the gilded cupolas of Zagorsk, that white-stone fairy tale of Russian architecture with its gold-sounding bells, rose up before the car as if from the depths of Russian history.

Girdled by a brick wall, the fortress of the ancient monastery of the Trinity of St Sergius stood high on the brow of a snow-covered hill; its powerful bastions were thrust forward from all four sides of the fortress until they overhung the deep moatlike ravines, as if giving warning of the certain doom awaiting any who would try to take this fortress by force of arms. And towers on the actual wall of the fortress awaited those who were bold enough to overcome the defensive fire of those outpost bastions. Since the overthrow of the Mongol Tatar yoke the Zagorsk fortress had been the northern defence of the state of Muscovy. But for those who came to the monastery as kind and dear guests there was the single solemn way into the fortress through the heavy cast-iron Uspensky gate . . .

A few monks stood in the gateway, their black cassocks wrapped around them against the frost, and greeted the general's cortège with reserved bows. The Patriarchate of the Russian Orthodox Church that was housed within the Zagorsk Monastery had been warned about the important visitor ahead of time, and access to Zagorsk was closed that day to all visitors, Russian and foreign.

The general's limousine did not stop at the gate, but reduced speed and followed the lead escort car past the Cathedral of the Dormition on the central square to the monastery's main attraction – the Cathedral of the Trinity; the general pulled on a pair of short warm boots and a dark grey overcoat with fur lining and got out of the car, courteously giving Virginia his hand.

Before the eyes of the important visitors stood the white-stone cathedral, constructed of hand-hewn blocks and decorated with an ornamental carved stone girdle. Its gilded cupola soared into the sunny sky and looked like the helmet of an ancient warrior. A light downy snow brushed against this golden helmet without sticking to it and descended to the portals of the white-stone steps leading into the cathedral. There were more young monks standing on the steps of the main entrance – pupils of the local theological seminary. They bowed deeply as the general mounted the stairs with his companion. The sound of matins could be heard from inside the cathedral.

As he went into the cathedral the general took off his fur cap.

Virginia was astonished – inside, the cathedral looked even more vast than from the outside. The high arches stretching upwards and the open drum of the cupola which was the chief source of light added more volume and airiness to the inside of the church. The ancient murals, the iconostasis with its red and blue icons in gold and silver frames painted by the famous Russian masters Andrey Rublyov and Daniil Chorny, with the stern eyes of Jesus Christ and the Mother of God flashing with Scythian fire, the seventeenth-century Royal Doors at the altar, covered with chased and pierced silver, behind which stood Pimen,

Patriarch of All Russia, silently and meekly, in robes embroidered with gold and jewels, the golden gonfalons over the altar, the priest conducting matins in his scarlet brocade cassock, the monastic male-voice choir singing with unspeakable purity and harmony: 'Thine hospitable memory, O Xenia, we honour . . . revering thee with love . . . we sing Christ who gave thee the power to heal . . . To Him we pray for us all forever . . .' – all this filled Virginia with a genuine religious agitation and ecstasy.

She observed that the general stopped at the cathedral door by the candle table, took two candles, but then with embarrassment began to fumble in his pockets and looked at the bodyguard following right behind him. This was probably the first occasion for many years when the general had needed some ready cash – everything else he was either entitled to or was given for nothing. The bodyguard immediately put his hand into the pocket of his black uniform trousers and paid for the candles that the general had taken.

With these candles, to the priest's measured reading of the life of Holy Xenia who 'led a truly angelic life, loved all people, helped all people as she could, was a benefactress of the poor, a comforter of the suffering, and an instructress of sinners', the general and Virginia approached the icons – the general that of St Nicholas and Virginia that of the Mother of God.

When the general first thought of showing Virginia Zagorsk a strange thought occurred to him; it even surprised him, but then it grew into a firm secret resolve. He was of course an atheist, and as head of the KGB did not believe in God or the devil. And the Department of Religious Cults at the Council of Ministers of the USSR was packed out with his KGB men and was therefore subject not so much to the Council of Ministers as to him personally. But the real possibility of attaining in the near future supreme and in effect royal power in the country brought the general up against that other power over the world – the eternal, the divine. And with his candle he went up to the icon of St Nicholas, protector of all Russian tsars and their pious undertakings. The candles burning beneath the icon were reflected in his glasses, and his firm gaze met the gaze of St Nicholas. He did not ask a blessing of the icon, he did not humble himself with a petition, but yet . . .

Virginia was looking into the deep, dark, anxious Semitic eyes of the Mother of God. And her lips uttered the soundless words of a prayer learned in childhood. She asked the Virgin Mary to bless her future child – no, not future, but already living, already kicking in her stomach!

'Glory to Thee who hast shown us light . . .' pronounced the priest, intimating the end of the service.

'Glory to God in the highest,' sang the choir, 'and on earth peace to men of good will . . .'

The service was finished, the Royal Doors opened, and two attendants led the Patriarch by the arms out on to the ambo. From there, using both hands in the ancient Assyrian blessing, he silently blessed the praying monks and the choir and, having waited for the choir and monks to leave the cathedral, turned his gaze upon the general and Virginia.

Now, looking quickly around and seeing that there was nobody left in the cathedral except his personal guard, the Patriarch and his small retinue, the general walked up to the Patriarch with a firm step, without servility, but without the usual arrogance he showed in public.

And there took place that mysterious, sacred act which the general had planned the day before, for which, indeed, this whole trip to Zagorsk had taken place and all visitors had been barred access to Trinity St Sergius Monastery with its museums and cathedrals. The Patriarch of the whole Russian Orthodox Church silently raised his hand and blessed the general. The Patriarch thought – for pious, moral deeds and a meek and sinless life, but the general knew it was for his reign. In just such a way Russian tsars, princes, and heirs to the throne had come throughout all the centuries of Russia's conscious history to receive the Patriarchal blessing before wars and campaigns, before carrying out great undertakings of State. And when the sign of the cross was made over the general's big grey uncovered head he realized it: he was *going* to inherit Romanov-Stalin-Brezhnev power in Russia!

And as he followed the guide round the rooms of the monastery museum he was already in a different mood, a cheerful, almost boyish mood. Virginia walked along beside him. Priceless treasures of Russian antiquity surrounded them. Old icons with stern faces, with green and vermilion clothing on a gold background, in silver and gold settings – St Nicholas the Miracle Worker, the Mother of God Hodigitria, the Vladimir Mother of God, the Last Supper, St John the Evangelist, St Nicholas of Radonezh, the Great Martyr St Barbara . . . Folding icons, silk icons . . . Silver candlesticks entwined with golden snakes and bunches of spun gold . . . Old porcelain . . . Ancient earthenware vases . . . Fourteenth-century royal robes embroidered with jewels . . . A gilded two-seat carriage presented to the Tsar of Russia in the eighteenth century by the Queen of England . . . Forged chain mail, helmets of old Russian warriors, portraits of Russian tsars – the whole of Russian history looked at the general and his companion from the wall, showcases and stands, and – he was sure of it – all this Russian history followed the Patriarch in blessing him for his reign. And he looked at the portraits of the former Russian tsars as their equal, as their rightful, almost blood-heir . . .

Then, after the museum they walked around the monastery. The fresh snow crunched beneath their feet. The prickly, frosty air was bracing, like dry champagne. Small snowflakes, not so much flakes as snowy sparkles, swirled in the air. In the deserted avenue of the monastery cemetery, among the ancient snow-dusted gravestones, the general motioned to the bodyguards to stay behind, and

Virginia took him by the arm. Round the next turn of the snowy avenue a view of Russian space opened before them from the top of the monastery hill – green and white fir forests, the narrow ribbon of an electric railroad, snow-swept fields and slopes with tiny figures skiing across them, then more fields, villages . . .

The future master of this land was happy, and from the plenitude of his feelings he embraced his foreign concubine, drawing her to himself and kissing her soft, obedient, slightly swollen lips. This woman had become privy to his secret, the ecclesiastical blessing that he had received, and apart from the covert male tenderness he had for her, he felt that now they were bound together by something different, something eternal.

But on the return journey from Zagorsk Virginia threw up. She just had time to shout, 'Stop the car!' She managed to leap out of the car with her hand pressed to her mouth and run down into the snow along the side of the highway, surrounded by the bodyguards who had come running up, but here on the roadside she could no longer hold back the vomit.

The general knew of course that she was pregnant, that she was already in her fourth month, but until that day her pregnancy had not disfigured her or spoiled their relationship. She did not have the swellings of the face that had accompanied his wife's pregnancy, nor capriciousness, nor compulsion for food, even her waistline had not increased enough to spoil her figure. He did not yet have any concrete plans for her child, he was not able to think about such things during the turmoil of the last few weeks, but he knew very well that there would be no more grateful, tender lover than Virginia if he allowed her to give birth and if he surrounded her baby with even the minimum of American comforts. And now, as he looked out of the car window at Virginia's doubled-up figure, at her convulsed body – it was not disgust he felt for her, but pity and tenderness.

And that frightened the general. Not the fact that sudden

attacks of nausea or other ailments of pregnancy might temporarily disrupt their carnal relations, not even jealousy over some other man's baby who, he knew, would take Virginia away from him from the fifth month – no. But the fact that he had caught himself feeling a tenderness that was not feigned or affected, or just the amusing prelude to an amorous affair. Worse than that, he had caught himself feeling pity – an unthinkable weakness of mind. That frightened the general, just as a brave teetotaller is frightened when he finds his legs carrying him for no apparent reason towards the tavern or his hands reaching for the bottle . . .

And having experienced that fright the general took a decision. Not against Virginia, but against himself. That woman had gained too great a power over his heart and he must stop it at once, sharply and decisively.

And as Virginia came back towards the car supported under the elbow by the general's bodyguard, pale, wiping her damp mouth with her glove, the general quietly said to the driver: 'To Mini-America . . .'

By the time they reached Mini-America Virginia had thrown up three more times and the general realized that the decision he had taken was the only correct one.

In Mini-America he conducted Virginia to her room himself, and carefully put her to bed – Virginia was feeling weak and exhausted.

'Sleep . . .' he said to her before leaving. 'It's nothing terrible. It's normal for the fourth month. I'll tell Colonel Stanley to take care of you . . .'

10

Meanwhile Saturday, 6 February, was going on elsewhere too. As if by special request of the birthday girl it was a lovely sunny winter's day, only minus ten centigrade. Early that morning a company of soldiers from the Household

Regiment of Soviet Army General Headquarters had arrived at Marshal Oparkov's Government *dacha* at Malakhovka. For an hour the soldiers had cleared the garden paths round the *dacha* with wooden shovels, sprinkled them with yellow crunchy sand, washed all the floors in the two-storey *dacha* itself, chopped up birchwood for the fire, and from nine in the morning Oparkov's housekeeper Aunt Klara, with two assistants under her, had been in the kitchen roasting, boiling, and baking the age-old delicacies of the Russian national cuisine – fish and rice *rasstegai*, *kulebyaka* fish pie, cabbage pies. And Stavinsky and Marshal Oparkov's adjutant, Major Ryazantsev, were plying between the Army Stores and Yeliseyevsky's grocery store, GUM and the Aragvi restaurant in an army jeep buying up imported and domestic drinks, Finnish and Austrian meat products, black and red caviar, fresh vegetables from the Caucasus, Pepsi-Cola from Krasnodar, Arabian fruit.

In the *dacha*'s small but comfortable basement cinema, a projectionist brought for the evening from the Ministry of Cinematography was threading the projector. One hundred and twenty Government *dachas* round Moscow are equipped for showing films and a special delivery service has been established at the Ministry of Cinematography to supply these *dachas* with films illegally acquired from abroad – here you can have *Superman*, *Last Tango in Paris*, *Night Porter*, the entire series of James Bond films, the latest films by Fellini, Antonioni, Godard, and Kosta Gavras. Admittedly, 'all these Fellinis and Antonionis' do not interest the inhabitants of the *dachas*, but then there is always a run at weekends on *Some Like it Hot*, *Deep Throat*, and the porno version of *Cinderella*. And while the whole Soviet nation is watching 'outstanding' works of Soviet cinematographic art – *The Epic of Siberia*, *Lenin in Paris*, *Lenin in Poland*, *Lenin in Finland*, and other films that have been awarded State prizes and Lenin prizes, the inhabitants of the Government *dachas* round Moscow, unafraid of the corrupting influence of bourgeois film art, and with a totally Communist steadfastness characteristic of inflexible Leninist Bolsheviks, test their morality on porno-Cinderellas, and the next day return to the attack on the depraved, corrupt West – but now with the knowledge of what they are attacking . . .

Galina drove straight to the *dacha* from the Enchantress beauty salon. She was in a wonderful mood – God, what a beautiful day, what sun, what silvery snowy woods all round, how delightfully the frozen river snaked through the forest, clad in its blue and purple armour of snow! And all this belonged to her! It actually did! She, her father, her husband, and a few dozen other such families – were they not the masters of the whole Russian land from the Baltic to the Sea of Okhotsk? No Rothschild, no daughter of Onassis ever dreamed of such wealth and such power – power over land, seas and rivers, the army, police, and all the people! Lord, how sad that her son could not see all this, could not see his mother in her new Volga and her new blue sable coat which her father and her husband had given her for her birthday.

The memory of her son was a stab in Galina's heart, but it was not a deep stab. Silly boy!

By five the long festive table spread with linen cloths was ready for the arrival of the guests, but even without seeing them, even from the sight of this table one could say with certainty that the true masters of the whole Soviet Union would be sitting at it.

There was so much food on the table that it would be impossible to eat it all. The hors d'oeuvre and first course alone consisted of Georgian *satsivi* and *suluguni*, Siberian partridges in Moldavian wine sauce, *omul* and grayling from Lake Baikal, trout from Lake Sevan in Armenia, a stroganoff of white salmon from the Ob, carp from Lake Ilmen cooked in sour cream, Caspian herring, Volga crayfish, *taiga* cranberries, Latvian cheese, bear meat from Altai, and, in two separate buckets – black caviar from the Far East and red caviar from Astrakhan. Besides, the faces of the guests who gathered at six o'clock from neighbouring *dachas* or came out from Moscow were an impressive testimony in themselves. After the death of Suslov there was not one thin person left in the Government and the so-called Government circles, no one whose thinness might cast aspersions on Communist plenty.

And the toasts that were heard at this table – 'To our Communist Party!', 'To our own Government!', 'To our army!' – these toasts were not routine phrases: they really were drinking to *their* Party, *their* Government, and *their* army that safeguarded their wellbeing . . .

But the main attraction of the night's programme of entertainment turned out to be, not the refinements of the Russian national cuisine, not the singing of 'Kings Can Do Anything', not the ride on Russian troikas with jingle bells, and not even the films *All That Jazz* and *Deep Throat*, but a video of an American TV show that had gone out over American and European television only a week earlier on 31 January, in protest against the introduction of martial law in Poland. The video of this show had arrived by diplomatic bag from Paris on 1 February, and in two days the jokers from the KGB's film section had altered the soundtrack and superimposed the voices of the famous Soviet comedians, Arkady Raikin, Tarapunka and Shtepsel, Shurov and Rykunin, on to the speeches of Reagan, Thatcher, Schmidt, and the prime ministers of Belgium, Norway, Portugal, and Luxembourg. Thus, between songs by Frank Sinatra and Barbra Streisand and other items, there appeared side-splitting speeches (especially if you happened to be drunk) in which American and other presidents and prime ministers glorified Jaruzelski in Russian and Ukrainian and slung mud and obscenities at Lech Walesa . . . A copy of this movie spoof was brought as a gift to the birthday girl by Ilya Andronov, leading expert on American affairs and son of the KGB Chairman.

'Galya,' he said 'you can regard this as a present not so much from me as from the American President. He spent half a million dollars on this show, but I think you are well worth such a present! And from me you'll receive a different present, but a little later on . . .' and with relish he bit into a pink-cheeked pear from Krasnodar.

Stavinsky saw there were pink traces of blood on the pear. Periodontitis, he thought to himself, a weakening of the gums. Strange that only people who have suffered from starvation and lack of vitamins or who neglect oral hygiene get periodontitis. But it was difficult to believe that this well-fed Party member with his chubby face, this forty-year-old expert on America and Canada with his stomach bulging inside his imported suit, had never been taught to brush his teeth, and even more difficult to suspect him of malnutrition. However, Stavinsky recalled reading in a medical book that periodontitis can also occur in people that have a hereditary tendency to diabetes.

And choosing his moment during the general conversation he went over to Ilya Andronov and said: 'A friend of mine has your disease – periodontitis. The doctors tried injections, but it didn't help . . .'

'It doesn't help me either,' laughed Ilya Andronov. 'In Madrid recently I had to break off negotiations over the Helsinki Agreement and go into hospital – it really knocked me for six!' He modestly refrained from mentioning that the main reason why the Madrid meeting was halted at the request of the Soviet delegation was his drinking bouts every night.

'Then the doctors tormented him with vacuum therapy,' continued Stavinsky with a smile.

'They do me too,' said Ilya. 'They suck the blood out almost every week, but it doesn't do any good.'

'And then an old woman advised him to rinse his gums with a soda solution. Two teaspoons of soda in a glass of warm water, and keep the foul mixture in his mouth for fifteen minutes.'

'Well?' inquired Ilya.

'And he never gave the doctor another thought. Try it now. Come with me,' and he took Ilya into the kitchen and immediately made him a soda solution, and fifteen minutes later Ilya Andronov was amazed to feel the nagging pain in his gums disappear. Stavinsky knew very well that that would happen – a soda solution does not cure periodontitis, but it relieves the pain in the gums.

'Listen, you're a magician!' Ilya said to Stavinsky, switching straight away to the familiar form of 'you'. 'And I've prepared a surprise for you too – you and your wife. But I'm not saying what it is now. Later.'

About two o'clock in the morning, when all the guests were either drunk or semi-drunk, Galya found her husband out in the wintry garden, on the verandah. He was whispering about something to Captain Kushchin, General Krasnopolsky, Head of Military Intelligence, and General Bogatyryov, who was in charge of prisons and camps.

'Sergey,' she called to her husband, and when he came over to her she whispered excitedly in his ear: 'Listen, Ilya Andronov is offering to take us for a spin to some absolutely fantastic place. Only it's completely secret. You, me, Ilya, and his wife Lyuda. Just quietly get away from those idiots and wait for me in the car . . .'

Twenty minutes later Ilya Andronov's Mercedes and the Yuryshevs' white Volga were rushing down the wintry night highway to the west of Moscow. Dark sleeping villages and illuminated glass and concrete militia boxes flashed past. At kilometre 47 on the Mozhaisk highway the Mercedes, followed by the Volga, turned off through an almost imperceptible opening in the wall of trees growing along the roadside. And then, just two hundred yards along this forest road, the Mercedes came up against a police roadblock. In the dark Galya and her husband saw a KGB captain come out of the box and go up to the Mercedes, talk to Ilya Andronov for a moment, then come over to their Volga and shine his flashlight on their faces and right round the inside of the car. Only after that did he wave to the soldier on duty at the barrier: 'Open!'

There were four more checks like that one: two in the

forest and two out in the open fields. At all four posts the guards recognized the son of the KGB head and let him and his friends through without any delays.

After that a strange cross between a town and a village opened up before them – its streets and houses shone with neon signs in English.

Swinging on to the main street of this odd micro-town, Ilya Andronov stopped his car outside the games hall and casino, walked over to the white Volga, and said in English with a smile: 'Welcome to America, my friends! This is my special present to you, dear Galya! You can spend a night in a real United States town!' and he started to sing: 'Happy birthday to you! Happy birthday to you! Happy birthday, dear Galya, happy birthday to you-u-u-u!'

Looking around him Stavinsky could not believe his eyes – this tiny town near Moscow was amazingly like Portland, and even the sign on the corner store said 7-Eleven.

11

The unusual amount of noise woke Virginia up. Outside on the Avenue of the Americas drunken voices were singing loudly in Russian:

> Gunners, Stalin has given the order!
> Gunners, our country is calling us!
> From a hundred thousand batteries
> For the tears of our mothers,
> For our country –
> Fire! Fire!

And then the same drunken voices switched to a folk song:

> Apple trees and pear trees were a-flower,
> River mist was rising all around.
> Young Katiusha went strolling by the hour . . .

Probably some new intake had arrived for their practical course, thought Virginia, glancing at the clock on her side table – it was 6.30 a.m. But why were they singing in Russian and no one was stopping them? Speaking Russian here was strictly forbidden, and Virginia was not used to hearing the sound of Russian . . . But the singing kept intruding through the open window – untidy, drunken, and very loud.

Two male and two female voices and the sound of dancing feet. And one of the male voices was surprisingly familiar. Really weird! It couldn't be . . .

Reluctantly Virginia climbed out of bed, wrapped herself in a blanket, and went over to the window. Outside the window two drunk men and two drunk women, illuminated by the red neon signs on the stores, were dancing on the snowy Avenue of the Americas. Dancing and singing.

The figure of one of the men dancing in the snow, dressed in general's uniform, looked strangely familiar to her. But even before she recognized him with her eyes she felt a fiery shock in her heart – Stavinsky! Stavinsky!!! Perhaps he knew she was there and had made all this noise to attract her attention?

Meanwhile the drunken quartet was dancing down the street (the women in front with hands on hips, the men following behind unsteadily and unsoberly) towards the two cars parked on the corner of the Avenue of the Americas and 7th Street – a Mercedes and a Volga. And Virginia realized that they would be gone in another minute.

Feverishly she pulled on her dress and boots, all the time looking out of the window – if only she could make it! If only they wouldn't leave! She did not even think about what it was that was pushing her, driving her towards him right now – after all, she had forgotten him, cast him out of her memory, as he had her. As he had her? But there he was now . . . Only what was he doing in that general's uniform? If only she could make it in time! Down there in the street Stavinsky and his friend had already got into their cars – Stavinsky behind the wheel of a Volga, the other man into a Mercedes.

Throwing her coat over her shoulders Virginia rushed out of the room and down the hotel staircase. As she was running through the vestibule she could already hear the engines starting up in the street. But there was still two hundred yards between the cars and the glass doors of the hotel, and Virginia stopped short at the door, waiting. Finally the headlights were switched on and the cars moved away from the sidewalk, accelerating down the street – nearer, nearer to the hotel. 'Now!' Virginia commanded herself, when the lead car, the white Volga, was only ten yards away. And, pushing open the door she ran out into the street right in front of the Volga. A screech of brakes, the Volga shied in fright over to the right (Virginia prudently went to the left), a dull thud as the front bumper hit the lamp post. Like one of the Furies, out leapt a handsome woman in a blue sable coat and screamed at Virginia in Russian: 'Where d'you think you're going, you stupid whore? Are you blind?!'

Having gone through the school of Russian obscenities in the juvenile delinquents' camp Virginia understood every word perfectly, but she answered in English, looking not so much at the woman as at the bearded general who had also got out of the car and, his face pale, was looking fixedly at Virginia.

'I'm sorry, miss,' Virginia said to Galya Yurysheva, 'but we are forbidden to speak Russian here.'

The woman in the expensive sable coat continued in Russian, choking with rage: 'We've ruined our new car because of you!'

Behind them the Mercedes also stopped, and out climbed a laughing, chubby-cheeked, respectable-looking man of forty vaguely resembling the head of the KGB.

'Great! A typical American accident!' he said to the general and his wife with a laugh. 'Now you've had the full range of American entertainments! Only you won't be able to claim because you aren't insured with the American Insurance Company!' and turning to Virginia he said to her in perfect English: 'Are you all right, miss? I don't think I know you. Are you new here?'

'Yes . . .' Virginia answered, still looking straight into the eyes of the bearded Stavinsky with his general's uniform. 'I came here recently, but for good, I'm afraid. You gave me such a fright that I might have had a miscarriage . . .'

'Are you pregnant?' asked the owner of the Mercedes.

'Yes, in my fourth month. I ran out to get something to eat. I sometimes get these urges for food because of the pregnancy!'

Stavinsky was stunned by this encounter and said nothing. He had constructed a complete intrigue, he had invited the head of all Soviet camps and prisons to Galya's birthday party so as to get friendly with him and eventually under some pretext find out which camp Virginia was in, and then suddenly – this meeting! Without any preparation, and in front of such witnesses too – Yuryshev's wife, Andronov's son!

Meanwhile Ilya Andronov had put his own interpretation on his silence and said to him: 'You nearly ran a pregnant woman over. In America she would have sued you straight away for about five thousand dollars,' and he turned to Virginia and said in English: 'May I introduce us, miss. My name is Ilya Andronov, and this is my friend Sergey Yuryshev and his wife Galina. It's her birthday today, so we're going out. I invite you to join us . . . We'll give you something to eat, and we'll have a drink. What's your name?'

'Virginia . . .' she uttered with difficulty, her tongue would not obey her: there before her stood Andronov's son and Stavinsky wearing Yuryshev's uniform, and with his wife too.

'No drinks!' Galina interposed in Russian, cooling off a little. 'You've already drunk so much you've smashed up the car!'

'Nonsense!' Ilya waved her away. This Virginia had clearly begun to interest him. He had already heard something about his father's involvement with some detained American woman, and now he realized that this was her. 'Galya, you don't have to drink, then you can drive, and Sergey and I will hit the bottle again. And besides, it's not good manners to abandon a woman you've nearly run over. Let's go!' He took Virginia by the arm and a few minutes later she was forcing herself to chew fried chicken in the deserted all-night café.

Stavinsky and Ilya Andronov drank whisky and soda as they watched Virginia, and their wives drank champagne. Stavinsky spoke slowly to Virginia in Russian, with pauses and choosing his words carefully, while Ilya Andronov translated: 'I am very sorry about this incident . . . But on the other hand I am glad that today happened to be my wife's birthday . . . and that our friend Ilya came to the party and then invited us here . . . because I have been able to make the acquaintance of such a charming woman as yourself . . .'

Naturally he wanted to say more than circumstances allowed. And this is what his eyes were crying out to her.

'I hope . . . No, I am sure you will give birth to a boy . . .' Then Stavinsky looked questioningly at Ilya Andronov: 'Can we come here again?'

'Not for another month when the new intake of students comes,' Ilya told him in Russian. Then he asked: 'Why? Are you afraid to fix up a date with her in front of your wife?'

'Oh, I just want to make sure that what happened tonight won't affect her pregnancy,' answered Stavinsky. 'Apart from that, I think it must be rather lonely for her in this tiny little town, and if we visit her as friends . . . What room are you staying in?'

'Thirty-three,' said Virginia.

'Don't worry, she's not lonely!' said Ilya Andronov, laughing.

'All right, boys, let's go!' said Galina getting up from the table, a clear note of jealousy in her voice. And she had reason – her husband couldn't take his eyes off this pregnant American.

'As a matter of fact I wouldn't mind having a dance with your victim,' Ilya said to Galya Yurysheva, feeling that his father didn't have bad taste at all.

'No, no, really, let's go!' said Ilya's wife Lyuda, also getting up. The two women were united in jealousy over the attention their husbands were paying this American, and, not suspecting that Virginia understood Russian, Lyuda added: 'In a month's time her belly will be twice as big as it is now. Then I'll allow you to dance with her. Now let's go.'

Without finishing their champagne both women walked demonstratively towards the door of the café.

Ilya Andronov made a helpless gesture, smiled, and touched Virginia's hand: 'See you soon . . . All the best . . .' and he turned to Stavinsky: 'Let's go . . .'

Outside, Galya Yurysheva had already got into the driving seat of the Volga, had backed the car away from the lamp post on to the street, and was now imperiously blowing the horn for her husband.

And realizing that he was not going to be given even a minute with her alone Stavinsky also touched Virginia's hand and repeated Ilya Andronov's words: 'I'll see you soon . . .'

They were looking into each other's eyes now, realizing that the last seconds of their meeting were slipping by. More sounds of the car's horn came from the street.

'Good luck . . .' Virginia said to them both, but she only looked at Stavinsky. And she smiled: 'Go, your wives are waiting for you.'

'Take care . . .' he said. 'I'll see you soon . . .'

Stavinsky turned abruptly and followed Ilya Andronov to the exit.

Virginia saw his wife lean across the seat and open the right-hand door of the car, and she saw him get in. Oh Lord, she thought, he's crazy, he's absolutely crazy! If he's found out – and it could happen at any moment – then the whole truth will come out and I'll be interrogated again, taken away from here to prison, to camp. And what'll happen to the baby? Why, why did he have to do that? Kamikaze twice over . . .

But perhaps he became Yuryshev so as to find her?

Kicking the snow up with its wheels the white Volga leaped away and raced down the Avenue of the Americas after the Mercedes, beyond the outskirts of the little town and into the open country to the control point.

Virginia watched the cars go and felt the nausea rising to her throat from all she had been through.

12

It went on for about three weeks: attacks of nausea followed each other in quick succession, especially in the morning. Colonel Stanley did release Virginia from classes with the new intake, and his daughter Mickey looked after her with unusual diligence and kindness. She went for walks with her, sat with her in her room in the evening, made her drink various natural juices. Virginia did everything her nurse told her, and all the time thought about Stavinsky. Would he really come here with the next intake at the beginning of March? And what if he stole her away from here and they both escaped from Russia? No, that was only possible in novels and James Bond films. If the real Colonel Yuryshev wasn't able to get out of the USSR by himself, then how was Stavinsky going to steal her out of a top-secret KGB school and get across the border with her? No, it was unthinkable.

Timid hopes of a miracle gave way to despair and further bouts of morning sickness that clouded her mind. Finally Colonel Stanley said he could not go on watching Virginia suffer and he was going to call a doctor from Moscow. That evening a tall dark-haired doctor of about forty called Musatov arrived from Moscow. With an anxious look on his face he examined Virginia, listened to her, and gave her two pills which he asked her to take before going to bed. He said the pills would take away the nausea and Virginia would be able to sleep normally.

Indeed, that night Virginia fell asleep very quickly and her sleep was deep, as if she had passed out.

She did not see or hear the doctor and Mickey coming into her room again just an hour after she had gone to sleep. Without fear of waking her the doctor removed the covers and gave her an intravenous anaesthetic. Then Mickey bared Virginia's stomach and with a long thin needle Musatov injected into her womb a rare imported drug called prostaglandin for terminating pregnancy. Even the KGB had taken three weeks to find this drug since the USSR had no drugs for terminating pregnancy.

Covering Virginia and putting out the light, Dr Musatov and Mickey withdrew.

At six in the morning Virginia awoke with a sharp pain in the abdomen. The second stab of pain made her cry out and sit up in bed.

She lay a little longer in bed, doubled up with pain and trying to stifle her groans, but when one particularly sharp pain made her heart miss a beat she realized she could not hold out till morning. Her legs tucked up, she lowered herself to the floor, threw on a bathrobe and still bending double, clasping her hands to the small of her back, slowly made her way downstairs to Stanley's room.

The colonel opened immediately to her knock as if he had not slept all night and was expecting her. Seeing the groaning Virginia he reacted immediately, laying her on the sofa and running to wake the doctor in the next room. Musatov appeared with a needle, gave her a shot of pain-killer, and confirmed her suspicions – it appeared she had gone into premature labour; that was what he had feared the night before.

Ten minutes later Colonel Stanley's personal car was already taking Virginia and the doctor to a hospital in

Moscow. On the way Musatov tried to calm Virginia down in broken English, saying they would stop the premature labour in the hospital.

Moscow was still dark as they entered at seven-thirty. The street lights illuminated groups of people hurrying to the metro stations with their red neon Ms shining over them. Shivering knots of people stood at bus stops, and equally silent dark groups queued at the doors of food shops that were still closed. Muscovites and people who had come on business from various parts of the country were getting on line for food.

The car swept through the centre of town, dived into a side street, and stopped in front of a high iron gate with a mantle of snow that had fallen that night. A soldier came out of the box wearing an army sheepskin jacket and felt boots and with an automatic over his shoulder. Surely they hadn't brought her back to the prison hospital?

The soldier sleepily stamped his felt boots in the fresh snow, looked into the car, and began checking the driver's documents.

'Open up!' Dr Musatov ordered him sharply.

The soldier indifferently gave the driver back his papers and went to open the gate.

The car drove along a snow-covered roadway into the hospital forecourt and Virginia realized that this was not the prison – they stopped at the entrance of a beautiful modern seven-storey building with a concrete awning over the main entrance and identical white curtains in every window on all seven floors.

Musatov and a nurse who had come out of the hospital helped Virginia to get out of the car. Holding Virginia round the waist, the nurse led her into the admissions room. Here the nurse on duty told Virginia to undress, for some reason weighed her on a large cold pair of scales standing on the floor, then pulled back an oil-cloth curtain and pointed to a shower. The painkiller was wearing off, and once again Virginia felt a dull pain below the stomach.

As she dried herself with the towel Virginia noticed she had started to bleed. She was looking in horror at this blood when the nurse on duty walked into the room together with an older woman with a military bearing who had a doctor's gown on and a lighted cigarette clenched between her teeth. This cigarette – not the Western type, but the Russian kind with its long paper mouthpiece and sharp smell of coarse tobacco – this cigarette between the woman's lips surprised Virginia.

Seeing the blood-stained towel in Virginia's hands the old woman ordered the nurse on duty: 'To theatre!' and tossing the cigarette on the floor she stamped it out with the toe of her calf-leather boot.

Another sharp pain made Virginia bend double, gasp, and cry out . . .

. . . She came round to the pungent smell of ammonia. She was lying on a table in the operating theatre. A number of people were standing over her in clean white gowns, surgical caps, and masks. They were exchanging curt phrases: 'Collapse . . .'

'Gravidity seventeen to eighteen weeks . . .'

The bright surgical lamp was directed on to the lower half of her body. Virginia could not see what was going on down there – a piece of gauze under her chin blocked her vision of the gynaecological surgeons as they worked on her. She tried to move her hand and felt that her arms and legs were tied down to the table. And she began to lose consciousness again. The last thing she heard was: 'A girl . . .'

'Normal foetus. Could have been a healthy child . . .'

13

The coded message from the tailor Volodya Ivanov in Moscow both pleased and amazed Daniel J. Cooper and David MacKerry.

'. . . According to Stavinsky's report NATO exercises in Northern Norway, manoeuvres by Swedish armed forces, the situation in Poland, and also the power-struggle in the Kremlin have forced Soviet Army Headquarters to postpone the operation of encircling Sweden with the new weapon. However, Stavinsky only consents to hand over the secret of this weapon and all relevant information on condition that you guarantee his and Virginia's escape from the USSR. Virginia is in her fourth month of pregnancy. She is just outside Moscow in a top-secret KGB school, and Stavinsky is going to try to get her out one night in early March. Her disappearance can only remain undetected for five or six hours. By that time Stavinsky and Virginia must be over the border. These are Stavinsky's conditions. I will inform you later of the exact date of escape. As confirmation of the importance of the materials at Stavinsky's disposal, in the near future a Soviet submarine will appear in Italian territorial waters thirty-five miles south of Taranto . . .'

Although Stavinsky's conditions posed the CIA a new headache, Cooper was delighted to hear that the NATO exercises had forced the Russians to postpone surrounding Sweden with some new strategic weapon. Hell, now at least he had taken a little revenge on the KGB for all his previous defeats. He considered as one such defeat the recent expulsion of the Soviet military attaché, General Vasily Shitov, from Washington, and the sudden disappearance of another Soviet Embassy official at almost the same time – Dmitry Yakushin, head of the entire Soviet spy network in the US. On the whole, all these public scandals over the expulsion of Soviet spies from various countries in January and February 1982 (Oleg Dokudovsky and Yevgeny Vopilovksy were expelled from Norway, the assistant military attaché Lieutenant-Colonel Sergey Yegorov and the head of the Aeroflot agency Aleksey Finenko were sent home from Indonesia, and also some Soviet spies were expelled from Portugal) – all these public scandals described luridly in the press did no credit to the security systems of those countries. Instead of 'taming' those spies, getting to know their habits, weaknesses, movements, connections, feeding them false information through plants, the security services would now have to spend years studying the new people sent out by the KGB to replace those that had been expelled. Of course, sometimes these Soviet spies were beyond the limit. The Soviet military attaché General Shitov, for example, had become so brazen that he started meeting his informers personally. But in the end, what the hell, let him meet them, Cooper was willing to tolerate this brazenness if there had not come an order from the White House to prove to the American public that Soviet intelligence agents really were operating on American soil. So this general who had overdone things a little had to be sacrificed on the altar of the Government's new so-called 'decisive' policy. And yet how convenient it would have been to pass the Russians another piece of false information through this general so as to delay the Soviets from surrounding Sweden with some new weapon a little longer – delay them just until Cooper got the documents on the weapon into his hands. For example, one could slip him some information that the US had supplied Sweden with a P3 Orion aircraft which was capable of detecting submarines and following their movements from the air.

Oh well, Cooper laughed to himself, there were several hundred other Soviet spies in Washington beside Yakushev and Shitov. He would have to work through them. Also, he would have to warn their Italian NATO partners to intensify their patrols in the Gulf of Taranto and not send their anti-submarine aircraft to the exercises in Norway.

Meanwhile MacKerry and Carroll were tearing their hair again trying to plan Stavinsky's escape from the USSR, just as they had the previous August. Only now, instead of just Yuryshev they had to get two people out – Yuryshev-Stavinsky and Virginia. And get them out in a matter of hours.

MacKerry and Carroll got down to work on the archive

materials. They studied dozens of cases of Soviet people escaping across the border over the last few years. Two soldiers had crossed into Finland and gone on foot right across Finland and Sweden, avoiding the Finnish police since the Finnish Government always hands Soviet refugees back to the Soviet authorities. Three Soviet dissidents had attempted to swim across the Black Sea. A group of Pentecostalists had stormed the American Embassy. An air force pilot, Lieutenant Belenko, had flown his MIG-26 to Japan. A fisherman in the Soviet Far East had sailed to Japan in a motor boat. Some Germans had escaped from East to West Germany in a balloon. Two students, Gilev and Pozdeyev, had hi-jacked an Aeroflot plane from the Crimea to Sinope in Turkey . . .

But all these escapes – each one more fantastic than the last – were useless for Stavinsky and Virginia. Even if Stavinsky actually succeeded in spiriting Virginia out of that intelligence school (how he proposed to do it was quite beyond them), a pregnant woman cannot walk across the Finnish border or swim the Black Sea. The group of Pentecostalists were still sitting in the American Embassy after umpteen years and the Kremlin was not allowing them to emigrate from the USSR, not because the Soviets needed these Pentecostalists so badly, but to discourage others from seeking refuge in foreign embassies. The Turks handed the hi-jackers back to the Soviet Union. And of course Stavinsky was not going to be able to fly a MIG-26 out . . .

The solution came unexpectedly when MacKerry and Carroll came across a story in the papers about a Soviet interpreter who had failed to return home and who, once settled in Western Europe, had twice tried to get his family out of the USSR. The method of escape was brilliantly thought out and quite simple, and it failed both times only because it was carried out in an amateurish way. But to use the idea and employ specialists . . .

Three days later MacKerry received from the Pentagon some beautiful and exceptionally detailed aerial photos of the frozen Lake Ilmen near Novgorod, about two hours' drive from Moscow; they had been taken by satellite and showed not only the actual lake but even tractor- and sleigh-tracks crossing the ice. On receiving these photographs MacKerry flew out to Switzerland, to the Alps, where a new Hollywood spectacular was being shot. The famous stunt pilot Lana Pett, owner of the firm Doubleur, a six-foot Frenchwoman with a coarse masculine voice who had executed the most intricate stunts in her tiny planes and gliders for dozens of films, listened to MacKerry, looked at the snaps of the lake, looked MacKerry up and down with her blue eyes, and suddenly said in perfect Russian: 'Do you really think I should risk my life for the sake of two of your agents in Russia?'

Lana Pett turned out to be Svetlana Petrovna Khudyakova – daughter of émigrés who ran away from Russia back in 1917.

MacKerry silently handed her the latest issue of the Swiss newspaper *Neue Berner Zeitung*. There was a big headline on the front page: 'Soviet submarine in Italian territorial waters.' The article continued: 'Taranto, Italy; 27 February (UPI). During patrols in Italian territorial waters yesterday the submarine *Leonardo da Vinci* detected the engine noises of a Soviet submarine that had penetrated the Gulf of Taranto only thirty-five miles south of the Taranto naval base, the largest base in Italy. When the Soviet submarine failed to respond to inquiries over the radio it was attacked with depth charges by the Italian air force in order to force it out of Italian territorial waters. However, the Soviet submarine chose instead to remain in the Gulf of Taranto and lay on the bottom at a depth of 1,000 feet (300m) with its engines stopped, and only after fourteen hours, at 2 a.m., did it leave Italian territorial waters at maximum speed. The anchorage in the Taranto region is regularly used by ships of the American 6th fleet . . .'

'So?' Lana Pett looked at MacKerry again.

'The people you could get out of Russia know what the

Russian submarines are after in Italy, Sweden, and other countries. It's to do with setting up some new top secret weapon around Europe,' MacKerry told her. 'And you are the only person who can help us find out what's going on.'

Lana silently took the photographs of Lake Ilmen out of his hand.

'All right,' she said with a sigh after a moment. 'We'll give it a try. Fools rush in . . .'

14

From: Colonel A. P. Muravina, Medical Service, Head Doctor, Special Hospital of the KGB
To: Major General P. D. Stashkov, Medical Service, Head of Medical Service of the Main Directorate of Corrective Labour Institutions at the Ministry of Internal Affairs

On 27 February at 8.17 a.m. the prisoner Virginia Williams, registered in camp 942-OP in the town of Syktyvkar, Komi Autonomous Republic, was admitted to the closed special hospital of the KGB.

The patient was brought in with vaginal bleeding and premature contractions in the fifth month of pregnancy.

All attempts by medical personnel to prevent premature birth proved unsuccessful. During the course of spontaneous abortion the patient's condition deteriorated sharply as a result of amniotic fluid embolism, acute pulmonary oedema, and post-partum haemorrhage.

In order to support the functioning of the heart the patient was given adrenalin, and to stop the non-coagulation of the blood she was given fibrinogen, but unfortunately this did not produce positive results and it was necessary to resort to direct blood transfusion.

In connection with the personal instructions of General

G. Andronov, Chairman of the KGB, all donors with the same blood group as the patient (B) were summoned from confectionery factory No 17 . . .

General Andronov stood at the window of the operating theatre and looked at Virginia. Through the thick glass he could clearly see her pale, swollen face with purple spots, the blue-black lips, and the dishevelled hair all over the pillow. This woman bore little resemblance now to the Virginia who had recently been so enchanting, soft, and touchingly trustful. Yet another donor from the confectionery factory was lying on the next table, and the transparent white cord with its pulsing scarlet stream united the donor's vein to Virginia's. Another surgical nurse and two assistant surgeons were now on duty in the operating theatre.

And next to the general stood the old female doctor in the uniform of a colonel in the medical service, a cigarette in her narrow clenched teeth. After a long pause she said briefly: 'Musatov tried too hard, Comrade General. He gave her too big a dose of prostaglandin . . .'

The general glanced at her, and she explained: 'It's risky medicine, Comrade General. Imported. God knows what doses you're supposed to give. The dose turned out to be too big for her . . .'

But the general did not need her explanations. He was just irritated by the peasant smell of bad tobacco and her *Byelomor* cigarette. And seeing him involuntarily tilt his head away from the smoke of her cigarette the doctor hurriedly walked to the back of the house surgeons' room and put it out.

He was left quite alone with this window and his thoughts. This was perhaps the first time he had stood face to face with his victim. Everyone who had been killed on his orders during his years of work with the KGB, those who 'actually' had car-crashes or who were shot by hired professional bandits and terrorists; all those who had been driven insane by enforced treatment for dissidence in mental hospitals and all those who were actually going insane right now; or who were freezing to death in Siberian camps or trying to fight him, the general, with long hunger strikes – he never saw their faces, their eyes, never heard their voices. Those people were just pawns in his big game for the security of the Soviet system, the dictatorship of the Communist Party, and his personal power. They needed to be swept off the chess-board – into the camp of the madhouse, the West or the graveyard.

But all his great power over Madam Death, who visited people at the exact time appointed by him as if she were one of the lowest members of the KGB staff, this power proved insufficient to command that other Lady – Life – not to desert Virginia's body.

And now he stood at the glass window of the operating theatre and watched the life ebbing, ebbing from her body. And at the same time he studied what was happening to his own heart. And he saw that he pitied himself more than Virginia. He was an old man already, he had lived a cruel life that had exhausted his nerves and his brain, and he had devoted the last forty years of that life to pursuit of the most intoxicating feeling of all – the feeling of complete, indisputable regal power. But did he really need that power now that he was already sixty-seven and the doctors were talking about symptoms of diabetes? The yoke of that power would descend on his no longer young shoulders in all its weight, and like all his predecessors he would change from being a hunter after power to a watchful animal listening for the approaching steps of the young hunters who were tracking him. If he did not watch out they would without a tremble of the hand let the blood out of his body just like that blood over there. And would even one donor come forward and give him the blood from his own young veins? Lord, what was Life? Was it really just those few litres of blood that could be pumped from body to body? Or was Life something else? Virginia's smile, the pine smell in the forest outside Moscow, the dappled shadows of the leaves in the park, the sun on the Black Sea beaches, and the simple joy of loving this woman?

No, he would not permit this death, he could not believe that he was powerless to stop it.

He turned to the doctor: 'You've got to save her.'

'I can guarantee she will live only as long as she continues to receive direct blood transfusion, Comrade General. But this is already the twenty-sixth donor, we've only got eight left.'

'There won't be any shortage of donors, I'll give the order. What's Dr Musatov's blood group?'

The doctor stared at him.

'If he has the same group as her,' said the general, 'he will lie down next and give her half his blood.'

'He won't survive that, Comrade General. The maximum dose you can take from a person . . .'

'I'm not interested in that,' the general interrupted. 'Tell him he has the same chance of survival as she does. That goes for you too, by the way. Call up the best doctors, any amount of donors. Remember, you're not saving her, but yourself.'

15

A bare-footed child, a tiny little girl with chubby little legs and white curls falling over her happy blue-eyed face, was running along the hot sand of a Florida beach. Laughing like an angel, she called Stavinsky to follow her. When he woke up in the mornings Stavinsky enjoyed going over these dreams in his memory. A girl! He was going to have a girl, another daughter! There was no disappointment that it was a girl after all, and not a boy. He was not alarmed that she ran away from him so lightly in the dream, her feet scarcely touching the ground, and that he could never catch up with her. Just a joyful, excited feeling that lasted all day and mild surprise that he should keep having the same dream every night.

And he felt that his excitement was helping him with everything – the tailor Volodya Ivanov had passed on to him the coded message from Washington: on the night of Virginia's kidnap a plane would be waiting for them on Lake Ilmen near Novgorod, and this morning Ilya Andronov himself had called up and invited him to the show *This is How We'll Conquer!* at the Moscow Arts Theatre. The show had been a sensation in Moscow's theatreland for the last month. It had apparently been ready long ago, but Suslov – the former chief ideologist of the Party – had forbidden the première. But now that Suslov was dead . . .

'You've just got to come,' Ilya said over the telephone. 'They say it's a fantastic show, and tonight there are going to be two shows, not just one.'

'What do you mean?'

'Can't tell you over the phone, you'll see for yourself. Pick up the tickets from the manager, I've ordered them for you. We'll meet in the intermission.'

Something strange certainly was going on in Tverskoy Boulevard, where the vast new areopagus-like building of the Moscow Arts Theatre stood. It had been sealed off to traffic from both the Gorky Street and Herzen Street directions, and the militia was only permitting access to ticket-holders. Of course, the general's epaulettes and the ID from Soviet Army General Staff helped Stavinsky and Galya to get through these cordons, but then there was nowhere to park near the theatre – it was all cluttered with Zhigulis, Volgas, and Moskviches belonging to Moscow's theatrical and government elite and black KGB Volgas with their steel radio 'whiskers'. Against all the rules cars were even parked on the pavement.

Stavinsky thought for a moment, then also swung on to the pavement.

Athletic burly-faced lads stood on the broad stone steps

leading up to the theatre doors – all of them in civilian clothing, but quite obviously KGB men.

Ignoring the KGB figures Stavinsky glanced at his watch. It was 6.59; he and Galya were very late, the show was beginning at seven. Another three minutes passed while Stavinsky got the tickets left by Ilya Andronov in the name of General Yuryshev.

Another run up wide stairs, to the theatre cloakroom.

'I'll go inside and get the seats,' said Galya. She threw her coat into Stavinsky's arms and rushed up a side staircase to the stalls.

The cloakroom of the new Moscow Arts Theatre was huge. Attendants in blue livery with gold braid nimbly took the clothing and issued numbers, opera glasses, and programmes. But the normal festive theatrical atmosphere had a nervous element in it today, owing to the fact that about eight hefty KGB men were hanging around in the cloakroom in standard dark-grey and dark-blue suits.

Stavinsky deposited his greatcoat and Galya's coat and made his way hurriedly inside the theatre. About forty men were crowding round the foyer; they were in no hurry, and it seemed evident that they were not planning to watch the show. More KGB guys, thought Stavinsky, what sort of a show was this?!

As he entered the stalls Stavinsky looked round the auditorium. He had never been in the new building; the theatre had moved here from Arts Theatre Street where the old building was after he had emigrated. But he remembered the theatre being built very well – it had gone on for twenty years, construction sometimes being halted for years at a time, and on Tverskoy Boulevard this stone box with empty eye sockets constantly stood out like a sore thumb, contemptuously dubbed by Moscow taxi-drivers the Crematorium, the Morgue, or the Second Mausoleum.

Now the vast auditorium was in that state of semi-darkness and living silence that comes a few seconds before the curtain rises, when the lights have gone down and the audience are settling back into their seats, having one last hurried, nervous cough into their hands.

And in the midst of this silence a loud female shout was suddenly heard: 'Sergey! Sergey!!'

Down at the front, in the fourth row of the stalls just below the Government box, stood Galya, waving her programme at Stavinsky and calling: 'Over here! Sergey!'

And the whole auditorium turned to look at him.

'Idiot,' Stavinsky cursed to himself. 'Wants to show off her dress, stupid fool!'

At that moment a heavy hand descended upon his shoulder and a man's voice said quietly in his ear: 'Quick, Comrade General, let's go . . .'

Stavinsky's heart turned to water.

But the KGB hand was courteously leading him down to the fourth row.

Stavinsky walked down the aisle accompanied by this hefty, solicitous KGB agent feeling hundreds of eyes upon him – like an unidentified aircraft in the night sky that has been caught in a crossfire of searchlights.

'I'll kill her!' he thought as he went, but just as they reached the fourth row, at that very second all the theatre spotlights came on and illuminated . . . no, not the stage, but that very box beneath which Galya was standing. A thunder of applause shook the vast auditorium of the new Moscow Arts Theatre. And it was only now, as he followed the wave of this ovation, that Stavinsky realized what in fact was happening that evening in the theatre – right above his head, ten feet from where they were sitting in the fourth row of the stalls, into the Government box walked Leonid Ilyich Brezhnev, Konstantin Chernenko, Andrey Gromyko, Georgy Andronov, and Dmitry Ustinov.

So that was why the theatre was surrounded by so many KGB guys today! And, as though at an unseen signal, from all four corners of the hall these KGB guys rose up together and began furiously applauding towards the Government box, growling through their teeth to their neighbours – the ordinary theatre-going public: 'Get up! Get up!'

And whether they were obeying this command, or whether they were lifted up by the general wave of loyalty, all the spectators in the auditorium, all 1,500 of them, stood up and applauded their own Communist Government.

And of course Stavinsky and Galya stood and applauded that Government.

Holding his hand suspended and bowing back to the auditorium with a slight nod of the head, Brezhnev lowered himself into his seat the way the residents of old people's homes sit down – slowly at first, as if bending his knees with difficulty, but then neither his hands grasping the arm-rests nor his legs were able to support the weight of his body any longer and he dropped into the seat. At the same moment, as if by a word of command, Chernenko, Gromyko, Andronov, and Ustinov took their places beside him . . .

The ovation died. The auditorium settled down quietly. The spotlights directed at the Government box were extinguished, and Galya thrust a programme into Stavinsky's hand. In the dim light coming from the red sign over the side door Stavinsky read: '*This is How We'll Conquer*! A play by Mikhail Shatrov. Produced by Oleg Yefremov, People's Artist of the USSR. Script by Ilya Rutberg. The part of Vladimir Ilyich Lenin played by Aleksandr Kalyagin. The action takes place in 1923 in the Kremlin, during V. I. Lenin's last visit to his study. Cast: Fotieva, Lenin's secretary – Yelena Proklova . . .'

Stavinsky did not notice the curtain go up as he was reading the programme, and his attention was only directed to the stage by a nudge from Galya's elbow. The open curtain revealed the humble décor of Lenin's study in the Kremlin. The heavy desk, the table lamp with its green glass shade, the tall grandfather clock, and the windows looking out on to Red Square.

In the total silence Lenin enters from the wings on the left almost inaudibly, an ill man, walking somehow sideways and looking round from side to side. Silently he surveys his study and his secretary, who sits wrapped in a downy shawl typing something.

And suddenly from the Government box Stavinsky heard Brezhnev's voice, drawling, querulous, and quite audible: 'Le-e-enin . . . Ought to cla-a-ap . . .'

Stavinsky and everybody sitting near him automatically turned towards this voice. Up there in the box one of Brezhnev's advisers was bending over and whispering something into his ear, but Brezhnev shook his head petulantly and said to the adviser: 'But that's Lenin! Ought to clap him . . .'

At that moment the music came in with a thunderous crash. The actors came on and like a whirlwind of Lenin's memories of the Revolution of October 1917 a pantomine of events burst upon the stage: the taking of the Winter Palace, the collapse of the German front, the Kronstadt rebellion, typhoid in the Volga region . . . To the rhythm of music symbolizing revolution the actors circled faster and faster round the sick, confused man who by the power of his genius had gathered into his small fist all the reins of history.

It was done so beautifully and powerfully that the theatre roared with enthusiasm.

And in the Government box Brezhnev straightened his bowed back and looked proudly at his retinue: 'I told you we ought to clap! I told you so!' and began to clap with the audience. Stavinsky and Galya were sitting so close to the Government box that they could hear Brezhnev's every word. The old man was convinced that the audience was applauding Lenin and that it was just his advisers that had prevented him reacting correctly to the show.

The pantomime rushed past and vanished. But what did not vanish was the feeling that the whirlwind of history that Lenin unleashed had acquired such centrifugal force that the frail, sick little Lenin could no longer control it, and that he realized it, realized that this scenic circle was hurtling round like the fly-wheel of a machine that has gone out of control. Something had to be done – save it, stop it, guide it! But Lenin no longer had the strength, with a bullet-wound in his lung, hardening of the arteries, and Stalin keeping him locked up in Gorki, forty kilometres from Moscow. Yes, he had secretly escaped from that *dacha*-hospital in Gorki, yes, he had secretly made his own way to the Kremlin and had come to his study to dictate his testament to the Party, but thoughts, thoughts about his country's past and future, became mixed up in his sick head. Then suddenly Yakov Sverdlov, his friend Yakov Sverdlov, first Soviet President, who died of typhoid in 1918, rose up in his feverish brain – also ill and dying. Lenin sat down at the front of the stage and talked to his dying companion-in-arms softly, almost in a whisper.

And immediately from the Government box the petulant voice of Brezhnev once again reached the ears of those sitting in the front rows of the stalls: 'I can't hear anything . . .'

Once again his advisers clung to him and Gromyko, who was sitting on his right, bent over and was whispering something to him, but . . .

'I can't hear anything!' exclaimed Brezhnev like a spoilt child, and he got up impetuously and left the box.

The advisers ran after him, and Chernenko darted out after him . . .

Five minutes later Brezhnev returned and sullenly, grudgingly sat down in his seat.

Only Moscow theatre-goers could imagine what would have happened if Brezhnev had really walked out of the show. The show would have been banned, the actor Kalyagin would have been thrown out of the theatre.

But everything was all right. Stavinsky heard a sigh of relief pass through the first rows of the stalls, and he too breathed out with the release of tension. He stole a glance to the side. To left and right sat square-faced KGB men with suffering written on their faces – it was painful to them that the 'simple people' should see the infirmity of their leader.

And only one man in that whole room seemed totally unmoved by what was going on. Georgy Andronov. Silent, motionless, his eyes hidden behind glasses and gazing beyond the auditorium and the stage into a space that was inaccessible to others, he sat in the box as though he were serving out an unnecessary and tedious spell of duty. That petulant, senile, deaf old man sitting next to him with his dyed eyebrows no longer even evoked irritation in him. At that very moment in the special KGB hospital a few blocks away doctors were waging a furious battle for Virginia's life. It had been going on for five days and there seemed to be some hope of saving her. Unless the doctors were deceiving both him and themselves. But if Virginia survived, Lord, if she survived . . . That would be divine Providence, and the life of the Russian people would be quite different under him from under Brezhnev. He had given himself a vow. He would do what that genius on the stage who couldn't pronounce his rs properly was unable to do.

Imitating Lenin's speech impediment, the actor Kalyagin was dictating his testament to the typist. He was warning the Party of Stalin's despotism, warning them that under no circumstances should Stalin be given supreme power in the country. He was talking of the abyss into which the logic of autocratic power led a country. Perhaps Brezhnev would leave such a testament about him, General Andronov? But history laughed at these scraps of paper . . .

Intermission.

The well-fed audience, who owed their wellbeing to those very people – Lenin, Stalin, Khrushchev, and Brezhnev; children of serfs who thanks to Soviet power had risen from rags to riches, and who possessed *dachas*, cars, mink coats, and the titles of honoured servants of the country – during the first act that audience had listened delightedly to the spicy lines with their blatantly anti-Soviet flavour, all those phrases by Lenin that the playwright had lifted out of various transcriptions of Lenin's speeches and then stood on their heads to make them relevant to the present day.

And now there they were, giving the cast a thunderous ovation, experiencing that secret enjoyment of slaves who see their masters ailing and dying. There was gratitude for you, the scum!

The general felt a wave of anger rise in his heart. And in an instant he had forgotten about Virginia and his vow. No, this audience wouldn't get any 'thaw' or any so-called 'democratic' liberties. They didn't deserve them . . .

Through his dark glasses Andronov slowly and intently examined the auditorium, memorizing those faces. He wondered who that little bearded general was in the fourth row of the stalls with the pretty, fidgety woman. Why had he been staring at him during almost the entire first act, and was now avoiding his gaze in such a cowardly way? Who did he remind him of? Ah. Yes! That was that colonel, Marshal Oparkov's son-in-law, the commentator on that secret film about Project EMMA, the seismic weapon. So, he was already a major-general, his father-in-law was advancing him fast! Incidentally, what was happening with that Project EMMA? A few days ago the proofs of a pamphlet by Marshal Oparkov entitled *Always Ready to Defend the Fatherland* had landed on General Andronov's desk, and his assistant had underlined some particularly interesting passages in the pamphlet which seemed to refer to Project EMMA, the project with which Marshal Oparkov's son-in-law, this bearded little General Yuryshev, was involved. Well, there was a grain of truth in the Chief of Staff's insinuations: no matter what intrigues you get involved in in your struggle for power, the might of the army must be increased and increased . . . 'One must increase its degree of readiness for total war.' He was right to say that . . .

Meanwhile the object of General Andronov's thoughts had already left the auditorium and gone into the foyer with the general stream of people. There was the usual theatrical hubbub of voices. The people were walking round the room in a circle, as at a riding school, showing themselves off to each other. The biggest stage and screen stars, like those with whom Stavinsky had flown from Brussels to Moscow, were wearing ostentatiously worn American dungaree suits, but their wives and the wives of the Moscow store managers, as well as the most fashionable and elite beauticians and cosmeticians, were in long evening gowns, with diamond earrings and necklaces, emerald pendants and brooches. And they smelled, they smelled of every conceivable cosmetic from France to Riga . . .

Ilya Andronov, dressed as usual in a conservative American suit from the famous New York store Brooks Brothers, his dark horn-rimmed glasses on a round face that closely resembled his father's, was also walking round in this circle. There was an arrogant, condescending smile on his lips, and there was arrogance in the way he thrust out his already impressive stomach. Beside him walked his wife Lyuda, Georgy Arbatov, the slightly balding Director of the Institute of the USA and Canada, and Colonel Pyotr Orlov, Head of the Tourist Department of the KGB, a handsome man with a military bearing dressed, of course, in a civilian suit.

Stavinsky and Galya went up to Ilya Andronov. He introduced them to his companions.

As he shook Stavinsky's hand Orlov said: 'I've seen you somewhere. Or am I imagining it?'

Stavinsky shrugged his shoulders. He had never met this man, but the devil knew where Yuryshev might have met him. As he had often done in such cases, Stavinsky looked at Galya with an inquiring smile – let her bale him out, you couldn't tell everyone you met that he had suffered concussion and loss of memory. And Galya did bale him out: 'But of course!' she said. 'We were all on holiday together in seventy-seven in Pitsunda, at the Central Committee sanatorium. Only Sergey didn't have a beard then, and you were with your wife and twins. Remember? How are they?'

'Right!' Orlov remembered. 'Oh, my girls are almost ready to get married! And how's your young man? I seem to recall you had a son with you . . .'

But this time Stavinsky came to Galya's rescue: 'Galya, do you have any cigarettes? I'm dying for a smoke.'

Both Orlov and Ilya Andronov offered him a packet of cigarettes, and they both laughed – they had the same cigarettes – American Marlboros.

'No smoking in here!' a soft, but firm, masculine voice said right next to them. 'Go to the smoking-room! Up the stairs to the second floor.'

Stavinsky liked the way Ilya Andronov reacted – he didn't argue, he didn't boast his relationship to the boss of this KGB man who had suddenly appeared from nowhere, he just smiled ironically and like an obedient schoolboy moved towards the smoking-room with all the others. There Orlov and Arbatov started to discuss the latest news from Washington; the ladies – Galya and Lyuda – went off to the ladies' room, and Ilya Andronov said to Stavinsky: 'Well, what do you think of the show? Not badly put together, I like it! Do you know the producer, Yefremov? No? A gifted fellow, we ought to take a trip to that place outside Moscow with him, remember? Take a few actresses . . .'

'I hear he drinks . . .'

'Yes, that's bad. He's a hard drinker. He'll hold out for a month and not touch a drop, but then if he starts drinking he's an animal. No, we can't go there with him, he'll get drunk.'

'How's your periodontitis?' asked Stavinsky, pretending to be quite indifferent to a trip to Mini-America and at the same time racking his brains for a way to steer the conversation back to the topic.

'Old man, you really saved me! Just imagine, my gums don't hurt any more. I rinse out with your mixture and . . .'

He stopped short. The theatre-going public was streaming past them from the buffet where they had been queueing for caviar sandwiches and boxes of chocolates that were in short supply just now in Moscow. And together with this general stream, arm in arm with a tall foreigner, into the smoking-room walked the beautiful, light-footed Olya Makhova.

As he followed her with his eyes Ilya Andronov said softly: 'Ye gods, look at that girl!'

'D'you want to meet her?' Colonel Orlov turned to him with a smile – it turned out he had been listening to their conversation with half an ear the whole time.

'Is she one of yours?' Ilya asked him.

'Of course!' said Orlov proudly. 'Olya Makhova, student at the Theatrical Institute, and with her is Mike Leonard, a Canadian, president of the biggest construction company in Toronto. He's leaving in a couple of days, so I can fix . . .'

Apparently sensing that she was being talked about and looked at, Olya Makhova – the late Major Neznachny's best 'cadre', his pride and joy – turned round and sent Colonel Orlov, Ilya Andronov and Stavinsky a long look of her naughty eyes. But if this bewitching glance merely caused Ilya Andronov to draw in his tummy in anticipation of the fun he would have with this sex-kitten, Stavinsky, on the other hand, felt his legs give way as Olya's blue eyes brushed against him. Olya Makhova – the very girl that Major Neznachny had been foisting on him at the National! And not only that – it turned out that this Pyotr Orlov was her immediate superior, a KGB man!

Meanwhile Ilya Andronov took a deep pull on his cigarette, blew out the smoke, and said almost indifferently to Orlov: 'Well . . . as long as you don't squeal to my father . . . I wouldn't mind . . . I have a little idea. Yuryshev and I are thinking of taking a trip out of town next Saturday, to the country . . . Does this beauty have a little friend?'

And Stavinsky realized that the trip to Mini-America would be taking place the following Saturday. And Olya Makhova would be with them.

16

At 3,500 metres above the Baltic, Lana Pett switched off the engine. Catching a head wind on which she could glide down to the Soviet border presented no difficulty. With her experience in aerial equilibristics she could make the machine do what she wanted. And it was not of course these minor technical details of flying that caused her to strain her eyes peering into the night. She was flying home – to the land which the descendant of every Russian émigré carries in his heart even if he has never been there, even if that land has never warmed his bare feet with its hot dusty country paths or stung them with the chill of its dewy morning grass. Russia was for Lana what Wonderland was for Alice. There in that fabulous country lived the music of Tchaikovsky, the poetry of Pushkin, the heroes of Russian folk tales – golden-haired Alyonushka, the Little Hump-Backed Horse, Vasilisa the Beautiful . . . Three times Aleksey Pavlov, the chubby-cheeked head of the Soviet Sports Committee, had invited Lana to gliding contests in the USSR – twice as a participant and the last time as a judge. But Lana would plead filming commitments and refuse. Actually her reason was a different one – in 1918 the Bolsheviks shot her grandfather, the Tsarist General Count Khudyakov, and for her to accept their invitation now implied acknowledging the legality of that execution. Of course that fat-faced Pavlov had more than likely never heard of her grandfather or of a Count Khudyakov being shot by some red military commissar in the Siberian town of Tobol. But Lana knew – and that was enough.

Now she was flying to Russia. If it were up to her she would have glided all the way to Tobol (well, perhaps she would have had to put the engine on a couple of times to get height), but her flight destination was quite different: frozen Lake Ilmen. And the fact that she – the granddaughter of a Russian general and count, and consequently Countess Khudyakova herself – had to sneak across the Soviet border secretly like this, like a smuggler, bringing her machine down from an altitude of 3,500 metres almost to sea level, then creep across like a shadow, being careful not to climb higher than 200 metres above the ground so as to avoid Soviet radar – this hole-and-corner method of coming back to her legitimate home country angered Lana more than anything now. Every detail had been worked out on a worst-case situation. If she was picked up by radar or arrested on landing, she had no Soviet charts in the cockpit, and her navigational instruments and engine could be sabotaged by simply kicking a button with her right foot. The fuses would go, the electric wire would catch fire, and everything would look very natural – the European glider champion makes a forced landing and asks the Soviet authorities, and Aleksey Pavlov personally, to help her repair the aircraft. Far more complicated was the return journey with two passengers on board. You couldn't make up any story then, you just had to beat it out of Soviet territory whatever happened! But no, there must not be any miscalculations! Under no circumstances! Even if they picked her up on the return journey they would not open fire straight away, they would send out planes to intercept her and try to force her to land on their territory. And then she would show the Soviet pilots what was meant by superior flying skills! She had a few aerial tricks up her sleeve . . .

But even so, despite all her experience and all her hereditary aristocratic courage (family myth obstinately claimed that her grandfather had managed to spit in the red military commissar's face just before he was shot, and even preserved the commissar's name – something like Neznachny or Nichtozhny), as she approached the Soviet Baltic coastline Lana was more nervous than she had been even during the most risky aerial filming. Her hands gripped the stick, her eyes were glued to the altimeter needle and the small screen of the infra-red night-flying instrument, but her thoughts . . .

To relieve the tension Lana switched on the radio. On this eve of Women's Day, 8 March, Soviet radio stations were broadcasting songs devoted to women. But Lana knew nothing about this Soviet holiday. Allowing the radio's self-tuner to range freely across the Soviet airwaves she was amazed to discover that the Russia which from far-away Paris she had pictured as a stern, frozen Communist prison or barracks – that Russia – sang! And not marches and Bolshevik hymns, but sprightly popular songs:

Today you brought me,
Not a bunch of white roses,
Not tulips and not lilies . . .
But today you brought me
These delicate flowers –
Lilies of the Valley . . .

Or:

Down Piterskaya Street and down Tverskaya-Yamskaya
Street,
On a little troika with a little bell,
Here comes my darling . . .

Lana froze. 'Down Piterskaya Street' – but that was a pre-Revolutionary song, that was a song her grandmother used to sing to her when she was little! So even these songs had been shamelessly taken over by her grandfather's murderers!

Thrusting the stick forward almost as far as it would go, Lana levelled out at the edge of the Gulf of Riga's coastline, and on the dark, snowy night of 7 March 1982 her single-engine sporting power glider slipped across the Soviet border like a noiseless bird; then one and a half kilometres inside the border Lana again caught a strong head wind and took her falling plane up in this air current. The old pre-

Revolutionary Russian song 'Down Piterskaya Street' filled the cockpit, and Lana even rocked the plane in time to the music. She was flying over her own country, over Russia.

17

A few hours before this event, at nine o'clock in the evening, a grey Mercedes drew up at the entrance of the students' dormitory of the Theatrical Institute on Trifonovskaya Street. Ilya Andronov sat at the wheel, with Stavinsky in the back seat where it was completely dark. There were also two black Volgas, a new Volkswagen, and a Lada standing in the snow near the entrance.

'Just like a diplomatic reception,' Ilya Andronov laughed to Stavinsky.

In fact there was no diplomatic reception at the student dormitory. It is simply that Soviet and foreign cars belonging to diplomats, big Party writers and Party writers and Party officials constantly drew up outside the student residences of Moscow's theatrical and film institutes. A young first-year girl in the acting faculty merely has to get herself on film especially in some musical part, she merely has to get her pretty little face on the screen, and she is transformed overnight from a poor Cinderella who lives on twenty-five roubles a month, darns her single pair of tights at night and eats on eighty kopecks a day – potatoes and watery tea – to a princess on whom wealthy admirers wait each evening at the entrance of her dormitory. And, borrowing shoes from one friend and tights from another, the young princesses excitedly run down the dormitory stairs, sometimes dragging along for company some of their not yet famous friends. A minute later the gleaming limousines dissolve in the Moscow night, carrying hungry film stars away to Government and non-Government *dachas* out of town – sometimes for several days. A few days later they return at dawn, drunk, with dark circles under their eyes, with a bottle of French perfume in their handbag or a bottle of foreign brandy under their arm. Swaying with fatigue, they drag themselves to their rooms and flop into bed – sleeping until evening, when a new lot of cars comes to pick them up. After a month the fashion for these particular film stars passes, the cars waiting at the students' front doors have new favourites, and the old ones are now used to alcohol and the gay night life and are prepared to rush off anywhere and with anyone in order to get it – no longer in private cars, but ordinary electric trains . . .

So there was nothing extraordinary about the appearance of Ilya Andronov's car outside the students' dormitory. Stavinsky, dressed in general's uniform, sat in the back seat in the dark. At his feet there was a briefcase with bottles of champagne and cognac, mandarins, and a thermos of hot coffee. The tailor Volodya Ivanov had provided Stavinsky with this thermos with a false bottom, and apart from coffee it contained three microfilms on which Stavinsky had photographed all the documents relating to Projects EMMA and EMBA at General Headquarters. The champagne also had its secret – white heroin. Stavinsky was counting on using this champagne to befuddle Olya Makhova's mind so that she couldn't recognize him as Robert Williams. This, however, was just another of his over-insurance measures. A scatterbrain like Olya Makhova would really have to strain her memory to recognize a Soviet general with beard and moustache as being the American client that never came through . . .

Olya Makhova and her friend Nadya, a student in the Choreographic Faculty, came fluttering out of the dormitory at 9.03. Colonel Orlov had warned them ahead of time that the people who were doing them the honour of spending that evening with them were very highly placed. Nadya had become a KGB agent only a month ago – Colonel Orlov, developing the theories of the late Major Neznachny, had 'consolidated' Olya Makhova with a friend – it always looks more natural if a student has her friend with her, and when working with foreigners it is more convenient. Now both young ladies were excited – hell, getting to know Ilya Andronov himself, son of *the* Andronov, offered no small prospect in life! They flitted into the car. Olya sat in the front next to Ilya and said a quick hello to some bearded general sitting in the dark in the back where Nadya had installed herself. The car moved off, and Olya immediately concentrated her efforts on chatting and flirting with her 'Number one client'.

By the time they reached Kutuzov Avenue the little company had already drunk the first bottle of champagne to lively music over the car radio, and they were in high spirits. Ilya Andronov was driving the car with his left hand, while his right hand was already on Olya Makhova's bared knee. Nadya was making active progress with the bearded general, and gradually began to take charge of the drinks, pouring out champagne into plastic cups for her friend and Ilya Andronov, and not forgetting herself. Stavinsky was in a state of nervous excitement. So far everything was going according to plan. At Kilometre 45 on the Mozhaisk highway the Mercedes turned off into the forest, and at the first control point the officer on duty recognized the owner of the car and instantly raised the barrier, even saluting the honourable company. The same thing happened at the second point. Stavinsky deliberately leaned out of the window so that these officers would remember his face. His plan was that in two or three hours' time it would be him, Stavinsky, driving the car, not Ilya Andronov. And Ilya Andronov and Olya Makhova, whom he would have to send to sleep with a strong soporific during their drinking bout in Mini-America, would be sitting in the back with Virginia. Five control points had seen Ilya Andronov arrive at Mini-America with General Yuryshev and two women, and they would quietly let the same four out again – the drunken son of the KGB head would be asleep in the back with two women in his arms, and no guard would risk waking them up to check if it was the same women or different ones. And Nadya would remain in Virginia's room, completely knocked out by the soporific, and would sleep peacefully there until morning. By that time Stavinsky would have nipped up to Lake Ilmen near Novgorod in the Andronov Mercedes and – 'Fairwell, unwashed Russia, land of slaves, land of masters!' Two days ago the tailor Volodya Ivanov had passed on to him a coded message from Washington: at 4.30 a.m. on 7 March a plane would be waiting for them at the western end of that lake. And yesterday Stavinsky had rehearsed the whole journey – he had driven from Moscow to Lake Ilmen in his own Volga in two hours fifteen minutes. That meant he must leave Mini-America no later than 2 a.m.

Ilya Andronov's Mercedes drove into Mini-America at 11.25. The dose of white heroin in the champagne that had been drunk on the journey was enough to give even a corpse a high. Very stimulated, Ilya Andronov stopped the car outside the Holiday Inn, sounded the horn, and immediately led the whole company into the hotel. He felt as if he owned this place. Exchanging a cheerful greeting with Colonel Stanley who had come hurrying out to meet him, he took the keys to two rooms on the second floor from him and dragged his own giggling beauty straight on upstairs – he could not wait to get her to bed.

'But what about supper, Ilya?' said Colonel Stanley in disappointment. 'Supper's waiting for you in the restaurant . . .'

'Later!' Ilya said dismissively. 'In an hour! We'll really be starved then . . .' and he laughed at his joke.

He disappeared with his Olya into room twenty-seven, and Stavinsky and Nadya got the room opposite.

Stimulated by the drug, Nadya obligingly began to pull off her clothes as soon as she crossed the threshold. Her slim figure and small ballerina's breasts were hellishly tempting, but Stavinsky was not in the mood for sex. While Nadya was having a shower and impatiently calling him to join her in the bathroom Stavinsky opened another bottle of champagne and tipped the soporific into Nadya's glass. Nadya came out of the bathroom naked, jumped into bed, drank to friendship with Stavinsky, and in the middle of unbuttoning his uniform fell asleep.

Stavinsky looked at his watch. It was 11.40. There was a little under two hours left for the whole operation. He buttoned up his uniform again and went off in search of Virginia so as to tell her the details of the escape plan.

Room thirty-three was on the third floor. Stavinsky knocked softly, but there was no answer. He tried the door handle – it was not locked. Stavinsky stepped into the room, felt for the switch, and turned on the light. The hotel room looked exactly like the one where he had just left Nadya – not lived in, with a neatly made bed, and with none of Virginia's things. Only a plastic doll and a little inflatable rubber penguin stood under the lamp on the bedside table – perhaps as ornaments for the room, perhaps forgotten by the last occupant when she left.

Seeing these toys Stavinsky felt the first stab of anxiety in his heart. Could a pregnant woman forget children's toys when she was leaving her room?

He switched off the light and went down to the hotel foyer to look for Colonel Stanley.

He found him in the restaurant sitting at the table set for the important guests, chatting with Louis Norton, the black teacher of Negro slang and pronunciation (he also doubled as bartender and waiter).

'Already? So fast?' Colonel Stanley asked Stavinsky in Russian with a smile of surprise.

Stavinsky made an embarrassed face, shrugged his shoulders, and joined them at the table.

'The girl's asleep, and I'm famished . . .' he said.

After a few minutes of chatting about the weather and Moscow gossip Stavinsky asked Colonel Stanley: 'Last time we were here we nearly ran over a pregnant American woman. I think her name was Virginia, or something like that. How is she?'

Colonel Stanley frowned, exchanging glances with Louis Norton. Then reluctantly he said: 'She's in hospital. She had a miscarriage.'

'A miscarriage?' Stavinsky exclaimed.

Stanley looked at him in surprise – General Yuryshev rather overreacted to the miscarriage of some unknown American woman.

But at the moment Stavinsky was not thinking about who he was talking to and where. He fastened on to Stanley.

'Did you say a miscarriage?' His face was white and frightened.

'No, not that time you nearly knocked her down, and not because of that,' Colonel Stanley said. 'It all happened later, a week ago. So you are not to blame at all . . .'

Stavinsky swallowed with difficulty. How could that happen? It was for the sake of that child and Virginia that he had gone through God knows what – he had thrown himself out of a train, had his arm broken and his teeth knocked out, lain in hospital pretending to have amnesia, risked his life every day impersonating Yuryshev, and had finally made it to this secret Mini-America so as to get Virginia out tonight – finally – and escape to the West with her. And she had had a miscarriage, and was in hospital! Impossible! It . . . And what about the plane at Lake Ilmen? Escape alone perhaps? The CIA were waiting for the materials on the new secret Soviet super-weapon. But to hell with the CIA! And to hell with the whole world, they could blast it with earthquakes tomorrow! He wasn't leaving the USSR without Virginia.

Before the amazed eyes of Colonel Stanley and Louis Norton he poured himself half a glass of brandy with a trembling hand and drank it down in one. Together with the burning liquid there returned also the sense of danger – Colonel Stanley and Norton were observing him with some surprise.

Clearing his throat, Stavinsky said: 'You scared me, I thought it was my fault, because of that incident. What hospital is she in?'

From far away in the hotel foyer came the sound of the telephone. Colonel Stanley sighed: 'New students arrive tomorrow, they'll be calling all night . . .' Round as a ball, he waddled penguin-like out to the telephone.

Norton watched him go and said: 'It's not your fault a all. It's just that she was General Andronov's lover and he didn't want her to have the child. They gave her some medicine . . .'

He poured brandy into his and Stavinsky's glasses. Sta- vinsky did not even notice how perfectly this black man Norton spoke Russian, without any foreign accent. Norton raised his glass and said: 'Why does he need a lover with baby? He's the master of the world. He can cause abortions he can kill anyone he wants. Only thing is, I don't know i they can save her now . . .' Stavinsky looked questioningly at him and he explained: 'She's in a serious condition. Only don't talk about it in front of Stanley. He's had a terrible time over this whole business. He must have had a soft spo for her, and we all liked her here . . .'

Stavinsky drank mechanically, not even tasting the brandy.

He didn't hear what this black man Norton was saying to him. He sat there, shattered, drained. A little barefoot golden-haired girl was running away from him across th hot sand of a Florida beach.

18

Two hours' drive from Mini-America, on the dark snowy ice of Lake Ilman stood Lana Pett's power glider. Lana kep looking at her watch impatiently. Time was running out - 4.15 . . . 4.18 . . . 4.22 . . . At 4.23 five obscure silhouette came out on to the ice. Dogs, thought Lana at first. The animals crossed the track made by the plane's skis, which had been greased with a special natural-fat grease, stopped and sniffed at the tracks, then came trotting towards the plane. On reaching the plane and sniffing at its skis, the first dog sat down in the snow just beneath the cockpit, lifted up its snout, and let forth a long, wild howl that resounded round the nocturnal lake. Immediately the others sat down next to the first and began to howl. 'Wolves!' Lana realized with horror. Her blood ran cold.

Lana could hold out no more. At 4.29 she switched on the ignition, the engine roared into life, frightening the wolves away, the plane took a short run along the lake's snow-covered ice and soared up into the night sky.

Part 5
Dive

1

At 0001 hours on 22 May 1982 submarine U-300, freshly painted after her recent refit left the jetty at the Baltiisk submarine base and in the grey twilight laid a course for the open sea.

Holding on to the rails of the conning tower surround were the Commanding Officer of the boat, Captain Pyotr Kushchin, the First Lieutenant, Oleg Kuvayev, the commander's Political Assistant, Vasily Danov, and the Project Officer from General Headquarters, Major-General Sergey Yuryshev (Stavinsky).

A cold sea breeze blew into their faces, the Baltic swell lashed the boat's hull, throwing heavy salt spray against their officers' pilot jackets. Behind Stavinsky lay the monstrous strain of the last two months, spent trying to steer Oparkov and Benzher round to the idea that he ought to be sent on this cruise as supervisor. The cruise was constantly being postponed, either by the Politburo or by General Headquarters, and it was not until the beginning of Margaret Thatcher's war for the Falkland Islands that Oparkov felt the moment was ripe for the operation – the attention of the entire world was taken up by the Anglo-Argentine war. On 21 May, when British marines began landing on the Falklands and the Royal Navy were shelling Port Stanley, with Harriers bombing Fox Bay, a radio message was received in Baltiisk from Marshal Oparkov: 'Proceed to execute operation at 2400 hours.'

The boat slowly rounded the northern tip of the Kursk-Neringa Spit and came out into the open sea. The lights of Klaipeda glimmered weakly through the low-lying night mist astern – the last lights of the Soviet mainland. In that Soviet land he was leaving behind the grave of former Colonel of the General Staff Sergey Yuryshev, buried under the name of the American tourist Robert Williams, the grave of the hapless Major of the KGB, Frol Neznachny, and the grave of Virginia. Virginia Part had died without regaining consciousness in the KGB hospital on 9 March of amniotic fluid embolism, pulmonary oedema, circulatory collapse, and cardiac arrest. Since then much had changed in the lives of our heroes: the new Plenum of the Central Committee of the Communist Party of the USSR had confirmed General Andronov as Secretary of the Central Committee and the general was now impatiently ticking off the last weeks of Brezhnev's life; Marshal Oparkov had made his choice – he had submitted to General Andronov a report on midget submarines with seismic weapons, and within a few days the USSR Ministry of Health had brought a large, million-dollar consignment of medical equipment from the US, including the TV eye that Benzher required, and in the Marine Institute Academician Benzher was put in charge of a group designing midget submarines on tracks; for his drinking in Spain and his orgies with the girls in Moscow Ilya Andronov had been deprived by his father of the right to travel abroad in case he should compromise his father's reputation as Galya Brezhneva had done; Olya Makhova had been permitted by Colonel Orlov to marry the successful Canadian businessman Michael Leonard, who was about to run for the Canadian Parliament; and after the death of Virginia, Stavinsky had spent the whole month of April at Oil Rocks in Baku, where he took part every day in the underwater trials of the new drilling equipment and in divers' training.

When the Falklands crisis began to get serious in May, Oparkov ordered submarine U-300 to take the Benzher energy transmission grids on board and await his command to put to sea. And while the British were preparing for war and Admiral Woodward's task force was heading for the Falklands, and while Marshal Oparkov was waiting for the decisive moment, and Galya Oparkova, having given up on her husband, had started up with another young student lover, in Baltiisk the twenty-year-old waitress Tanya, lingering, doe-eyed, smelling of apples, would silently enter Stavinsky's hotel room every night and quietly, without any words, relieve his nervous tension – he was afraid that at any moment a radio message might come from General Headquarters cancelling the cruise or recalling him to Moscow. Like a true Russian woman, Tanya healed Stavinsky's nervousness with her own body.

In fact all submariners are treated to such caresses by their girls before going to sea. And since no crew member knows in advance his exact date of departure, each night spent with a woman is treated as if it were the last and is correspondingly ardent and tender. Landlubbers – those who do not sail away from their girls for half a year, sealing themselves off from the world with the steel armour of the ship, wireless silence, and many fathoms of ocean water – landlubbers who in the morning say goodbye to their wives and loved ones until lunch, or at the latest until supper – such landlubbers do not know those nights that submariners enjoy with their women before departing.

A small vibration ran through the hull of the U-300 – the boat's nuclear-powered engines were working hard, though not nearly at full power. This vibration combined with Stavinsky's nervous trembling – up to the very last moment he had been expecting Marshal Oparkov to remove him from the cruise. But obviously the old man had put his own interpretation on his son-in-law's desire to 'get a breath of air for two or three weeks at sea' – let him get his breath of air, let him miss his wife a bit, then when he got back he would love her more.

'Nervous, Comrade General?' inquired the thirty-three-year-old Political Assistant Vasily Danov. His round Volga face shone with a sly, peasant smile.

Stavinsky had no time to reply – the voice of Captain Kushchin was heard: 'Flood main ballast tanks! Open for'ard valves! Dive!'

The bow of the vessel slowly began to bury itself in the phosphorescent, moonlit water.

'That's it, Comrade General,' Danov said to Stavinsky. 'Take your last mouthfuls of fresh air and let's go below.

We're diving.'

Stavinsky breathed a sigh of relief. In a couple of minutes the boat would go below the water and radio contact with the shore would be severed. The plan of operation worked out at General Headquarters specified that for the purpose of secrecy the boat would go on to wireless silence on approaching the outer limits of Swedish territorial waters. And now nothing – or almost nothing – could spoil his escape plan. Now only this pushy Danov would get on his nerves – was he trying to show how keen he was to a VIP from General Headquarters, or could he smell something wrong about Stavinsky with his Party nose, something alien maybe? During preparations for the cruise Stavinsky had established easy and even friendly relationships with all the other officers of the U-300. Essentially young officers of about thirty, with a high degree of military and technical training, each one was a first-class specialist in his own trade, and this removed the need either to curry favour with their superiors or to assert themselves with the other ranks by standing on formality or pulling rank. Most of them were on familiar terms with the sailors, and the sailors were familiar with them too – just like in the Israeli army . . .

But this Political Assistant Vasily Danov was quite a different matter. With no technical education, all he had under his belt was a military political training. Even the sailors who had joined the navy straight from secondary school were better educated than him. But then he easily made up for his technical inferiority complex with a strict Party sense and Party power. He was proud of the fact that he – a simple peasant lad – had been entrusted by the Party with keeping a watch on the Party consciousness of all 112 members of the ship's company – from the Commanding Officer to the last sailor. Dozens of internal political instructions, Party manuals, memoranda, and circulars emanated from the Main Political Directorate of the Soviet Army and Navy, and he studied every line of them; he read the whole of *Pravda* – the highest printed organ of the Communist Party – from the front-page leading article to 'News from the Collective Farms'. And now before this cruise, apart from the compulsory Party instructions, he had filled his cabin with bundles of literature – the magazine *Communist*, the pamphlets *Always Ready to Defend the Fatherland* and *The Party Agitator's Aid*, Brezhnev's books *The Rebirth*, *At the Sound of the Factory Whistle*, and *Dire Straits* and General Andronov's most recent speech at the April celebration of Lenin's birthday. And during loading he would look out of the corner of his eye at the Project Officer from General Headquarters – did the general see his diligence and high degree of political activity, or was he like all the other sailors and officers of the submarine, just watching the loading of food supplies – chocolate, butter, wine, dried soups, and the Captain's supply of brandy? Stavinsky realized that as a representative of General Staff he would be obliged to visit Danov's daily political classes with the sailors from time to time during the cruise, and then even to praise Danov for his work. And the mere thought of this made Stavinsky feel ill . . .

Gripping the rails he lowered himself down the ladder – without naval panache of course, but also without losing his footing – and followed the executive officer into the control room.

'Flood after tanks! Secure all hatches!' came the command from Captain Kushchin.

2

Vodka's gone up to six and eight,
Never mind, we won't stop drinking!
Tell Leonid Ilyich
We can even take ten!

But if the price goes any higher
They'll have a Poland on their hands.
If it gets to twenty-five,
We'll take the Winter Palace!

In the cramped mess deck sailors not on watch were playing dominoes, and one of them was quietly singing popular ditties about price increases and accompanying himself on the guitar. On an upper bunk freckle-faced Seaman Sinitsyn was reading a dog-eared copy of Dumas' *La Reine Margot*, while on the next bunk Ruchkin, a torpedo rating, was trying to set up a cockroach race in a cardboard box. Unlike surface vessels, submarines are not permitted to keep dogs, cats, or birds, they do not even have rats; but no amount of disinfection can save them from cockroaches. Cockroaches are the only form of life that voluntarily sets sail with the submariners on any voyage, even round the world. And the submariners feel something in the nature of a tenderness towards the cockroaches – after all, they are something alive amid this eternally dead electric light and steel bulkheads lined with air purification hydrogen cartridges. The cockroaches were fed on the remains of the sailors' ample dinners, they were given nicknames, and periodically cockroach races were organized.

Three blasts on the siren – short, long, short – brought the sailors tumbling out of their bunks.

'Fucking hell, another NBC alert!' Ruchkin swore, closing the cockroach box and pulling his respirator out from under his pillow.

And in his cabin, a tiny cabin, but an individual officer's one none the less, Stavinsky also swore as he put on his gas mask. He was already used to these practice alerts by now – five of them a day: NBC (nuclear, bacteriological and chemical) alerts, aircraft alerts, fire alerts. Then there were political classes, radioactivity checks, cleaning of sections, watches – the sailors were given no time to be bored.

Sailors' boots could be heard thundering down the corridor, then all was quiet – mechanics, missile ratings, planesmen, torpedomen, and sonar ratings had all dispersed to their action stations.

Stavinsky came out of his cabin wearing his respirator and walked along to the control room. The section was small – four metres long by two metres wide – and into this small space were crowded the Commanding Officer, the First Lieutenant, the Navigating Officer, the Communications Officer, and of course the Political Assistant Danov. It was a working situation, routine – no fuss, no nervousness. Kushchin sat on what looked like a rotating piano stool at the periscope, which at this depth was idle, the Navigator stood by the hydroplanes, the other officers watched the navigational instruments, the echo sounder and the long-range sonar scan. Not one of the instruments indicated the presence of any ships above the vessel or near it, but Kushchin calmly announced over the ship's broadcast system: 'Enemy attacking with torpedoes, crash dive! Flood midships tanks! Port seventeen! Engine room increase revs! Speed twenty-four knots!'

And immediately toneless male voices were heard over the broadcast system from every part of the boat: 'Seventeen degrees of port on!'

'Midships tanks flooded!'

'Speed twenty-four knots!'

Stavinsky felt the boat tipping forwards and to the right, and his ears began to get blocked from the rapid dive. Through his partial deafness he heard the executive officer's voice, as if through cotton wool: 'Depth eighty metres! . . . ninety metres! . . . 100 metres! 120 metres!'

The blood rushed to his face, and even through the glass of his gas mask Stavinsky could see that the blood had come to the faces of the other officers inside their respirators.

But Kushchin continued the dive, altering course: 'Enemy attacking with depth charges. Port thirty . . . Starboard forty . . .'

'Depth – 140 . . . 150 . . . 160 . . .' reported the First

Lieutenant.

In the nuclear reactor compartment the signs over the door shone with a dry red light: 'No Entry. High Radiation.' In the engine room the thin thread which the sailors had stretched athwartships was hanging slack, indicating the amount of pressure that was now squeezing the vessel – none of the ship's company apart from the Commanding Officer and his closest officers was permitted to know what depth the boat was at, and sailors in every submarine in the Soviet Navy have devised a method for calculating the dive depth according to this thread stretched from one side to the other.

'We're down about 150 metres . . .' said the freckly motor mechanic Sinitsyn, glancing at the thread.

'Blow for'ard and midships tanks!' came the command over the broadcast system: 'Crash surfacing!'

The vibration of the engines caused the hull to shudder, the bow tipped sharply upwards, and the boat began to surface rapidly. The blood rushed back out of Stavinsky's head and his stomach felt as though he were going up in a high-speed elevator. No wonder, he thought, all submariners get varicose veins and go deaf . . .

About twenty minutes later Kushchin finally gave the all-clear. Exhausted, sweating, his legs weak, Stavinsky pulled off his respirator and limped back to his cabin. The sailors and officers off watch walked down the corridor with him. They looked tired too as they made their way to supper – the officers to the wardroom, the sailors to the galley. As they walked along a group of sailors were counting on their fingers to see who was going to get today's bottle of wine: each submarine seaman gets a dinner ration of fifty grams of red Kagor wine per day, but there is no pleasure in drinking wine in such miserly quantities, and the sailors – ten men per bottle – either toss up among themselves for the whole bottle or draw up a strict rota. To drink a whole bottle before you go to bed even once in ten days – that's real enjoyment!

And although the officers did not have such restrictions on wine and Stavinsky knew that Kushchin would be happy to pour him as much brandy as he could wish for from his own supply in the Captain's cabin before supper, he did not go either to the wardoom or to Kushchin.

Reaching his own narrow little cabin, he collapsed on to the bunk. These constant dives and surfacings, these alerts and exercises at sea were finally beginning to wear him out. But now was the time he needed his physical health more than ever! What he had thought up, the one possible means of escape which he had prepared, demanded tremendous physical endurance. After sailing the Baltic for eight days with frequent changes of course to throw off any possible surveillance, the submarine would approach Sweden in order to lay down the last two matrices of the 'Swedish arc': one at the island of Muskö to destroy Stockholm and the whole Stockholm archipelago, the other at the Väddö Peninsula to destroy the huge industrial complex at Uppsala. Sweden's remaining military and populated centres – Götteborg, Malmö, Karlskrona, and Sundsvall – were already covered by grids installed by Kushchin the previous October.

Before leaving Moscow at the beginning of May Stavinsky had managed to give the tailor Ivanov only approximate dates to pass on to Washington when some small fishing vessel should be standing by for him near Muskö Island in Mysingsfjärden Bay at a position 59° North, 18° 07′ East. The period he suggested was during the two weeks from the outbreak of hostilities in the Falklands. But would MacKerry keep watch round the clock for two weeks at sea, waiting for Stavinsky?

And as he lay face downwards on his bunk Stavinsky felt so exhausted that he did not even notice a new Morse signal on the siren: dot-dot, dash, dot-dot.

Silently, without a knock, the door of his cabin opened and the Political Assistant Vasily Danov looked in. For several seconds he looked intently at Stavinsky lying on his bunk, then said politely but firmly: 'Let's go to the shower, Comrade General. Radioactivity check.'

3

'Welcome aboard the *Jurianna*!'

This large coloured sign was attached to the snow-white superstructure of the two-deck private yacht. Although Stavinsky had requested through the tailor Ivanov that he be met at Muskö Island by some simple little fishing smack, MacKerry felt that after all his misadventures in Russia Stavinsky deserved a far more luxurious welcome. Apart from that, one couldn't spend two weeks bucketing about in the sea in a fishing tub, without any rest or basic conveniences. The *Jurianna* was quite a different matter; it belonged to Jacob Stevenson's lover Anna Jurins. Two sleeping cabins, a saloon with colour TV, stereo, and bar, a galley with refrigerator, gas stove, toaster, and coffee machine, a hot shower, air conditioning, and two toilets.

This was now the fourth day that MacKerry, Carroll, Jacob Stevenson, and Anna Jurins – a twenty-seven-year-old blonde with long legs and slim hips – had been waiting by Muskö Island, sunbathing, fishing with spinners, frying delicious fish steaks on the gas stove, and they were not in the least bit tired. The four of them had already got a good tan under the May sun; Anna had sunbathed topless since the first day and now her small breasts were almost as dark as her chocolate-coloured nipples, while Jacob had filled his eighth notebook – MacKerry had been giving him a detailed account of how the plan to abduct Yuryshev had failed and of how they had sent Stavinsky and Virginia off to Russia. Jacob assured him he would alter all the names of real people in his novel and was already looking forward to the book's success. And why not! He had been in on the beginning of this operation, he had been the first person to meet Colonel Yuryshev in August last year, then he had met his look-alike Stavinsky-Williams and his 'wife' Virginia in Moscow, and he himself had sent Colonel Yuryshev the tickets for the train from Leningrad to Moscow. On top of all that, he had witnessed the deaths of Colonel Yuryshev and Major Neznachny of the KGB at Sheremetyevo Airport. And now he was going to be present at the dénouement of this whole story - he was going to meet Stavinsky here on this yacht and finally learn the secret of why Soviet submarines had appeared round the coasts of Sweden. Any professional journalist's hand would be itching at the thought of such a scoop. Of course, if he published a series of articles or a book about this operation, then however much he changed his name the KGB would have no difficulty in establishing that he had had a personal hand in the operation; and then it would be goodbye to Moscow for him until Soviet power came to an end in Russia. The hell with it! How long could one go on hanging about in that country being constantly watched by KGB 'guardian angels'? It was time to move across to the editorial side of the paper as Hedrick Smith and Robert Kaiser - correspondents for the *New York Times* and *Washington Post* - had done after their best-sellers on Russia.

Hell, where was that Stavinsky? Was he really right now somewhere below them in the depths of the sea, escaping from a Russian submarine which had once again penetrated Swedish waters? But jeepers-creepers, how could you escape from a submarine? Neither MacKerry, Carroll, nor Stevenson knew. The Anglo-Argentine war was in full swing, and they kept running inside to the hired skipper, Martin Raben, to check if the wind or current had carried them off target, and they would take turns keeping watch on deck, gazing into the green sea. At night the *Jurianna* switched on all her side lights, as well as two powerful spotlights fixed to the upper deck.

Early the next morning, 25 May, the skipper, puffing on his pipe, silently indicated the horizon to MacKerry.

'What's up?' MacKerry asked Anna, his interpreter in conversations with the skipper. Raben did not know a word of English, neither did MacKerry know a word of Swedish.

Anna exchanged a few words with Raben and translated for MacKerry: 'He says the sky's gone red, and there's going to be a gale.'

'So?'

'He says if it gets to more than force five or six he'll have to take the *Jurianna* back to port.'

'That's impossible! We can't leave this spot until the end of May! Whatever happens!'

'Even if it gets up to force ten? Hmm!' said Anna. 'I'm not about to die here for the sake of your spying business! One's enough – Virginia.'

'Get him to request a weather forecast over the radio,' said MacKerry.

Anna had another brief talk with Raben and told MacKerry: 'He's already done that. According to the forecast there's going to be a light breeze, but he doesn't believe these forecasts. He says there's going to be a gale.'

'All right, we'll see . . .' said MacKerry sullenly.

An hour later, as he sat with a spinner over the side, he suddenly heard the winch motor start up and then saw the anchor cable being rapidly hauled in.

He rushed to the wheelhouse. 'What's happening?'

Anna was not there – she and Stevenson had withdrawn to their cabin: as a true journalist Stevenson was not wasting any time.

In the wheelhouse skipper Raben grimly started the yacht's two diesel engines and put them to full ahead, and immediately the two powerful screws shot the *Jurianna* away from the island northwards towards the small port of Sandemar.

'What's happening?' MacKerry yelled again, and for good reason – the sea was a dead calm, there was not a breath of wind. And no clouds in the sky.

'*Om tio minuter vil stormen börja,*' said Raben grumpily.

MacKerry only got the international word 'storm' and once again looked about in disbelief. Only now did he notice that there were none of the pleasure yachts and fishing boats about that had been criss-crossing the sea yesterday and the day before, and more important – there were none of those raucous, impudent seagulls that for the past four days had fed on everything that was chucked to them from the *Jurianna* and had even boldly landed on the guard rails and the forward deck. The calm before the storm, thought MacKerry.

Indeed, fifteen minutes later as the *Jurianna* was dashing at full speed for Sandemar, the Baltic was hit by a force ten gale.

. . . Two hours later a heavy seiner shoved off cumbrously from her moorings in Sandemar and shaped course for the gale-torn sea.

4

Coded Signal

To: Marshal Oparkov, General HQ, Moscow
Info: Gorchakov, C-in-C Naval Forces
Reached stand-by position 29 May 1908 hours. Awaiting further instructions.

Kushchin

Coded Signal

To: Kushchin, Commanding Officer U-300
Info: Gorchakov, C-in-C Naval Forces
Aerial reconnaissance reports that despite gale conditions a seiner fishing boat has been in your operating area near Muskö Island for the last few days without any visible signs of fishing activity.

You are to change the sequence for laying down EMMA and to start the operation at the second point, in the region of Väddö in the Gulf of Bothnia. After completing work at this point you are to proceed to international waters to receive further instructions.

Your country sends warm greetings to the whole ship's company and wishes you success.

Marshal Oparkov

When the telegraphist brought this signal to the Captain's cabin and read it to him Stavinsky blanched. 'Idiots!' every nerve in him cried out. 'MacKerry and Daniel Cooper are idiots!' He had specifically requested a small fishing boat! Lord, what was he going to do now?

Meanwhile Kushchin was dictating to the telegraphist:

Coded Signal

To: Marshal Oparkov, General HQ, Moscow
Info: Gorchakov, C-in-C Naval Forces
Your order received. Will execute. Ship's company thanks the country for confidence shown.

Pyotr Kushchin, Commanding Officer, U-300

And with a wink to Stavinsky he went along to the control room to carry out a crash dive. Stavinsky was left alone in the Captain's cabin. A great wave of despair came over him and seemed to block his vision as he looked around at the Captain's small, but comfortable cabin, the table with large-scale charts of Swedish territorial waters laid out on it and sea-bottom charts, the bottle of brandy on the table and the photograph of Captain Kushchin's wife and two children on the wall. Feeling drained of all willpower, Stavinsky closed his eyes and sat at the table on the metal chair riveted to the floor. Muffled diving orders reached the cabin over the broadcast system: 'Recover radio buoy! . . . Flood for'ard and main tanks! . . . Slow ahead! . . . Port . . . Increase revs . . . Steady . . .'

The boat was descending into the depths of the sea. Through the metal bulkheads the dull noise of water flooding the ballast tanks could be heard in the cabin.

Stavinsky opened his eyes and looked blankly at the charts left behind by Kushchin. He did not need these charts – he had long ago studied them down to the finest detail in Baltiisk and at General Headquarters. The second point for laying down EMMA – near Väddö Peninsula – was at a depth of ninety-seven metres. It was utter folly to risk surfacing from such a depth in one go. Even in a diving suit the sharp drop in pressure was bound to cause the bends and rupturing of the ear drums and blood vessels in the nose. It was quite a different matter at Muskö Island. There EMMA was to be laid down at forty metres – and it was from this depth that Stavinsky had been planning to come to the surface, by leaving the boat through the torpedo compartment together with the divers – the drillers and the fitters who were going to set up EMMA, and coming out on to the bottom of the Baltic Sea. Even if one of the divers chased after him, and in order to evade pursuit he would immediately have to get rid of his lead weight-belt and his heavy lead-soled boots which keep a diver on the bottom – in other words, even if there were an emergency and he had to shoot up to the surface like a cork, and lost consciousness because of the drop in pressure, he would be picked up by the fishing vessel which he had requested from MacKerry and Daniel Cooper. It was not for nothing he had done three weeks' training with the underwater drillers at Oil Rocks on the Caspian Sea. But now they had blown it all! Blown it all . . .

Somebody knocked at the door of the Captain's cabin. Probably that Danov again, thought Stavinsky lazily. And indeed, a second later the irritating face of the Political Assistant appeared round the half-open door of the cabin.

'I've been looking for you, Comrade General. Right after this dive we're having political classes. I wanted to ask you to give the sailors a talk before the operation. On behalf of General Headquarters. The men have been waiting for a long time . . .'

Stavinsky gazed at him with melancholy eyes. Then, very slightly swaying, he reached for the bottle of brandy and before Danov's very eyes took two deep swigs right from the bottle, wiped the drips off his beard and moustache with the back of his hand, and said huskily but audibly: 'Fuck off, you stupid prick!'

'Hmm . . .' Danov sniggered, turning slightly pale. 'I think you are a little drunk, Comrade General . . .'

And in the depths of his grey peasant eyes there was a gleeful, vengeful spark. After all, he had tried so hard throughout this cruise. At the daily political classes he had worked so hard with the sailors on Comrade Andronov's speech in honour of the 112th anniversary of Lenin's birth that they knew every paragraph of the speech by heart and could answer unhesitatingly any questions on the aggressive plans of the American imperialists, the Chinese hegemonists, the Afghan rebels, the Israeli Zionists, and the Polish counter-revolutionaries. And the representative of the army's General Staff, Major-General Yuryshev, had not been to one of these classes – now it was obvious why: he was drinking.

Stavinsky slowly swung the bottle back and over his head – and hurled it at the Political Assistant.

Danov managed to get the door shut before the bottle crashed against the metal.

5

At the entrance to the Gulf of Bothnia the submarine bottomed. In the two torpedo compartments – in the bow and stern – eight drillers in diving gear were already lying in the four torpedo tubes, preparing to go out on to the sea-bed. The compressors were working hard, gradually bringing up the pressure in their diving suits. Kushchin, Stavinsky, Danov, and Raizman, the Torpedo Officer, were in the forward torpedo compartment and in the after torpedo compartment, the First Lieutenant and the Electrical Officer were monitoring the divers' preparations for leaving the boat. Dull metallic signals could be heard from inside the torpedo tubes – the divers were tapping with spanners to indicate that they were adjusting normally to the high pressure. Stavinsky knew that each diver was now breathing hard through his nose, what the divers called 'blowing the nose', to get used to the high pressure.

When the pressure gauge needle was pointing to ten atmospheres Raizman switched off the high-pressure air hose to the diving suits and the divers transferred to their independent oxygen supply. Now their only link with Kushchin was the intercom system. Kushchin motioned everyone out of the torpedo compartment. Danov and Raizman left Stavinsky and went with Kushchin to the control room.

'Ready aft?' Kushchin asked into the intercom.

'Ready!' came the reply over the radio.

'Secure torpedo compartments!' ordered Kushchin.

'For'ard compartment secured!'

'After compartment secured!' came the reports.

'Open torpedo tube valves!'

In the total silence, with the boat's engines stopped, the water could be heard rushing into the open forward and after torpedo compartments. Stavinsky knew what was happening there just now, and the brief radio reports by the petty officers in the two diving parties completed the picture: 'Half flooded . . . three quarters . . . Flooding complete, Comrade Commander!'

After the compartments were completely flooded the divers went down the torpedo tubes as if they were on a toboggan slide, and out on to the sea floor.

'We're on the bottom, Comrade Commander. What a mess, it's a fucking garbage dump!' Petty Officer Rogachov reported over the radio.

'Stop swearing!' ordered Kushchin.

'Aye-aye, Comrade Commander! The bottom is terrible – slime and rubbish. Do they tip out all their old tins here or something?'

'Look for a place for drilling.'

'We're looking, Comrade Commander.'

The eight divers moved slowly across the sea bottom, searching for a more or less level area for drilling with the powerful spotlights attached to their chests.

'Well, it looks as though we might be able to do it here, Comrade Commander.'

'Where?'

'About twelve metres from the boat.'

'Are you sure?'

'U-huh . . . all right . . . It's all right here, Comrade Commander. We'll just clear it up with our feet and it'll be fine.'

After a few minutes, during which the divers cleared the rubbish away from the place they had selected, the petty officer in charge of the party reported: 'That's it, Comrade Commander. We can take out the equipment.'

Kushchin looked at Stavinsky, gave him a merry wink, and asked: 'Well, Comrade General? God-speed?'

Stavinsky nodded.

'Open port missile compartment!' Kushchin ordered into the microphone.

Once again there was a dull, turbulent noise of water as it rushed into the gigantic port side section of the submarine – that section where normally the long cigars of long-range nuclear missiles stand upright in their shafts. But now there were no nuclear missiles on board the U-300. Instead, out of the long missile compartment powerful pneumatic jacks slowly pushed a steel platform up against the rushing water carrying, beneath a protective covering, the drilling rig that had been assembled in Baku.

When the water turbulence round the missile compartment had subsided above the submarine, all eight divers approached the platform and, taking hold of the drilling rig on all sides, slowly moved it from the boat to the selected spot. The water lessened the weight of the equipment; a horizontal screw propelled it forwards. In a few minutes it was standing on the level platform. Now the divers hauled across the electric cables and the rubber high-pressure fresh-water hose for cooling the diamond bit during operation.

'Ready, Comrade Commander,' the petty officer reported.

'Engine room!' ordered Kushchin. 'Power for the drilling rig!'

'Ready, Comrade Commander!'

'Compressor room?'

'Ready!'

'Sonar, what's on the surface?'

'All clear, Comrade Captain.'

Kushchin looked at Stavinsky again, and Stavinsky nodded silently again.

'Rogachov, switch on!' Kushchin ordered the petty officer in command of the divers.

'I wouldn't mind a smoke, Comrade Commander,' Rogachov joked over the radio.

'I'll smoke you, you son-of-a- . . . ! Switch on!'

'Aye-aye!' the voice replied cheerfully.

Even without hydrophones one could hear the whine of the high-speed diamond drill.

There, twelve metres away from the boat, ninety-seven metres down on the bottom of the sea, and only six miles from the Swedish coast the sharp, stinglike diamond bit bored into the sea-bed, preparing a shaft for the seismic weapon. Half a metre . . . one metre . . . one and a half metres . . .

Suddenly the sound of laughter and the strumming of a guitar came down the corridor leading from the control room to the other sections of the boat. Kushchin turned to the Political Assistant, annoyed: 'Danov, give the men something to do!'

'Aye-aye' Danov saluted, dashed out of the room and

immediately started bellowing at the skiving sailors who had set up a cockroach race in the corridor: 'Stop it! All hands to political classes! All hands!' And with the sole of his officer's shoe he crushed three record-breaking cockroaches, including torpedoman Ruchkin's pride and joy, the prize-winning cockroach Reagan.

'Why did you have to squash Reagan, Comrade Political Assistant?' said Ruchkin with tears in his eyes.

'I'll give you Reagan! I'll give you such a Reagan when we get back on shore! Quick march to classes!'

And while the diving party was drilling the Swedish sea-bed outside the U-300, the men of the stand-off watch were in the mess answering the Political Assistant Danov's stern questions clearly and without hesitation: 'Motor mechanic Zakharov, how do the Soviet people respond to attempts by the aggressive forces of imperialism to achieve military superiority over the Soviet Union?'

'"In response to attempts by the aggressive forces of imperialism to achieve military superiority over the Soviet Union,"' motor mechanic Zakharov immediately began to quote Comrade Andronov's report, '"we shall maintain our defensive capability at the level necessary to ensure reliable security for our country and for the whole socialist commonwealth."'

'Sit down. Torpedoman Ruchkin, what would happen to our planet without the firm, peace-loving policies of the Soviet Union?'

Twelve metres away from these political classes the diamond bit continued to chew into Swedish soil: two metres . . . two and a half . . . three . . .

6

Stavinsky lay in his cabin, his hands behind his head, staring at the metal deck-head. The last few hours of the

U-300's stay in Swedish waters were running out. If he did not take the risk of escaping now the opportunity might not present itself again. The new Secretary-General of the Central Committee, General Andronov, was personally supervising the construction of midget submarines on tracks, and with his protection Benzher would get these boats made, not in a year but in a few months – the best designers at the Marine Institute had been put on to the job now, and some bright fellow had even suggested fitting a rubber fish-tail to the keel so as to smooth out the track-marks on the sea-bed . . . Yes, when those remote-controlled mini-subs came into use there would be no more deep-sea drillers coming out of submarines on to the sea-bed, and the last chance of escape would have gone . . .

Stavinsky got up and went through the Navigating Officer's cabin. It was just next door – the other side of the bulkhead. The Navigating Officer had nothing to do while the ship was on the bottom, and so to occupy himself he was compiling lists of boys' and girls' names – his wife was due to have a baby in a week, and now the whole ship was involved in choosing a name for the new-born boy or girl. The next time radio contact was established with the shore the Navigating Officer was planning to radio the two names – male and female – that the ship's company had voted for. The Navigating Officer got up when Stavinsky opened his cabin door, as was proper with a general, but Stavinsky waved his hand lazily for him to sit down again.

'Comrade General, can you suggest some pretty girl's name?' said the Navigating Officer, worn out from days of choosing names.

Stavinsky shrugged his shoulders, then laughed: 'Virginia.'

'What?' asked the Navigating Officer.

'It's one of those American names – Virginia . . .' said Stavinsky. Then he casually asked the Navigating Officer: 'Listen, what's the weather like on top?'

'Dead calm, Comrade General. Less than force one.'

'But there's a gale at Muskö Island?'

'When we made contact three days ago the forecast was bad. But that doesn't affect us in the slightest. We're under water – no sea-sickness!'

'That's right, too . . .' said Stavinsky pensively, thinking that David MacKerry probably had not managed to hire a fishing boat because of that gale. In any case, there was no other way to explain why a large seiner should be patrolling Muskö Island. But if that seiner was going to hang around there any longer General Headquarters would not permit the submarine to approach the island.

Captain Kushchin poked his head round the door. 'Comrade General, the drilling is completed,' he told Stavinsky. In front of subordinates he always used the polite form when addressing Stavinsky, though in private they had long ago switched to the familiar forms. 'We're going to begin installing EMMA. The fitters are preparing to exit. Are you going with them?'

Kushchin was evidently pleased with himself – he had brought his vessel to a perfect location, the drillers had done a first-class job, and now only the last phase of the operation remained. And during those few seconds Stavinsky was deciding his own fate.

'Yes, I'll go!' he said at length. That was of course why he had come as Project Officer on this cruise – to monitor the installation of EMMA. Otherwise his being on the cruise could look to an outsider like a meaningless joy-ride, and to refuse to go out with the fitters would look like cowardice. Of course he could wait to go out until the second point Muskö Island, but would they give the boat the go-ahead for the second point, or would they just order her to lie to in neutral waters until that Swedish seiner left the island? Or perhaps they would order her to return home altogether and then . . . No, Oparkov would not let him go on a second cruise. 'I'll go!' Stavinsky repeated.

And he went to his cabin to change.

7

Thin woollen stockings . . . Thick woollen socks . . . long woollen pants . . . Two thick woollen sweaters and a woollen cap to fit inside his helmet. Opening the false bottom of the thermos flask, Stavinsky took three small microfilm cassettes out of the secret compartment. With sticking plaster he attached them under his left armpit. Then on top of the warm clothing he put on a light overall. So. Everything all right, it seemed . . . With a last look round the cabin Stavinsky turned quickly and walked out into the corridor. In the fore part of the ship the fitters were already putting on their diving suits in the torpedo compartment that had been 'blown' for them. Stavinsky was surprised to see the Political Assistant Vasily Danov putting on a diving suit with the others. Since Stavinsky had thrown the bottle at him Danov had kept out of sight, deliberately avoiding him, and now all of a sudden here he was putting on a diving suit! Stavinsky looked inquiringly at Kushchin.

'The Political Assistant decided to be a hero . . .' Kushchin said with a shrug of the shoulders.

'Cancel it!' said Stavinsky calmly.

'What do you mean?' Danov flared up indignantly, looking at Stavinsky now with unconcealed hostility.

'Just that. Political Assistant Danov is not going out!' repeated Stavinsky imperiously. 'You are not trained.'

'I have forty-nine hours' experience of underwater work with submariners! I've been out in the Atlantic and in the Arctic!' Danov objected.

'I didn't see it, take off your diving suit!' ordered Stavinsky. 'Apart from that, you don't question commands from a senior officer!' He needed to get it off his chest, so when Danov had taken off the diving suit he ordered him: 'Attention! About turn! Leave the torpedo compartment, quick march!'

'Aye-aye!' answered Danov, giving him a curt, angry salute, and with a pale face left the section.

'That was a bit steep . . .' observed Kushchin, evidently displeased. 'Watch out, he'll put in a bad report on you to the Political Directorate . . .'

'I am responsible to General Headquarters for this operation, and I don't need any surprises,' said Stavinsky, putting on his diving suit. Heavy boots with thick lead soles attached to them, belt with lead weights, pack with two oxygen bottles, another belt with fitting tools, knife, and spotlight battery. Two men of the watch on deck helped Stavinsky kit up. The fitters were already lying in the other torpedo tubes ready to leave the boat. In another minute that same Raizman, the Torpedo Officer had switched on the compressors. The thin rubber hoses leading to the divers' suits became inflated, and Stavinsky felt the atmospheric pressure in his suit increasing, crushing his whole body. He began to blow out hard through his nose . . .

The pressure increased. It was as if some powerful, heavy object had come down with all its weight on Stavinsky's body as it lay stretched out in the torpedo tube. 'Breathe!' Stavinsky told himself. 'Breathe!'

At last he felt that the increase in pressure had stopped. With a movement of his hand he switched the valve at his side to the independent oxygen supply on his back. Then with the handle of his knife he gave three short taps on the casing of the torpedo tube. And immediately he heard the cheerful voice of Captain Kushchin in his headphone: 'Well fellows? Everyone alive?' And then the senior fitter's reply: 'All alive, Comrade Commander!' So, thought Stavinsky, that means Kushchin is already in the control room and has switched over to the radio intercom. Now they would begin to flood the compartment.

And indeed, slowly, very slowly the clincher bolt in the ship's side moved back a fraction of an inch, and the cold, heavy Baltic water came rushing through the crack into the dark torpedo compartment.

Stavinsky counted off the seconds to himself: eight . . .

nine . . . ten . . . eleven . . . At the same time another thought was pounding through his head – perhaps he should not run away after all? Perhaps he should return to Russia to live the opulent life of a general with Galya Oparkova? After all, it was sheer folly to run away here, at such a depth. Even if he made it up to the surface alive he would not be able to swim even two miles in that heavy diving suit, those expert fitter-divers would catch up with him.

'Sergey Ivanovich,' Kushchin's voice came through his headphone. 'How are you feeling?'

'Fine . . .' he tried to answer as cheerfully as possible.

Meanwhile the petty officer in command of the fitters was reporting to Kushchin: 'A quarter flooded . . . half flooded . . .'

Stavinsky could hear these reports through his headphone. And when the water level reached his back he bent down to his boots, overcoming the weight of his back-pack, and on each boot unfastened two of the four clips securing the thick lead soles. If he did decide to run away it would be easier to undo the rest of the clips in the water.

A new command from Captain Kushchin in the control room came over the headphone: 'Open starboard missile compartment!'

Against the water rushing into the compartment the powerful pneumatic jacks now thrust up yet another platform, this time bearing Academician Benzher's horrific invention – the sections of the energy transmission matrix, trail-blazer of Soviet seismic weaponry.

8

The bottom of the Gulf of Bothnia really was dirty, littered with slime-covered metal barrels, cans, and other junk. In the dense, opaque depths one could see only two or three yards ahead with the aid of the powerful spotlight attached to the chest.

But at the working platform where the sections of the grid were being installed in the sea-bed it was lighter. The rather cumbersome structure erected on the platform looked like a small oil derrick. Four powerful stationary spotlights were fitted to the top of this oil rig, powered by the submarine's generator. These spotlights illuminated the working platform for the divers, and the fitters were able to work without hindrance. With precise, practised movements they lowered the metre-long sections of EMMA into the shaft. Special equipment screwed the sections together when they were already in the shaft.

Stavinsky saw these lethal sections disappearing in the shaft one by one. Not only that – together with the other divers he himself dragged the sections over to the working platform from the submarine. Section four . . . five . . . six . . .

In the pauses between work Stavinsky looked up, and even swam up a little way, pushing himself off from the bottom with his feet and hanging weightless for a while, peering into the dense water above his head. But the thick leaden water was completely opaque. There was almost a hundred metres of water above him and it would be absurd to escape from such a depth. Even if he didn't go up all in one, but in steps, gradually shedding his tool bag, lead soles, spotlight battery, and other heavy articles, and even if the fitters were so occupied with their work that they did not immediately notice his disappearance, he still would not make it to the shore in that cold water, and wearing a diving suit as well. It was out of the question!

Even through the diving suit with its special battery-powered heater the sepulchral cold reached his body. The sea-bed was dead – no seaweed, no fish. And the number of sections of Benzher's energy transmission column was decreasing all the time – there were only three left, then two . . . Soon the fitters would be installing the last one, then they would be sealing the shaft with a special grout that absorbed radio waves so that Swedish seismic reconnaissance would not detect the matrix. Having sealed the shaft, the divers would drag the drilling rig back to the boat's port missile compartment and . . .

And suddenly the lights on the drilling rig went out – all four of them. And immediately the rig's machinery was turned off. In their headphones Stavinsky and the fitters heard the authoritative, but obviously worried voice of the commanding officer, Kushchin: 'Stop all work! Switch off body lamps! Switch off intercom and don't move! A ship is passing overhead!'

The lamps on the fitters' chests went out. In the pitch darkness the boat lay on the bottom in total silence, all her engines shut down so as not to betray her presence by any metallic or mechanical sound. At that moment she was like a giant hiding fish.

And Stavinsky realized – this was his chance! Some ship was moving overhead. Not a yacht, not a fishing boat – such small fry would not cause Kushchin to halt the work – but a large vessel. It didn't matter what, thought Stavinsky. Swedish, Japanese, Canadian! A ship – that meant rescue! In any case, it was his last chance, the decisive moment! There was no need to swim to the island, no need to go shooting up to the surface like a cork at suicidal speed from this depth – nobody would notice his disappearance in the total, pitch darkness with the intercom switched off, and it would be twenty minutes, if not half an hour, before Kushchin was satisfied that that ship had gone far enough away from where they were, and that there was not another one following in her wake. And maybe there was?! Maybe it was a convoy of merchant vessels? Rescue! Rescue! They would pick him up when he reached the surface and Kushchin would not risk chasing him, he wouldn't risk exposing himself!

All these thoughts went whirling round in his brain. And a moment later Stavinsky was already slowly easing himself away from the working platform and the fitters. Just one more step, and . . . A fair bit of water separated him from them now, and he was already invisible, but he was in no hurry to begin the ascent. Easy does it! He'd already been buried twice - once under his own name in a cemetery in New Jersey, and again somewhere in Moscow under the name of Robert Williams. He must be sure to escape this third grave as well! Do everything in the right order! He was already thirty feet away. Now was the time to do it! Down with the metal clips holding the lead soles of his boots!

No sooner had he undone them, than the water pressure began to push him up and away from the sea-bed. He seemed to be completely weightless and he soared thirty feet in a few moments. But then he stopped. The heavy instrument bag, the pack on his shoulders containing the battery and his lead weight-belt all stopped his upward progress and brought him to a halt, floating there in an absurd upside-down position. He had to shed the belt and the instrument bag as quickly as possible. But the lock on the belt wouldn't do as he wanted. He started to empty the bag of spanners and wrenches. He could feel himself beginning to rise again, but the most important thing still remained to be done: releasing the strap holding the battery and the belt with the lead weights. No diver is able to undo those locks by himself without help from somebody else. Meanwhile, he could feel the blood rushing to his head, and it was becoming more and more difficult to breathe. A knife, that was what he wanted! Stavinsky withdrew his Finnish knife from its sheath and began to hack away at the lead weight-belt. Just take your time! Do it properly! It only needs one careless shake of the knife, and that will be that. The water would come flooding into the diving suit.

As soon as he had cut through the belt, the water pressure hurled him towards the surface again. He didn't even have time to move his arms and change positions. It was like going up in a high-speed elevator. He caught his breath, and his heart started thumping. Oh God! Let me stop, or else

I'll get the bends and my blood will begin to boil. Oh God! Let me stop!

He stopped. His ascent slowed down by itself, and there he was, hanging in the water, held down by the pack containing his oxygen cylinders and the battery for his lamp. Taking short gulps of air, Stavinsky tried to relax. Gradually his heartbeat returned to normal. He wondered how far he had ascended. The water around him was brighter and a shoal of tiny fish darted away from him in all directions. Aha! If there were fish around, that meant he must have risen quite a distance. Should he take a breather and get used to the pressure at this depth, or risk another jump immediately? Of course, he ought to adapt himself and get accustomed to this new depth by remaining there for at least fifteen or twenty minutes, but the ship might have sailed away by then! The sonar ratings on board the U-300 had most likely detected the vessel as it was approaching the submarine. They would have calculated its course and decided that it would pass either right over them or come very close. But he, Stavinsky, had no idea what speed the ship was doing, or when it would pass over him.

But suddenly . . . God, what was that enormous black shadow above him on the left? It was the ship! The ship! He might miss it!

Forgetting all about the danger of getting the bends, Stavinsky started to hack away at the strap securing the battery and cylinders. Then suddenly he felt something that he had dreaded, a tiny pin-prick from his own knife beneath one of his ribs. He immediately noticed a flurry of tiny air-bubbles rising past the glass visor of his helmet. The air had started to escape from the chest section of his diving suit. And the next moment he could feel the water pressing against his chest, like an iron hoop, preventing him from breathing. Part of the suit had lost its buoyancy, and now Stavinsky could feel himself being dragged down, while the pressure on his throat became stronger and more unbearable. He was held in an inexorable, icy grip. Unable to breathe any longer, he gave up all resistance and gradually lost consciousness, after realizing quite clearly that he was about to die a senseless death . . .

It is so much stuff and nonsense, this idea put around by idle writers who have never experienced it themselves, that when a man is at death's door, he relives his whole life in microcosm. Not even for a split second does a dying man think about anything other than the desire to live. Even when he knows full well that death is upon him, and even when his broken will and fading awareness tell the organism to surrender, every muscle in his body seems to act instinctively, according to some biological programming of its own, and disregard the instruction from the brain by continuing the fight for life at any cost.

So it was that when Stavinsky succumbed to the inevitable, when his heavy battery, the oxygen cylinders and his leaking diving suit began to drag him down to a watery grave, and his fragile ribs were almost breaking under the pressure, his hands continued to act by themselves and succeeded in performing the one desperate movement that could save his life at that moment – in a final burst of convulsive activity, they cut through the last bit of strap . . .

Four seconds later Stavinsky came crashing up out of the water into the direct rays of the setting sun. He was hurled six feet into the air and then dropped back into the water with a heavy, painful thud. He took a severe blow to the back, and even before this, the sudden change in pressure had sent blood streaming from his nose. But he was alive, *alive*!

As he floated there, choking in blood and almost fainting from the pain in his back, feeling the icy water through the rent in his diving suit and for some reason still clutching the Finnish knife in his right hand, Stavinsky suddenly saw the ocean liner *Viking* forty yards away from him, as white as snow, its decks covered with brightly lit awnings. Although he didn't know it, it was a Swedish cruise ship, which travels up and down the Baltic, making short stops at Stockholm, the Åland Islands, Helsinki, Leningrad, Riga and Gdansk. But it was passing him by, passing him by . . .

Stavinsky gestured weakly with one hand and made a gurgling sound through his blood-filled mouth: in his clouded mind he thought that he was waving, waving at the ship for all he was worth and shouting at the top of his voice.

But his hermetically sealed helmet suppressed his cry . . .

Meanwhile, there was music coming from the liner. Carefree couples were dancing on the promenade decks, while a floor-show was just beginning in the ballroom. Up on the top deck there were still a few half-naked sunbathers, their sensitive noses protected by bits of paper, squinting in the rays of the dying sun, which of course never completely sets during the white nights in this northern latitude. And all these idle Americans, Frenchmen, Canadians, Swedes, Brazilians, Japanese, and God knows who else, were heading east, and looking forward to seeing the Hermitage and the Kirov Ballet in Leningrad, and the quaint alleyways and cafés of old Riga.

Deep below them, on the bed of the Gulf of Bothnia, Soviet submarine U-300 was installing a new seismic weapon, capable of reacting at any time to a radio signal from Moscow to destroy the houses and villas of these carefree people, their offices and factories, the whole of life as they knew it. In a few weeks, or at the very most a few months, similar energy grids would be installed in the sea-bed around Japan and off the coast of France, England, West Germany, America . . .

And the man who had come to warn the future victims was begging silently for their help, at a distance of no more than forty yards from their ship.

The vessel passed by and disappeared slowly and inexorably from view.

9

Coded Signal

To: Marshal Oparkov, General Headquarters, Moscow
Info: Gorchakov, C-in-C Naval Forces
At 19.40 hours on 1 June, while EMMA was being positioned off the Väddö Peninsula, your representative, Major-General Sergey Yuryshev, made an unauthorized ascent to the surface. Acting in accordance with Instruction ED-01, which forbids the abandonment of classified equipment, all installation work was immediately halted and we achieved periscope depth at 21.39 hours. Poor night-time visibility has made it impossible to carry out a search for Yuryshev. I await your orders.

Kushchin

Coded Signal

To: Commander, submarine U-300
You must find Yuryshev at all costs. In order to divert the attention of Swedish naval forces for the next half-hour, submarine E-40 will head along the Gulf of Bothnia, north of your position. Using code E-2, make contact with her and co-ordinate your movements.

Marshal Oparkov

Coded Signal

To: Commander, submarine E-40
Surface immediately and reveal your position, in order to divert the attention of the Swedish navy from U-300. Contact the U-300 Commander using code E-2 in order to co-ordinate your movements.

Marshal Oparkov

Coded Signal

To: Marshal Oparkov, General Headquarters, Moscow
The body of General Yuryshev has been spotted drifting into a narrow fjord at Arholma Island, floating near a

cave. Impossible to recover the corpse owing to the appearance of Swedish naval helicopters.

Kushchin

EXTRACTS FROM NEWSPAPER AND AGENCY REPORTS, I

Stockholm, 5 June Swedish air and naval forces are still attempting to apprehend an unidentified submarine, detected at the southern end of the Gulf of Bothnia. Officers manning three observation posts spotted the presence of the submarine on 2 June, north of the sixty-foot-wide channel at the southern end of the Gulf of Bothnia. A second unidentified submarine was detected by fishermen and radar installations a hundred miles further to the south . . .

Stockholm, 8 June Naval helicopters have been dropping depth charges around the probable location of an unidentified submarine, in order to force it to surface before it can leave the area around the Väddö Peninsula. Approximately one hundred military planes and helicopters, together with coastguard vessels have been carrying on the hunt for two unidentified submarines, believed to have entered Swedish territorial waters.

The Commander-in-Chief of the Swedish Navy, Emil Svensson, made the following statement: 'Six or even seven foreign submarines have appeared in our coastal waters since a Soviet submarine ran aground off Karlskrona in October, 1981. This is unprecedented. We have absolutely no idea what these foreign vessels want in our territorial waters.'

Coded Signal

To: Commander, submarine U-300
Leave Swedish waters immediately. Observe wireless silence.

Marshal Oparkov

EXTRACTS FROM NEWSPAPER AND AGENCY REPORTS, II

Stockholm, 11 June A representative of the Swedish armec forces has announced that the search for the two unidentifiec submarines will be continued for another week at least, anc that the Swedish navy will blockade the entrance to the Gul of Bothnia until it is certain that the unidentified submarine have quit Swedish territorial waters.

FROM SOVIET ARMY GENERAL HQ CLASSIFIED CORRESPONDENCE

PRIORITY
TOP SECRET
BY MILITARY COURIER

To: Chairman of the KGB Lieutenant-General V Fedorchuk

Submarines U-300 and E-40 have now left Swedisl territorial waters and are returning to their base ir Baltiisk.

In accordance with your personal instruction, all worl on installing EMMA off the Swedish coast has beer halted, until you have finished investigating the circum-stances surrounding Major-General Yuryshev's attemp-ted defection.

I am enclosing some materials discovered in Genera Yuryshev's safe addressed to me. As you will see from th note in Yuryshev's own hand and the confession of m daughter, appended to it, the reasons for General Yury-shev's attempted defection appear to be entirely per-sonal. Although this in no sense justifies his treasonabl act, it does give reason to hope that he acted on impuls and alone, without having made prior contact wit enemy intelligence. Since General Yuryshev is no dead, we may hope that the enemy has no knowledge o Project EMMA.

Respectfully yours,
Soviet Army Chief of Staff
Marshal N. Oparkov

Enclosure: General Yuryshev's handwritten note and the confession of Galina Yurysheva-Oparkova
Moscow, 11 June, 1982

TOP SECRET
PRIORITY

Headquarters of the KGB
2, Dzerzhinsky Square,
Moscow

To: Soviet Army Chief of Staff,
Marshal N. Oparkov
. . . The fact that a Swedish seiner was present off the island of Muskö directly above the point chosen for the installation of EMMA, and the fact that this vessel remained anchored in the same spot throughout the operation, leads us to assume that the Swedish boat may have been waiting to rescue your son-in-law, the traitor, Major-General Yuryshev.

I suggest that you supply me personally with a list of anybody who had any involvement at all with Project EMMA, together with another list giving the names of everybody who came into contact with the former Major-General outside his official work.

At the same time, I suggest that you do everything in your power to maximize the secrecy surrounding the development of the new strategic seismic weapon, code-named EMBA.

KGB Chairman,
Lieutenant-General V. Fedorchuk
Moscow, 11 June 1982

Epilogue

Headquarters of the KGB
2, Dzerzhinsky Square
Moscow

To the Head of the CPSU Central Committee
Defence Industry Section
Comrade Igor Fyodorovich Dmitriev

TOP SECRET

. . . After a long and painstaking investigation of the circumstances surrounding the attempted defection of Major-General S. I. Yuryshev, the Assistant Director of Strategic Planning at Soviet Army General HQ concerned with top secret projects EMMA and EMBA, the KGB have established the following:

> During the month of June 1981 Yuryshev suffered a severe trauma caused by the adultery of his wife and the suicide of his son . . .
> . . . His colleagues at work all agree that after his son's suicide and his own accident, Yuryshev's character underwent a substantial change . . . These facts together with circumstantial evidence of various kinds (e.g. the testimony of his wife and a statement from his last mistress Tatyana Logina, a waitress in Baltiysk) lead us to suppose that General Yuryshev committed his treasonable act on impulse as a result of severe mental depression. Careful examination of all the people with whom General Yuryshev came into contact – from his colleagues at General HQ to the son of the Secretary to the CPSU Central Committee, Ilya Andronov – has excluded the possibility of their having any links with Western Intelligence. According to agents' reports in Sweden, the

Swedish fishing vessel anchored off Muskö island between May 25 and June 7 had experienced engine failure and was being repaired. General Yuryshev's body disappeared in a Swedish fjord and evidently sank to the bottom of the sea.

Reports from our KGB agents within the CIA and other foreign intelligence services indicate that Western Intelligence knows nothing about Project EMMA. This is also the view of the Soviet Army Main Intelligence Directorate . . .

My recommendation is that you complete the 'Swedish arc' as quickly as possible by installing EMMA off the island of Muskö as planned.

Chairman of the KGB
Lieutenant-General V. Fedorchuk.

Moscow, September 20, 1982.

EXTRACTS FROM NEWSPAPER AND AGENCY REPORTS

Stockholm, October 5, 1982
Swedish helicopters and ships are continuing to search for the unidentified submarine, sighted last Friday, October 1, three hundred yards off the Swedish naval base on Muskö Island, only twenty miles south of Stockholm.

Stockholm, October 6
A swedish naval representative has declared that the foreign submarine which illegally entered Swedish territorial waters last week most probably belongs to the Soviet Union. He claims that the submarine has been trapped in Hörsfjärden Bay, ten miles from the entrance to the Baltic, and that Swedish ships and helicopters are making every attempt to force the submarine to surface. The Muskö naval base contains strategic radar equipment which enables the country's Eastern sea-board, facing the Soviet Union, to be

kept under constant protective surveillance. Part of the island's defence installations are located underwater in a system of caves which would be safe from attack even in conditions of nuclear war. As far as the Soviet Union is concerned, this base is of particular strategic importance because it is ice-free throughout the year and, in the event of war, would control the entry of ships to and from the Atlantic Ocean. In those circumstances, the NATO allies would aim to trap the Soviet Baltic fleet in its bases and cut off access to the Atlantic.

Stockholm, October 7
Some forty Swedish naval vessels and ten helicopters are now concentrated in the area of Hörsfjärden Bay in an attempt to discover the whereabouts of the foreign submarine believed to have entered Swedish territorial waters. The entrance to the bay is now completely sealed by nets and metal booms. The helicopters are firing depth charges to attack the submarine which is believed to be lying on the sea-bed.

Stockholm, October 8
According to Swedish naval representative, Commander Sven Karlsson, the submarine made an attempt to break the blockade and escape into the open sea. The attempt was apparently unsuccessful as the vessel ran into the metal booms and was then forced to retreat through the line of depth charges. The newspaper *Dagens Nyheter* reports that the submarine suffered damage and is at present situated on the sea-floor near the coastal settlement of Arst Havsbad at a depth of 250 feet. It is said to have five days' supply of air.

New York, October 8
This was the author's forty-fourth birthday – an event of little significance which he decided to celebrate by informing Swedish television of the real reasons for the Soviet

submarine's incursions into Swedish territorial waters. Neither this information nor the no less reliable information about the author's date of birth was actually broadcast.

Stockholm, October 9
(UPI) The Swedish naval fleet, aware that its professional reputation is at stake, has decided at whatever cost to force the submarine to the surface.

Stockholm, October 12
The Commander-in-chief of the Swedish Armed Forces, General Lennart Ljung, has issued a statement disclosing that the offending submarine has apparently managed to give its pursuers the slip and escape into the open sea.

Moscow, November 1
(TASS) Yesterday saw the death as a result of a sudden heart-attack of Marshal Leonid Ilyich Brezhnev, Secretary General of the CPSU, Chairman of the Presidium of the Supreme Soviet and Chairman of the USSR Defence Council.

Moscow, November 12
(TASS) A plenary session of the CPSU Central Committee unanimously elected Comrade Yury Vladimirovich Andropov as Secretary General of the Communist Party.

Saña, December 14, 1982
(TASS) According to official sources, the severe earthquake which occurred in North Yemen yesterday has led to the death of some 600 people. The worst loss of life and the greatest damage occurred in Dhamãr province. Eleven villages were completely destroyed while another eighty suffered severe damage.

(No news agency in the world appeared to notice that TASS was the first to report this earthquake in non-

Communist North Yemen and the first to provide exact information about damage and casualties.)

Kabul, December 16
Afghanistan was hit this morning by a strong earthquake. Seismic stations registered subterranean tremors measuring 6.3 on the Richter scale. The epicentre of the earthquake was in the foothills of the Hindu Kush, an area containing heavy concentrations of anti-Communist Afghan tribesmen. Underground tremors were also felt in the region of Peshawar in Pakistan, where camps housing refugees from the Communist Afghan Government are situated.

Taipei, December 17
An earthquake measuring 6.5 on the Richter scale was registered in Taiwan this morning. Information is awaited concerning casualties and the damage inflicted.

Washington, February 14 1983
Two large Soviet naval vessels appeared in US territorial waters today, fifty miles out from the mouth of the Mississippi River.

SWEDEN WARNS MOSCOW OVER SUBS AND TEMPORARILY RECALLS ITS ENVOY

The New York Times, Wednesday, April 27, 1983
Stockholm, April 26 – Sweden protested today against 'the gross violations of Swedish territorial integrity of which the Soviet Navy has been guilty' and threatened to sink any submarine that enters its waters without permission.

In an unusually strong series of actions for a neutral nation, the Swedish Government sent a stiff diplomatic note to Moscow, temporarily recalled its Ambassador there, Carl de Geer, and indicated that official visits between the two countries would be cut back sharply. Prime Minister

Olof Palme said Soviet military activity off Sweden's coast should 'be roundly condemned by all.'

Vessels 'Probably Involved'

Mr Palme acted after a five-member commission, appointed to investigate a submarine incident in the Stockholm archipelago in October 1982, reported that six Soviet vessels were 'probably involved,' including three manned midget submarines of a previously un-reported type with the ability to 'crawl' on the sea bed by means of tracks. The incident occurred near the Muskö naval base, about 20 miles south of Stockholm.

Official sources said there had been at least two further incidents this year.

Although they conceded that they had no proof, the investigators said they had abundant technical and circumstantial evidence indicating that the culprits on each occasion were Soviet submarines. The most important evidence was obtained by photographing and studying patterns left on the sea bed by the submarines, the commission added.

'We represent a united nation in our sharp protest,' Mr Palme said at a news conference. 'It is crucial to the credibility of our neutrality to show that we can defend our own territory. Violators in the future can count on the Swedish Government to order the military to sink the intruder at once.'

Describing himself as 'indignant and disappointed' by the conflict between Stockholm and Moscow, Mr Palme held out little hope that the Russians will admit the violations. That, he said, was not so important; what was critical was 'that they stop these grave breaches of international law so that we don't have to waste time chasing their submarines around the archipelago.'

Mr Palme said he did not know when the Swedish Ambassador would return to Moscow.

Delicate Balance in Area

For the Swedes and the other countries in the area, the danger in the dispute is that it could upset the delicate strategic balance. The Soviet Union is by far their most powerful neighbor, and each of the small Nordic states has had to work out an individual way to survive.

It is not entirely clear to the investigating commission or the Government what the Soviet subs have been up to. The Prime Minister said it could be 'a form of espionage,' but Adm Bror Stefenson, chief of the defense staff, disagreed. He suggested that the violations were the result of Soviet naval maneuvers to test new equipment.

'Prior Knowledge and Consent'

The commission's report mentioned 'the probability of motives of a military operational character' and added, 'After what has taken place in recent years the foreign submarine operations in Swedish waters cannot possibly have been carried out by military authorities only, without prior knowledge and consent on the part of their political leadership.'

Sweden said Soviet submarines were off Muskö in 1982. One went aground near Karlskrona in 1981.

Moscow, April 28 1983

(TASS) Last autumn the Government of the USSR made a public statement affirming that no Soviet submarines were, or could have been, situated in the region of the Stockholm archipelago. We are forced to conclude that the present campaign concerning mythical 'incursions' by Soviet submarines into Swedish waters is aimed at damaging relations between the two countries. Apart from that it is a blatant attempt to attract extra funding for the Swedish armed forces.

Afterword

The author must tell the reader immediately that he thoroughly dislikes afterwords, particularly those in which the writer attempts to communicate what he did not manage to convey successfully in the book. This is like a film director or scriptwriter jumping up in front of the audience at the end of a film and saying: 'Friends! Don't put your coats on yet! I want to explain to you what the film was about! . . .'

Literature is a hard task-master: either you expressed everything which you wanted to express in your book, or you are a bad writer . . .

Nevertheless, at the risk of gaining a reputation as the latter, I must append a few extra lines to my novel. More than that, I must admit to the reader that I myself am not the real author of this book – or rather, I was not the one who invented seismic weapons, energy transmission grids, midget-subs or caterpillar tracks and all the other technical marvels which the reader might think were pure fantasy. Having been brought up on Socialist Realism and being the screenwriter of seven entirely realistic films made in the Soviet Union, I don't have such inventiveness in me.

So who did invent all these fantastic elements, if we can call them that?

Before emigrating to the West in October 1978, I was a fairly well-known Soviet film-writer. I am not boasting when I say that. I merely want the reader to understand that while in the Soviet Union I was part of an élite professional group which sometimes had access to spheres of knowledge beyond the purview of ordinary Soviet citizens and the Soviet press. For example, there is a Special Cinematographic Committee attached to the USSR Council of Ministers which regularly arranges closed seminars and conferences for this small group of film directors and writers. Apart from being given the opportunity of watching prohibited Western films like *Last Tango in Paris* and *8½*, these privileged few are also introduced to leading members of the Government and the Communist Party. This is done in order to keep the Soviet movie élite abreast of real events both at home and abroad. For example, one of the advisers to the CPSU Central Committee's International Section, Comrade Sverdlov (brother of the first president of the USSR) gave us a fairly frank account of Soviet policy aims in the Near East, in Africa and in other parts of the world. And the Metallurgy Minister told us about the men involved in metal production throughout the country and asked us to produce a film depicting the heroic labour of steel foundry workers. Similarly the head of the All-Union CID tried to persuade us to make a film about the Militia or the Public Prosecutor's Department, and I remember an official from the Ministry of Agriculture once asking us to make a film singing the praises of milk-maids so as to attract more young people into that 'profession' and thereby increase the volume of milk available for consumption in the USSR.

I particularly remember one such seminar which took place near Moscow in 1978. It was held at Bolshevo, a retreat owned by the Union of Cinematographic Workers, where I spent some of the best years of my life. We were addressed by a representative of the Soviet Army's Political Directorate, a Major-General Pavlyuk or Pavlyuchenko – I can't remember exactly. On the other hand, I *can* remember what he told us extremely well. He was trying to persuade us to make a series of films about the Soviet Army – tank drivers, missile technicians, that sort of thing. But he particularly wanted us to emphasize the role of the young officers and military engineers. Apparently young people have been very unwilling to enter officer training schools over the last few years. And young people with talent and engineering skills have been even less willing to put their skills to work in the area of military technology. But what if you were to make films emphasizing the *romantic* side of life as an officer, said the General, or films showing the excitement involved in inventing new types of weapon . . . After that, he went on to tell us about four such strategic or, as he put it, 'ultimate' weapons which Soviet Army scientists were working on in 1978. One of them was a seismic weapon, just as I have described in this book. This is what he had to say about it.

'The theoretical problems involved with creating this seismic weapon have all been solved. It is possible to position explosive material of great destructive power beneath the ground in so-called energy transmission grids which, at a radioed signal from us, will be able to cause a controlled explosion at a distance of 400 kilometres from the place of installation. If such an earthquake were to take place in a specially chosen area, then it would be possible to destroy all the enemy's missile silos, power-lines, telephone cables, water supplies and so on. After this "natural calamity" our forces would enter the enemy territory bringing food supplies, water and electricity to the suffering population, as well as hot food from mobile army kitchens as well as medical aid. And the grateful populace will greet us with flowers, just as the Czechs greeted the Soviet Army in Prague in 1945 . . .'

One of the scriptwriters asked him how the 'energy transmission grids' could be installed on enemy territory. The general smiled and said that as soon as they had solved the technical problem of transporting such large amounts of explosive material in a more manageable form, then the problem of transporting the 'grids' abroad would no longer arise. It would be possible to position them on the edge of enemy territory with the aid of submarines . . .

That was all. We didn't get him to go into greater technical detail because, as you can imagine, none of us wanted to be granted special access to military secrets. If you do that you are automatically deprived of the right to travel abroad. I actually forgot about the lecture quite quickly, although the idea of a seismic weapon had made a strong impression on me, especially this amazing notion of occupying enemy territory through peaceful means by pretending to help the victims of an earthquake which the helpers themselves had actually caused. And the populace, suspecting nothing, would greet their saviours with flowers . . .

In October 1978 I emigrated from the USSR. In October 1981 Soviet Submarine No U-137 ran aground a few miles from the Swedish naval base at Karlskrona. It was then that I remembered the General's lecture. 'What if the Soviets have already solved the problem of packing the explosive in a more manageable form?' I thought. 'What if they already have this seismic weapon?' And I sat down to write the present novel, fully convinced, to be quite frank, that what I was writing was at least half way to science fiction, if not pure fantasy.

While I was busy with the first two parts of the novel, however, describing Stavinsky's attempts to return to the USSR, Soviet submarines began appearing more and more often off the coasts of Sweden and Italy, and also along the seaboard of the USA, particularly at the mouth of the Mississippi river. And these were only the submarines that people found out about! How many others had passed undetected? In other words, what at the beginning seemed even to the author to be nothing more than a fantastic hypothesis gradually began to take on a real and more frightening form. Especially when the Swedes eventually discovered that Soviet midget-subs, equipped with caterpillar tracks, had been crawling around the bed of the fjords literally a few miles from Stockholm. At this point reality and literary invention seemed to have closely coincided to make me feel quite at a loss! Could it really be, I thought to myself, that the Swedes still hadn't realized that these midget-subs hadn't disappeared from their waters at all? Equipped with remote control, these submarines can simply hide away in the fjords near Swedish military bases (not only Swedish bases: every base in NATO is at risk), waiting for a radio signal from Moscow to activate their seismic weapons! . . .

And even if you are of the opinion that the seismic weapon described in my book is a pure figment of the imagination, then would it really make any difference? It doesn't much matter whether these midget-subs are filled with ordinary dynamite or an atomic bomb. At a signal from Moscow, the effect would be the same: Swedish, Italian, British, Japanese and American naval bases could still be destroyed, especially those which are impossible to destroy by atomic or conventional attack from the air. I don't think the Swedes will be any the better off for discovering eventually that one of these midget-subs is filled with a few tonnes of dynamite instead of *EMMA* . . .

Amazed by the way my own predictions appeared to have become reality, I gave an interview to a correspondent of Associated Press on May 4, 1983. 'Just imagine,' I said to him, 'if midget submarines armed either with this seismic weapon or ordinary dynamite have been positioned near every NATO naval base and every important port in Europe, America and Japan, what will Andropov do next? Knowing that he could cause earthquakes in these countries whenever he liked, Andropov might well make all kinds of disarmament proposals to Reagan, involving the reduction of nuclear weapons and missiles, the withdrawal of Soviet tanks from Eastern Europe, and so on. In the eyes of the world he would immediately be seen as a pacifist and a peacemaker . . .'

I could tell from the AP correspondent's eyes that he was full of scepticism. I was just one more Russian emigré, trying to frighten the West by exaggerating the extent of the Soviet menace.

Two hours later I switched on the television news and

saw the familiar features of Yury Vladimirovich Andropov who had just made a speech advancing a new 'peace' initiative aimed at reducing the number of nuclear warheads in Europe.

That evening a friend of mine said to me: 'Listen, if your books are so close to reality, please don't ever write about a Third World War.'

So now I make a solemn promise to the reader: I will never write about World War III, the end of the world, the invasion of Earth by creatures from another planet or any other unpleasant occurrences which might put paid to this carefree life of ours in the West.

Edward Topol
14 May, 1983.

THE END

The heart-stopping novel of international suspense and intrigue by the author of *The Windchime Legacy*.

Michael Gladieux thought he'd finished with The Group, a highly specialised unit he'd served with in Vietnam . . . until his father is murdered, his body found with a note accusing him of Nazi collaboration during the war and a glass pendant anchored to his heart with a shiny steel spike..

Who was Michael's father? Why are Washington and The Group so interested? Michael's search for answers leads him on a terrifying quest – to find his father's killer. What he uncovers is far more deadly, as he becomes the one man capable of stopping the twisted legacy of THE SALAMANDRA GLASS.

Rivals Ludlum at his best!

0 552 12417 6 £2.50

CORGI BOOKS

ALFRED COPPEL

THE APOCALYPSE BRIGADE

A world on the brink of disaster . . .
A private army willing to fight to the death . . .

The Apocalypse Brigade describes the world as it may be a decade from now, where superpowers are held in thrall by both terrorists and OPEC. It is a world on the edge of apocalypse, where private citizens are prepared to act when their weakened governments are not . . .

"Mr Coppel is a wily writer. He knows how to keep things churning . . . and he knows when and how to spill a little blood and when and how to turn back the bedclothes . . . That he has a certain and unswerving understanding of the true nature of the world today is clear almost from the very first page"

The New Yorker

0 552 12079 0 £1.95

CORGI BOOKS